Earth
Made
of
Glass

Tor Books by John Barnes

Earth Made of Glass
One for the Morning Glory
Kaleidoscope Century
A Million Open Doors
Mother of Storms
Orbital Resonance

Earth
Made
of
Glass

John Barnes

A TOM DOHERTY ASSOCIATES BOOK
NEW YORK

EARTH MADE OF GLASS

Copyright © 1998 by John Barnes

All rights reserved, including the right to reproduce this book, or portions thereof, in any form.

Edited by Patrick Nielsen Hayden

This book is printed on acid-free paper.

A Tor Book
Published by Tom Doherty Associates, Inc.
175 Fifth Avenue
New York, NY 10010

Tor Books on the World Wide Web:
http://www.tor.com

Tor® is a registered trademark of Tom Doherty Associates, Inc.

Library of Congress Cataloging-in-Publication Data

Barnes, John
    Earth made of glass / John Barnes.
        p.   cm.
    "A Tom Doherty Associates book."
    ISBN 0-312-85851-5
    I. Title.
PS3552.A677E28   1998
813' .54—dc21   98-5246
                                      CIP

First Edition: April 1998

Printed in the United States of America

0 9 8 7 6 5 4 3 2 1

To the memory of my mother,
Beverly Ann Hoopes Barnes
1932–1996

For now we see through a
glass, darkly, but then face
to face; now I know in part;
but then I shall know even as
I also am known.
—Paul the Apostle

Dislike of Realism is the
rage of Caliban seeing his
own face in the glass
—Oscar Wilde

Like many of the upper class
He likes the sound of broken
glass.
—Hilaire Belloc

Let a man commit a crime and
he finds the earth made of
glass.
—Ralph Waldo Emerson

Part One

Jaguar
Quitze

Neytal

Jaguar Quitze: first born of the people, hence beginnings.
Neytal: The white water-lily.
In the *akam* poems: The seashore. Sunrise. The place of the crocodile, shark, and gull. The people sell salt and fish, swim in the sea, and eat fresh fish. Anxious waiting. Desire for the lover mixed with doubt about the lover's interest and one's own attractiveness.
In the *puram* poems: *Tumpai,* battle, the moment of decision.
A world dominated by Varunan, a guardian god, an all-seeing warrior-king, sentinel of the heavens.

It was hard to believe that Rufeu had been killed nine years ago. As he sat with us over a glass of wine, he barely looked six years old today. "It's honestly getting better," he said. "In this last year I've finally gotten some fine motor control, and as the corpus callosum grows in, I've begun to be able to think more coherently. Still, puberty's a long way away."

The joyous obscenity of his grin made me glad we'd taken the trouble to visit. The travel time was literally nothing—you stepped through the springer, and there you were. But Margaret and I got so few vacations from our work for the Council of Humanity that usually all we wanted to do, during the weeks between assignments, was to go to ground at the home of any tolerant relative, spending our time sleeping and loafing, seeing no one but our families and not going out for anything.

The last time we had been back to Nou Occitan, two stanyears ago, Rufeu still had not been downloaded from his psypyx into his clone-body; instead, I had talked to Johan, who was wearing Rufeu's psypyx, by com every day.

I suppose I felt responsible because I had been there when Rufeu died, on a climbing trip up in Terrbori during the long vacation home that Margaret and I had taken, just after our first mission as full-fledged Council of Humanity diplomats, so the time from his death to the present virtually spanned our careers; he had started on this long journey of his, back to physical adulthood, at the same time we had passed our probation and begun our careers of wandering from one trouble spot to another around the thirty-one settled planets of human space. We had seen sixteen of humanity's twenty-five suns while he had sat in the back of Johan's mind, waiting for his new body to finish growing.

"It must feel like a big hole in your life," Margaret was saying sympathetically.

"That pretty much describes it," he said. "Could have been worse, of course—they say if you die when you're fifty or so, you can still be trying to get everything back off your emblok when you're thirty. Memory only moves so fast and the more of it there is, the slower it moves. As it is, they say I'll be off this thing in less than five stanyears more." He fingered the black knob, no bigger than the nail of his little finger, behind his ear, from which all the copied memories of his first lifetime played back slowly into his child's brain; till he had reincorporated all of them into his brain structure, when he needed to recall something of his first twenty-five years, he had to reach across the interface and pull it in from the emblok. "But really, I'd rather not spend our whole visit talking about my, er, medical problems, eh? I know you don't stay in touch with the old crowd—"

"Just you," I said. "And I kept in contact with Johan while he was wearing your psypyx, because we both thought it was important for you to stay in touch with as many people as possible, but . . . well, he's always blamed me for Marcabru's death."

Rufeu nodded. He looked like a six-year-old pretending to be grown up. I squelched that thought. He didn't want to talk about his situation, but it was pretty hard not to think about it.

At last he said, "Well, I never blamed you. Marcabru was a depressive drunk. He was going to either kill himself or find someone to do it, and all that drinking made such a mess out of his psypyx recordings that there was no way he could reconstitute."

"I'd been, uh, thinking of asking—" Margaret said, looking pointedly at Rufeu's wine.

"I take scrubbers," he explained, finishing his glass and signalling for another round. "I can get drunk, then come down off it fast and clean. No damage to my tender young brain, as far as they can tell." He raised his glass to us and said, *"Atz fis de jovent."*

"Atz fis de jovent," we agreed, and drank with him. It could

mean "to the death of the young man," but it was more likely he meant another of its senses—"to the end of youth."

"It does get all of us, doesn't it?" I said.

"It does, Giraut. Though I was hoping that an occupation like yours would be different—"

Margaret snorted. "Go ahead, Giraut, tell him about the romantic way you and I spend our time out among the stars."

"Well, there's filling out forms," I said. "And asking questions so you know the answers to fill out the forms. And asking questions so you understand the answers that you need to fill out the forms. And—"

"Stop, stop, I need to retain some romantic illusions about you two. I prefer to imagine you spend all your time standing down local tyrants, rescuing hostages, getting rescued by the CSPs, maybe meeting intriguers and plotters in back alleys—"

"Absolutely," I said. "We tell the local tyrant that he hasn't filled out his permission for despotism form properly, we get the names and com codes of all hostages and fill out the request for rescue forms for them and the CSP—"

Rufeu laughed, not as if things were funny, but more in appreciation for a quick response. That killed the conversation for the moment, so I sat back and looked out over the broad terrace.

Rufeu lived on the east coast of Nou Occitan; I had grown up on the west coast. The cities over here were newer, so they showed some significant Interstellar influence in the architecture—excessive practicality here and there, the occasional spire, arch, window, or door not quite carried to the extreme conclusion that we Occitans had reveled in, before Connect. I liked my *very* excessive and extreme hometown, Elinorien, better, but still any Occitan city was a rest for the heart and eyes. Villa Guilhemi was not a bad place at all.

We were on the seaside edge of town, and the restaurant where we had met Rufeu looked across the beach down to Totzmare, the great world-ocean that encircled Wilson. We had been fortunate here, we Occitans, for we had gotten a whole planet to ourselves. Most cultures were jammed together, scores to a planet. But on Wilson, Nou Occitan was the only permanently habitable piece of land large enough for a colony; the two small polar continents, driven by the steep axial tilt of the planet and its slow, twelve-stanyear orbit, alternated between being burning deserts and glacial wastes, and were beyond the possibility of being made permanently habitable.

Hence Nou Occitan was the only culture that looked up to the tiny dot of Arcturus as our sun, its brilliance forever shielded and reddened by the vast amount of fine carbon dust in our upper atmosphere. Beyond the edge of the terrace, the soft white sand sloped down to the dark-green sea, which was gentle today, and warm as it always was in these equatorial waters. Children played in the shallows; further out, a yacht race was in progress, or perhaps it was some elaborate game of tag the sailors were playing.

For the thousandth time I wondered why I had ever left.

"Well," I said, "absent friends and old days."

Margaret looked at me a little strangely, but Rufeu raised his glass, I raised mine, and she joined us in drinking off the rest of the toast.

Of the friends of my *jovent,* Rufeu probably was the only one I really wanted to be in touch with, or could be. David was a professor now and as dull a pedant as I'd ever seen. Raimbaut had died in a dueling accident not long before I first set off for the stars, and since his personality had not been transferable, his psypyx was still stored in the Hall of Memory, waiting for the improved technology that could bring him back. Marcabru had died unrecorded. Aimeric was now the prime minister of Caledony, a culture on Nansen, six and a half light years away. Excepting Rufeu, all had gone into death, personality storage, or adulthood—the one true grave of youth.

And as for the *donzelhas,* well, a young Occitan worshipped women, but he avoided knowing them. My last *entendedora,*

Garsenda, had by some twist of fate become Margaret's friend, but she was generally offworld these days, pursuing one business deal or another as head of Nou Occitan's largest trading house, and when she and Margaret visited each other they only rarely invited me.

It wasn't the absent friends, really, that I was drinking to or missing; it was the time of my life when I had thought they were my friends, and that I was theirs, and that that would always matter. So Rufeu and I drank and chatted away the afternoon, talking about times long gone and what had become of people we used to drink and chat with, and Margaret politely sat there and drank along with us. Finally as it turned toward supper time, and the sun began to sink behind the mountains, I shook hands with Rufeu again (he didn't get up—but then if he had, he'd have had to jump down from the chair), and we said we mustn't let it be nine years again, even though for my part, anyway, I didn't care much whether it was another week, or forever.

Neither Margaret nor I spoke as we walked back to the springer station. Villa Guilhemi was very much a provincial town, and it was already settling in for the evening, the few who cared for it going out to sit in the cafés, the rest sitting out on terraces and balconies to enjoy a fine evening. It was so quiet, I could hear Margaret's full skirt rustling, and the light crunch of my boots on the brick street. When we got to the springer station, the first star, Mufrid, was just visible.

"Look," I said, "home."

It was an old in-joke between us. Just as Mufrid, the sun of her home planet of Nansen, was the brightest star in Wilson's sky, Arcturus was the brightest star in Nansen's sky, and thus we could always "see each other's house."

We put our card into the springer and stepped through into the bright sunlight of the Elinorien town square. Elinorien was a full fifth of a radian west of Villa Guilhemi, and it would be more than an hour before the sun set here. Still we said nothing; I wished I knew, offhand, whether this was because we were leading up to a fight, or because we were comfortably enjoying each other's company. Lately it could be either.

I stole a glance sideways at Margaret. She was not beautiful by anyone's standards, even mine, but I had grown to like the way she looked—to crave it the way an addict wants his drug, I thought sometimes. Her almost-white hair was cut short; her forehead and mouth were what most people would call too wide; her body square, muscular, and squatty; breasts small and not firm; buttocks large and saggy. More than ten years of experience had taught me that hers was the only body I really wanted to touch, but at moments like this—as I noticed so many of my fellow Occitans glancing at her once and then dismissing her—I could still, sometimes, wish that she could turn a head other than mine.

I was quite sure that telling her I wished she were better-looking would not have been a good way to start a conversation. Especially not now; there had been . . . oh, almost a stanyear of fighting about I-didn't-know-what, then making up, then fighting again. She seemed angry half the time and sorry for me the rest of it, but whatever the matter might be, even when she tried to explain it, neither of us was able to put it into words.

As we entered my parents' house, the sun was still shining brightly, and I blinked for a moment as we came into the darkened vestibule. My father would be out in the garden tending his tomatoes and grape vines, and probably hadn't noticed our departure any more than he would our return; my mother had had an engagement with some friends and was staying somewhere in Noupeitau overnight, so there was no one to say hello or ask how the trip had been.

Margaret went into the bathroom. I went into the guest room, where we were staying, to sponge off and freshen up for the evening, whatever that might turn out to be (most likely, a game of chess with my father, or a walk down to the beach with Margaret, or some lute practice—I had been neglecting that badly).

I cleaned up, changed shirts, washed my face, and swallowed an alcohol scrubber to get the last of the afternoon's wine out of my system. I combed through my hair again and looked into the mirror at the emerging monk spot on top of my head.

"Sinking into melancholy again?" Margaret asked, coming up and putting her arms around me.

I dropped an arm around her wide, strong shoulders and leaned a little against her. "*Ja*, you could say that. *Trop de tristejoi.*"

"*Semper valors,*" she said, hugging back. "It's funny how hard vacations are on you; you get so tired of work, but after a few days away from it you sink into this."

"I suppose I miss the *jovent* more here," I said. "Even though it's in your culture that I left it."

She stiffened; I had said the wrong thing again. My going to Caledony had led to two things, besides my personal end of adolescence: Margaret became the most important person in my life, and my life became the work did for the Council of Humanity and the Office of Special Projects.

But now and then—well, every day—my thoughts would begin to turn to my old *jovent* days, and though I was too old for it now, and anyway the old *jovent* life was gone and no one in Nou Occitan did it anymore . . . I wished I hadn't had to leave the party so early. I wished I were back. I wished a lot of stupid things. And Margaret had been with me for so long that by now she knew every stupid thing I wished, whether I voiced them or not.

"Sorry," I said.

"Sorry you said it, you mean. You still think it."

"I can't help that."

"You could try." She wrenched out of the one-armed hug I had been giving her and was through the door before I could think of anything else to say. I heard her stamping down the hallway.

I knew that Margaret and I would be trying to make it up within an hour or less. Lately, though, I often had the feeling that a day would come when making it up would no longer seem worth the effort. And what then? I sat on the end of the bed, feeling sorrier and sorrier for myself.

I heard the swift thudding of Margaret's feet in the hallway.

She threw the door open, smiling as if she had it in mind to tease me. "Hey, husband, are you still pitying yourself?"

"Uh, not for any longer than I can help. What—"

"It's Shan. We've got another assignment."

She was gone down the hall again, forcing me to run after her to my parents' parlor, where the image of Shan, twice life size, looked patiently from the screen toward us.

"Aha, Giraut, there you are," he said. A slight twitch at the corner of his mouth told me I must look disarrayed. It happens when you allow your personal grooming to be interrupted by fits of melancholy. "I hope that neither of you has any pressing commitments more than four standays from now?"

"None really," I said. The Dark was going to fall soon—the time when Terraust's forests and ranges would burn, and Wilson's sky would be darkened with the fine soot that chilled the world every six stanyears. I had enjoyed the Darks I could remember, when everyone in Nou Occitan stayed home and did creative work or held long parties with friends. But there would be other Darks, and besides, right now I had far too much time to think, anyway.

"Well, then," Shan said. "I have a thoroughly bad situation. If we succeed I suppose it will be a feather in all our caps and you will be in line for some promotions and commendations, but that is because no one expects us to succeed. Is that intriguing enough to make you interested in taking the job?"

Margaret made that flapping noise with her lips that sounded like a disgusted horse. "You know perfectly well that all we're doing here on leave is sitting around getting on each other's nerves and bickering. This is a job for the Office of Special Projects, isn't it?"

Shan grinned with something that might have been the glint of battle, or just his usual appreciation for Margaret's cut-the-crap approach. "Right. You're both secretly activated as of now in your appointments with the Office of Special Projects. As always your cover story will be that you're there on Council of Humanity business—as far as the Council, or any outsiders, are concerned, you're going to be cultural envoys again, which is something you are both experienced and effective at. It should be a good cover for you, because, in this particular case, the ability to roam about freely—or at all—is going to be critical. You're going to just about the worst trouble spot the Council has to deal with, and I'm not even going to pretend that you're likely to like it. In addition to two impossible local populations and a lot of complicated politics, you're going to be coping with high gravity, intense humid heat, foul air, and way too much shortwave ultraviolet. Not a bad looking place on postcards but that's all the closer I'd ever want to get to it. Have I scared you off yet?"

Margaret said, "You want us to go to Briand, don't you? Of course we will."

I felt a cold chill even before Shan slowly nodded yes. "I thought you'd guess it from that description. And I can't tell you how grateful I am that you accepted the job. Yes, it's Briand. Right now I have several of the OSP's field agents there, and we need more, as even a casual scan of the news would tell you. Unofficially, let me add, it's far worse than what the news depicts."

We made the arrangements quickly—shipping our personal effects from Wilson, and our furniture and warm-weather clothes from storage on Earth, to Briand in forty-five standays, setting up our appointment at the training school on Earth, for the rapid orientation we had to have first; and arranging concierge services for all the myriad of weird small things that always crop up in jumping tens of light years.

After that, there wasn't much left to talk about, and Shan rang off. Margaret got on the com to send a fast letter to her mother in Caledony and tell her we wouldn't have a chance to jump over for another visit on this vacation. I went back to my parents' guest room, stretched, and set about finishing my toilet. The hair finally wouldn't lie down till I put some antistatic on the comb, and then it took all the more effort to fluff it properly, and no matter what, that little hairless patch on top, like a death's-head

surfacing from a sea of hair, could not be made to disappear or
fit in.

But I was cheerful as I worked on this, and I could hear Margaret's fingers clattering away on the keys quickly and forcefully,
not because we were in a hurry but just because she too had a lot
of extra energy. All it took to banish depression, fighting, bad
sex, and the tendency to drink a lot, in either of us, was a call
from Shan with a job. It had been that way for some stanyears
now, and I still had no sense of whether that was a blessing or a
curse.

Neither of us knew much about Shan. Though I had known
him for a decade of stanyears, I didn't even know if "Shan" was
his given name, family name, patronym, matrenym, clan, generated name, or what. He had no other name I was ever made
aware of. As I had advanced in both my covert and overt positions, I had found myself at more formal receptions and on more
platforms with him, and become steadily more aware both of
how little I knew him, and how far-reaching his political power
really was.

But even though I listened ever more closely for clues to his
origin—or just to his full name—always it was the same.
"Ambassador Shan." "Envoy Shan." "Minister Shan." Once, in
a blistering hot graveyard on the beach of a salt-saturated sea,
local officials had called him "Colonel-Commander Shan," but
that culture had had no army for more than three hundred
stanyears, and out of the seventeen cultures on that planet that
had had armies, not one had ever had any such rank. I knew because I had checked.

So I knew Shan the same way that everyone did, as far as I
could tell: not at all. And probably I knew almost everyone who
knew him, across all the human-settled worlds.

The Council of Humanity's diplomatic service embraces a
small bureaucracy on Earth, not more than four hundred people
in all, plus the ambassadors to the Thousand Cultures (of which
there are actually 1228), plus the Embassy staff—and each staff

might be at most ten people, with three being much more typical. The Council Special Police, the military muscle behind Council decrees, number just twelve thousand. So the whole personnel roster of the Council of Humanity, from the three secretaries-general down to the lowliest private, is probably not as large as the population of most culture capitals.

The Office of Special Projects, within which Shan was not only my senior colleague but also my direct supervisor, never had more than a thousand personnel, and almost all of them also held jobs with the Council of Humanity.

Yet within either of those very small circles, no one I knew, who knew Shan, knew anything about him. It may have been no more than that he was very private, I suppose. Whatever the reason, despite the way in which he utterly shaped my life, I can't say I really know a thing about him, even if years later I could instantly remember his appearance down to his particular way of twitching an eyebrow or the slight pursing of one side of his thin lips that always meant he was looking forward to surprising some deserving *toszet* with bad news.

I *was* reasonably sure he liked me, and Margaret as well. Since we had entrusted our whole existences to him, that mattered.

That evening, after dinner with my parents, when we had told them that in four standays, just under five days local, we would be off yet again to do what we could to keep the human race together, Margaret and I sat out on the little terrace my father and I had built, enjoying the reflection of the stars on the calm black sea far down the mountains from us. "There are times when I wonder why I ever left," I said, "and then there are times when I wonder why I ever come back."

Margaret shrugged. "I feel the same way about my parents' house in Utilitopia. I guess next vacation it's their turn to put up with us."

"That's the system so far," I agreed. "I suppose we could

change it sometime, and probably we should, but so far it's been very comfortable, don't you think?"

"If it's comfortable not to have to make any decisions, well, sure, I suppose." She sighed and leaned against me; I slipped an arm around her and waited. Usually, anymore, this was the start of a fight. "Giraut, if you had stayed here, what would have happened to you?"

"Hmm. What would have happened to me? Well, I suppose, oh, I'd probably have been a drunk like poor old Marcabru, maybe even killed myself the way he did. Or I might have died in a duel like Raimbaut, or been killed in a sporting accident like Rufeu. Poor *toszet;* I'm always afraid I treat him as if he were mentally six years old, rather than just physically. At least he had the good sense to get killed after the modern psypyx came along; nowadays I guess it's what, eighty percent of the time they can manage a transfer of the last recording to the cloned body? He only lost a few weeks—"

"Giraut, my husband and lover," Margaret said, *"quiet!* You're babbling. I know it's because you're nervous, but it's only making *me* nervous and I don't think it's helping you. It's making us sound like an old couple gossiping at a news broadcast."

"Right as always, *midons.*"

"Now could you stand it if I ask you the same question seriously?"

"Perhaps." A skimmer was crawling slowly out on the black mirror of Totzmare, running on his electric motor, no sail up and no sound coming to us two kilometers above and behind him. The black shape cut forward like a knife blade across the sea, and the stars reflecting in it danced in mad circles as his slight wake stirred the water. "Ask again, then."

"What I meant was what you might be like if you had lived. You described dying, or having to restart from a psypyx. I mean, what sort of person might you have become?"

"Well, I think I'd have grown old deploring everyone around me, especially as the old *jovent* lifestyle was being abandoned, and then found some quiet corner to retire to where I could detest everyone else, plus myself, more and more. Maybe become a solitary drunk. I don't know. Nothing good, anyway, Margaret." I shuddered. No Occitan is really fond of the truth when anything more attractive is available.

"Kind of what I thought, too. And you know what would have happened to me, back in Caledony? I would have gotten married to some nice older man who would take a plain-looking woman like me. I'd have spent my work time on some clerical job and my off time going to church and raising kids, I guess."

"Do you want kids?"

"God, no. That's not the issue. It's just . . . " She sighed. "I never seem to be able to explain it once I lead up to it."

That had been true for at least a stanyear's worth of these conversations, so I let her have a long silence in case she might happen to think of what it was that she wished she could say. But she didn't, that night, or any of our remaining ones in Elinorien.

Just before dawn on the fifth day following, with our bags already sprung to the Office of Special Projects prep base at Manila, we hugged my parents and then walked the kilometer into Elinorien, where we went to a public springer. With no particular reason to delay, we stepped through the gray featureless fog of the springer, going from Elinorien's deep red dawn (stained by the permanent cloud of carbon particles that hangs above Wilson always) to the blazing greens and blues of Manila at 10 A.M. (whenever possible they try to have you do long springs between times of day that are not too far apart; it supposedly minimizes spring lag).

Twenty-five light years is a long way, and I was glad that the Office of Special Projects budget was picking up the cost of springing us. Nonetheless, although the springer had to instantaneously burn four and a half times the equivalent energy of the cube of the gravitational potential between a 7 AU orbit around

Arcturus and a 1 AU orbit around Earth, this was one of the gentler springs between the settled systems: the surface-to-surface gravitional change wasn't much—Earth's surface gravity is about four percent less than Wilson's.

That was a great benefit, because Margaret is as susceptible to springer sickness as I am blessedly immune, and the little change of gravity didn't do more than make Margaret stumble and retch.

We had arrived at an ordinary public springer near the newer business district of Manila, from which we could walk to the nondescript office building that is the training headquarters for the Office of Special Projects. Somewhere, our special springer passcards had just run up an enormous bill that would be quietly erased from the record; the passcards that OSP agents carried while on mission, so far as I knew, were unique, in that they overrode all security and credit checks—any springer with access to enough energy could send us to any other springer, even fifty light years away. As long as it was on OSP business, we could spring to anywhere in settled space on no notice at all. Shan had once mentioned that we could spend up to seventy times our annual salaries on the longer springs, but I'd never heard of anyone getting into trouble about overspending the card.

The public springer was just down the street from the training center, and our luggage had gone there the day before; we walked the short distance at a leisurely pace, since it was four hours till our first class. The sea in the distance, it seemed to me, was so blue that it was vulgar; the scraggly looking palm trees seemed washed out in the harsh, pale light. I was back on Earth, and, as always, already working up a defensive dislike for it.

Earth is old and crowded and awfully beat up. Most of the population lives in little concrete boxes for years on end, circulating from the kitchen to the bathroom to the virtual reality hookup, over and over, for all except their lifetime's seven "outside years" during which they supposedly earn enough money to pay for their ninety-odd years on the dole. (I knew from some figures collected by the Office of Special Projects that it cost more to keep the Earth people outside doing supposedly productive things—done better by robots—than it did to keep them in the concrete boxes, but the people in the boxes were voters, and, true or not, they wanted to feel they had earned their supposed keep.)

Manila is a startlingly ugly city of nineteen million, an agglomeration of huge concrete blocks that stretches all the way around the bay, down to Cavite, and up to Malolos, making it look like a large squashed bug from orbit. The old center city was bombed out in the Slaughter, so the "new" capital area—just over five hundred years old—is a collection of post-reconstruction stained concrete pyramids and domes, remarkable for its dullness and its interchangeability with other places of the same era. Still, at least it's on the sea, near the equator; we had once had to spend a sustained period of Olympic City, a transpolis of seventy-five million surrounding Puget Sound that could make anyone appreciate Manila.

Manila had always been a capital or administrative center—first for different native kings (one of whom had been lucky and smart enough to kill Magellan), then for the Spanish, American, Japanese, Indian, and Javanese Empires at various times, for a while as a province of Australia, of Old America, of Alaska, sometimes as a nominally independent country but usually under someone's domination. Until the Slaughter the people there had done fairly well during most changes of hands.

Now they were one of several international cities that the Earth Administration leased to the Council of Humanity, and their main job was consuming the dues payments that came in from the Thousand Cultures by employing human beings to do the filing and recording that could be better done (and had to be checked) by a computer.

The Office of Special Projects training facility is just a large office building with some pretty good neuroprojection setups and a lot of temporary apartments. It's where you go to study before going on a mission, to learn the basics that you're going to need and get the situation firmly into your head, so that your first few weeks can be reasonably gaffe-free. "Is this our tenth time here?" I asked Margaret, after we collected our key from the front desk.

"Why, are you hoping we'll get our next trip free?"

"I was hoping it was still possible to tell them apart."

"Hmm. Well, then, no, it can't be our tenth. We had our initial training here, right, two sessions, and this is our twelfth assignment, but five of the previous ones were just regular Council assignments, and we didn't come here for those. So that's two for training, six for previous OSP missions, and this would be our ninth. Next time is our tenth."

"Remind me to pack champagne."

We inserted our card key into the lobby springer; the gray field formed in front of us and we stepped through into our suite. A moment later, the card ejected onto the floor behind me. I stooped to pick it up.

"Do you think they gave us our old room?" Margaret joked. It was exactly like every other suite we had ever been in here. I saw at a glance that our luggage had all made it. A quick check of the kitchen showed that they had stocked it to our specs, as well.

"Three and a half hours till we do anything," I said. "Guess we might as well get moved in."

That took five minutes—like any diplomats of the last 1500 years, we travel light and everything is set up for quick packing and unpacking. I took another minute to confirm that my lute and guitar were in perfectly fine shape, and then we truly had nothing to do except eat lunch and wait for our language class at two P.M.

I killed some of the time by calling up a short briefing and going over it a few times. Briand was unusual in so many ways; perhaps if I looked at it often enough, it would stop looking so strange.

Even if the two cultures there had been made up of gentle, tolerant xenophiles who could hardly wait to be assimilated to Interstellar, Briand would have qualified as an outpost of Hell. It was the second planet (of six) of Metallah, an F6 star forty-six light-years from Sol. Most of the colonized worlds circled big red K stars, and were the remnants of destroyed gas giants that had lost most of their mass in the Faju-Fakutoru process; a handful were Earthlike worlds circling G stars, like Sol. Briand, on the other hand, was one of four that roasted under the fierce actinic light of an F star, lit by a harsh blue-white glare and with its upper atmosphere lashed into a chemical frenzy by ferocious short-wave ultraviolet.

Most of the worlds humanity had tamed had been bare rock with abundant ice before we started terraforming them; Briand before terraforming was a nightmare soup of complex organics that might or might not have been alive. It was a sort of intermediate case between Venus and the Earth, with seven atmospheres of pressure above the dense salt-saturated seas that covered most of its surface, very active plate tectonics (with many more and smaller plates than Earth), and a great deal of volcanism. Over most of its surface, a madly active atmosphere constantly roiled and burned, as local concentrations of reducing and oxidizing gases ran into each other at those high temperatures and pressures; the results dropped into the seas, keeping them forever a saturated cauldron of more exotic material than anyone could catalog.

It would have been a world of only scientific interest, except that late in the colonization era, with so many worlds already settled and with most of the decent real estate near Earth taken up, someone had noticed that Briand did have some terraformable features. Near its South Pole, volcanic hotspots like those that had formed Iceland, Hawaii, or the Yellowstone on Earth blasted up through the high crust of a mountain range, forming a few immense plateaus—really islands in the sky—that reached twelve kilometers above average surface altitude, well up into Briand's stratosphere. (The stratosphere was a great deal lower on Briand than on most habitable worlds, because the gravity there was a very high 1.3 standard, and the ferocity of Metallah's actinic light plus the highly reflective cloud cover at ground level forced the tropopause down considerably lower as well). Air pressure on those islands was a perfectly tolerable 1075 millibars, on average, and the surrounding mountain ranges, like great bulging shoulders leading up to the plateaus themselves, trapped most of the toxic matter that rose up from the lower atmosphere.

The South Pole was at an almost-bearable average temperature of 33° C daytime, 15° C nighttime, year-round because Briand, with the least axial tilt and the most circular orbit of any inhabited world, had no distinguishable seasons. The locals tended to use the stanyear as their time unit since there were no seasonal changes noticeable without instruments.

The permanent polar high sitting over the plateau excluded virtually all weather other than local; just after every sunset, hot wet air would rush up over the mountain tops and release fierce storms. The water would then run back down over the plateaus in brief rivers that lasted only till noon or so of the next day.

Briand had been right out at the edge of what had been legally colonizable during the age of settlement, back in the twenty-third and twenty-fourth centuries when the decisions were being made. Some bright *toszet* had figured out that genetically tailored nitrogen- and oxygen-releaser plants could grow on the mountains surrounding the South Polar plateaus, and the polar high could thus become a breathable space at a bearable temperature. To enhance the effect, the lowlands had been seeded with a weird mix of microorganisms that thrived in a corrosive, high-temperature, high-pressure environment, constantly releasing oxygen and nitrogen; they were still doing their job, but an unforeseen side effect had been that water and carbon dioxide interacting with some of the raw new rock surfaces around the many volcanoes sometimes released methane or hydrogen "bubbles" that exploded in the lower atmosphere. In the high pressure, the shockwaves travelled hundreds of kilometers, but fortunately there was no one down in that hellish environment to be harmed by them. The planetary scientists were learning a lot about the hitherto-unknown process of "sonic erosion."

At the time the colony-spaces were sold, there had been two chains of sky-islands in Briand's antarctic, on opposite sides of the pole, each of which could—by stretching the rules until they nearly ripped—be classified as fitting the minimum requirements for a salable colonizable space: 550,000 square kilometers of land, at least 40% buildable, capable of being modified to have a temperate-zone type climate. The reality was that Tamil Mandalam had gotten less than 410,000 square kilometers (many unusuable small mountain peaks had been counted to make up the difference), of which perhaps 15% was buildable in the sense of "flat ground someone would want to live on," and the climate was measurably worse than that of New Guinea. Kintulum had fared even worse, with a smaller area, only one sky island that was not subject to occasional toxic storms, and a location considerably farther north and thus more subject to extremes and to toxic incursions.

All the same there had been ferocious competition for Briand's little patches of habitable dirt. Those two culture-areas had become available for bids just as the process of colonization was winding down, and hundreds of applicant cultures were receiving notice that no space could be found for them and that they would not be sending a colony ship to the stars; their descendants would be allowed to practice their cultures just long enough for a full record to be made, and as soon as a group of Earth Administration bureaucrats decided that the recordings were adequate, they were to be forcibly assimilated.

The early twenty-fifth century had been the most intense and rigid period of the Inward Turn, the great systematic cultural integration of humanity in the Earth system. At the time it was strongly felt that the cultures planted across the nearby stars were already more than enough for whatever diversity there needed to be—if indeed there needed to be any.

The winning bids for Tamil Mandalam and Kintulum had

provoked riots, for they were both literary cultures, and there had been a strong feeling that the last colony spaces, regardless of the outcome of the bidding, should be granted to ethnic cultures.

When a colony ship was sent out to plant a culture, the culture it carried generally derived from one of three sources. Among the early colonies, the most common were ethnic cultures, like New Buganda, Chaka Home, or Tonkin, founded by an ethnic group trying to preserve its traditional way of life and identity. Next most common were literary cultures, like Nou Occitan, my home culture; these were generally founded by wealthy people in the richer parts of Earth, who had fallen in love with some piece of humanity's recorded past and wanted to revive and preserve it as a living tradition rather than as a dust collector in some library. Finally, in a few cases, some of the true believers in one utopia or another, fearing that in the general cultural integration their ideas would be lost forever, had had enough money to successfully plant ideological cultures like Thorburg, Ecoarete, Hedonia, Sparta, or Margaret's home culture of Caledony.

In general, by the late 2300's, the ethnic groups that were still trying to save some version of themselves had been the poorest of the poor. Any ethnic group with enough wealthy members had already had the resources to buy a cultural space on some distant planet, and furthermore—as wealthy people have always tended to do—already been thoroughly assimilated. Thus groups like the Samoans, the Salish, and the Miskito had the most genuinely divergent cultures remaining on Earth, but were too poor to preserve themselves.

Their protests that the few remaining cultural spaces should go to "real" cultures in danger of dying, as opposed to rich people's hobbies and fantasies, had crashed headlong into vast indifference. No one really cared, since colonization was winding down anyway, with all the terraformable worlds that could be reached by the half-lightspeed suspended animation ships of the time already being terraformed and already spoken for. The protests of the various tribes and nations who were slated for assimilation had only brought on a crushing repression that—when they bothered to know it was happening—had apparently not disturbed the sleep of the great majority of people on Earth.

In a way, my family had been one of those most affected, in the present age, by those decisions of four hundred years ago. My mother was a well-known scholar and expert on the subject of the Archived Cultures—the groups that had, ever so quietly, been wiped from living human memory.

As for Briand, whatever the claims of justice might have been, rich hobbyists had pursued their dreams. One group had been lovers of the fine old Cankam poetry of the ancient Tamils. "Cankam" meant something like "school" or "academy"; in the early centuries of the Christian era, in the southern tip of India, an extraordinary set of poems had been produced, attributed to the members of an artistic academy or a league of poets of some sort, from which the poetry took its name. Anthologized a thousand years later, the poems had lain largely undiscovered by anyone who did not read Tamil, until almost another millenium had passed, but in the polyglot, xenophilic culture of the last decades before the Third World War, the poems had been widely translated and read, and had taken their rightful place as some of the world's great literature.

True, at the time Tamil Mandalam won the bid, there were already two Tamil cultures planted among the stars, but those were ethnic cultures, dedicated to preserving the continuity of the Tamil way of life; now, thanks to millions of lovers of poetry, there would be a world where the Tamils were not the Tamils of the present, but those of millennia before: people, it was hoped, who might eventually found a new Cankam and bring forth new poetry. The ship had been dispatched to found Tamil Mandalam, with its capital at New Tanjavur, in the eastern part of Briand's antarctic. On the ship went ninety-six hibernating teachers, all fluent in the ancient version of the Tamil language and charged to raise every child to be monolingual in it; a million frozen embryos of the "purest" Tamil descent then available; and the whole of recorded human knowledge, carefully edited by aintellects to insure that any course of study would eventually lead to a feeling that the Cankam poems—and the moral verses in the later book of proverbs called the Kural—were of necessity the pinnacle of human achievement. It took them almost a century to get there, and by that time the robots, racing on ahead at speeds not available to ships that had to carry biological material, had landed, terraformed Briand, and grown New Tanjavur in its allocated place, so that when the ship arrived, the ninety-six awakened teachers had found their rooms ready to move into, and the decantery already set up to begin maturing the first embryos.

The other group of wealthy eccentrics had had, if anything, a weirder passion. There was already a Maya culture planted among the stars, for although few Maya had survived the Asian blasting of Central America, the small number of survivors had included many financiers, industrialists, and bankers; the Maya were quite secure in that sense. But, said the group that had won the bid for that last precious patch of terraformable ground, the Maya who are going to the stars have been influenced by the Spanish settlement during Renaissance times, by the American commercial conquest in the Industrial Age, by the wave of Russian refugees in Central America after the Third World War and the Islamic commercial connections (and later, Reformed Islam itself) that they had brought with them. These are the Maya of today; we want the old, pure, fascinating, pre-Columbian Maya, not these half-Islamic half-Catholic entrepreneurs who speak a creole that never resounded from the great stone pyramids in the jungle, they said. Give us the Maya of the ancient texts and inscriptions, and what is missing in the data we will make up from here and there, and create a culture of priests, warriors, athletes, farmers, and dancers, who will live as the only culture representing an uncontaminated Western hemisphere people.

And so they had sent a ship, physically identical to that of the Cankam enthusiasts, to plant its teachers, embryos, and library in the great stone city, grown through long decades by quintillions of nanomachines, on the one part of their territory where human beings could reliably breathe. The city was named Kintulum—after "Tulum", a ruin whose name might have had a Maya derivation, with "Kin" meaning new—in the western hemisphere of Briand, a tenth of a radian north of the south pole and a good 900 km from New Tanjavur.

If fate had been kind the two groups could have stayed there, ignoring each other, out of touch with the rest of the human race, for hundreds of years until the springer suddenly reconnected humanity in this present generation. But fate was not kind. In 2714, a volcano, known to both cultures as Old Grandfather, had erupted in the mountain valleys just below Kintulum, burying it in ash and rendering the air around it unbreathable; at first they had moved into pressurized tunnels under the city, and hoped the eruption would not last, but new and frequent eruptions, and major lava flows down in the valley, rapidly removed the hope that their sky-island would be habitable again any time within the next couple of centuries.

An arrangement had been worked out with the Tamils; at first the Maya, who numbered a fraction of what had been planned had lived as refugees in Mayatown, a large camp just touching the northwest corner of New Tanjavur. A decade later, after a city had been grown for them on a hastily-deeded bit of formerly Tamil territory as far from New Tanjavur as possible, most of the Maya had moved to the newly grown Yaxkintulum.

But for reasons understood only by the Maya, a remnant had elected to remain in Mayatown, and as New Tanjavur and Mayatown had grown, they had jammed against each other. Relations had never been good anyway, and the Tamil felt that having already lost one city site of their culture space to the construction of Yaxkintulum, they should not then have to endure having the Maya also take up room in the largest Tamil city.

No one knew what the Maya thought, for they seemed not to respond to any attempt to negotiate the removal of the

Mayatown people to Yaxkintulum, nor to be in any hurry to solve any other problem connected with living together. Reading between the lines of Ambassador Kiel's short summary, it appeared that the Maya did what they did and explained nothing; the Tamils were abundantly communicative about their desire for things it was impossible to do for them or to give them.

A few generations of such relations had brought on pure, honest hatred between the two sides.

Thus Briand had acquired several other uniquenesses in the Thousand Cultures. It had one of the largest ethnic ghettos, two cultures with the smallest land areas under their control, one of the most precarious ecologies (since another major volcanic eruption could well make the whole planet uninhabitable)—and the hightest level of ongoing ethnic violence in the present day, numbers so bad that New Tanjavur ranked with a roster of shame among the cities in which day in, day out, people persisted in killing and assaulting each other for belonging to the wrong group, and every decade or so whole blocks burned and the gutters were piled with bodies as outright warfare exploded: twentieth-century Belfast and Sarajevo, twenty-first century Montreal and Los Angeles, twenty-third century Nagoya and Honolulu.

On the average there was a hate-inspired murder every eleven hours in New Tanjavur, most of them gangs of Tamils killing Maya, but with a substantial minority of cases of Maya killing Tamils. About every twenty stanyears an outbreak of rioting might reach a level of 2000 people dead in that city of eight million.

Into this mess the Council of Humanity had brought the springer, the idea reaching New Tanjavur and Yaxkintulum by radio broadcast just in the last year. Tamil Mandalam had constructed a springer almost overnight; there was now a large Council Embassy in New Tanjavur. Yaxkintulum had remained silent but occasionally communicated by a single representative who lived in New Tanjavur and served as both their official representation to the Tamils and to the Council.

Normally the Council would have insisted on opening up a Trade Bazaar and getting Tamil Mandalam integrated into Interstellar trade just as quickly as possible. Wherever that had been done, however, it had always resulted in a short but very severe economic depression, followed by skyrocketing inflation, followed by an ugly boom and bust cycle that took a decade or so of stanyears to damp down. The social dislocations and uproar associated with that would have been intolerable in a city that lived always on the brink of civil war, and so for the first time an exception was made. Tamil Mandalam would keep its isolated economy and economic home rule, at least until someone could figure out how to defuse the situation.

If springers came into wide use in both New Tanjavur and Yaxkintulum, placing the two cities in instantaneous contact, it would be possible for a genuine war to be fought between the two populations, probably culminating in the massacre of one or the other.

Every springer in the universe can address every other—that's the physics of it—and you can't lock any connection out, because the equations don't allow the springer to know the address from which the cargo arrived. A physicist explained that to me once as "conservation of destroyed information" and "paraentropic balance," which left me understanding no more about springers than I ever did, but you don't always need to know what makes a thing work to understand how to use it. If there were a springer in each city, no springer that was turned on could be blocked from receiving whatever was sent to it, whether that was a package of laundry, a man visiting his aunt—or a madman with an automatic weapon, or a battalion of soldiers, or for that matter an atomic bomb with 0.0001 second left to go on the detonator's timer. The hundreds of kilometers of nice, safe, isolation would vanish immediately, and anyone with the price of a ticket could leap into the rival city, and back, at will.

The Maya of Mayatown were small in number, not well-armed, and dominated by their Tamil neighbors; the Maya of

Yaxkintulum were not, and if the Maya built springers (as they might do at any time, for the devices weren't complicated once you knew that you could build them in the first place) then suddenly eight million armed and bigoted Tamils would be, effectively, next door neighbors to two and a half million armed and bigoted Maya.

There had been wars in the Thousand Cultures, even ethnic wars—over the long run one could hardly *not* have wars, if human beings were involved—but none since the invention of the springer, so no one knew what difference instantaneous travel might make if ethnic fighting tipped over into a full-fledged planetary civil war.

The news and government channels, for the last stanyear, had been buzzing with the possibility that we might find out, and though Briand was the second-least populated world in human space, mentions of Briand on all 200,000 news channels across human space were running second only to mentions of Earth itself.

So here was the job Margaret and I had agreed to take on; to go to Briand and do whatever we could for peace. As I often did at times like this, I found myself repeating a phrase that I had first heard from an old Caledon preacher, the father of a friend of mine, and that Shan had adopted as his own—that we were "only called to try, and success or failure are not in our hands."

"Reverend Carruthers's favorite phrase," Margaret observed. It's a good one."

"Whoops," I said. "Didn't realize that I spoke out loud." I looked at the clock. "Still an hour till the first class. Want to take a break from studying and get something to eat?"

"Fine by me. The more I learn, the more depressed I get. Have you been reading the overall survey too?"

"*Ja, midons.* I keep hoping that Ambassador Kiel tends to exaggeration, but I don't think he does."

"Did you see the *Culture Tips?*"

"No. What do they say, expect to be shot at any moment?"

"Well, that of course. But there does seem to be one thing that both cultures agree on. You're going to love it." She might have wanted me to guess, but judging from the evil smile she was giving me, it seemed best to just wait for whatever unpleasant surprise she was about to give me. After a moment she said, "Air conditioning is for the weak and the ill. Foreigners who use air conditioning reveal that they are weak and unfit by doing so."

I shuddered; Manila, outside, in the midday sun, was pleasantly cool with mild humidity compared to the daily weather in either Yaxkintulum or New Tanjavur. "I don't suppose it says anything about that in the Kural," I said.

"I must have missed what the Kural is, in my reading," she said. "Is that the Tamil for 'how to make foreigners uncomfortable?'"

"On the contrary. There's one whole section devoted to the requirement for treating strangers well. It's an anthology of proverbs and wisdom, dating to some time after the Cankam. Morally speaking it's about as good as any other book about ethical behavior ever written—that is, if everyone followed it the world would be a better place, and everyone who has read it or studied it probably knows this, and the one thing everyone refrains from doing is following it. And like every other relatively reasonable, workable moral code ever devised, it now has a whole gang of experts who spend all their time elaborating on it and interpreting it—teachers, gurus, rabbis, call 'em what you want. So I'm sure somebody somewhere has considered whether air conditioning is contrary to his interpretation of the Kural, and worse yet probably arrived at a definitive answer."

She sighed. "Well, I suppose traditionally—"

"The interpreters are about as traditional as using nanos to grow the temples in the city," I said. "At least according to the *toszet* that wrote the note, nothing's really known about how the Kural was originally conveyed to the people. It might even just be a list of 'smart things Tamil people said to each other,' put together by some enterprising spirit." I reached into the refrigerator and found the fast-rising olive bread and a reconstitutable chicken-soup-for-two. "What do you think for lunch? Mediterranean all right?"

"*Stip-agr*-Mediterranean-*subj,* yum-*max,*" Margaret said. She was playing around, as she sometimes did, with her old culture's language, Reason. "If we have any pesto, I'll be in heaven."

"Your wish is my command, *midons,* or at least the refrigerator's," I said. "Lunch-a *tropa bo, venietz* right up."

Long, long ago, when we had first been married, little games with each other's culture languages had been great fun. Like everyone in the Thousand Cultures we had grown up speaking the convenient, universal Terstad, but when we had gotten married we had made a concerted effort to become fluent in each other's culture languages, me in Reason and Margaret in Occitan. Playing about in those languages had become an interesting, complicated way to flirt, and our pidgin of both languages plus Terstad had also been our language of love. It made me feel good to stand there, playing around in both languages, as we waited for the food to be ready.

We ate at the little table that for some reason was put in the bedroom, washing down the meal with strong coffee since we would need to stay awake that afternoon. "Have you looked over the fashions for Briand?" I asked Margaret.

She made a face. "Women who look like me typically don't have to worry about that."

"Oh, really, Margaret," I said, "I adore you, you don't have to please anyone else, and besides there are plenty of clothes around the Thousand Cultures that are very flattering to you."

"There was a time when I used to love the way you'd argue with me about what I look like," she said, getting up and going over to the window with the last of her coffee. "Nowadays it mostly just makes me wonder if I married someone who is blind, perverted, or stupid." She took a long sip, not looking at me. I contemplated her big, drooping buttocks, and the way her pale skin had aged rapidly, and thought a number of spiteful things that I immediately felt ashamed of. After she had finished the cup, she turned back to me and said, "I'm sorry, Giraut. I know you were trying to be nice, really. I guess it's not your fault that it doesn't work any more. Tell me about their fashions."

I swallowed twenty angry thoughts, because I wanted peace between us, and who knew how long this mood would hold? Then I said, "Oh, nothing really. It turns out that dress codes are moderately strict in both cultures. So the only thing we're going to be wearing is Council uniforms; everything else is significant in so many different ways that we'd be accidentally saying all kinds of things we didn't mean to. And, well, for the fun of it I asked the aintellect simulator to pretend to be a Tamil and guess what occupation went with the traditional costumes of my culture and yours. It looked at Caledon clothing and said 'Prisoner'—"

"You thought the same thing the first time you saw it," she pointed out.

"Till I found out how practical it was. And the Occitan outfit came out as 'Boy prostitute.' "

Margaret chuckled a little, and walked into the next room without saying anything. Now that I had told the story, it seemed silly and pointless to me; but at the time I had been so happy to find something amusing to talk about with her. I kept wondering which one of us was to blame—Margaret, me, or the universe.

After a while it was time to go to the class; we set our cards for the appointed number and sprang there. The room was small, with only about twenty seats besides the teacher's chair at the front of the room, but there was only one other student there when we arrived. "Hello," she said, so accentlessly that I couldn't place where in the Thousand Cultures she could be from, "My name is Paxa Prytanis. Are you here for Tamil class too?"

"*Yap*," Margaret said. It's the strong affirmative in Reason; it's also, at least in some circumstances, a real conversation shut down.

I wondered what Margaret was reacting to? Perhaps to Paxa

Prytanis's appearance; she was a little younger than we were, perhaps in her mid to late twenties, petite in all dimensions, with gold-brown hair of a shade that pretty much had to be genetically engineered, coffee-colored skin, wideset bright green eyes, and perfect teeth. Clearly she was from one of the cultures where they reshaped everyone's genes *in utero* for health and beauty; in her case the reshaping had really taken.

"Well," she said, "I understand it's difficult but it's a picnic compared to Maya."

"Mayan, I think," I said. "Apparently the noun and the adjective for the people are both 'Maya,' singular, plural, possessive, nominative, and objective, but the language is 'Mayan.' Just talking about it in plain old Terstad is a lot of work," I said. Paxa Prytanis smiled at that; Margaret rolled her eyes at me as if telling me I was making an ass of myself. Probably I was, but now that I was in the conversation I might as well keep going. "You're going to be taking both languages?"

"Not to completion," she said. "I'm posted to Briand in fifteen days. How about you?"

"We get forty," I said, sliding into a chair. "Not enough for proficiency—really just enough to load up the emblok so we can practice it all off later." For study, most people wore the emblok, a little black button that stuck behind one ear, near where you'd put a psypyx, which temporarily gave you an eidetic memory for anything you loaded into it. Unfortunately, because individual neural codes were unique, the only way to get information in or out of it was via the particular brain with which it worked. Furthermore, it was still too slow to allow for things like natural conversation; the memories in the emblok had to be copied, by repeated retrieval and practice, into the brain's ordinary memory, before it was possible to really use the knowledge. Supposedly they were working on better ones, and there was talk someday of a universal emblok that would learn your brain's code and could read directly off a database, so that instead of learning and practicing in a way that was more accurate but hardly more efficient than what a Roman ambassador might have done, they could just slap a new language straight into your head. Now that the Second Renaissance was underway, and all the old claims about limits to knowledge and impossibility were collapsing, who knew what might be around the corner?

Meanwhile, however, I would have to teach Tamil and Mayan to my emblok, which was based on a design three hundred years old, and then practice both languages back out of the emblok and into my permanent memory, which was based on millions of years of evolution—though to judge by the way my nervous system was reacting to my wife, this stranger, and the interaction between them, that too had not been improved in a long time.

"Anyway," I said, "I'm Giraut Leones, and this is Margaret, my wife."

Paxa Prytanis squinted for a moment. "Your name is Groutlio—er—?"

Margaret suddenly beamed. She knows it discomfits me that so many other cultures find my name hard to pronounce, and apparently right now anything that discomfited me was all right with her. "Gear Out Lee Owe Nuss," she said. "And my full name now is Margaret Leones. It happens we both come from cultures that rename one of us, and his family slightly outranked mine, as near as we could work it out comparing social positions across cultures."

"I see," she said. "Well, anyway, you must call me Paxa—I'm a Hedon, you know, and we really only have surnames so as to give people something formal to call us—and—"

"We'd be delighted if you'd call us Giraut and Margaret," Margaret said. "I wonder where—"

At that moment the teacher entered, a tall thin woman who looked nothing like any Tamil I had seen any pictures of. She turned out to be our instructor in both languages, and the Office of Special Projects agent who had originally gone there decades ago as part of a delegation, by sublight-speed hibernation ship, and then returned once the springer became available. Unlike almost any other language classes I had ever had, hers were conducted like a military drill, with no sense of warmth or fun in communication. After having spent the better part of two decades on Briand, she hated both languages and everything about both cultures. It didn't seem like much of a recommendation.

We kept studying anyway; the day after Paxa's last day of class, we took one day off to lie down in a dark room, let them fit helmets over our heads, and let them take psypyx recordings of us. This was the first time we'd ever had to do this before a mission, and since its whole purpose was to make sure there was a recording to be loaded into our clones in the event of our deaths, that too told us something about the mission we were going on.

We knew the mission documents by heart by the time that Shan had us come in to talk to him. That was normal. He rarely met face-to-face except to confirm that everyone had understood the written documents and the com calls; it was not his style to be chummy.

"Well," he said, as soon as Margaret and I had taken seats, "I assume that the job description makes sense and that the only problem is that the job itself is impossible."

"Of course," Margaret said. "If I'm reading the reports accurately, the Tamil culture is very eager to share itself with everyone but doesn't want anybody else polluting it; and no one knows what the Maya think because they're refusing any contact except the purely commercial, and even that's restricted to about a dozen vendors in the capital city, who virtually live under house arrest. So it isn't promising, and we knew that when we took the job. The two questions that are bothering me are whether you really think this is going to work and what the real mission is if it's not."

Shan grunted, looking down at his hands, folded on the desk in front of him. "I am reserving judgment about its working. Besides yourselves, as of yesterday we have nine different OSP missions on Briand, and each one of them is working on the problem from an angle of its own. I don't think any of them has *no* hope of success, and there may be synergies between what the different projects accomplish, so that it's possible they will do more together than the sum of what they do individually. That's the best I can tell you.

"As for the reasons why we don't just abandon Briand and let whatever happen—well, let's start with the problem that we think there are at least five alien ruins in the Briand system, the most ever found in a single solar system. If one of our bright fellows in xenolinguistics is deciphering other indicators correctly, the Metallah system may have been a regional capital or administrative post. So at a minimum, if we get permission to really explore Briand and the other planets in the Metallah system, we may very well bring the total number of alien ruins, derelicts, and probes recovered up to twenty-six. And it's always possible that a 'regional capital' or 'administrative center' will have bigger or more interesting ruins than we have seen before, maybe enough to get a start on really understanding them.

"Furthermore, if it was an important place to them once before, then it's always possible that—*if* they still exist—they might return there. So Briand, out of the twenty-six solar systems of human space, has a slightly higher than average probability of being the place where we finally contact the aliens." He smiled at me, inviting me to remember. "I don't suppose you realized what you were starting, Giraut."

I shrugged and smiled. It's a perennial embarrassment, since I can take no credit for anything and I don't know any more than any other educated layman, but by pure accident I had been present on Nansen, the very first time I worked for the Council of Humanity, before Shan recruited me for the OSP, when the first alien ruin had been found and it had been realized that humanity was the *second* intelligent species to terraform Nansen. It had been a mere fluke—two Caledons and I had been driving through a roadless mountain pass on an urgent errand and seen the gateway of what turned out to be a small compound, apparently left by the aliens 17,000 years ago when they were forced to survive on Nansen under primitive conditions.

Once the archeologists knew that there were alien ruins in the tiny corner of the galaxy explored by human beings so far, and had some idea of what to look for—and with the vast expansion of scientific research known as the Second Renaissance—alien sites had been turning up all over, as had their ancient space probes and dead, drifting ships.

The oddest thing was that although they had maps and charts in great variety, they were illiterate—so far we had yet to find anything recognizable as a book or a text, not even a label above a switch, but there were plenty of other things to examine in the meantime. And perhaps matters would resolve in another nine stanyears, when one of our springships would reach what was believed to be their homeworld. "I understand that that's part of our permanent assignment. Get the human race's act together before we contact aliens. And yes, having a world go up in ethnic warfare would be pretty bad, but I still don't see—"

"If you merely think it would be pretty bad, then there are two things you're neglecting," Shan said. "Number one is that we'd rather be represented in our first contact with an alien species by a culture that is reasonably representative, and we don't want human beings trying to enlist aliens for any ethnic war. And the second thing is even more important—the power of example. Did you know that we've had copycat murders and bombings in various trouble spots around the Thousand Cultures, ever since contact with Briand was established and so many people learned how to hate their neighbors in new and creative ways?"

"I didn't but I'm not surprised," I said.

"Well, now. Imagine what every bigot out there in the Thousand Cultures can say if we have warfare and genocide on one of the settled worlds, with constant coverage by the news media. Regardless of which side wins. It will all amount to pointing at

Briand and urging everyone to 'do unto others before they do unto you,' but that's quite persuasive enough to people who already fear and hate their neighbors. On the other hand, if war is averted, the Council and the OSP both are making such large efforts on Briand that it may get into popular mythology that we never let anything of the kind happen—which builds everyone's sense of security and makes the next job a lot easier."

"The next job?" I asked.

"We have only one more contact to go. For reasons known only to themselves, the ninety-two cultures of Addams, out in the Theta Ursa Major system, have not yet built a springer. Yet we know from ongoing radio contact that—at least up until forty-two years ago, when the radio signals left Addams—there was a fairly normal situation there. So they may make contact at any time—they've only known how to build a springer themselves now for six years—and once they do, chances are it will be a routine Connect. After that one, our first task will be done— we'll have all of humanity under the common umbrella of the Council, with everyone at least nominally accepting collective decision making between the Thousand Cultures and the Sol System. But that's only the first step, and hard as it's been, it's the easiest one.

"After all, in the long run the mission's always been to get humanity headed outward again, to return to innovation and exploration and all the things that have been largely abandoned ever since the Inward Turn—yet at the same time we don't want to bring back war, or any of the other social evils that the Inward Turn let humanity escape from. In a way it's the question of whether or not we're mature enough as a species to be able to go out into the unknown again without having to be afraid of losing ourselves there. And just as a recovering drunk can't afford to think about booze, we're a recovering violent species and we can't afford to think about ethnic bloodshed."

Margaret nodded. "You do know that you're preaching to the choir?"

Shan's eyebrow rose and his lips twisted. "Yes, I know. But repeating it helps me to keep believing it."

"Can you tell us what the other missions are doing so that we don't cross them up?"

"In a general way. We have intelligence missions surveying both cultures. A very nice police assistance program that is teaching the cops of New Tanjavur to be professional, loyal only to each other, and not provocative to the Maya anymore, so that in the event of rioting they'll get in between the factions, not act as shock troops for the Tamil side. Some people getting cross-ethnic study groups and clubs going in both cities. That's five, eh? Well, there are four others, and they're more secret. I don't think you'll bump into them."

Twenty seconds of guessing would have allowed me to figure out as much as Shan had just told me. "Couldn't you have just told me you preferred to keep quiet about the entire issue?"

"It would have gone against all my training as a diplomat," Shan said. "Which bring us to our last point. Ambassador Kiel is not the man I would have chosen for this job, but he's the one we had to accept; the Council diplomatic service no longer gives the Office of Special Projects a free hand, after a couple of unpleasant incidents with which I am very happy to say I had nothing to do. Kiel will bring those up at every opportunity, along with a number of unfocused but deeply felt accusations. You can't really expect cooperation from him. He's so old that he made his first trip out in a sublight hibernation ship. He believes in working entirely through local authority, by which he means local *government*—because it has never penetrated his mind that the nominal state is not necessarily where the power rests in a given society. If we had sent him to Nou Occitan, he'd have spent all of his time trying to talk to your ceremonial king, and ignored your whole art world. If we had sent him to Caledony, he'd have ignored the church and concentrated on the civil administration.

"Now, since in Tamil Mandalam the real power is in the rival schools of poets—all hoping to be declared the next Cankam officially—and quibbling Kural interpreters, and in Yaxkintulum the real power is in the temples and the extended lineages (we think), this doesn't do us much good. It doesn't do Kiel much good either, but he's not able to see that. Almost all of his reports are recountings of what the local cops and bureaucrats tell him, which he repeats upward with an innocent belief that would be charming in another context. When he does talk to someone who has real prestige or influence in the culture, he doesn't listen. Rather, he tries to get them to pledge to remain loyal to the state, even if the state pursues a peace policy; he thinks of that as securing the cooperation of nongovernmental institutions.

"So to state the obvious, emphatically off the record, you will have to work around him, not for him. You are going to have office space in the Embassy, and quarters there, because it's the only place in New Tanjavur where cultural envoys could be permitted to live, but this is happening very much over his protests, and I am forced to emphasize that he will probably obstruct you when he can. Therefore, don't even let him know what *you're* doing, let alone what any other Office of Special Projects team is doing, except in the most general of terms."

"That shouldn't be hard," Margaret said. "Because the truth is we don't have a clue what we're going to do."

"Of course you do," Shan said. "You're going to figure out what I would have ordered you to do, if I really understood the situation and knew exactly how two cultural reps could improve it. That's your first task. Your second is to follow those orders I hypothetically would have given. Now, given that my impression is that no matter what you do, the Tamils won't listen to you and the Maya won't talk to you, I do not expect overwhelming success. I expect a damned good try."

He rose, which indicated that the interview was over. When I had been younger I had taken these vague missions as votes of confidence, declarations that he felt he could rely on our judgment; later I had come to think of them as ways to insure deniability if anything went wrong, and to make sure that we didn't have any standing orders in the way of doing what would work. Nowadays I just regarded it as a ritual we did before every mission.

Once again, our baggage and furniture had gone on ahead of us and robots were unpacking it, probably at this very moment, in the Embassy in New Tanjavur. So having concluded our interview with Shan and shaken his hand, we made a final trip to the restroom, Margaret gulped a large dose of an antinauseant, and we did the obligatory last-minute check of our personal baggage. After confirming that everything was there, we went to one of the many springers in the OSP's transport section, registered and confirmed our destination, and watched them power up the rectangular empty doorway in front of us; it became dark and opaque, then light gray and featureless. "Yet another world," Margaret said.

Forty-six light-years in one step, we walked through the gray nothing of the springer, face-first into the brilliant glare of Metallah, as far from Earth as any human beings had yet gone to live.

For ceremonial reasons—even though local media were barely covering it—we had been sent to the springer that was used for formal receptions, on the terrace of the Embassy at New Tanjavur. We arrived at about mid-morning—the time when the terrace was hottest. All I could see was the terrible glare off the concrete at my feet, and the black silhouettes of the people standing in front of us.

I clapped on protective glasses from my pocket—beside me, Margaret, who had been careful to spring across that 30% increase in gravity with nothing on her stomach but a couple of nausea suppressants, had stopped retching and was standing up straight, pulling on her own protective glasses. The burst of pain in my eyes subsided and the glasses began to find their proper adjustment. Behind the still-dark shapes of the party receiving us, the whole city of New Tanjavur spread out before us. Backlit as it was by the harsh light, it was a confusing, jagged range of spires, pyramids, peaks, and domes, in black outline against an indigo sky.

"Hello," a voice said at my shoulder. I turned away from the glare in front of me, and the protective glasses had dimmed enough to let me see a tall, thin, white-haired man clearly. He had the palest skin I'd ever seen, paler even than that of Margaret or some of the other Caledons, so pale that in the harsh light I seemed to see every vein. His hair could have been white or platinum blond, and the spray of fine lines on his face could be the way his skin was naturally, or the effects of the alien sun, or many years of life. His eyes were pale blue and large, nose long, thin, and delicate, and he was very thin. He was wearing the standard bureaucratic uniform for the Council of Humanity—the same uniform Margaret and I wore, since it seemed impossible for us to find civilian clothes that wouldn't offend anyone on Briand.

"I'm Ambassador Kiel," he said, sticking out his hand. His grip was firm, and his hand was dry and oddly callused.

"Giraut Leones," I said. "Office of Artistic Interchange. This is my wife Margaret Leones; she's your new Bureau of Tourism Development rep."

The Ambassador nodded. "That is the pronunciation? Gurret Le Yoniz?"

"Close," I said, smiling—I'd heard worse. "Gir*aut* Leones. A-u dipthong and long e." I did wonder why no one ever had trouble with "Margaret."

"Well, no matter how you're pronounced, we're all pleased to have you both; your records have preceded you here and we know we've gotten two special people." He turned and gestured to the row of five people behind him. "My chief staff officers, and our guests from the government of Tamil Mandalam. Ms. Skine, Political Section, my second in command." She was a short, light-brown-skinned woman, wearing an unpressed standard bureaucratic uniform without any medals or badges of rank, her head shaved. She looked very bored and as if she were hoping to escape at any moment. In the heat and the glare, that made me think she might be the sanest person here.

"Sir Qrala, Advisor for Ethnography." He was tall, bulky, and balding, with a burned-red skin that indicated that he had a lot of trouble remembering his sunblock. He was probably originally the color of most of humanity—light coffee—which is to say he was considerably darker than Margaret or I, and yet he had that sunburn. I made a quick mental vow to be careful about covering up before going out into Metallah's direct light.

Qrala had one of those dead-fish handshakes that some large people develop for fear of crushing anyone's hand. He lightly placed his left hand on the back of mine, and I felt his middle finger tap my hand twice. I did the same.

Good; the second in command, at least, was with the OSP. I wondered why Shan had not told us that; perhaps he was letting Qrala decide who to approach. "Let me make sure I pronounce it correctly," I said. "Kh'rala?"

"Qrala. No aspiration; begin with a glottal stop and slide into a soft k. Let me assure you that practically no one other than the people I grew up with can do it. And Giraut Leones?"

"Perfect."

Kiel seemed a little impatient; he steered me to the next person. "Doctor Urruttiran, spokesperson for the People's Assembly of Tamil Mandalam, which is our host culture here, to the Council of Humanity."

The man was small and slight in build, with a graying mustache and close-cropped hair; he had skin as dark as any I had ever seen. He inclined his head slightly and said, "And may I present my assistant, Kapilar, who Ambassador Kiel has been good enough to hire as your personal assistant? Kapilar has been editor of a couple of significant journals of opinion here in New Tanjavur and is well-known in artistic circles, and has been described by many of the senior critics as one of the more profound exponents of the *akam* poems of the Eight Anthologies; a man who can guide you through the city, the Cankam poets, or the bureaucracy with equal facility, though I must add that only the city and the Cankam poetry are apt to be beautiful. But listen to me babble—I'm sure he'll please you, at least as soon as I give you a chance to become acquainted. Should Kapilar not please you, you need only let me know and we'll find another talented and hardworking young man."

I had been listening closely and thought I had figured out the pronunciation; Interstellar receptions seem to inevitably require brief language lessons, but it's so unpleasant to hear your name mispronounced—at least it is for me—that I try very hard to get it right. "Kapilar?" I asked, letting the *p* be slightly voiced, so that it was almost a *b*.

"Just right," Kapilar said, "and I've been a junior assistant long enough to be used to being addressed as 'you' in any case." He was about average height, so that he looked straight into my eyes. I judged that he was better muscled than I had ever been, even ten years before when I had been something of an athlete; that was hardly surprising on a high gravity world.

Like Doctor Urruttiran, Kapilar was very dark-skinned. He wore a neat mustache and a wisp of an underlip goatee, and his curly hair was pomaded close to his head. His fine-boned features and big, dark eyes were startlingly handsome. His white, thigh-length shirt, beautifully decorated in a wild swirl of colored embroidery, fit him with the perfection that requires both a fussy client and a fussy tailor; instinctively he stood in a way that draped the sleeve elegantly on the arm. The soft baggy black pants, and the elegant pointed slippers, too, seemed to have been formed on him by some loving artist. I rarely saw any young man dress so well away from my home culture; at that moment I had a surprising realization that there might be some things here that would make me feel very much at home.

Ambassador Kiel cleared his throat and said, "And our other person here is Tz'iquin, who is. Hmm. Who is Tz'iquin, for the moment, at least."

I smiled at Tz'iquin-who-was-Tz'iquin, and he returned the

smile in a way I liked, as if laughing at the whole situation, as I wished I could. He was a tall, strong man with features that might have appeared in any of the Maya carvings we had studied as part of our preparation. Just as the Tamils of Tamil Mandalam were probably the last unmixed Dravidians around, the Maya of Yaxkintulum might well be the very last of the pure Amerinds, at least until whatever mysterious problem cleared up on Addams and we got springer contact out there. Tz'iquin wore a white tunic and trousers, a broad-brimmed black hat, and sandals, devoid of decoration except for some tiny embroidery around the cuffs and at the neck.

"Well," Tz'iquin said, "the Ambassador is kind. To be very precise, I am the Maya who the Tamils call on when they need to talk to the Maya, and so I have taken over the job of talking to Ambassador Kiel as well, since he wanted to talk to a Maya, and he could only do it through the Tamils, and I was the only one *they* could talk to. But no one, least of all the Maya, has seen any way to give me a title that I can answer to without doing something politically unwise. Indeed I cannot even tell you whether I am speaking to you as a friend of the Tamils, as a prominent resident alien in Tamil Mandalam, or in any capacity for Yaxkintulum. So I remain very much myself, just as the Ambassador so discreetly put it. However, if it is any consolation, as myself, I'm very happy to meet you."

As official introductions go, all of this so far had been reasonably pleasant, but already my feet and back hurt in the higher gravity. As if on cue, Ambassador Kiel said, "I believe we should step inside and take comfortable seats. Our guests cannot be used to our gravity, heat, or light. And I understand that they have some exertion ahead of them this afternoon."

Margaret and I glanced at each other since neither of us had heard any such thing, but we followed along as the ambassador and the others led us into the main part of the building, behind us.

The furniture in the main conference room was squat and ugly, but that had to be expected. 1.3 gravities means almost a third again your weight, and to both carry that load and support it comfortably, every chair in New Tanjavur was shaped like an old-fashioned acceleration couch, curved up like a banana lying on edge so that you could see the faces of others while your lower back was supported. As soon as the ambassador and his two senior officers had gotten onto their couches, I sank into mine, letting myself stretch as much as protocol permitted.

The room was a standard Council of Humanity embassy meeting room with almost nothing that wouldn't have been there in any other such room, anywhere else throughout the Thousand Cultures. It had the standard decoration for the main meeting room in an embassy—fifteen second vus from all over the Thousand Cultures. They were even the standard vus—Arcturus setting over Totzmare from Montanha Valor, of course, from Wilson. Nansen was represented by a vu of the Gap Bow, a gigantic double rainbow that formed in an enormous fjord at noon most days. Both were spectacular, but in a fifteen-second vu, with such limited motion, you didn't get much of an appreciation of them, and anyway the images were so common that they had become visual clichés. They were good choices, since the room was calculated to give offense by nothing, not even by its blandness.

Ambassador Kiel signaled for drinks, and shortly all of us had been presented with a glass of punch, running wet with condensation. I took a sip; the mix of mango, coconut, and tamarind, sweet, cold, and grainy, tasted rather like a liquid pear. I was startled at how cold the drink felt in my hand, and how wet the glass was; now that my spine and feet didn't hurt, I finally noticed that the room we were in was un-airconditioned, with only a big, slow ceiling fan to circulate the damp, stifling air. If a desire for air conditioning was regarded by both Tamil and Maya as offworlder weakness, I liked weakness.

"Well," the Ambassador said, "I imagine you were briefed on our situation here. It might be of some benefit for you to hear how our representatives understand our problems; perhaps that would make matters clearer."

Tz'iquin spoke first. I listened closely because I had liked his sense of irony out on the terrace, and because it seemed likely that a person who could not fit into the language or concept set of either culture was likely to have an insight or two. "I am a little alarmed, in an already volatile situation, to discover that we have people here to encourage tourists and artistic exchange," he said. "These are often fine things, I'm sure, but none of our Maya are going to want to see tourists in Yaxkintulum, and since Maya decoration is illegal in Mayatown—a Tamil law I have been working on getting changed—the Maya of Mayatown are not going to get much benefit from tourism. As for artistic exchange, we would be most pleased never to read anyone else's books, or hear their songs, or whatever, in exchange for never having them meddle with ours. So I shall be very happy to be friends with our new representatives, indeed I am happy to be friends with anyone, but I truly cannot see any way in which I will ever want to arrange anything for them." He never stopped smiling while he said it, but the firmness of his tone was unmistakable.

"My job isn't to judge or to serve," Margaret said. "Some cultures want tourism, and I teach them how to encourage it. Some are indifferent, and some, like yours, want to keep it out. My job is to make sure, among other things, that if you don't want it you won't have it. I can help you a great deal with keeping it out, while maintaining reasonably good terms with the Council of Humanity."

Tz'iquin's smile deepened. "Well, then, perhaps Ambassador Kiel was right that I would want to attend this meeting. And you—er, is that Sir Leones, Mr. Leones—?"

"I've answered to practically every common title," I said, "but in my home culture the polite prefix is *donz*."

"*Donz* Leones, then. Are you able to offer something similarly of value?"

"If you don't want contact we can steer away creative artists who might otherwise come here to work," I said, "and help you draft polite notes of refusal when scholars ask you to let them come here and study either you or your art. If you want to maintain isolation, we can do many things to help you maintain it."

"I think you may be our most popular offworlders," Tz'iquin said.

Doctor Urruttiran smiled too broadly, in a just-slightly-too-friendly way; after Tz'iquin's blunt honesty, it wasn't a good act. "As you doubtless are very well aware, and must be concerned about," he began, "On Briand only Tamil Mandalam has elected to invite an embassy from the Council of Humanity. But I want to assure you—you most of all, Grout and Margaret Lyo Nyess, since it is you who have responsibility for art and for people coming here to experience what is unique about Tamil Mandalam—that we are very, very happy to have opened the Embassy and we look forward greatly to the benefits it will bring to the human race. We think that the other Thousand Cultures need to become reacquainted with the beauties of true Tamil culture, the pure culture of the Cankam era, and thus we are eager to share. We would like to have visitors of all kinds and I'm sure Kapilar will be eager to work the details of that out with you," he said, nodding at Margaret. "We Tamils are much more outgoing, you know, than the Maya we share Briand with. We are a people who live in our public spaces, in constant contact with each other and our ancient works, and I am sure you will be glad to know us. We often say we live in public shadows because the harsh light of Metallah keeps us from venturing outside more than we have to, so we have constructed many, many patches of shade, making our city civilized, cool, and comfortable, a place where anyone who wishes to study or to learn to create may come."

He wasn't saying a thing about learning from anyone else; he spoke as if 1227 other cultures had just come knocking on the Tamils' door for no reason other than to learn how to be Tamil, which they would want to do. In the long run the Maya might be easier to deal with.

He spent quite a while explaining the many advantages to Earth and the Thousand Cultures that would be made manifest by our contact with Tamil Mandalam, and I hardly had the heart to point out that there were two other Tamil-derived cultures already in the Thousand Cultures and that the poetry he was so proud of was taught in college courses from here to places as far as seventy light-years away—I had read parts of it myself, though in Occitan translation, in a Survey of Human Poetry course at school in Elinorien.

As I was thinking that point, he answered it by discussing how the other two Tamil cultures—by falling away from the true Velalla tradition—had given us all a debased impression of the noble Tamil world of the Cankam poets, and that Tamil Mandalam, where every Tamil was truly Velalla and thus a farmer-warrior-artist, was the only place where true understanding had been preserved. Urruttiran knew that the Cankam poems were already known across human space, but until they were known properly, they could not take their rightful place at the top of the great pyramid of literature. He would be happy to help us to understand, any way we needed him to.

Finally he wound down by observing that the best way for us to appreciate the greatness and beauty of New Tanjavur would have to be by walking through it, and that fortunately Kapilar would be taking us on a walk right after this meeting, if that was all right with us.

We agreed that it would be, and Dr. Urruttiran, apparently satisfied that he had done everything we would ever really need, got to his feet and left. A moment later Tz'iquin said, "Well, that is all that I needed to talk with you about at this moment. But I shall be happy to call on you tomorrow, later in the day, if that is all right." Then he was gone as well.

That left us, Sir Qrala, Ms. Skine, the ambassador, and the silently smiling Kapilar.

"Kapilar," Ambassador Kiel said, "if you don't mind, we're going to hold a private conversation for about ten minutes, and then you can take that walk through the city with your new supervisors if the three of you wish. And Qrala, there's no need for you to be here unless you wish to, so don't let us detain—"

Qrala shrugged. "There's always work I can be doing," he said, and got up, along with Kapilar. The two of them went through the door together.

Ambassador Kiel checked to make sure that the soundproofing for the room was turned on, and then said, "All right, let me just explain our situation here. I'll start with a few standing orders to make them official, but I have no doubt that they're unnecessary for people with your degree of experience, and so I'll make them brief—ask if you need any clarification.

"One, you are to wear only uniforms, or the *suit-biz,* anywhere in public. Big billowing robes—basically nightgowns—are acceptable within the Embassy or when entertaining any close friends; I've taken the liberty of providing your quarters with them. You'll find they're very cool and comfortable, but unfortunately they are only suited for very informal occasions. I've worked to establish them as normal breakfast clothing, and for drinks on the terrace after dark, so invitations to those occasions permit the robe unless I specify otherwise.

"Two, under no circumstances allow any Tamil or Maya to directly observe you using air conditioning. When local staff are in the Embassy, turn it off and keep it off. They can tell when it's being used in private quarters, and they check. We had an economic attaché here about forty standays ago who forgot that; the Tamils suddenly stopped greeting him as an equal and broke off his section of the trade talks. They did talk to him a bit—but only to offer crude sexual propositions. So far as I can tell air-conditioning here is found almost entirely in brothels.

"Three: avoid any references to food, hunger, or starvation when you are anywhere near Mayatown, or when any mass media might pick up what you say. The Tamils have gotten a belief from somewhere that the Maya routinely deliberately starve large parts of their population, and that accusation is an offensive ethnic stereotype here. No Council personnel must ever be seen uttering anything that could be construed as referring to starving Maya. Let me point out that just last week a nine-year-old Tamil boy pointed at a group of Maya teenagers returning to Maya-town from a shopping trip, and called them 'starvers.' They kicked him to death. The Tamil judge did not permit the insult to even be entered in the court record as a possible mitigating circumstance, on grounds that any Tamil had the freedom to say what everyone knew to be true. This is not the first such case I have seen since I arrived here, so do not mention anything about hunger or starvation anywhere in public; and let me add you can expect anything you do say to be taken severely out of context.

"Four, some businessmen, both here and out in the Thousand Cultures, have been asking us when the Bazaar will open here. The official answer is that we're waiting for an appropriate time; the unofficial answer is probably never—our economists tell us that a Connect Depression, followed by a Connect Boom, would be so disruptive that it might be forty stanyears before all trade barriers can be relaxed. So if you are asked, be utterly noncommital; refer them to the official answer but make it clear that you don't know and in any case it doesn't matter much to you, since we don't want them to keep coming back to you about it and risk their figuring things out via repeated contact. Or in short: do not, under any circumstances, encourage any business person to even think about the opening of a Bazaar.

"And let me repeat again, I know all this was part of your briefing. My only reason for giving direct orders like this is so that, if—all gods forbid—it should happen that the Council has sent me a pair of incompetents, I can fire you at once for disobeying orders. And I am well aware that they have done no such thing, so please forgive the long, dull lecture."

My mind had been drifting away, contemplating how different the perspectives of different people—even within a community as small as the Council's permanent staff—could be. When Margaret and I were young, and I was a mere assistant to a Council economist in Caledony, the Council had boldly opened the Bazaar *because* it would cause disruption. The sudden impact of all the bounty of Earth, the space colonies, and the Thousand Cultures, available right now for immediate delivery—vast quantities of high-quality imports at very low prices—had shattered the Caledon economy, provoking a coup that put the stiffnecks briefly into power, then drove them to desperate acts that had justified sending CSPs—the Council's marines—to support a revolution. In the aftermath, one way or another, every important politician with any anti-Council feelings had become permanently retired. Caledony was still Caledon—but no more likely to resist the Council of Humanity than Earth itself.

The new thinking—or the old thinking reasserting itself?—was that oppressive quiet was better than noisy freedom, and that the top people belonged on top, at least as long as they could be suborned to the Council's will. Maybe it was just relic of my time as a wild *jovent,* ready to get into a fight for art and just possibly get killed for no more reason than the freedom to do pointlessly beautiful things. Maybe, once having been a revolutionary agitator, even by accident, I would never quite look on the top people with the proper reverence. Or perhaps my earlier selves were merely whispering, to my present self, that Kiel seemed like an old windbag of a paper-pusher and anus-tonguer, and I wasn't seeing any way to argue with that.

I kept a straight face anyway, and appeared to listen. Now that he was satisfied that he had fulfilled his official duty, he shrugged and got down to business. "The truth is that we have been managing to suppress many of the media reports concerning our constant low-level violence here in the city. Copies of the true numbers will be waiting for you in private, eyes-only files on your office computers. Do not let any Tamil, or Tz'iquin for that matter, see them.

"You will at once see that in the thirty-day interval figures for the last three years, with which I have supplied you, there is very little change in the numbers so far, but I do expect they will be going down soon—the New Tanjavur city authorities are doing a better and better job of containing the brutality, and I fully expect that we'll eventually see the city pacified. Not that it will be easy. The Tamils are deplorably culturist on the subject of the Maya, and the Maya won't communicate at all so far except to tell me that my messages to them are unwanted—all of us here, I think it's fair to say, have come to doubt that the Maya will ever communicate at any significant level with the Council of Humanity directly. We don't even know the names of their chief government officials, or their rivals if any, or of anyone of any importance over there, except insofar as the Tamils sometimes share their guesses with us. So, between one culture of bigots and another of hermits, it hasn't been easy, and I am afraid I have yet to secure face-to-face talks between the governments, but that is what I am working toward.

"Now, as to where the pair of you fit in, there are two possibilities I can think of. One is that for some insane bureaucratic reason, I have been sent an artistic exchange person and a tourist relations person, perhaps because every embassy gets one, or for some equally silly reason. In that case you will quickly discover that nothing you are trained for matters here. I would suggest you can win us some good will, for example, by finding some highly respected exponent of the Kural, studying with him, and then exclaiming frequently and in public that the proverbs you have learned represent a great leap forward in your moral development and have helped you learn to admire the Tamil people even more. Or you might take up some special study in the Cankam, or arrange for a new set of commentaries on the Cankam to be prepared and shipped to libraries all over the Thousand Cultures—anything that will flatter them, and keep you harmlessly out of the way. I am afraid we must keep you out of the way; we have no need for cultural envoys here and there is no possibility that you will do anything of value. This is undiluted pure power politics, and it's really just a matter of talking the local governments into cooperating to restore order and then backing them while they do it. So far the Council has sent me any number of equally useless specialties—economics, military, scientific, ethnographic, and now arts and tourism, all sorts of people that are irrelevant to any really effective peace process—and you two would seem to be their highest achievement in uselessness thus far.

"The other possibility, which I rather strongly believe thanks to other sources, is that you are actually working for Shan in the Office of Special Projects. Don't bother to deny it, since you would in any case. Let me just tell you what I have told everyone else here. We have a very delicate situation. The top people, in both cultures, I believe, are either committed to handling it properly, or can be persuaded to do so."

This was a bit much. "If you don't know who the Maya 'top people' are and they won't talk to you," I asked, "how do you know that they're 'committed to handling it properly', and how will you 'persuade' them if they won't listen or speak to you?"

Kiel glared at me. "I am not accustomed to be interrupted while I am giving orders. I can dismiss people for insubordination, and put them right back through the springer where they came from, and Ms. Skine can attest that she has seen me do this many times."

I glanced at Skine; she was nodding eagerly, as if perhaps she hoped to see this happen at this very moment. *Perhaps due to my long association with Shan,* I thought, *I am not accustomed to being given orders and told to shut up.* I managed not to voice it; I sat still. If Kiel was waiting for an apology, he didn't get one from me.

After glaring at me interminably, he finally took a long sip of his drink, and when he spoke again his tone was if anything harsher and less conciliatory. "Now, what we need to do is make sure that *the top people become completely persuaded* to make a commitment to peace, and that *they stay on top.* Capture the leadership of a culture, back them to the hilt, and the culture eventually does what you want it to. That's how it's always worked for me. If the leadership wants peace and works for peace then there will be peace. So—don't fuck with me."

"I beg your pardon?" Margaret asked.

"Don't fuck with me. Don't try to run games behind my back. Don't go developing networks out in the city that undercut the people I'm working with. That's another thing Ms. Skine can tell you I don't tolerate, and she will be watching you to see that it doesn't happen."

Ms. Skine nodded again. I was beginning to wonder if that might be her entire job. After another long sip of his drink, Kiel went on. "And to make this unofficial order completely explicit: don't create a pretext here for Shan to pull one of his famous runarounds, subvert the legitimate government, and create yet another Office of Special Projects satrapy here. I know how many times he's done it, and a Caledon should know just what a disaster it is when the legitimate government is overthrown with covert aid from Earth."

Margaret and I had been *saved* by the overthrow of the Caledon government, by what I now knew had been an OSP operation, back before I had ever been recruited. Furthermore the "legitimate government" there had been a crazy theocratic despotism, and the "top people" had been stiffnecked puritans with only such imagination as they couldn't strangle and an ugly habit of regarding everything they didn't like as treatable insanity. From what we'd seen since, we had often remarked to each other that the Office of Special Projects really didn't overthrow *enough* cultural governments. I managed not to voice those thoughts to Kiel, but I enjoyed the slow wink Margaret dropped me.

"Have I made myself clear?"

"You have," Margaret said.

"And have you anything you want to say?"

"Not a thing," I said, "but I do have a question for you. What are your real reasons for hiring Kapilar as our assistant?"

"He happens to be Dr. Urruttiran's nephew, and when he proposed that I find his nephew a job, I took the opportunity. Dr. Urruttiran may well be the next Prime Minister, you see. As for the rest—well, suppose Kapilar is a spy, and you are the innocent cultural affairs people that you are supposed to be. Well, then, without insulting Dr. Urruttiran, I have put his spy where he will have the least opportunity to do any harm. If on the other hand, as I think likely, you are Shan's people, well . . . then whatever harm Kapilar does, he can do to Shan's organization. And in either case, if Kapilar is not a spy, he still has a very nice job, which should please his uncle and get us closer for the next round of negotiations. I only wish Tz'iquin had a couple of eligible blood relatives in the city."

"Thank you," I said. "I really was curious."

We got up and left. Down the hall and up a flight of stairs, we found the internal entrance to our apartment; Qrala was leaning against it, a bit too casually. "Lecture?" he asked, softly.

"Some," I said.

"He bring up Shan?"

"Yap," Margaret said.

Qrala shrugged. I doubted that any aintellect scanning for conversation would have noted that exchange; I had no idea why Qrala had wanted to know. I pressed my thumb to the door's plate, and it opened, but before I had quite gotten inside, Qrala asked "He redfaced? Took a lot of sips off that drink?"

"Now that you mention it, yes," I said.

Qrala leaned forward to whisper; as I leaned forward to hear, I smelled alcohol on his breath. "None of us here ever takes a scrubber with a drink," Qrala said. "None of us longtermers anyway. When you never take a scrubber, that's when you're really adapted to Briand."

He ambled off. As soon as we had closed the apartment door, Margaret said, "Skine looked pretty unfocused most of the time too, and her whole drink went into her. I guess they just figured we'd ask for alcohol in ours when we wanted it."

We did some fast unpacking—the robots had been able to figure most of it out, so there wasn't much left to do—stored the luggage, and were at home for the duration, whatever that might be. After a bathroom break and a damp sponging of our faces, we heaved our already-tired bodies upright, placed an internal com call to Kapilar, and told him that we were at his disposal and he ought to show us as much of the city as he thought good. He was there in less than a minute; he must have been just down the hall somewhere.

The brief glimpse I had caught of the city as we arrived had revealed silhouettes but not much else. The platform had faced east into the midmorning sun, with the nearer parts of the buildings in deep shadow, for despite the ferocity of Metallah's blue-white light—it was almost twice as bright in Briand's sky as Sol was in Earth's—Metallah was only about half the apparent width of Sol from Earth. Thus shadows were not fuzzed nearly as much by light from different edges of the sun, and since the mainly blue light had a very short wavelength, shadows were all but pitch-dark unless a light-colored wall or pavement reflected light into them.

Hardly any light came from the deep indigo sky; above the bubbles of nitrogen-oxygen mix that clung to the antarctic mountains, Briand's atmosphere still retained traces of its old witches' brew mixture. One trace gas or another absorbed almost every color, so the light that took the long way down, bouncing around the sky, did not scatter in one color more than another, like the reds of Wilson, the blues of Earth and Nansen, or the green of Ducommon; rather, almost all of it was absorbed and re-radiated as heat, so that the sky was dark and hot. The blinding dot of Metallah was ringed by a circle of blue that quickly faded into the uniform deep indigo.

Briand had a 22 ⅓ hour day that was close enough to a standay for human beings to adjust to it easily, and given its almost perfectly circular orbit and lack of axial tilt, no matter where you were on the planet, the sun always rose at five hours and forty minutes after midnight, hit noon five hours and forty minutes after dawn, and set five hours and forty minutes after noon—five hours and forty minutes before midnight—year in and year out, with no trace of seasons. The harsh regularity of its light stamped it as a place where nothing changed, where each hour was a copy of many other hours, some other time, years or days before this one, and all of them were hot, vivid, and painful to the eye.

By the time we walked out the Embassy door into the city, my color vision had already adjusted; the brain works from relative color, and there was enough white light to allow me to see a full spectrum, though it had an oddly cold and washed-out look, like stage-moonlight.

"I really suggest you both put on hats, at least," Kapilar said.

I fished in my tunic and found my old collapsible broadbrim; Margaret beside me did the same. Metallah is an F6 subgiant, second only to Procyon for size and ferocity among the stars humanity lives around, and the halogen compounds in the upper atmosphere prevented Briand from ever forming an ozone layer; exposed skin burned in five minutes or less.

Heat seemed to bounce between the white street and the dark sky. To look directly at Metallah was flatly impossible without severe damage to the eyes (fortunately the pain from even looking close to it was so intense that one quickly got out of the habit of even glancing in that direction).

I put on the self-darkening glasses and blinked for a moment, until my eyes stopped smarting and I could see comfortably.

"Right ahead of us," Kapilar said, "is a long row of temples that leads to one of the main thoroughfares, and it leads through the city center. You may trust me, I think, that since you want to understand us, you will want to go to the temple of Murukan first."

Even though she was wearing her dark glasses, I could tell that Margaret was studying him with the intense look that she had used to peer into presidents, chairpeople, councilors, kings, and bureaucrats of every stripe. I wondered what about him fascinated her.

Kapilar conducted us up the broad avenue between the temples.

In the whole city of eight million, only eight of these wide malls and boulevards pierced through the four vast circles of buildings—four to connect the centers of the circles, and four to reach from the centers of the circles into the spandrel between the circles. The spandrel itself, and occasional squares, were open as well, but mostly the streets were narrow and the thick-walled buildings jammed against each other. In a city where heat is a problem, and bounced light is painful, it pays to put buildings close together to supply the maximum possible shade. Many of the streets of New Tanjavur were so narrow that sunlight never reached all the way into them and, because Metallah's light scattered so poorly from the sky, it was necessary to light them even at midday.

As we walked along the shady side of the wide avenue, Kapilar said, "I am presuming you have been told that we are Saiva Hindu, that we are Dravidian in ancestry, that among us it is the Velalla and not the Brahmin that are the dominant caste—indeed we have no Brahmin here, and that we were founded to live the life depicted in the Cankam poetry?"

"We read some of your Cankam poets when I was in school," I said. "They are literary classics throughout the Interstellar metaculture. Beautiful stuff, subtle and very deep. Are you all Velalla?"

Kapilar nodded. "One of the few advantages of a culture invented from shards of the past is that no one has to be born into the bad parts. So we have no one assigned by birth to tasks that we hold to be degrading, we practice a very loose and un-ascetic form of Hinduism, and we have no special need for experts in purity. Since we are all Velalla, in theory we are all farmer-fighter-lovers, working hard in our fields, rejoicing in our festivals, boldly fighting our enemies, and eternally conquering the bodies of new lovers, as the characters in the Cankam anthologies are. The truth is that robots do all the farming, there is no one to fight but the Maya and they are not the sort of opponent that honor demands, and as lovers . . . well, we *do* manage there."

Margaret laughed more than I thought necessary. Well, I had known her, many times, to draw men out by pretending to find them fascinating. *Deu,* when she used it on me, it always worked.

By the time I had finished thinking that, Kapilar had engaged Margaret in chatter, which she was either feigning intense interest in, or perhaps had really found interesting. I would find out which later; I could be sure it was whichever would do the mission the most good.

I was glad that Margaret had distracted Kapilar, for I was getting fascinated with the temples, now that I was seeing them up close for the first time, and I wanted a chance to form an esthetic judgment without the burden of having to make conversation. I was distracted enough by the fierce heat and humidity. My uniform was drenched; rivulets of sweat, like racing ants, were working their way down my chest, belly, back, and legs.

In one way this place was very familiar. Just as my own culture had done in Noupeitau, the Tamils had grown New Tanjavur's buildings out of a deliberately soft stone so that they would "ruin" faster, because the appearance of being ancient was a vital cultural value. There was a slight melted edge to the temple that now reared above us to my left. Its sloped sides had at first made me think it was pyramidal, but now I saw it was a series of pillared terraces. Most of those were open to the air, stretching nine levels upward to an airy, domed cupola.

The pillars were statues of people, animals, and animal-headed people, some with many pairs of arms, legs, breasts, or heads. They were dancing, talking, posing, bearing weapons, all in such wild confusion that though the lines of the temples from a distance had seemed simple, clear, and harmonious, very nearly classic in the way the pyramid rose to its capping dome, the effect up close was a wild rococo, so complexly interrelated as to defy perception of any whole, each individual figure clamoring for the eye's attention, as if all the statues together were so many excited eight-year-olds and the observer a camp counselor.

A voluptuous woman, bare-breasted, wearing a half-meter tall helmet, held out a bunch of flowers. Next to her a figure whose gender I could not guess extended four arms and danced with four legs, its concentration all turned inward into the moment of its dancing. Beside that a tiger crouched between two cobras. On the level below, Ganesha (the elephant-headed god), danced around the Bo tree, hand in hand with a figure that looked a bit like Buddha and another that looked much like Christ but was probably one of the Saiva saints.

Even one row of statuary pillars was too much for me to grasp fully. Figures rode rearing horses and carried children, played peculiar musical instruments and stabbed each other with spears.

It was drastically different from the art I had grown up with, the baroque gingerbread of Occitan culture just before it had collapsed into Interstellar and been assimilated. Our architecture had been a wild profusion, but of classical curves forming a harmonious whole, fractal and ordered. These figures were allowed to be noisy, to disrupt the space around them, rather than required to harmonize with it. And yet it was also absolutely opposed to the clean lines and simplicity I had learned to appreciate on Caledony, or the elongated restful poetry of the neoclassical sculptures in Trois-Orleans.

I had the odd feeling that if I could only stand here and look long enough, everything I might ever want to know about myself or others, past, present, or future—*everything* was in the pillars of cosmic dancers making up this single temple. And yet it was only one of the smaller temples in a city of hundreds, if I had seen accurately from the Embassy terrace. *"Bella, zenzar, que gratz,"* I said, reverting to Occitan as I often did when visually overwhelmed, *"Deu,* what a sight New Tanjavur is. I don't think you will have trouble drawing tourists if you really want them."

"I am no connoisseur of visual things," Kapilar said, "but I am told that as we approach the city center, the temples are in ascending order of magnificence. And most magnificent of all is the temple of Murukan where we are going, for Murukan was very much the special god of the Cankam poets. Is the heat getting to you yet? We have some distance to go, and there is a much cooler way we can walk."

"I'm all in favor of a cooler way of getting there," I said.

Kapilar turned to the right down a narrow street, and walked through what at first looked like an open doorway in the side of an otherwise nondescript building. We followed him, and found that inside the doorway, a set of stairs descended in a leftward spiral; it was cool and dim on the first few steps, but then light coming up from below quickly made it pleasantly bright. Three steep turns of the spiral, following Kapilar's back, brought us down to a broad floor.

I had already realized we were going to a "tank"—there had been pictures of them in our training, along with short lectures about the etiquette of tanks. They had seemed like a minor peculiar feature of Tamil Mandalam, to be visited sooner or later, at the time I had looked over the pictures of them; the only report about them that I had read had been classed "C6," a category that meant "interesting trivia about a culture—read to improve your conversation."

"If you want to understand us," Kapilar said, "the tanks are a good place to start. And congratulations—you're only the second and third Embassy people who have had the sense to come down here and see it."

"Who was the first?" I asked.

"Sir Qrala."

"Ah."

I looked around the space, taking it in more easily now that the initial confusion had worn off. The space was the size of a gymnasium—smallish for a tank, I was later to learn—with a ceiling about two-and-a-half stories high. It was oval-shaped, with a gently vaulted roof, and the inside was painted with an elaborate mural scene, as busy, colorful, and visually noisy as the temple I had seen out in the street; the themes were just as incomprehensible.

The floor in front of us gently sloped down to a wide, low

stone wall, no higher than my knee, and within the wall, coming to a handsbreadth from its top, was a wonderfully clear pool of absolutely smooth water, glowing a deep Cerenkov blue as if someone were running a reactor at the bottom of it—but the bright column at the center revealed the secret: a shaft of Metallah's brilliant sunlight came straight down into the center from a skylight high in the ceiling. We walked toward the pool, ignoring for the moment the little café tables surrounding us, and I saw that on the concave bottom of the pool, perhaps five meters down, there was a blue convex mirror positioned in the center of the beam, so that it spread the beam across the whole surface of the pool.

"The light comes from a mirror tower," Kapilar said, gesturing at the skylight. "Those are the thin spires that visitors mistake for minarets. In the open space at the top of the tower, a lightweight parabolic mirror, three meters across or so, tracks Metallah on its way across the sky. Then an inner mirror takes the focused light and turns it into a collimated beam; another mirror deflects the beam into a mirrored tube that brings it down here, and voila. Just above that skylight, if you could look into it, you'd see a lens system that recollimates the beam."

It was very simple when he described it, and yet the effect was overwhelming. "And of course," I said, realizing, "if you vent that tube or do something to cool it, only the visible light comes down—the infrared that would make it hot in here gets trapped in the mirror tube and expelled back outside. But you're right, it's not the engineering that's wonderful—a sixteenth-century architect could have done that—it's the art. Is this part of Tamil tradition?"

"Well, there weren't any plans in the ancient manuscripts," Kapilar said, grinning. "No, this would be one of those cases of improvising something different and quite accidentally creating an entirely new thing in a culture." He explained that the tanks were modeled on the tanks of India on Old Earth, which had been the public water system—big reservoirs where anyone could fill a jar or bucket. Back on Earth, a few tanks had been built below ground, with arched or domed stone roofs over them, lighted by skylights and filled by indirect rain gutters, presumably to keep the water cleaner and cooler. And it happened that one of the designers of New Tanjavur had seen photos or holograms of those, and fallen in love with the way that light played through the skylights and reflected off the water to provide soft, cool, delicate indirect lighting in the space.

Thus even though the subterannean tank had been fairly uncommon in India, and nobody was sure that any of them had even been really Tamil rather than the work of conquerors in Tamil country, here they were the truly unique feature of the city, the thing that every Tamil who traveled elsewhere became homesick for.

Materials science had advanced a great deal in nearly twenty centuries, making it possible to have virtually the whole city sitting on the roofs of the tanks. The great vaults and domes that underlay the city covered a vast system of underground plazas which stepped down to wide, deep pools of very clean cold water. I'm told that a large part of the city's energy budget went to keeping that water cold enough, that they didn't rely on nature as their ancestors might have had to do, and an enormous amount of electricity went into circulating and cooling the water.

If so, it was an extremely sensible investment. The cold water, kept always pure by a discreet filter and electrolysis system, was beautiful to the eye, and dozens of marvelous optical effects could be worked with the combination of skylight and pool. Further, the chilly water also served as a heat sink and a chemical trap, so that the underground spaces were comfortable at all but the hottest times of day, and the little whiffs of sulfur, chlorine, and ozone, and the burnt smells that were everywhere on Briand, were absorbed and processed away, leaving the air in the underground spaces the best-smelling on Briand.

The tanks were the heart of the city's social life. They provided thousands of good sites, out of the weather and the heat,

for cafés, bars, restaurants, concert spaces, rental libraries, tres-
tle stages, public podia, and all the other accouterments of civilized life. To a great extent, New Tanjavur slept upstairs and
lived downstairs.

"The tanks do many things for us," Kapilar said. "They are
comfortable during the day—many of us only go home to sleep,
and prefer to live and work in the public spaces around the tanks.
Since many of them are linked, for our immediate purpose they
provide a way to walk across the city without melting in the
heat. And most of all the tanks help to keep the Tamil way of life
public. That's perhaps the most important thing the tanks will
teach you about us. We live in public; we spend almost all our
time in public view. And it is in the spaces around the tanks that
we do it. Reputation, honor, appearance, everything, are all determined down in those spaces."

As we walked from tank to tank via the passages between
them, we came to wide, brightly lighted spaces that seemed like
the best promenades of the romantic cultures; cool, tall spaces
full of shadows and texture, gothic in feel; bright geometrics in
primary colors; warm earthcolored spaces full of soft, natural
shapes; and always, everywhere, the glorious pools, fountains,
waterfalls, basins of every description. I found it hard to believe
that we were the only Embassy people who had come down here,
apart from Qrala, and said so.

Kapilar shrugged. "I'm an Embassy employee now; it's not my
place to criticize."

"You're our employee now," Margaret reminded him, "and
you're being paid to tell us what you think."

He shrugged. "Well, it's Kiel, of course. He's so strong on his
idea of non-interference that I don't think he wants to know very
much about us; he just wants to be assured by our government
that they're doing what he thinks is the right thing. And . . .
well, I don't know . . . how many cultures is the government important in?"

"Across the Thousand Cultures?" Margaret asked.

"Define important," I said. "Most places they provide police and environmental-hazard protection, drinking water, basic transportation, a minimum income, public spaces—the basics of civilized life, anything you don't want people to have to buy a ticket to. But I've only seen a handful of cultures where the government is central to what people are interested in doing."

And, I added to myself, I had only seen a handful of cultures in which people were interested in doing much of anything. Wherever you went in the Thousand Cultures, mostly you found people trying to come up with something to do other than sitting around watching old entertainment programs from the past several centuries. Government could deliver what was needed to keep people alive, healthy, and reasonably safe, at a reasonable cost. It could not give them a reason to live—any more than art, sports, religion, business, science, or any of humanity's other timekillers did. But this was leading me into one of my depressions, and I had a beautiful new city to explore in front of me, so I resolutely shoved the big picture away and let myself enjoy each tank as we came to it, thinking as little as I could, letting the colors and shapes soak into me.

Clearly the tanks specialized to some extent; we passed through one that was almost entirely a playground, with a big transparent wall surrounding the water so that children couldn't get into it; there must have been two hundred mothers gathered on the benches talking, and none of them looked up as we went by.

"Where are the fathers?" Margaret asked.

"Hmm," Kapilar said, clearly embarrassed, and then thought of one of the most basic diversions. "Then it's true what they say about Earth and most of the Thousand Cultures, that the fathers and mothers are supposed to divide the work of child-rearing—"

"Never mind the rest of human space," Margaret said, "and stop trying to change the subject. Where are the men?"

I didn't hear his answer just then, because I was busy looking at the space. I figured that Margaret was going to corner him and extract whatever the truth might be; this place was at least as gender-divided as Nou Occitan had been during the years I grew up there. That would change. Perhaps half the Thousand Cultures had been somewhere far over toward patriarchy at the time they were founded, but patriarchy had been eroding in a lot of them for a long time, the Interstellar metaculture was at least officially non-sexist and anti-sexist (though I could think of several exceptions, and I would have bet that Margaret could think of several hundred), and anyway as soon as a culture came into contact with one that was more egalitarian than it was, usually the women's revolution took no more than half a generation to start. From the defensive tone in Kapilar's voice, I could tell that if it wasn't underway already here, it would surely be as soon as Margaret got to spend some time talking with Tamil women.

Though, too, I reflected, when you consider how many proverbs in the Kural seemed to deal with male pride and incompetence, probably the women here had caught on to the game just as much as they had anywhere else. Maybe on our next vacation we would go to Hedonia, just to take a look at humanity's most officially egalitarian culture; Margaret might like that and I'd never met a Hedon I didn't like.

At last Kapilar directed us up another long stair, and we emerged in the square in front of the temple of Murukan. By now his argument with Margaret was over, and the two of them were talking to each other animatedly; apparently Margaret was making a friend of our new employee, and that was a relief—on these missions she was sometimes depressed until she could find a few friends.

The temple of Murukan was at its best at about an hour and a half past noon, and that was when we saw it first. To this day I am amazed to think what it was like, and that it was there for us to see; we had no sense yet that it would shortly be one with the hanging gardens of Babylon, the Colossus of Rhodes, St. Peter's, or Manhattan's skyscrapers.

It was best at this time because the light was coming from high up and northwest; the whole west wall was lighted with plenty of small shadows, so that all the outlines were defined sharply but almost all of the brilliant colors were exposed to full daylight. Darkened reds and boosted blues predominated, but in almost every spot there was the whole spectrum—where an Occitan, or almost any Westerner would have carefully tried to balance and harmonize, to keep colors from clashing by taking out a primary, the Tamils of New Tanjavur had instead jammed all the saturated colors together, forcing clashes. The contrast was sharper, too, for Metallah's light, the nearly black sky, and the glare off the white stone around the statues put everything except the sculptures themselves into brilliant monochrome.

The temple was octagonal with its main entrance facing solar west, which in those high southern latitudes was almost northwest. The corners of the eight sides, going up eight levels, had been reinforced with columns in animal shapes. Just below the top, tigers with huge jutting teeth and grotesquely protruding eyes stood on the next level down and heaved against the lintels above them as if afraid it might fall at any moment. The level the tigers stood on, in turn, was held up by delicate elephants (also with strangely bugged eyes) who danced gracefully with each other, on their hind legs, their front feet still elephantine but somehow more handlike, their molars and tusks exaggerated and extended, their bodies elongated till they had something of the grace of deer, all this while balancing the level above them on their heads like a water jar. Horses with huge ears, teeth, and eyes, oddly sleek, their front hooves reaching up to brace the stone terrace above them, reared in bridle and saddle as impossibly muscular human riders fought them. Gods, animals, and people danced in a mad confusion of bright colors.

I think we spent an hour standing and staring in sheer awe. As the sun came around to take the front wall of Murukan's temple full on, many shadows vanished and the statues no longer cut into space with the same vividness; now it was merely splendid. At last, having let us drink in the whole thing visually, Kapilar said, "It's in honor of Murukan. He's not a primary Hindu god and though he was always important to us it was only when we came here that we elevated him so far in the pantheon. If you understand Murukan, you understand us. The temple is eight-sided to symbolize the eight anthologies that make up the Cankam texts, the Ettutokai; the temple of Siva on the other side of the central square is ten-sided, in honor of the Pattuppattu, the Ten Epics. The temple of Siva is fine, but it is not like this; our heart and soul went into several works, but the core of us—and the heart of Murukan—is in the Ettutokai. On this temple each statue and relief in some way or other illustrates one of the poems, or depicts one of the poets, or shows Murukan's delight with his people's poetry. So you could say that the whole literature of my people is there in painted stone. And once you really know the Ettutokai, you can find your way around the surface of the temple with just a copy of it, reading the icons by the poems and vice versa. It takes several days to do; I myself have only done that three times."

Despite my aching feet and back, I could hardly tear my eyes from the sight. At last tiredness, the soggy heat of the lengthening afternoon, and the outright ache of carrying so much weight in the high gravity, forced Margaret and I to admit that we needed to get back to the Embassy.

"Well," Kapilar said, "the springer station is right over there, just around a corner and down the street. Sorry I didn't tell you it was available; I had assumed that since your note said you like to walk through a new city to get the feel for it, that you would want to do that today. I hope that was all right?"

"We wouldn't have missed it," I said, sincerely. "And thank you. I suppose we'll need to see you in the morning, so that we can get started, formally, on the mission."

He nodded. "Usually the Ambassador has new staff have breakfast with him the first morning. I shall come by around the time that I would guess that that will be concluding."

I noted, as we strolled to the springer, that his long white shirt and dark trousers were still perfect; they had fine tailors here, and fine designs, I was sure, but there's also something about the way a person wears things, so that the most attractive garment in the world will look dumpy on a person who doesn't stand right, and a person with real style can make a plain tunic and pants look like a work of art. That too warmed my heart to the Tamils; the evil cult of comfort and practicality had spread far and wide in the Thousand Cultures, resulting in a vast amount of stylelessly graceless clothing, but clearly, like Nou Occitan, Tamil Mandalam was fighting back bravely.

"Until tomorrow, then," Margaret said. We turned and stepped into the springer. Moving from one point to another on a planetary surface, there is no sickness since the gravity doesn't change much, and the experience is very much like going through a door—except that you can't see what's on the other side of the blank gray sheet until you contact it. After that the induced pseudovelocity is so high that it seems as if your front toe barely touches the field, and then there you are, standing with a different gray field behind you, in the place you were going. It was like that this time, as always, and in an instant Margaret and I were standing in our private quarters in the Embassy.

We were glad we had already unpacked, for the combination of high temperature and high gravity had worn us both out. We had no more appointments that day, and the Embassy guest list showed that all Tamil workers had gone home and none were expected that evening, so I said "Air conditioning on" and a moment later there was a gratifying whoosh of cool air. For almost an hour, it seemed that all we could do was lie in the reclining chairs, the neuroducers set for pain relief, and let our spines decompress and our bodies cool. As soon as we could get up the ambition, we both took cool showers, ate a quick meal, and lay down on the bed, exhausted, not touching each other.

"Kapilar seems like a pleasant *toszet*," I said.

"Well, he's witty and friendly," Margaret said. "And my god he can dress beautifully."

"That takes talent," I agreed.

"Is that what you call dressing well?" Margaret asked. The edge in her voice made me hesitate. "I guess it looks that way to you. God, Giraut, do you ever even think what it feels like to be stuck in bureaucratic uniforms for the next stanyear or so? Nothing flatters me but in those damned uniforms you can see everything that's wrong. Or maybe I . . . just . . . lack . . . *talent!*" She turned on her side, away from me; I rolled over and tried to hug her, but she jabbed an elbow into me, hard. I moved back to my side of the bed and lay still. I guess I fell asleep sooner or later.

The next day, Margaret and I got up quite early, two full hours before dawn. As Kapilar had suggested there would be, there was a short note from Ambassador Kiel inviting us to an early breakfast on the morning terrace, and though we hadn't liked him much when we met him the day before, we decided that we needed to allow him a chance to prove that we could work together with him, or that we couldn't. We sent back a yes and started getting ready.

Just as we were almost dressed, the computer pinged and I said, "What is it?"

"Reminder—turn off air conditioning in your quarters before coming to breakfast. It is possible that you will not be back to your quarters until after the first Tamil staff arrive and it is possible for Tamil staff in the building to tell when a room is being air-conditioned."

"Thank you," I said, and started to button up the uniform tunic. At other times Margaret and I had competed to come up with how best to describe Council of Humanity uniforms—one of the better descriptions was "looked like the marching band returned it and asked for their money back"—but after the uproar of last night, I wasn't going to say a thing about them today.

"Kiel must have set that message to be sent to us this morning. Wonder if it was just for us or if it's automatic for everyone every day?"

"Or automatic until he decides you're smart enough to cross the street without him holding your hand," I said.

"Either way. This job is going to stink, Giraut." She didn't look at me as she said it. "What impression did all the art give you yesterday? You were raised to think about esthetic things; I didn't really see anything other than church art till I was past twenty. Did you get an impression that told you anything about these people?"

"More or less the same impression I had from all the pictures before we came. South Indian, colorful, bewildering. I don't really understand it. But the temple of Murukan—now, that's just beautiful. As fine a building as there is in human space. Didn't it leave you with any feeling at all?"

She sighed. "I think it's just because I grew up in Caledony. I hope that's all it is. But you know, the temple of Murukan would have been really offensive to me if I had still believed in Rational Christianity. All that wild passion and emotion was bad enough, but it's very hard not to see it as idol-worship, as well. And to me it seemed like all those creatures with bugged-out eyes and huge teeth were demons of one kind or another. So it read, to me, as a temple of wild worship of demon-idols. Not a comfortable thing for a woman who spent her first twenty years going to church four days a week. More like child's blasphemy."

"Child's blasphemy?"

"You know, the way small children sometimes experiment with offending their elders by just reversing or negating everything they are supposed to believe. 'I believe god is a weak mother, and didn't make heaven or earth, and in Jesus Christ, one of many bastard children . . .' and like that. My older brother used to get himself spanked for doing that; now he's a preacher." She sighed and looked at herself in the mirror. "I guess this is what I have to look like for the foreseeable future. Anyway, I just saw the temple of Murukan as a slap in my home culture's face, and I know that's silly because they had no such intention, but it made me feel creepy and nervous. Everything so far in New Tanjavur makes me feel creepy and nervous."

"It's great art," I said.

"I didn't say it wasn't," Margaret said, glaring into the mirror and not looking around at me. "I said it made me feel creepy and nervous. Like this is a place where something bad happens. In the abstract, I agree, it's magnificent, and if we ever really do get tourism to Briand going, it will be one of the things people come here to see. Ready to go down and eat?"

"Starving," I said, "and my back seems to be all right this morning, too. Maybe the beds here are designed for the high gravity?"

"Could be," she said. "I slept beautifully too."

The hour before dawn in New Tanjavur is astonishing. There's no moon, but because Metallah is such a bright sun, and all four of the more distant planets are highly reflective gas giants, the planets, which hang low in the polar sky, are awesomely brilliant, many times brighter than Earth's Venus. The pale light, coming from four different directions, sets up a dense interplay of shadows on the flamboyantly varied surfaces of the city, a pattern that slowly changes even as you watch it. The south pole of Briand points into the Milky Way, so it's always high overhead.

Better still, morning is cool and pleasant. During the early part of the evening, the tropopause bounces up above the city, and hot water-saturated air rushes up the mountainsides and creates a gigantic storm, refilling every cistern, catchbasin, and temporary lake, and bringing the Kaveri River, which roars down through the city into the abyss below, to full flood. When the clouds have drifted off, Briand's still-hot sky swiftly pushes the tropopause back down, and it becomes clear and dry. For the last three blessed hours of the night, the air is cool but not cold, as heat radiating from the sky slowly rewarms the stones chilled by the thunderstorm.

Also, at that time of day, the traces of complex organics are almost gone, and the air actually smells sort of fresh and clean—

at least the sort of fresh and clean you would get on a nice day near a tar pit on another world.

The ambassador had had a good table set, of warm pastries and chilled fruit plus coffee. He and Sir Qrala were waiting for us, and we all sat down to the table with good appetites. "You missed the evening storm, I suspect," Kiel said, "but it was a good one last night. Dumped its whole load of rain within a couple of hours. Very impressive."

"This is a beautiful place," Margaret ventured.

"Exactly. And if we do this right, there is no reason at all why this *can't* be a place for tourists and art scholars. There's a lot here and it would be a pity to see it lost to human pigheadedness and stupidity. Which brings me to the report I hear from Sir Qrala every day at breakfast—unless either of you has a weak stomach or doesn't care to be upset at breakfast?"

"Not too weak a stomach," I said.

"I don't like to be upset at breakfast, but I can cope if it's necessary," Margaret added. "What's in the report?" She lifted a sweet roll to her mouth.

"Daily incidences of significant violence," Sir Qrala said. "Significance is determined by local reactions; if no one talks or whispers about it, it's not significant. Today is a better than average day, but not unusually so. We have four incidents, nine injuries, and no deaths.

"Item one. A Maya family living in central Mayatown was reputed to have purchased several gallons of paint in various colors. A mob of about twenty Tamils arrived at the house and battered its outside walls with sledgehammers, with no effect except frightening the family. Police arrived and dispersed the mob. Two of the mob resisted arrest and are being treated for bruises."

"Now, wait," I said. "Because there was a rumor—"

"That they had bought paint in different colors," Sir Qrala said. "It is illegal to display anything non-Tamil in public in Tamil Mandalam. Thus all the houses in Mayatown are plain white boxes. There is a recurring rumor that someday the Maya are going to paint their houses in Maya decorative patterns, and thus make their area look Maya. Any time that that is rumored, we have riots and angry mobs. As it happens, the family had not bought paint of any kind, and we are not sure why they were made the victims of the rumor."

"You do see the problem with accidentally giving offense?" Kiel asked.

"Certainly," I said, the most sincere answer I had given him since meeting him.

"Proceed with the report," Kiel said, spreading butter on a warm roll.

"Item two. Two Maya boys, ages fourteen and seventeen stanyears, returning from shopping in the northwest circle, were said to have loudly commented on the breasts of a Tamil girl, aged fifteen stanyears. A dozen Tamil youths chased them back to the edge of Mayatown, where a group of Maya attacked the Tamils. The Maya boys got away unharmed but three of the pursuing Tamils were injured in the brawl, none seriously. It is believed by the Tamil that the boys did this in order to trap the crowd that chased them. It is believed by the Maya that the girl invented the story.

"Item three. Four Maya children travelling in a trakcar between school and the shopping center where they were to meet their mother were attacked by a crowd of Tamils, who tipped over the trakcar and pelted it with stones before police arrived and drove off the crowd. All four children were injured; boy thirteen cut over eye, boy ten bruises—that's age ten, not bruised ten times—girl nine broken arm caused by her brother landing on her, boy six bloody nose, possible concussion. Current joke circulating in New Tanjavur is that it was a waste of effort because the boy was already old enough to starve the other three to death, quote if they had just let nature take its course unquote."

"*Deu,*" I said.

Kiel grunted. "At least there were no deaths. Then we could

have counted on several days of stoning along the line between Mayatown and New Tanjavur proper."

"Item four. Maya woman in Mayatown was approached by a Tamil man who quote 'made a crude sexual suggestion and offered to pay money' unquote. She screamed for help and the man was chased for several blocks before getting away. New Tanjavur police say her description of him matches a sex offender that they've been looking for, not previously known to attack Maya. They were rather huffy with me about including this case in my report, on grounds that it was quote not really ethnic violence unquote.

"And that's it. No doubt there were a lot of minor scuffles and name calling but we wouldn't necessarily have heard about those, since everyone on both sides regards the smaller incidents as so normal that they don't excite much comment. Per Ambassador Kiel's request, I only report the ones where our informants have brought back rumors and I was able to find something that matched them in the police reports."

Kiel grunted, took a sip of coffee, and swallowed his bite of food. "That is because on any given day to hear about everything that is being rumored would take until about lunch time." He poured another cup of coffee. "Well, there you have it. In short, it's a mess. Between us, the authorities in New Tanjavur and the Embassy manage to keep much of this away from the news outlets, and we think that helps at least a little; there's no point in having the Council throw a fit and send in a few hundred CSPs to give both sides someone new to hate, there's no reason to generate any more political pressure than there already is on the Council, and locally it would be inexcusable to encourage others to copy that behavior."

"Do you need something copied?" Kapilar asked, joining us. The Ambassador looked irritated, but passed the tray of food in the young man's direction. Kapilar merrily ignored whatever offense Kiel might be taking, grabbed three large rolls and a cup of fruit, and poured himself a cup of coffee. Qrala glanced at me; I

couldn't be sure in the dim light, but the slight twitch at the edge
of Qrala's mouth made me suspect that Kapilar inviting himself
to breakfast was a regular event here. It made me like both Qrala
and Kapilar better.

"Well," I said, "we've established that there are tourist attrac-
tions, many of which are art, around here. What's our next step
in getting to know your culture?"

"I thought I'd take you out and meet some of it," Kapilar said.
He nodded to the ambassador. "With respect, sir, I was planning
to introduce them to Kannan and his crowd."

"Is he dressed for it?" Qrala asked. "They've been known to
take exception to our diplomatic uniforms being seen in public."

"But if he dresses like a Tamil, it will be worse," Kapilar said.
"Get the clothing wrong and it shows a lack of culture and breed-
ing; he would seem to be trying to ape us and not succeeding. Get
it right—with the real Tamil flare for fashion—and it would
seem that the Council of Humanity is finally taking a lesson on
the proper way to live from the Tamils, and while, speaking personally, I wish you would, I don't think it would be at all good
to be seen taking it from Kannan and his people in particular. So
I think a decent uniform is probably the thing least likely to get
us into trouble."

The ambassador sighed. "Well, there you have it. Here, it's
not even possible to dress politely for everyone; you have to decide who to offend every day. And I suppose offending Kannan's
people might even be the way we *want* to begin with them." He
thought for a moment. "Giraut is the one who should probably
make that contact—it's an artistic and cultural group, and I suppose we should be able to talk to them, just as we should be able
to talk to anybody." He sighed again. Clearly this was a subject
he just didn't like to think about at all. "Still, I would really
rather keep Embassy staff just as clear of them as we possibly
can. And Kapilar, you did right to check in with me about this
first."

"What's wrong with them?" I asked. "Bigots? Radicals?"

"You're right so far," Qrala said. "I've found unofficial contacts with them very helpful, and I've also noted that they are spoken of with great respect, both in the artistic and the general community. Like it or not, they're an influence, but given how extreme their, ah, ethnic partisanship is—"

" 'Ethnic partisanship' being Qrala's polite way of telling you that they're hatemongers," Kiel said. He wasn't looking up from his cup of chilled mixed fruit, seemingly more intent on spooning up the last juicy bits than on what he was saying. "Being a bit more specific, so far our whole staff here at the Embassy, one way or another, has had political duties, and we dared not appear to have the slightest contact at the political level with Kannan and his gang. Yet at the same time they are influential and important. Well, here we have a cultural envoy, someone whose whole job is to communicate about art—nothing political at all in that, you see?"

"It lets you open another door," I said. "You said about art, rather than art and tourism, so I take it you prefer that I pursue this by myself?"

"I prefer that you be the initial contact. How you divide the work between you does not matter particularly to me, so long as appearances are kept up; the one thing we must not do is anything that would allow anyone, even the most paranoid, to think we might be taking sides, or that in any way we endorse Kannan's bid for the Fourth Cankam."

"I don't know what you're talking about," I confessed.

Kiel's glance was cold and sardonic. "Then you're really perfect for the job," he said. He stood up, filling his coffee cup to take with him. "Kapilar can explain that more thoroughly than I possibly could," he added. "But I'm not being facetious when I tell you that not understanding too much, and needing to have things explained, might be one of your greatest strengths in this. Ask about everything, endorse nothing." He glanced at Kapilar. "When were you supposed to meet Kannan?"

"Sunrise plus two," the young Tamil replied, through a

mouthful of food. Clearly he was enjoying his free breakfast a good deal. "Time enough for a full explanation before we go—maybe not too full, if you prefer."

"I would at least like to know what a Fourth Cankam is if I'm not supposed to endorse or support it," I said.

Kiel grunted. "It's a piece of foolishness if ever there was one. That's the short answer. Kapilar will explain the rest." He lifted his coffee cup in salute, and went inside the Embassy.

"I do trust you won't pay too much attention to our leader," Sir Qrala said, after Kiel had gone. The way he said "our leader" dripped with skepticism, but there was an odd affection to it; later I was to learn that despite spying for Shan for all these years, Sir Qrala was also Kiel's best friend. "He objects to the Fourth Cankam because he thinks every culture should be falling all over itself to go Interstellar, and that all cultures should be eagerly participating in their own assimilation. No matter what he says about respecting local rights, the truth is that he thinks that if all cultures were allowed to do what they wanted, they would all want to be Interstellar. Furthermore, several times the local politicians have broken off talks with him, sometimes for periods of as long as twenty days, in order to participate in the ongoing debates about the Fourth Cankam, and he is offended to the core to be told that what he conceives of as the state is subordinate to the needs of poetry. He can recognize that it is but he can't help judging that to be very silly."

Kapilar nodded emphatically. "And if you are to do anything important here in Tamil Mandalam, you have to understand that with us what really matters is the upcoming Fourth Cankam. We are trying to build a culture here that is so steeped in our poetry that we can again reassemble the Cankam, as it has been before."

I thought about that for a moment. The Cankam was, in the roughest possible description, an academy or school of poets and scholars; the term was applied both to the classical poetry in the Eight Anthologies and the Ten Long Poems (or Ten Epics, or Ten

Lays, or whatever other translation you preferred), and to the era in which they had been written; the Cankam could be the period, its literature, or the academy that had governed it, depending on context.

The first two Cankams were mythic, and if their datings were taken literally they would have extended back to almost 8000 BCE. No archeological trace of either era had ever been found on Old Earth.

The Third Cankam was the Cankam from which all of the Cankam poetry derived, which had flourished in the early centuries of the Christian era. Even for the Third Cankam period, it wasn't clear whether there had ever really been a Cankam as a formal body, or just a retrospective grouping by the scholars, centuries later. In any case, the Cankam was made up of poets and scholars, each of whom had been known as a *canror*, a wise man or a person of power and knowledge. The poets and scholars who made up the Cankam had probably been concentrated within a period of six generations, ten at most—if there had ever really been a Cankam at all. It was quite possible that the whole idea of a Cankam originated in twelfth-century misunderstandings of some obscure fourth-century hints.

"So the Fourth Cankam is an attempt to reassemble the old Cankam?"

Kapilar nodded. "That *is* the basic idea, but it's much more than just an attempt to reassemble the Third Cankam. The idea is that once we get an overwhelming majority to agree on a single body of critic-leaders, we expect to create a new Cankam that will last a few centuries. The Fourth Cankam will establish the standards that every poet can seek, and that will give us a chance to reach perfection. It is what the culture was founded to do, and we aim to carry out our mission, despite the distractions of the Maya invasion of our lands, or your Interstellar metaculture's Second Renaissance, or anything else that might try to get in our way."

It was clear that the bias in both the Council of Humanity and the Office of Special Projects, towards thinking of politics as primary, military and economic matters as secondary, and everything else as minor and trivial, had tripped us up yet again, as it had been doing ever since Margaret and I had gotten into this ridiculous occupation. No one had bothered to tell us that the Tamils were working to form a Fourth Cankam, even though—if they did—it would mark the completion of the project the culture had been founded for.

The money to purchase a ship and a colony space for Tamil Mandalam had been put up, not by the Tamils of Nallur or of Tamil Nadu (who had already purchased and settled two colony spaces the century before) but by a group of eccentric scholars and their quadrillionaire backers, who had wanted to see the Cankam poetry flourish again as a living tradition. Thus for centuries New Tanjavur had been struggling to give birth to a new Cankam, who would at last declare that it was time to begin producing a new set of works in the Cankam tradition.

I had known that; I hadn't known that the Tamils thought they were almost there. I had been given the impression that disputes over prosody, subject matter, the distinctions between *akam* and *puram* poems, the landscapes critical to the old Cankam poetics and how they might be translated to a world that didn't offer the same landscapes, had so flourished that it looked like a consensus would never be reached, let alone the overwhelming consensus required to establish the Fourth Cankam.

And now that I had gotten oriented, mentally, to what this was all about, I could appreciate just how serious the situation might be. "Are you telling me that this Kannan, and his 'gang,' as the ambassador calls them, are likely to be the nucleus of the Fourth Cankam?"

Kapilar sighed and smeared jam on a pastry. After taking and chewing a big bite, he finally said, "Well, what Kannan's group is doing is successfully bypassing most of the problems that have always dogged that project. They allow a wide range of poetic expression but they also compare everything critically to the Ettutokai and to the Pattuppattu, so that there aren't rigid rules, but there's a powerful central tendency. They treat the ancient distinctions more as expressions than rules. Things like that."

"It sounds like they're just liberal syncretists."

"They are, poetically speaking. Politically they're deeply reactionary, worshippers of despotism, with a list of demands that begins with the physical expulsion of Mayatown and eventually demands that the Maya abandon Yaxkintulum and return to old Kintulum in the other hemisphere."

"But Kintulum is—"

"Uninhabitable for a few centuries yet to come. Absolutely. That's the point. Depending on how you interpret what they're saying, Kannan and his group are calling for anything from genocide to systematic exile. Beyond that, since the Maya won't leave Mayatown, let alone Yaxkintulum, it's a plan to start a war."

"The ambassador believes this is all nothing to worry about," Qrala chimed in, "because there's not a political arm to the movement and no public officeholders are involved. So he has a tendency to think that it can't really be taken seriously, at least not at this point. But—well, Kapilar, tell them what happens when the Fourth Cankam is formed?"

Kapilar was caught with a mouthful of food, and it took him a moment to swallow. Finally he said, "Oh, well. I'm not sure how seriously we should take it. But the Fourth Cankam was supposed to replace the state. So if they do succeed in forming the Fourth Cankam, they theoretically take over everything. But you know, I can't imagine that any of the poets and critics will really want to worry about electric power, or subsistence allowances, or street maintenance. I think most likely, whoever the Fourth Cankam turns out to be, once they take over they'll just deputize the existing state and have it look after all that. Part of the point of *having* a Fourth Cankam is to get the most important people in society focused on the things that matter most, and away from daily trivia. So all of Kiel's current administrator buddies in the Tamil government would still be doing whatever they were doing before—they would just be subject to loose supervision from the Cankam." He poured himself another cup of coffee.

Margaret and I had been glancing at each other, and at Qrala, with more and more worry; reading between the lines of what Kapilar was telling us, it seemed virtually certain that sooner or later—probably without Kiel's seeing it until it happened—there would be a de facto coup, and the minor flunkies to whom he had devoted himself would be subordinated to the real powers in the culture.

Qrala did nothing to reassure us. "So you see," he said, "we've needed people who specialize in artistic affairs here for quite a while, because we need to have contacts in place in the event of any sudden reversals of the status quo. Which is why I had been voicing, in my reports, for some time, a concern that we had no such people on hand."

He didn't mention who those reports had been to, but I could make a guess that it hadn't been to Kiel, nor to any of the regular Council of Humanity diplomatic offices.

"We can certainly understand that," Margaret said.

Kapilar nodded. "With us the Fourth Cankam is everything, it's the purpose we're building towards, and since that is the case, it doesn't matter how much of the government Kannan doesn't have, or how few of the ordinary politicians join up with him. If he defines the Fourth Cankam, he defines what it is to be Tamil—and that means that the core of our culture will get built around these ideas of cultural purity that he's been promoting. It's just not a good thing, and I think you should get a close look at him, either as a matter of knowing your enemy, or perhaps because he may really win and your Council of Humanity may have no one else to deal with."

"So," Sir Qrala said, "I finally prevailed on the ambassador to agree that a contact with Kannan's group might be valuable—and then made that policy operational before he could change his mind again. I also found it necessary to point out to him that since, Giraut and Margaret, he regards you as highly suspect, should anything go wrong it would be trivially easy, to, er—"

"To shift the blame to Shan's organization," I said. "I realize that. All right, I'm deniable, I'm not in a vital job, I speak art, I'm good at sneaking around. I'll go meet this *toszet.*"

Then all of us except Kapilar gasped. Margaret said. "Oh! *That's* a sunrise!"

Briand rotates slowly for an inhabited world, almost as slowly as Earth itself, but Metallah is a small and intensely bright object in the sky. Because we were on the west terrace we couldn't see Metallah directly—it came up behind the Embassy—but that kept us from being blinded by its onset.

Most of humanity's inhabited worlds are like Wilson, the terra-formed bones of former gas giants, circling big reddish K or G stars; they orbit very far from their primaries, and they rotate very fast, so that the tiny disk of the sun bounces up over the horizon in almost no time at all. Thus sunrises on them look very much like what I had grown up with: suddenly a light comes on. Earth was one of the few worlds that had a real sunrise: the disk of the sun was wide enough and the rotation slow enough so that the light came gradually, creeping slowly down from the high mountains into the valleys. Indeed, the problem with Earth was that the sunrise came so slowly that you had to sit and patiently watch it; at any given instant it didn't look like anything was happening.

Briand was a perfect intermediate case—an appreciable disk of Metallah (but not nearly as wide as Sol) and a fairly slow rotation (but not as slow as Earth). What we saw looked like a tropical sunrise on Earth, but three times as fast. Furthermore, due to its nearly black sky, Metallah's contrasts between light and shadow were far sharper than on most other worlds.

So first the stars and planets dimmed; that was what had caught our attention. Then within the space of a minute, light swept down the spires and domes of New Tanjavur, so that the upper parts blazed with light while the lower stories, streets, and alleys remained in near-black purple shadow. Before us, from the top down, the city sprang into vivid existence, until finally the few broad avenues and squares, too, glowed with the harsh blue-white light.

The light raced out across the boundaries of the city, bouncing off the flat white roofs of Mayatown, racing down the mountain slopes around us. In a matter of a few minutes, color erupted across what had looked like a dark sea far beyond us, as the light touched the nearly opaque mixture of colored gases that filled the abyss. Somewhere down there, in the shallow levels, on top of mountains and plateaus, bioengineered life was waking to begin its daily battle to maintain Briand's oxygenated antarctic stratosphere; somewhere deeper than that, perhaps, a different biology, that of the abyss itself, struggled to maintain the part of the planet we had left to it.

Finally, Sir Qrala said, "Well, I suppose we do have to get on with the day, even if it can't possibly be as beautiful as the morning."

My meeting with Kannan was set for a little café in a large tank; that part of town didn't yet have public springers, so after springing to the station behind the temple of Murukan, Kapilar and I walked around to the stop in front of the temple—it was hard to believe how hot it was already, even in the shadow of that huge building—and called for a trakcar. While we waited for it, I treated myself to the view of the temple backlit by Metallah; the white glare around it formed a kind of halo, and the shape of the temple itself was an intricate black fractal tangle that kept the eye moving no matter how long you looked at it.

"I'll get you pointed toward the right door," Kapilar said, "but after that if you're to have any chance of success, I'll have to get back in the trakcar and be gone in a hurry. Kannan will eventually find out I work for you, but it's best he doesn't know while you're still getting acquainted."

"Is there bad blood between you?"

"Quite a lot. I think I could forgive *him*, but I'll never know for sure, because he won't forgive *me.*"

"What do you have to forgive each other for?"

Kapilar thought for a moment. Then he shrugged. "It may sound silly and trivial, but if you want to understand us Tamils, perhaps you should hear what it is that we can stay angry about for years."

"I'm an Occitan; we pride ourselves in our exuberant anger about trivial points."

"Fair enough. Well, to begin with, I worked for his little journal for a while, and I was in line to get promoted to being his second in command, when I happened to undergo some changes of principles—or a recovery of sanity, whichever way you prefer to see it—and therefore departed before he could fire me. I'm not sure whether he felt more betrayed by my quitting or by my disagreeing with him.

"Then there was the smaller but much more emotionally intense matter of Auvaiyar, who worked at the journal at the same time I did. Have your briefings, or any of the people you've talked to so far, mentioned her yet?"

"I know that, like most of you, she's named after one of the Cankam poets. At least in the other cultures, Auvaiyar is the best known woman in the Eight Anthologies."

"Well, that's a start. The Auvaiyar in the anthology traditionally is pictured as a mature woman, what I've heard the ambassador call a 'woman of a certain age.' The Auvaiyar I'm talking about— which is of course the one most important in avant-garde poetry circles, there are plenty of other Auvaiyars around in all sorts of other professions, just as I run into twenty men named Kapilar every day—is still quite young, I should guess no older than twenty-five stanyears. And she's different from her namesake."

"Different how?"

"Beautiful. Brilliant. Secretive. The avant-garde's most respected, not to say feared, critic. And New Tanjavur's best-known slut."

"If I meet her I'll try to confine the relationship to her work as a critic."

"Good idea. You may find that it is much more difficult in practice than in theory. Just to assist your resolve, *Donz* Leones, I should add she has a knack for convincing each new man that he's going to be different from all the previous ones. It might even be true. But they all finish the same way.

"Anyway, she's a painful element in Kannan's past, and an excruciating part of mine. Kannan happens to have been my successor in her affections, and at the time I was upset enough to tell him exactly what was going to happen to him, just as it had happened to me. We might still have been friends, I think, except that unfortunately everything I predicted came true, and I am *not* the big-spirited sort of person who can refrain from saying 'I told you so.' So on the whole it's a very sore subject. Don't mention her name and don't quote anything she said in any of her reviews anywhere near him."

The trakcar pulled up to the stop in front of us. Though it had no air conditioning, it did have windows and vents, so that as long as it was moving through the streets, the temperature in it was merely uncomfortable, as opposed to the oven it became when sitting still.

We rode in silence, mostly. I watched the scenery and mentally reviewed what I had learned by reading translations of a few back issues of *Palai*, Kannan's journal, back at the training center. It had mostly made me cross, so that I had quarreled with Margaret. Now that I had been reminded that Kannan edited *Palai*, I had a grudge against him.

Unfortunately, he might well develop into one of just a dozen people or so I talked to regularly here. As the Artistic Exchange person in the team, I was supposed to go out and make contact with the significant artists and critics in a culture, and so I usually was very well-acquainted with a very small number of people. I could only hope that I was picking the right ones.

Meanwhile, Kapilar went over the notes that Margaret and I

had scribbled about things Margaret wanted to visit and subjects she wanted to discuss that day. Because Margaret worked in Tourism Development, she had carte blanche to go look at virtually anything that wasn't religiously sacrosanct (and often at those as well). Since she could go anywhere and look at anything, she generally supplied the breadth in our reports, just as I supplied the depth. Shan had once told us that he used our reports in just that way—he read Margaret to understand what was going on, and me to understand how what was going on was manifested in people's lives.

Shan had always assigned us together for every mission, because he liked the way our reports dovetailed and he knew we preferred to work together. I wondered if Margaret would soon be requesting that we be sent on separate assignments, and if we were, if that might not be the death of the marriage right there.

I shoved that thought away like an annoying, yapping dog, and forced my attention back to the review of instructions with Kapilar. Margaret would be going with him to several of the largest and most-frequented tanks in New Tanjavur, to establish at least a nodding acquaintance with the city's business community and to see how ordinary people spent their time. Later in the afternoon they were to return to the office and he was to assist Margaret in preparing a first draft of an RSRM—Reticulated Societal Response Model—a polydimensional chart that helped us track who was likely to learn of an event first, who they were apt to pass on the knowledge to in what form, and what was the likely response as information moved out through the network of human interconnections. At least that was what I thought it was for; Margaret thought it was probably just a bureaucratic hangover, one of those documents that keeps being prepared years after its uselessness has been well established. Neither of us knew what they were actually used for.

The trakcar came to a stop, and Kapilar said, "Well, that doorway there—just below the mirror-tower—is the entrance to the tank. Go down the stairs you'll find there, turn left, and walk toward the fountain you'll hear. Kannan will be at a large round table, probably with several of his staff. It's the place he uses as his office."

The trakcar slid away behind me before I had taken two steps; I was on my own for my first time since getting here. On most missions the first moment of handling it all myself seemed exciting and I looked forward to it; as I dragged myself up the alley, sweat seeming to gush from every pore and my legs already aching from standing up in high gravity, I couldn't remember why.

The stairs down from the tank entrance were gently curved and well-lighted by mirror-glows above them, so that though I couldn't see where I was going, I could easily see the next few steps. As I trudged down the stairs, feeling better now that I was out of the heat, I reviewed the thumbnail summary of the culture, still loaded in my emblok, one more time.

The ratio of critics to artists was part of what took me a lot of effort to understand. In Nou Occitan, where I grew up, there were many artists and a few critics, and the critics were looked down on and rather pitied, as people who couldn't paint, sing, write, or whatever. It was a point of honor for Occitan artists to ignore critics, or else to chastise them rather than to reply to them. I myself had once pummeled a man unconscious for saying that many of my songs had pleasant melodies and forgettable lyrics, and dueled with another (to the first blood only, to be sure) because he had used the word "heavy-footed" to describe the dancing of my *entendedora* of the time (had her name been Azalais? I thought it was Azalais, anyway, and remembered a freckled straw-blonde who had been somewhat clumsy, but tender and affectionate, though too shy for me to remember much else about her . . . why was my mind wandering back to my youth? Maybe it knew where all the fun was).

In Nou Occitan the critics, as a class, were kept on the run and treated like dirt. This allowed truly atrocious artists to have someone that they could look down on, since any real Occitan would rather make a rotten work than a sound argument. Better still, given how bad our art was, it kept the number of people who might point that out so small that they could not possibly get around to looking at most of it.

Here in Tamil Mandalam, though, it was quite the reverse. The critics were so numerous and so respected that hardly anyone dared any art; what there was of new works was highly polished and refined little gems, bits of formal perfection, which were nevertheless attacked regularly for their triviality. Where the mostly-young Occitan poets were sloppy, emotional, often bathetic, and prolific far beyond demand, the Tamil poets labored for decades to become brilliant specialists, masters of prosody with not much more feeling than most people associated with chess masters.

I myself enjoyed rereading the Ettutokai and the Pattuppattu, in the elegant Terstad translations now available, much more than I enjoyed any of the contemporary work. I was pretty sure that when the old poets had described the breasts of a young girl undressing, out in the fields, for sex with her lover, they had in no way been trying for a perfect description of a perfect breast on a perfect woman undressing perfectly; but a few centuries of critics had established those poems as being just that, and so one reason Tamil poetry was going nowhere fast in New Tanjavur was that all the possible perfect work had already been written.

Supposedly Kannan and his followers were working to change that; as an artist I had to sympathize with them.

At the bottom of the stairs, a doorway opened into a very large octagonal tank. The group of tables nearest me were in an area sunk below the main floor level by perhaps two meters, and water ran from the main tank down through a series of waterfalls to a dimly lighted blue pool on one side of the sunken area. A scrawny young-looking Tamil, whose clothes fit him badly, sat at the table nearest the waterfalls. He got up and walked toward me. As he approached, I saw that his neck was bowed forward, he walked as if not quite aware of where his feet were going, he stared straight at my face without scanning for any obstacles between us, his arms hung limp at his sides—in short he looked like a man who thought mostly about words and concepts all day. "I suppose you are Kannan?" I asked.

"I suppose I must be," he said, smiling. "And you are Gurgrutu Lehonanasu?"

"Giraut Leones," I said, firmly. "Two syllables, then three. No glottals."

"Ah," he said. "Let me try again. Girutuli Onisu."

"Perfect," I said, realizing from the thickness of his accent in Terstad that this was as good as it was going to get.

"Join me at my table, then." He turned and went back to where he had been seated, not bothering to look at me to see if I was following, or if the idea was agreeable to me. On the table in front of him there was a pocket terminal and a large cup of tea. He took a sip of it as I sat down across from him. "Or perhaps I should have said, step into my office. That is the Terstad expression, isn't it?"

"This is your office?"

"This table. Yes. We Tamil live in public, see each other, debate and discuss everything, all the time. If my comrades and I are to form the nucleus of the Fourth Cankam, we can't do it inside a sealed building; we have to be out where people can see us, drop by, talk to us at any time."

"Then you do aspire to form the Fourth Cankam?" I asked, hoping the question was not too blunt.

"Every Tamil here does. I am told the Tamils of other worlds are different, but they have not adhered strictly to the classical culture, as we have. The time has come, I think—and so do all of us who write for *Palai*—to move from mastering the works supervised by the Third Cankam into creating a Fourth Cankam and completing the project."

"Completing?"

"We are not like your silly romantics on other worlds. We don't aim to add works to our anthologies just to be original or just so there can be more names. But we know that there are feelings and ideas not fully explored in the existing body of poetry, and the time has come to write those added works. And for a Fourth Cankam to tell us when we have truly finished and can then live out the implications of perfection."

"What are the implications of perfection?" I asked, feeling more and more bewildered.

"Ah. First we must produce perfection. Then we shall know." His smile seemed like nothing more than a tactic. Here was a man who wanted to offend me, or baffle me, and thereby reinforce his claim that we could never understand him. Or perhaps a very young artist—artistically if not chronologically young— who longed for a response so much that he didn't care whether or not it was his art that drew the response. I had been one of those, when I was seventeen, and could understand it, but not like it.

"You are thinking," he said, "that I am jamming my superiority into your face for some tactical political reason, or in an attempt to drive you away, or perhaps because I just want to offend you. Aren't you?"

"The thought crossed my mind," I said. I signalled a robot passing by and it poured me a cup of dark, strong tea; I made a minor point of really settling my weight into the reclined, padded chair, as if I might stay right there in Kannan's "office" for the next ten stanyears. "But in my experience, if someone is rude to me without provocation, whether it is in the great cities of the Inner Sphere or out here in a backward cultural capital, it always turns out that they are longing to tell me why they are rude to me. So why don't you just tell me and spare me hours of speculation?"

Kannan seemed taken aback. So far so good. He pulled his tea toward him, like a dog securing its bone, and clutched it between his hands in front of his chest. "Well," he said. "I thought all Council diplomats sat politely, and listened intently, and accepted every insult, and went away with no idea about us."

"I doubt that I'm as different from them as all that," I said. "And my understanding was that no one from the Embassy had talked to you."

"No one has. But one hears things."

"Only if one listens. Which is not always worthwhile. Now, are we going to spar, or are you going to tell me why the author of that editorial in the last *Palai* would want to talk to me, or anyone like me?"

"I run many editorials, and they're never signed—"

"*That* editorial," I said. "Let me remind you of a phrase or two. 'Representatives of the mongrel civilization.' 'Decadent beings who have the Eight and Ten in their libraries, without understanding it, now come here to force us to intermarry with squalid savages who starve their women and children.' 'A Velalla does not need to know what sort of animal it is that has come into his farm and is leaving its foul excrement in his fields; he only needs to know how to drive it off.' That editorial."

He shrugged. "Am I expected to deny it? Or to try to explain it away?"

"For one who doesn't want to be influenced by outsiders," I said, "you certainly seem to be worried about meeting my expectations." I signalled the robot waiter and ordered a cold lunch, though it was quite early and I wasn't remotely hungry yet. It was one more little way to tell him that he could talk, or not; explain, or not; but I would be at the table and I wasn't breaking off talks first.

"You are not my idea of a diplomat." Kannan didn't look at me.

I shrugged anyway.

He went on. "You barge in to talk to me, knowing well how much I must dislike your alien, invading, barbaric, stupid, graceless Interstellar metaculture, and you make no effort to win me over, you become more insulting than I have been, you bluntly demand to know what I want as if that were your business. Now you sit there."

"That would seem to be an accurate summary."

"What are you going to do when I get up and storm out of here?"

"I will eat my lunch and then go home," I said, "And then come back here tomorrow morning, and sit at this table, and wait for you to tell me why you want contact with us, so that I can begin to figure out whether it is worth our time and effort to talk to you. I will do this until I become convinced that you won't talk to me without these silly games and clumsy insults. Or until you do talk to me."

"Enjoy your lunch," he said, and got up and left.

I picked at the food for about forty minutes, just in case he was hanging around somewhere nearby to watch me. While I ate, I watched people, and admired the whole institution of the tanks once again; the whole functional city, full of workplaces, sleeping quarters, markets, and the ordinary rest, rested on the roofs of all these extraordinary beautiful water-places, like a work-coverall worn by an angel.

Finally I got up and caught the trakcar back to the springer, and then sprang into our private quarters. I took a quick freshen-up shower, and then got Shan on the com. "I met with a local bigot and insulted him," I said.

His eyes twinkled and he stroked his chin; his crows'-feet deepened as well. "Any results yet?"

"No idea," I said. "But it got a reaction, anyway." I told him the whole story.

"So far so good," Shan said. "Of course we don't know yet if there's the faintest risk of the Fourth Cankam being declared at any time. But if it is, all our old contacts will be of no value, and if Kannan heads it, or if his faction dominates it, it will be very useful if they feel compelled to explain to us. Do you think he'll be at that table tomorrow?"

"I'm going to be late, just to make him impatient," I said. "I'm sure he'll be there within a few days. People who don't want to see you don't waste time trying to explain or offend. There's something he wants from the Council, or the Embassy, or maybe just from me, very badly."

The next morning, Margaret and I had breakfast together on the terrace; again the air was cool and pleasant with only faint traces of the smells of complex organics, and the dawn came up like a searchlight sweeping down the spires and towers of the city. It must be very impressive, too, inside a tank, when sunlight hit the mirror towers and reflected down into the water. I resolved to get a look at that sometime soon.

We had been mostly silent during breakfast; all the necessary conversation for business had happened the night before, and there was little to say now. As the light came up over the city, I glanced at Margaret, who was picking at her food idly and staring into space. "What are we musing about today?" I asked.

"Musing? Oh, I wish I *were* musing. No, I'm just sitting and enjoying the morning, waiting for it to get much too hot. And enjoying feeling comfortably full. And . . . oh, I don't know." She yawned and stretched. "I just feel good this morning, Giraut, can't we leave it at that?"

Now that I looked more closely, her skin glowed as if she had just been exercising. There was a little upturn at the corner of her mouth, just enough to put a dimple in her cheek, and her eyes were far away. Whatever she had found to like on Briand, or whatever there was that was special about this day, it really had hold of her now. I might as well have been back on Wilson for all she knew. Still, it was better to see her happy, and if—

She turned and glared at me. "Must you stare at me? I told you it was nothing."

I looked down, startled and feeling guilty. "I didn't mean to stare. I thought you looked happy. I like seeing you look happy."

"Sorry," she said. "I'm just very edgy and tense. This planet gets to me."

But when I dared to sneak another look at her, a minute or so later, she was smiling into space again. Years of worry and stress seemed to have dropped off her. I couldn't imagine how her serene smile could mean she was edgy or tense.

She almost caught me staring again, for at that moment there were footsteps behind me and she glanced toward them. I turned to follow her gaze. Kapilar had arrived; he was wearing another long shirt, this one with vivid cobalt-and-rust-colored embroidery, over a pair of soft gray trousers that fit him perfectly; at his neck there was a silk scarf. I dress well, usually, and I'm not one of those men who is easily intimidated by other men's finery, but I had to admit that every time I saw him, Kapilar's sheer style overwhelmed me.

"You look very fine this morning."

"Thank you, *Donz* Leones. Well, you will be happy to know that the town—or rather the poets' quarter—or rather the tiny corner of the poets' quarter that regards Kannan as important—are all abuzz with arguments about the significance of your quarrel with him. Good day, Margaret."

"Good morning, Kapilar. Do you need breakfast this morning?"

"I always need breakfast," he said, and sat down.

I was mildly startled that he had addressed Margaret by her first name, but then he was working closely with her, and she was Caledon—so automatically democratic that I'd always had to argue with her about maintaining protocol. If she was comfortable being familiar with an assistant, I wasn't about to make a quarrel of it, especially not considering her recent touchiness.

I finished the last cup of coffee while they chatted idly about what they would see that day. New Tanjavur was a big and interesting enough city so that Margaret would need several more days to take it all in, even though Kapilar was steering her away from all the northwestern part near Mayatown, where the violence tended to happen. (At least she had said that that was what she thought he was doing).

The day before their exploration had concentrated in the

southwest circle; New Tanjavur was made up of four huge circular areas, each a little over thirteen kilometers across, surrounding the central spandrel where public buildings and the more important temples were located. The plan was to visit all the circles, about one per day, and then to spend at least four days exploring the spandrel. From the excitement in Margaret's voice I gathered that she was finding the city delightful.

"Giraut," she said abruptly.

"Sorry. I was wool-gathering," I said. "What was the question?"

"Just wanted to give you a few notes if you're really going back to see Kannan," Kapilar said.

"Why wouldn't I be?"

"Any number of reasons. Maybe he disgusts you. Murukan knows, he disgusts me. Maybe you don't expect him to ever show up again, because you frightened him too much. I would like to believe he's a coward, since I've never seen his courage tested."

I shrugged. "It's a good idea for diplomats to keep their word in small matters. It makes the later complete betrayals more of a surprise." I got up and nodded to them. "And I suppose I should be moving along. Enjoy your day; I have high hopes mine will be spent reading and waiting."

I wasn't that fortunate, as it turned out, but the morning started off pleasantly enough. I went downstairs and stepped through the springer in our quarters to the springer behind the temple of Murukan, using my Office of Special Projects passcard habitually—aside from its unlimited credit line, which allowed me to spring anywhere in human space that a springer had room for my mass and volume, it also was untraceable, and after the first couple of days here I had slid over into the working paranoia you get in a hostile culture; I left no more trail than I had to, despite being highly visible to people who already hated me.

The square in front of the temple was just beginning to warm up, and was not yet unpleasant. I put an audio clip in my ear and said "News." I was rewarded with barrage of rapidly spoken Tamil. "News in Terstad." A moment later I was listening to a

Tamil announcer with an accent thicker than Kannan's proclaim that the terraforming project was slightly ahead of schedule and that background toxics were at their lowest level ever. He went on to announce that seventeen new groups had filed applications to found the Fourth Cankam that year, but reminded listeners that most such groups folded long before the board of examiners could investigate them, and that in any case it took two years to get a candidate on the ballot, and that only five votes had ever been taken, all of them overwhelmingly defeated. "The prospect of a Fourth Cankam in our lifetime remains dismal," he added.

Then he started to talk about violence in the city. I had read Qrala's report that morning before breakfast, and after Kiel's explanation I wasn't surprised that of the fourteen incidents the Embassy knew about, only two had made it onto the news broadcast: the stoning of a trakcar full of Tamil children that passed through Mayatown, and the mob of Tamils that had cornered a Maya woman, grabbed the bag of fresh vegetables she was carrying, smashed the vegetables on the pavement, and smeared her clothes with the nasty mess. What startled me was the way the announcer linked the events—the tone of horror as he described the stoning (none of the children had been physically hurt and the trakcar had carried them out of harm's way at once) and the clear gloating satisfaction as he described the mistreatment of the Maya woman (he finished with an extremely unfunny joke that implied that her lazy husband would not touch her unless she was covered with food). I clicked off the earpiece, angry at myself for having listened for that long.

The trakcar pulled up and I got in; today's ride was as uneventful as yesterday's, and I spent it people-watching. I suppose I was watching for an incident of ethnic violence, though surely I wasn't hoping to see one. In a city of eight million, the small number of violent incidents every day was lost—an ordinary citizen might see one in a year, or be directly involved in one in a decade—but over time everyone knew people who had been involved in them.

I saw nothing other than the occasional pedestrian and a few open shops. The trakcar came to a stop outside the same alley as yesterday. I got out and, now that I was outside the shade of the trakcar and air was no longer blowing over me, felt instantly hot and damp; the sun was higher and the glare around the edge of my dark glasses was already slightly painful. I walked quickly to the door and down the stairs to the tank, enjoying the immediate return of comfort. That must be why everyone I had seen on the street was hurrying: most of them were probably just taking a shortcut between tanks, or going from a trakcar to a tank as I just had.

The table was vacant and I got a pot of coffee and pulled out a Terstad translation of the Kural, a little pocket edition. Here were all the usual injunctions of wisdom literature everywhere: be gentle with the weak. Be brave, especially when you don't feel brave. Tend your own garden. A small precaution now is better than a big repair later. Trust others if you want to be trusted. Success and failure are less important than they appear. Respect your parents. Don't do things that you know you will eventually want to stop doing. Treat people the way you want to be treated.

Almost every culture in the Thousand Cultures had some wisdom literature, and much of it was the same between any two cultures. When I had been younger, and out on my first couple of missions, that had seemed like a reason for everyone to get along, a reminder that we were all on the same side. Now I felt that the observation was interesting, but pointless. Cultures tend to be alike in much of what they think are the basic virtues, but one of the ones they are most alike in, though it rarely appears in their book of wisdom, is: Distrust strangers, fear foreigners, dread novelty.

That was a sour thought on a day when I was determined to be in a good mood, so I ordered rice with condensed milk and mango slices, and a fresh pot of coffee, and had a second breakfast while I read some of the Tirumurukarruppatai, the "Guide to Lord Murukan" that was one of the Pattuppattu, the Ten Long

Poems. It seemed so wildly voluptuous to me that I became fascinated; first one read of a whole countryside of slaughtered fat animals, trees groaning with fruit, and then of all of it pouring into an inconceivably rich and beautiful market, and the best of that went to a single family, whose single daughter prayed in Murukan's temple . . . and the focus of all this bounty was a ripe, rich, utterly feminine being who waited patiently for Murukan . . .

"Nakkiranar does not really do Nakirranar justice," Kannan said, sitting down beside me. "Do you, Nakirranar?"

Startled, I looked up to find I was surrounded, by Kannan and several others. It took me a moment to catch that Nakirranar, now shyly looking away as he stood in front of me, was the translator into Terstad of the poem I had been reading—which had been written, almost three thousand years ago in India on Earth, by the poet for whom he had been named.

By the time I figured out the feeble joke it seemed there was little point in even smiling at it, but since Nakirranar seemed shy, I smiled at him and said, "Sit down, please. Everyone join me. Can the Embassy expense account buy you all some breakfast?"

They agreed it could, as one might expect of any crowd of poets in their twenties.

Nakirranar was only shy until he warmed up; a bony young man with a larger nose than most Tamils, and a rather extravagantly curled mustache, he quickly became eager to explain to me how the images in that particular poem tied it closely to the type of *akam* poems called *kurinci,* which dealt with lovers' unions, and the puram poems called *vetci,* which dealt with the inciting incidents of a war (almost always the cattle raid).

Murukan, as the god of both successful erotic love (which the Cankam defined as a mixture of knowing infatuation, warm friendship, and very vigorous sex) and victory in battle (or perhaps of glory?), was also intimately connected with those two types of poems, so the connection was hardly surprising, Nakirranar said, but he then spent ten minutes explaining why it wasn't surprising—while breakfast arrived, and everyone ate, and during which I wasn't even introduced to the other three strangers at the table. I wondered if I was going to have to hear a literary lecture with every introduction.

"Has this planet ever seen a cattle raid?" I asked, to break up the flow of Nakirranar's exposition.

"May I say that that is precisely the kind of irrelevant question that Council diplomats always raise and that causes many of us here to suspect that you really favor the Maya?" another young man asked. He was muscular and squat, like a lightweight wrestler, and his clothes were notably less rumpled than those of the others.

"You may say anything you like," I said, "my job is to listen. And may I ask your name?"

"Villakaviralinar," he said.

" 'The poet of fingers around a bow,' " I quoted. It was one of the few names I recognized at once. "And what exactly is irrelevant about that question? In my home of Nou Occitan, there is a fine old ballad called 'The Wild Robbers of Serras Vertz,' that speaks of bandits who live high in the dense, impassable forests of a mountain range, and how no one can catch them, and how the King sends his soldiers against them a hundred times without success. Yet our terraforming is only now reaching the point where the trees are starting to grow there, and our King has no army and wouldn't have any power over it if he did, and the only robberies in Nou Occitan were committed by mental patients generations ago. At the time the song was written most of the mountains it refers to were still covered by kilometers-thick glaciers. And yet, knowing all that, we do treasure the story and think it very fine. So I wondered, perhaps idly, if anyone here raided for cattle, or even had any cattle."

"But that is why your question is irrelevant. You dream of your wild robbers because you never had any and thus you have to make a dream about them. We never had any cattle or any cattle raids, because having the Cankam poems, we already knew everything important about how to herd them or how to fight over them, and thus the actual cattle were irrelevant. Your question was about actual cattle—"

"And a question whose answer refers only to an irrelevancy is an irrelevant question," I finished for him. "I see."

He went on for a while longer; once I realized he was the political theorist of *Palai,* I stopped giving him any attention. The other two young men whose breakfast was being bought by the Council of Humanity were Uloccanar, who was an exponent of the Kural, and Venkorran, who was the only one in the group who wrote new poems as opposed to expounding old ones. I must have done something that indicated I approved of this, for he hastened, shamefacedly, to assure me that his poems so far were of little account, mere technical tricks he was mastering, and would remain so until there was a decreed Fourth Cankam that could definitively tell him what to write. He hoped that when that happened his practice would pay off, but most of the other members of the circle were of the opinion that writing poems, as opposed to the important business of criticizing them, was merely an odd hobby until there was a Fourth Cankam, and when that happened everyone with talent and taste—emphatically including themselves—would begin to write brilliant poetry.

I forebore mentioning that in the other two Tamil cultures it was generally accepted that the Cankam, if it had ever existed as a body, had come into existence long after the poems, and had been selectors and expositors, not prescribers. "What if," I asked, "the difference between Cankam poetry, and your current poetry, is that the Cankam poets wrote of things they saw every day, the way they saw them, and you write about the experience of reading?"

There was a long silence.

Villakaviralinar responded first. "Absurd," he said. "We can all feel the power in the words and phrases of the Cankam. They are the same words and phrases that we use today. We need only put them together in the right way—as a Fourth Cankam can teach us to do—and we will produce great poetry too."

Ulocannar was nodding vigorously. "A set of perfect poetic objects, and a perfect syntax of poetry, ultimately will generate all the perfect poetry there can be. And why meddle with less than perfection? You ask us if we have had a cattle raid. I hear the sneer in your mind, as if we write about what we know nothing of. But a real cattle raid—if anyone here were trying to keep cattle, and were armed to defend them—would be an experience of almost nothing but physical exertion, fear, confusion, and the like. One can't write a poem in such a state. It would only confuse us. The essence of a cattle raid, and what's important about it, is what's in the poems, and it is with that that we must be familiar. I suppose you might argue that those times when we fight with the Maya in the street might make poetry. It takes real courage to stand up to savages and teach them a lesson, you know. And we are not weak and soft like you are; we don't record ourselves onto psypyxes and leave little frozen chunks of our soul around in case we should die. We face the real danger just as it is, the possibility of dying, the possibility of being laid up in a hospital for three weeks, bored and stupefied, while a limb is regrown. We could make heroes of ourselves with poems about the battle with the Maya—but that battle is low and mean, an affair of rocks and sticks, of teaching manners to people who aren't much more than animals. It is not a fit subject for a poem; not the way a cattle raid is. Not the way the cattle raid has become. Think of the talent our ancestors must have had, to have had real sweaty dangerous dirty bloody cattle raids and yet to have written only the essentials about them. Perhaps the Fourth Cankam can teach us how to abstract the essentials of suppressing the Maya, and make that into poetry—"

I noted that all of them were nodding and agreeing with this, so I said, "And thus besides writing, as your ancestors did, about the heroic theft of potential shoes and steaks, you can glorify ganging up on a woman to destroy her groceries."

There was a stunned silence.

"As I told you all," Kannan said, "it appears to be the intention of the Council to insult us. But perhaps *Donz* Leones is merely making a tasteless joke."

"If I were," I said, "I would make a funny one. I heard a number that were not funny at all on the news this morning."

Nakirranar shook his head. "You don't understand at all. Those newscasters are not our educated or intelligent people; they have no desire but to be notorious for themselves. Of course his jokes were tasteless and stupid. Of course it was wrong to smear smashed vegetables all over a woman who was doing no harm. These are vulgar things that debase the entire Tamil cause. They make us ashamed too, and we will thank you not to mention them.

"But nonetheless, a courageous fight with a Maya is honorable, and by enough of them we can scrub our city clean of the Maya. You know it is only the sight of backward people, and the necessity of dealing with them, that has forced the long delay in creating the Fourth Cankam. Just consider that, like cattle raiding, farming is something better learned through poetry than practice; if we are to be truly Velalla then we need to know how to *feel* like a farmer, not grub in the dirt like one. And yet how can we think of these ideals when right on the edge of the city, everywhere under Mayatown, where decent people would dig tanks, there are actual farms? And these dirtgrubbers live off what is raised in them, and when their sordid little farms fail they starve their women and children rather than eat normal, wholesome food from a foodmaker. How can we teach our children the straight truth about what is important about farming when they are constantly confronted with people who eat plants grown in dirt—when they eat anything at all? Don't you see how the presence of so much fleshly detail degrades and erases the pure essence of what the life of the farmer-warrior-poet is about?"

"You are poets of farming and war," I said, "and of love, and I must confess as an outsider I would say that since you do no real farming, and fight no real wars, that I am forced to conclude you know no real love and that is why you write no real poetry."

That triggered an eruption and an effect that I later described to Margaret as "serial sermons." As they took turns lecturing me, they all ate a great deal more on the Council's tab, and meanwhile I maintained an alert expression while letting my eyes enjoy the play of the waterfalls and the mirror-skylight. How anyone could create such perfect places in which to enjoy doing nothing, and then work up the ambition to assault their neighbors, seemed more inexplicable than ever.

For six hours that day, interrupted by meals and introductions to more writers affiliated with *Palai*, I was harangued about Tamil poetics (about which I knew very little), the internal politics of the movement (of which I knew less), and the need for a "final solution" to the Maya problem. That last disgusted me; there were several ugly historical precedents for that expression, and I couldn't believe that a group of people so hyper-attuned to words was using such a phrase without knowing about those precedents. Furthermore, when I demanded to know what it was that they hated about the Maya, they told a number of bizarre stories, claiming that forced labor and torture were regular parts of life both in Mayatown and in Yaxkintulum. And despite its being obvious that all of these could only be mere urban legends, they believed it absolutely.

When I got home that day I was tired and heartsick. Margaret was acting as she had at breakfast—if anything more so—humming and smiling to herself one moment, gay and friendly to me and to everyone, and then abruptly cold and rude. Because she told me she didn't want to eat and didn't want to see more of me, I ate with Sir Qrala that night in the Embassy's dining room, and we talked far into the evening; he confirmed virtually every impression I had already formed, and had no more idea of how to make headway than I did.

When I returned to our apartment, Margaret wasn't there; a quick trace revealed she was in the office, and I figured that since she had seemed very upset, she was probably working off the stress by cataloging her observations from the day. The trace also showed her to be in an extended com conversation with Kapilar; clearly she was still at work on her report. I envied her the ability to produce that much material; if I had had to write my final report that minute, all I could have said was "everyone here is hopelessly *ne gens* and I want to go home."

I was just going to bed when she came in; she seemed startled to find me half-undressed in the bedroom.

"Good evening, *midons*," I said, trying to sound offhand as much as possible, not wanting to provoke trouble when I was tired.

"Thank you for waiting for me for dinner," she said, sarcastically. She turned and began to strip off her clothes for bed.

"You said you weren't hungry and didn't want to eat with me."

"You take everything too literally. And you're very whiny, Giraut, lately everything I do seems to bring up this grudge you have against me."

I didn't know what to say; I was angry and thought about storming out to sleep on the couch, or shouting—but what would I shout? And I wanted to make up, not estrange her further. Suppressing a sigh, I finished undressing and got into bed, turning away so that she couldn't accuse me of staring at her.

A moment later the lights went out, the door thudded, and I heard the creak of the couch in the parlor being pulled out to make a bed. Margaret had decided to sleep without me.

Yet the next morning she seemed cheerful and more or less her old self. While we enjoyed breakfast on the terrace, we went over our experiences of the day before in some detail, making a cross-reference of names of people we had both heard. When Kapilar turned up to conduct her on her next tour in the city, and it was time for me to take the springer and trakcar back to another meeting with Kannan, Margaret and I still hadn't said anything about the tiffs of the night before, but I felt that they were forgiven, forgotten, and past us. If I was wrong, I didn't want to know that yet.

I met Kannan and his followers daily, and endured three more days of lectures on poetics and culturist harangues, while buying them a great number of meals. At times I felt as if they were competing with each other to see who could say the most obnoxious thing about the Maya, perhaps as a way to drive me off, perhaps to make the Council complicit in their nastiness.

While I was doing this, Kapilar and Margaret cataloged tourist sites for the city, and Margaret picked up a lot of gossip. She thought she was making some headway in understanding the informal systems of prestige exchange that were the focus of so much of young adult life in New Tanjavur. She seemed happier every evening, though disinclined to talk. Now and again she would snap at me, and we'd have a brief fight.

As her work progressed, and mine became more depressing, I was beginning to envy her assignment, but I did my best to fight the feeling down; it was the one thing in which she'd had no choice, and if it meant that her job was fun and mine was not, well, she had been unhappy lately, and perhaps the pleasure she was finding in her work would help. It couldn't hurt.

One evening, a few days later, we had been going over each other's notes. (Poor Margaret couldn't suppress yawns at my reports—how many different ways are there to say "I met with several bigots and they said hateful things about the Maya?") As we got into bed, I rolled over and put an arm around her. "Margaret, are you used to the high gravity yet?"

She hit me, a hard blow in the ribs, which left me gasping. "Oh, god, Giraut, I bet you thought that was so damned clever that you spent a whole day planning to use that line on me."

"It's not exactly a line," I said, rubbing my chest where it hurt. "You're my wife. I was only suggesting—"

"You were only suggesting that poor old Margaret must need some sex because she isn't pretty enough to get any, any other way, than having the noble Giraut nobly sacrifice himself—"

"I didn't say a damned thing like that!"

"You thought it."

"I—this is impossible. I don't know what you want from me."

"Well, I know that you don't want me."

"I just made a pass at you—"

"Which you did so I wouldn't find out that you don't want me. I'm tired of all the pretending, Giraut. I watch you in the evenings, practicing your lute and playing songs you wrote more than a decade ago, and I know perfectly well you're wishing you were a *jovent* again, with nothing to do but fight and make verses and fuck pretty girls. God, I don't even blame you. I look at the young Tamil men here, easily a decade younger than you are, and the gorgeous way they dress, and the sheer style of them, and— well, it just brings everything back. You were such a gorgeous *jovent* and I ought to know. It's why I fell for you in the first place.

"But every time I hear you singing one of your old songs, the good popular ones from before you started writing those weird dirges about being discouraged and tired and so forth, even if I'm just listening to a recording of it from years ago—every time I do that, every time I hear your voice singing, I know what's going through your mind when you look at me, or when you touch me in bed, and I can't stand to be touched by a man who thinks of me like that."

She got up and went out into the living room; I heard her un-folding the couch.

Did I think of her like that? I couldn't decide. What exactly did she mean by "like that?" That I was seeing her as a mature woman? But I didn't "think of her like that," did I? I liked the way she looked, I liked her, I wanted her to like me. Or was she aware of something that I didn't consciously realize? And if so, what? That I would still enjoy a younger woman's body given the op-portunity? But I'd *had* opportunities, here and there, and had turned them down, and—well, I was back at the start. I went around the circle of confusion so many times that I lost count, as I lay there in the too-large bed by myself, listening desperately for any sound from the couch—a sob, a sigh, a groan, a swallowed scream of rage, just a change in her breathing. There was nothing.

It was a very long night, and I doubt I slept more than an hour of it. The next day I felt so sick and tired that I commed Kannan and the Embassy staff, pleading illness, and just stretched out on the couch to nap most of the day. That seemed to make Margaret even more angry with me, though I didn't understand why since she was going to be in the office all day, or out seeing more of the city with Kapilar, or something like that. Whatever she was angry about, I told myself, I didn't care, I absolutely didn't care, I just wanted to sleep, no matter what unremembered nightmares and vague discomforts might attack me.

I got up late in the afternoon, and without asking Margaret whether she might want to come along, went to an early dinner with Sir Qrala, at a place he suggested, and had half a bottle of wine, while he had a whole one. "Damn Briand," he said, as we set up what we had agreed would be our final glasses of the evening.

"Damn Briand," I agreed. "It makes everyone weird and dangerous."

"Some of us more than others," Ambassador Kiel said, coming over to sit at our table. He was a little drunk himself; fortunately the restaurant was a discreet, high-priced place, and there were few people other than us there. "Hope you don't mind my inviting myself. Just spent the early part of the evening meeting with a group of high level bureaucrats, which is to say I spent all my time hearing about men's mistresses. Half of them bragging, half of them griping, none of them bothering to be with their mistresses, or their wives. Same old crap you find at any post, eh? In more egalitarian cultures you can hear women complain about men, as well, but that's all the difference there is. Nothing new under twenty suns."

"Same old," I agreed, mostly because I had reached the point of feeling numb and content, and didn't want to spoil it with an argument.

"Unofficially, how's talking to poets going?"

"Unofficially? Well, it's a mess, sir. I suppose there's a real danger that Kannan and his little gang might take over if they ever put together a bid for the Fourth Cankam and manage to get the votes. But if they do it will all be a mess."

"Damn straight. Poets make messes. Tamil Mandalam's already a mess. They'll make it a bigger mess."

"Not just poets," Sir Qrala said.

I was afraid for a moment that Qrala would burst into a denunciation of Tamils in general; there were a few present in the room, and a diplomatic officer has no preferences for one culture over another, or if he does he stays quiet, or if he doesn't stay quiet he is quickly fired.

Either he drew back from the boundary or had never been going there in the first place. He went on. "Intellectuals. Talent. The whole thing. Only happy people I know are stupid. That's the great thing about alcohol; it makes you stupid. Alcohol, love, some stupid hobby like collecting something. All the problem is smart people." He looked at us blearily. "Let me just tell you one thing. Don't ever, ever marry a smart person. Smart person gets unhappy. Six hundred years of nothing to do, all over human space, six hundred years of people trying to kill time by developing themselves, and here they are all developed and nothing to do. That's why the system is coming apart. That's why smart people are bad for getting married. They have to find . . . have to find . . . "

"Unofficially, Sir Qrala," Ambassador Kiel said, "You are very drunk and we are somewhat depressed. One problem or the other ought to be solved."

"Absolutely," I agreed.

"Perhaps we'd best spring back to the Embassy," the ambassador added. "We might have a nightcap there if you'd like. I have a private stock that, I flatter myself, is better than anything they have here."

We got up, and with Kiel and me guiding him, we got Qrala to the springer in the restaurant lobby. Kiel and I set the springer for the ambassador's main office and sprang Qrala ahead of us, then stepped through ourselves, nearly falling over him since he had stumbled and gone headlong on the floor in front of the ambassador's springer. "I think," Qrala said, getting to his feet, "that perhaps, maybe, I've had a bit much. Maybe I should just go back to quarters."

Kiel nodded at me, and I grabbed Qrala by the arm and hauled him up. "See him into bed, and I'll be in my private quarters when you come back," the ambassador said.

"I can find my own . . . Well, I can find it." Qrala said, to no one in particular, as I guided him down the hall. I was disliking high gravity more than ever; the weight of the big man on my shoulder felt like a ton, and in my own partial inebriation, the floor sometimes jumped at me very aggressively. I managed to keep my feet but I could tell my muscles weren't going to forgive me in the morning. Well, maybe I could be sick two days running. Nobody here seemed to care whether I did any work, anyway.

"Smart women, that's the whole problem," Qrala said.

"I'm sure you're right," I said, trying to soothe him as I guided him toward his apartment through the long corridor.

"No!" he said, loud enough so that I expected other Embassy staff to hear him. Then "No," very softly. "You are *not* sure I'm right. At all. You don't believe me. But you look at Kiel, divorced three times, you look at me, divorced twice. And your real boss, Shan, now there's a story, isn't it? Could that have happened unless the woman was so damn smart? And you look at . . . what was his name, three posts ago? I was on Roosevelt. Funny that we used to think Roosevelt was a big-trouble world till we got this one . . . anyway—what's his name?—no matter, the point is that the poor stupid spawn of a pig was married for forty years. Happy man. Happy woman. Both dumber than potted plants. Secret to happiness." He was drifting into mumbling. I kept guiding him, hoping this would be the last I'd have to listen to. We were almost to his door and I was beginning to look forward to it, when he loudly said, "But it's not just women."

"Shhh," I said, "what's not?"

"Smart women are a mistake." He whispered, exaggerating his quietness. "Smart men are a mistake. Smart people. You think you'd be having this problem if she hadn't married a smart man? You think she'd be . . . ah, hell." With that he staggered to his door. "Kiel's third wasn't that smart, you know, but she was still too smart not to get bored, and *Kiel* was too smart. Way too smart. She married him for him to be smart and there wasn't anything for him to be smart about. So that's why she did all that. And that's why she's doing all that. And don't you think it will get better. I've been in the corps twenty years and once it starts it doesn't get better. She did, I mean, and so did lots of others, and they will once they do and—" he started to giggle. "What this sentence needs is a couple of proper nouns and a specific verb," he said, "doesn't it?"

"You need to get to bed," I said.

He pressed his hand against his doorplate, and the door opened. I guided him into his bedroom and left him sprawled facedown across his bed, head hanging over. If he threw up I didn't want him to choke; he was about the only friend I had here. On the other hand, I figured duty was discharged without going so far as to undress him.

Walking back through the long, winding hallway, I worked hard, in the obsessive way the truly drunk do, to get Qrala's words out of my head. By the time I got to the Ambassador's door, I was pleasantly untroubled.

He answered my knock at once, and guided me over to his table. I noted that he had gotten ahead of me on the wine, but to judge by the big glass he shoved into my hand, I'd be catching up soon if I wanted to.

One sip told me Kiel had a grand taste in wine. Hedon Gore lies warm and fruity on the tongue, with a full body and a hint of smoke, and seems to glide down the throat; so gentle that you are surprised to find that you are hanging desperately onto a spinning floor without any idea how you got that way. I took an appreciative sip and let it warm my throat and heart.

"Have a seat," the ambassador said. "How are you feeling?"

"Better for the wine," I admitted. "Life's been depressing lately."

Kiel made a face that wasn't quite a smile, and his shoulder moved just enough to be a shrug; if he had a comment to make, he was holding it till I asked for it. "Well, the Embassy's not a big building. Everyone hears things and knows things, you know. Eventually everything." He sighed and took a long drink.

"That's my experience everywhere else," I said. Well, obviously, everyone knew that I was fighting with Margaret, and it was nice that they were bothering to worry—though frankly I hoped Margaret was getting more attention, since she was the one, it seemed to me, who was acting strange and distressed. Drifting through the pleasant fog of alcohol, a thought crossed the distant horizon of my mind: Qrala had said something about Shan, and a clever woman, and I had no idea that Shan had ever had any connection with any woman. I thought perhaps I'd get one more piece of the mystery about my boss cleared up. "Ah, I got the impression from Sir Qrala that you had known each other for a long while?"

"Twenty-six years. Met him at Council Headquarters on Gobat. Believe it or not he was once about the best ethnological specialist you could imagine. I suppose I should find someone to replace him, but . . . well, years and years together. And hell, I'll be fired soon enough, if Shan and his office have their way. No, don't try to disagree. Maybe you're not high up enough to know what's going on, and maybe you do but you're about to lie to me, and either way I'd rather just talk a bit, all right?"

"All right," I said, taking another sip of Hedon Gore. A beatific fire was starting in my belly, spreading throughout my body, and just now I would be happy to listen to an old man reminisce.

He leaned forward in his chair; I saw that his hand trembled a little as it held his glass, and the glowing red of the wine reflected off his paper-white, wrinkled skin, and off the platinum hair that clung to his skull as if it were glued down. "I suppose this world is a test case and I suppose Shan is going to win. He's had his reverses, but he's going to win here, and I'm quite sure that you and your so-friendly-to-locals wife are going to help him win it, though for the life of me I don't understand quite how he intends that to happen. She is really your wife, isn't she? I don't suppose you could possibly be so upset if she were not."

"Yes, she's really my wife. Met her about the same time I met Shan," I said, taking a large swallow. I thought distractedly that I might really like to tell this nice old fellow about how I happened to meet and marry Margaret, but on the other hand it had been in the middle of the Caledon crisis, and from a previous conversation I knew he had been opposed to what the OSP had done there, even if it had saved our lives. So I missed a few words while I thought about telling him that story, and then caught up with him a moment later.

"—quiet and peace," he said. "In the centuries since the Inward Turn, the human race has killed fewer of its own members, in war, riot, and murder, than were lost in any one year of any of the big wars between 1900 and 2250. Sure, the world is less exciting. Some of us *like* it being less exciting. Sure, there's another civilization out there somewhere and someday we'll meet them. Why be in such a hurry? And why act like we've all got to be alike before we can meet them? And why is it so bad if some cultures just stay the way they are?" He sighed. "I don't know why I'm asking you. When did you get into this stupid game, anyway?"

"I went active duty for the Council in 2820. Margaret and I were in the same class," I said. "But we'd both been irregulars a while before."

"And I went out on a starship, in suspended animation, to Gobat in 2730," Kiel said. "When I got there I looked twenty-two, but I was getting on toward fifty by the clock. Eleven years there. Then to Ducommon in 2766, another thirty years in the tank. During the thirty years while we had crawled from 61 Cygni to Alpha Centauri, the radio message explaining how to build a springer had passed us, so that when we reached Ducommon the first thing we did—after burying the six people who had died in the suspended animation tanks—was report home for leaves, via the springer, in the blink of an eye. My first wife went through the springer just once, and wouldn't go again; it wasn't an uncommon phobia in our generation. My second, I met after I was reposted to Gobat, and lost . . . oh, I suppose it was on Roosevelt, sometime around the time you were enlisting. There was a third as well. Human marriage was never meant to last for so many decades as we've been living since the twentieth century, and most especially not for having our lives uprooted this way. I've known one very happy very long marriage—an old diplomat who was retiring at my second posting. She and her husband always put in for the first transfer they could get, back in the old starship days. So they had been married over two centuries but they'd been asleep for almost all of it. Excellent system!"

"Everyone tonight seems eager to tell me how inevitable it is that my marriage will collapse," I pointed out. I was poised somewhere between cool amusement and wretched self-pity, not sure which way I was going to fall.

"Well, Qrala and I have seen a lot," he said. "And the one thing that really seems to be true is that people who blame themselves don't do themselves any good. Maybe we just wanted to tell you we've both been there, or maybe we didn't want to drink alone tonight." He finished his glass; I finished mine. "If you'd like another, help yourself. I've had enough to be sure I'll sleep without dreams, and that's what I wanted."

"I should go back while I've got the energy and focus to find my way down the hallway," I said. "I appreciated this very much, sir. I hope we can be better friends."

"Probably we can't," he said; his blue eyes stared off into space far away. "Different organizations, different priorities, and Shan won't let you be overt about what your real mission is. But I hope you share my regret that we've turned out to be on different sides."

"I do," I said, and staggered to my feet. We shook hands the way I used to shake with my opponents back in Noupeitau, during my *jovent,* just before a friendly, trivial, *atz sang* duel. Then I made my way down the hall, back to our apartment. The world whirled wildly, and the high gravity made every misstep a potential disaster. I fell more often than I could count. But I got there, staggered in, and discovered that Margaret was mysteriously not there at all. A trace showed she wasn't in the Embassy, either, and as I didn't want to be nosy I let it go at that.

I could have taken an alcohol scrubber but it seemed like such a waste of Hedon Gore. Instead, I took a hot shower, which felt wonderful, toweled off, and went to bed. Just before I fell asleep, I heard the springer activate in our living room, which must have been Margaret coming home from wherever she'd been. I drifted up into consciousness but didn't seem to be able to form anything to say.

She came into the room without turning on a light, kicked off her uniform boots, and stretched out on the bed beside me, fully clothed, her hands under her head, as if she intended to study the ceiling in the dark. My eyelids dropped slowly, and she disappeared into the dark void; after a while I dreamed, but I don't recall of what.

A few days later I sat down to a lunch at the Embassy, in a small, comfortable inner room, with Tz'iquin, the lone representative of the Maya to both Tamil Mandalam and the Council. Since everyone from Kiel on down had assured me that there was virtually no prospect that any Maya would ever want to talk directly to us, it was about time I at least established some connection with their envoy, if only to confirm for myself that I could go no farther.

We had a pleasant enough chat about New Tanjavur while we

ate. Tz'iquin seemed genuinely to like the place, even though his every day was a series of insults and snubs. He acknowledged that life there was difficult for him, but maintained that the city itself was beautiful and that he found much to like about individual Tamils. We talked a little about the Cankam literature, which both of us were struggling to master. I found it reassuring that with his many years of practice, Tz'iquin still found it hard. "The problem," he said, "is in that dense coding; virtually everything signifies so much in so many different ways that every poem seems to write itself, as if the first few words dictated the solution right through to the outcome."

"I wasn't raised to think that way," I said. "Dense coding is pretty scarce in human literatures. Thank goodness, or we'd never be able to talk to each other, and we'd all have the same problem their contemporary poets do, of never being able to say a new thing in an established idiom."

"Are you so sure it would be good for the two sides to understand each other better, here? Do you really think that Briand's problem is that the Tamils and the Maya don't know each other? And what makes you think any of us wants to say a new thing?"

The questions hung there, and I thought about them for a long moment before I decided that the last thing I wanted to do was answer. Feeling reckless, or perhaps just wanting something to start to change so that I could look forward to getting off Briand, I said, "I've now heard a great deal of Tamil bigotry about your people."

"You could hardly avoid it. I hear it all the time as well."

"The claims are very odd and nasty, and I am baffled as to why—"

"Oh, most of them are true," Tz'iquin said. "We really do keep most of the nonaristocratic population in ignorance, and some of them do starve to death now and then."

I stared at him. The machinery that made food for human beings—which could support populations a hundred times that of any existing settled solar system, including Earth—had been

known for more than five hundred years. It was as if he had confessed that they practiced circumcision, crucifixion, or infanticide
routinely.

"Don't gape," he said. "I've reached a decision of sorts and the
first phase of the decision is to tell you as much of the truth as I
can. While I'm at it, here's the answer to the mystery of why
some Maya stay in Mayatown: during that three stanyears when
our whole surviving population lived there, some people had
births, deaths, marriages, things like that in the family. The places
where such lineage events happen are sacred, and junior branches
of the lineage were assigned to stay on, to preserve those places.
Then their children had more such events, in the same places, and
so they stayed. And so to this day, the houses that were blessed
by special events are still occupied by the descendants of those
families. You see? Just a matter of keeping our sacred spaces
sacred, and meeting our obligations to our ancestors."

I stared at him. "I'm sure there are rules and principles of
sacredness that anyone would—"

"Oh, yes. The whole thing could be explained. Could have
been explained a long time ago. Probably some of the Tamil
would have understood, or tried to, or said they did anyway. My
people have a tendency, however, to decide that the way we do
things is nobody else's damned business, you see. A thousand
years of being hounded by anthropologists produces that perspective—or so we say in the upper class. We make a special
point of claiming to have been exploited by anthropologists. I
think that's because the one thing we won't admit at all is that the
origin of our culture is in the speculations of archeologists and a
highly selective reading of the ideas of some anthropologists and
linguists. As long as you don't directly say to us that we originated in white people's books, in what they wrote about our
cousins and what they dug up of our grandfathers' cities, we are
not offended. We just don't feel like explaining any of it. It makes
us uncomfortable to have to do that. But we really don't mind
someone else's knowing the explanation."

"So may I tell the Tamils the reason that—"

"If you think they'll believe you. And while we're at it, you can com me and ask me anything, if you like. I've gotten approval to speak frankly with you, and no restrictions on what you repeat. Go right ahead, from now on." He stretched his big frame. "I couldn't have been born a short squatty man with the stumpy legs that make sense for this miserable gravity, eh?" Leaning down to rub his calves and knees, he wasn't looking at me, and I couldn't see his expression, when he added, "And here's the real issue. I want to see if maybe I can arrange for you to meet with some people over in Yaxkintulum. Because you talk about stories and philosophy and so forth, and those are the sorts of things they might want to talk to you about. With luck maybe I can get Kapilar included too. I am assuming you would not want to include Kannan?"

"I would think you wouldn't. Kapilar at least is trying for understanding—"

"But Kannan *needs* it. Well, perhaps you are right anyway, and good intentions matter more than good effects. And I *am* limited—they will only let me invite one Tamil." He grinned and leaned forward. "The question is whether I'd rather have Kapilar openly jealous, or Kannan secretly jealous, and in either case make them hate each other more. You know they don't like each other—the little crack between them of artistic differences, on the one hand, and the great chasm of Auvaiyar on the other?"

"One can hardly avoid knowing that."

"Right, then. And I suppose there are other reasons why you might prefer to take Kapilar along. The journey will be long and filled with anxiety, I suspect, and you might rather have him with you, than Kannan I mean." Tz'iquin took another big sip of the hot cocoa he had ordered with lunch. "Interesting that this is a sweet drink for children with you. Different approach to things. Perhaps we can learn to learn from that; my brother's children might like the recipe for this as a gift."

"It's yours." I looked at him curiously. "And just like this, all of a sudden, your people and mine will begin to talk?"

"It only looks sudden from some places. Running off a cliff is sudden if you don't know it's there, even if you have been running toward it for days."

"That's not a reassuring metaphor."

"It isn't meant to be. But I do think I know someone who would talk to you, who could take some kind of action—if he decided to take any—that might get you out of this stuck-in-dead-center situation. He is already considering it. If he decides to do it, he will need to meet with you, and will want to do it before anyone can see what he is up to. So if we offer, are you going to accept? Within a day or two at most?"

"I'm a professional diplomat. I talk to anybody."

"Get Kapilar to promise too if you can. It will help me to make my case. You might see about getting him some of your diplomatic uniforms, since they're apt to create less of a stir than the clothes he would usually wear; good luck getting him to wear it, though." He got up. "Thanks for lunch. Thanks more for the company. I get really tired of eating alone."

That evening I got Shan on the com. I was distracted since I wanted very much to ask him what it was that Qrala and Kiel knew about in his past, the mysterious "clever woman" on which Qrala blamed the equally mysterious "trouble." So I made my report in a perfunctory way, explaining that the opportunity had opened up to talk to some of the Maya face to face, that it might be a minor gesture, or a tentative feeler, or even what Tz'iquin had said—if they were going to talk to foreigners they wanted to talk about stories and philosophy, rather than trade or politics. I added that apparently they were now going to be more open with us, and that I had been given leave to try to dispel a little of the Tamil bigotry against them.

"You don't know that for sure," Shan said.

"I beg your pardon?"

"You don't know for sure that their reason for giving you the permission is to decrease bigotry. It could just as easily be to increase it, or to shift its direction."

I shuddered, knowing he was right, and then asked, "Do you have any reason to think that's true?"

He shrugged. "The Maya have had a system of quiet, monopoly relationships with a few fortunate traders from the outside world for the past half stanyear. We've been able to get about half of those traders to pass on information to us. One of them is your old friend Garsenda, by the way. And what we've discovered from that effort is that we are no good at all at discerning the motives of the Maya for anything. So I find it very interesting that they are now making an approach to you through channels, just as if they wanted to have a normal relationship with the Council and with the rest of the Thousand Cultures. Either they have changed their minds, or changed their strategy . . . or perhaps we should just say, they've changed."

The next day I had another meeting with Kannan. When I descended to the tank, he was sitting by himself at the table, looking quite morose. "What's wrong?" I asked.

"Oh, some of it's foolish," he said. "A woman I used to know, Auvaiyar—used to be close to, I should say—wrote a long and scathing letter to *Palai*. She's making fun of our position on the Maya question. Says our whole argument is self-contradictory."

"You have to expect criticism."

He took a deep gulp of tea. "I do indeed. On the other hand I'm very bothered by the fact that she seems to be absolutely right. And very few of my staff agree with me on that, so they are all accusing me of still being in love with her. Which is unfortunately true, you see—well, perhaps not in love, but at least still sexually fascinated. Still, a careful reading of her letter has convinced me that she is right. So first of all I must persuade my more partisan but less analytic followers that she is right, since the contradiction she has pointed out will doom us if we don't fix it before we go in front of the board of examiners to propose a Fourth Cankam. Indeed she may very well have saved the whole *Palai* movement by bringing this to our attention. Now all I need to do is persuade my staff, who don't like her and know that I am still in love with her, that she *is* right and that the reason I am reluctantly forced to agree with her is *not* that I am in love with her. It puts me in an extremely confusing position."

"It must," I said. I stopped a robot and ordered tea and sweet rolls. "Does this mean your position on the presence of the Maya has to soften?"

"I still want them to go away. It's just that Auvaiyar has made it very clear that my reasons for wanting it contradict each other."

"Well," I said, "For what it is worth, yesterday I learned why you are unlikely ever to get the Maya of Mayatown to leave—voluntarily, anyway." I explained to Kannan what Tz'iquin had told me, that every year more sites within Mayatown had become sacred, until finally they were bound there by a web as tight as the one that held most Maya to Yaxkintulum.

"Well," Kannan said, "making the very large assumption that that savage told you the truth, then I suppose we can be reassured on two points: their desire to stay is not irrational, and they are not just doing it to twit us. But from the viewpoint of *Palai,* you know, all it means is that we have to be much more dedicated about destroying Mayatown once we evict them. We can't have other peoples' sacred sites cluttering *our* city, after all. That's precisely what the essence of the Tamil way is: purity and coherence. In the same way that no critic would allow a borrowed Maya word into a poem—"

"Why not?" I asked.

"By now you know us well enough—"

"Pretend I don't. Tell me why a Maya loan-word can't be in one of your poems. None of those decisions really counts until it is made by the Fourth Cankam, does it? Till there is a Fourth Cankam, it's just everyone's guess as to what the Fourth Cankam is eventually going to decide. What if they decide to admit Maya loan-words? What if they decide that sharing your land and this city with the Maya is central to the Tamil experience, and a fit subject for poetry?"

"They wouldn't decide that!" His now-cold tea splashed over his hand, and his cup fell sideways as he banged it down.

"Could they?"

"No, they can't."

"But isn't the Fourth Cankam sovereign—"

"Subject to what is in the Eight and the Ten plus the Kural, and not—"

"Hold it. None of those contain any reference to the Maya, or Mayatown, or Yaxkintulum—or even to Briand." I was beginning to enjoy this. If Kannan was intellectually honest enough to be tied in knots by Auvaiyar's critique, then perhaps I could score a few more points and disable the *Palai* group further.

He sighed. "This is the problem with the whole business. Pull out one idea and it begins to unravel. The Kural doesn't say that it only applies to relations between Tamils, but if it doesn't, then we have to be brothers and friends with people who deliberately starve their children."

I was about to retort that that was probably pure legend, when I recalled that Tz'iquin had assured me that most of the stories about the Maya were true, and had even specifically said that some of them, sometimes, did starve. Not knowing what to say, I let the moment go by.

"Perhaps," Kannan added darkly, "you should have conquered us, and let us find our own way to deal with military occupation."

"The Council of Humanity doesn't do that," I said.

Even as I said that, I found myself thinking of what had happened on Wilson, and Nansen, and every other planet that I had visited: the Embassy was built and staffed, and then as shortly as possible afterward, the Bazaar opened at the Embassy—and the Bazaar was nothing less than forced free trade, a market protected by troops where the wares of all the Thousand Cultures were for sale, not subject to local control at all. It was the end of economic sovereignty for every culture on every planet where it happened.

We had refrained from doing that here, but it hadn't been because we respected the rights of these cultures. Only our fear that the violence that already wracked New Tanjavur would grow worse as the Connect Depression destroyed the local economies that had prevented us, thus far, from ramming free trade down their throats, as we had done to everyone everywhere else.

Those thoughts gagged me; I had no more responses to Kannan, either in defense of the Council or to further attack his ideas, and while I sat there he rebuilt the whole structure of his anti-Maya bigotry in front of me, rambling through sentences and ideas too fast for me to follow. I bought him lunch, and watched as he ate, gesticulated, and dictated to his pocket computer. Whatever hope there had been of collapsing *Palai* collapsed right there, and I couldn't for the life of me see a way to change that.

Worst of all, when he finally got up from lunch, he thanked me, and said that he really thought he saw a way that contact with the rest of the Thousand Culture could "help the Tamil become so Tamil that a Fourth Cankam is inevitable." He walked away with a cocky strut, clearly reassured that the problem that had seemed so insoluble to him a few hours before was now fully resolved.

Not having anything else to do, I caught the trakcar back to the springer station. I got home in mid-afternoon, tired and discouraged.

To my surprise, Margaret was in our quarters; she had called in sick earlier that day, it seemed. I nodded to her—she lay on the couch—and asked, "Are you all right?"

"No," she said. "But I'm more tired and unhappy than sick."

"I can understand that feeling," I said. "I'm going to get a shower. Is there anything up in the office that I need to deal with?"

"I told Kapilar to call me if anything came in," she said, "and I'm sure he will. Part of what has me so exhausted is that we had a long argument about the Maya and the Council and everything, and it made me see that even though he seems more liberal on cultural purity than most Tamils, Kapilar's still a steel-bound bigot. And I was very frustrated and there was really nothing to do."

"You had an afternoon like mine, I think," I said. "I thought I was winning an argument with Kannan and ended up confirming him in his bigotry. Has the ambassador said we can approach Kapilar about going to Yaxkintulum yet?"

"Not yet. He's still thinking. But I can't think of anything that he could get out of saying 'no,' and several things he might get if he agrees, so I'm sure once Kiel's thought it through and worked out the angles and political traps and so forth, he'll approve it." She stretched and yawned. "I wish I could make myself care about it more."

"I wish I could, too. Well, something will happen—it always does."

"It might have already. Did you hear there was another rape of a Maya girl? Only fourteen years old. And it was definitely by Tamils."

I whistled. "Any rock-throwing yet?"

"The police are keeping a lid on it and the rapists are being held incommunicado. We were very lucky—they got it all wrapped up before anything else happened, and it's under prior restraint, so there will be no news coverage. First anyone will hear of it is when the sentences are announced—hopefully personality erasures, but at least fifteen years in the pen."

I nodded. "That's not what I had in mind, but you're right that it's not wise, around here, to wish for things to happen. Most of what can happen is bad. Anyway, I'm going to get that shower, and then maybe we can do something relaxing this evening, or just go to bed early."

"Right now that sounds good," she said, and turned over, facing into the back of the couch. That seemed to close the conversation, so I went and got the shower. Many times warm water, soap, and a simple task seem to wash away the bad feelings of a day and leave me feeling renewed.

This was *not* one of those times.

When I stepped out of the shower, Margaret was standing there. She handed me a towel.

I was mostly dry before she came back into the bathroom, naked. "I don't know how long the mood will hold," she said, "but right now I'd like to try, if that's all right with you. It's been an awfully long time and if it works it might improve things between us."

I took her in my arms and kissed her; she responded eagerly, and I guided her to the bed. But due to overeagerness, losing each other's rhythm, the bad day we had each had, or perhaps just leftover anger, though we tried, I didn't become erect and she didn't get aroused. In a few minutes we finished, not with a gasp, cry, scream, or grunt, but with a mutual shrug. She turned away from me on the bed, and when I reached to put an arm around her, she pushed it away angrily. I lay on my back, hands locked behind my head, and stared at the ceiling, trying to figure out how much longer, at most, we'd have to endure this miserable situation.

I had arrived at no answer half an hour later when the com chimed. Blanking out the visual because we were still not dressed, I answered.

"Kiel here," a voice said. "I need to meet with both of you for some discussions."

We dressed quickly and sprang to his office, hoping we looked presentable.

"Sit down," he said. "This may take some time. I've reviewed your notes about your contact with Tz'iquin, and little as I like it, I'm forced to concur that you should be the one who makes the contact, Giraut. That worries me a great deal—"

He blathered on for more than an hour about Maya politics (which he knew only from sources as secondhand as Shan's, or anyone's) and the need to work toward full contact at an appropriate level (by which he meant direct talks with him) with the responsible people (by which he meant bureaucrats and politicians). Dr. Urruttiran had been very pleased at the selection of his nephew as the Tamil delegate, so it was affirmed that I was to take Kapilar along.

Then Kiel delivered a series of platitudes to Margaret about not upsetting me with such a critical mission in hand, and the importance of no dissension within the team. It was utterly obvious, the sort of thing I wouldn't have bothered to say to the greenest agent on the most sensitive mission; I couldn't imagine why the subtle, clever man I had recently gotten drunk with, now cold sober to all appearances, was being so heavy-handed. I wondered if for some obscure reason he wanted this picked up by a hidden camera or microphone—and for some reason subtler than that, he wanted no one to believe him sincere.

Whatever it was that he intended, the only effect it had was that he upset Margaret even further. Unable to find anything to talk about that did not lead to a fight, we went to bed early. I took a turn on the couch, listening, off and on all night, to her getting up, pacing around the bedroom, and collapsing back onto the bed. Though she was quiet, and never voiced a sound, her footsteps woke me every time.

The next morning when I went in to break the idea to Kapilar, he and Margaret were in the small reception room we had been granted as part of our offices. It could seat about four normal sized people, facing each other on the two couches that took up the two longer walls, or maybe six midgets. They had papers spread out all over the place but they didn't seem to want to talk about what the project they were working on was; they only said it had proven to be a dead end.

I told Kapilar about what little I knew, and that we would have to wait until we heard from Tz'iquin again before we would really know anything. "So—" I said "—if I go, you can go. They specifically invited you. Do you want to go?"

"Well," Kapilar said, "at least they asked for me in preference to Kannan, which shows more taste than I'd otherwise have believed they possessed. Perhaps they just prefer someone who is better dressed, but then that commends them as well, now doesn't it? It would mean some time away from society, and as they say, once you get out of a tank it isn't so easy to get back in. But on the whole . . . well. You know, their idea of inviting Kannan was not so silly as it might have seemed—it was pretty shrewd. The only mistake they made was that they underestimated just how much Kannan and the little gang of sycophants around him hate the Maya—how irrationally and how deeply. You have to accept some kind of equality before there can be any compassion, and I don't think Kannan and his crew will ever do that. It's a pity, too, because this is an idea that, presented in the right way, could spread wildly through the cafés, and pretty well take over the culture. Done right, in another generation you could make tolerance and interracial harmony the orthodox interpretation of 'Concerning Lord Murukan'—I've worked that out myself from time to time, but I would never be so crazy as to publish it."

"Why not?" Margaret asked.

He shrugged. "I know my people. I like being able to go out in public without being harangued—or stoned. I am about as liberal on the Maya question as anyone. But all the same, this morning I was waiting for a trakcar, and I heard someone say, 'How does a Maya pediatrician reassure a Maya mother?—Nothing to worry about, ma'am, as long as you don't feed him'—with three Maya standing right there. And along with all the other Tamils, I laughed. You see? It goes deep here."

"It goes deep a lot of places," I said. "The first step is to say you don't want it to go on."

"I'm not sure I can say that, honestly, yet," Kapilar said. "But perhaps that is why I *should* go to Yaxkintulum with you. I may be different when I return. And regardless of everything else, it would be an adventure, wouldn't it?"

After he left for the day, Margaret seemed more than usually upset, so I slept on the couch. It was beginning to feel like home.

The official invitation from Tz'iquin took a long time coming. He let me know every few days that it was still a live possibility, but I had only his word for it. I went on with my duties, trying to broaden my contacts with Tamil artists, but now that I was hopelessly connected to *Palai,* in the minds of most of them, only Kannan's group would really talk to me.

For the next few days I went and let Kannan harangue me in the morning (if he wasn't too busy getting out his next issue, in which he revealed the need to "cleanse" New Tanjavur of Maya lineage shrines), or sat and drank coffee in the cafés in various tanks. Now and then someone would walk up and begin to talk to me, generally to denounce the Interstellar metaculture. They seldom stayed long enough for me to say anything to them, or even to learn their names.

In the evening I would go home and Margaret and I would fight, or not. If we didn't fight, we would often attempt to have sex—which would fail, and *then* we would fight—except for three blessed times when we connected, somehow. Then it was wonderful, as good as or better than it had ever been. After all three of those occasions, she demanded to know why I thought I had to do favors like that for her, I said something silly—for example, that I loved her—and we got into a howling fight.

Whenever I talked to Shan on the com, I had nothing to say to him. Once I was ordered to a debriefing with Paxa Prytanis, who nominally ran a small trading company negotiating for import entry, but actually served as Shan's Number Two in New Tanjavur. I knew her slightly from the training base back in Manila. We went over everything I had told Shan. She got exactly what Shan had gotten, bought me a couple of drinks, and listened to me talk about my general boredom and unhappiness for a while; then she told me about hers. Both of us agreed that Briand was a place where promising careers went to die.

For forty standays I listened to bigots, tried to persuade my wife that I loved her, wandered around trying to find someone else to talk to, and reported to Shan. During that time there were 379 incidents of intercultural violence, according to Sir Qrala's reports. My feet, ankles, knees, and hips ached all the time from the gravity, and my eyes sometimes felt dry and inflamed—supposedly a natural reaction to all the ultraviolet light, which slipped in past even the best goggles. I got a tan that made it look like I was wearing a mask. I learned to interpret (in a very elementary and crude way) one whole side of the temple of Murukan. In short, I passed time less and less productively, as Margaret and Kapilar amassed more and more data, and the prospects of a contact with the Maya seemed to grow steadily dimmer.

I kept trying to talk to people, and waiting.

When the com finally came from Tz'iquin, it was an anticlimax. Could Kapilar and I, six days from now, please meet Tz'iquin at New Tanjavur's airfield, for a trip to Yaxkintulum, to learn about the Maya and to discuss important matters with some of them? We said yes. There was no more information forthcoming, so we would have to do all our learning once we got there.

I broke all my appointments with the various denizens of the café art scene. I reread all the known material about the Maya (there wasn't much, and since a lot of it was from the founding of the colony, it was potentially out of date by 450 years). And even when Margaret slept on the couch, or when I volunteered for it, I was as friendly and affectionate as I could manage. It's amazing what having something to accomplish, soon, will do for your spirits.

Part Two

Sudden Jaguar

Mullai

Sudden Jaguar: Second born of the people. Always there, and yet never out of the company of the other first people. The present, the moment, matters as they stand.

Mullai: Arabian jasmine.

In the *akam* poems: The forest. Evening. The place of the deer, hare, jungle hen, and sparrow. The people till their plots, watch their flocks, dance the kuravai, fight bulls, and eat boiled millet. Patient waiting; joyful and confident anticipation of the lover.

In the *puram* poems: *Vanci,* muster, the marshalling of forces for war.

A world dominated by Mayon, known also as Tirumal, called in Sanskrit Vishnu, the creator.

As we sat outside over breakfast in the cool, pleasant predawn, Metallah was streaking the black sky with indigos and deep magentas, and the southeastern horizon was vivid red. We sat listening to New Tanjavur come awake below us, and watched the shadows and light lunge across the landscape in that rapid sunrise. Margaret and I were trying very hard to make each other comfortable with the situation. Since Kapilar was not due to come by till midmorning, and we had nothing to do until he and I departed, we continued to sit, sometimes eating the cool fruit. The city's glare against the black sky was filtered out by our dark glasses; perhaps to some extent they filtered Margaret's facial expressions as well. I couldn't be sure.

The temperature rose steadily now that Metallah was up, and still we didn't speak. I don't know why Margaret didn't, but I didn't want to spoil the companionship. Finally, Margaret sighed and shrugged. She drew the bandanna from her sleeve and wiped her face. "The heat," she said. "I think it bakes the brains right out of everyone, and that explains half the behavior we see. God, I could just live on ice here. Want to sneak in some air-conditioner time before Kapilar shows up?"

I took a final gulp of the tar-dark local coffee, salty with the sweat already soaking my mustache. The loose robe I was wearing had gone damp with my sweat in the time it took to drink half a cup.

"With you right now," I said, pushing myself out of my chair, not sure whether it was the sex or the air-conditioning that made me feel eager. Despite the arch supports in my slippers, my feet and calves ached and my back was sore around the small, already. Briand was a planet where everyone was always going to feel old.

I took her hand as we went inside, spoiling it for myself at once by worrying about how this was going to go. I was trying to have no thoughts at all. Nothing will make a mess of sex like trying to put meaning into it, I knew, yet I couldn't help also knowing that if we could have a good quick one everything would get easier between us, at least for a while, especially since we'd have something good to think about during the time I was away.

On the other hand, another abortive, angry episode would make things that much worse, with no time to make up before I left for Yaxkintulum. Was I trying a long shot to get things right with Margaret, or trying something sure to fail so that I would have yet another excuse when the inevitable happened? And why was I thinking about it at all when I knew thinking was exactly the wrong thing to do?

Well, Shan had always said that in any multiple choice about human motivation, the real answer was always "all of the above."

We hadn't bothered to put on uniforms because we had no reason to expect any company—at least that had been the reason at the time. Now, holding Margaret's hand as we went back to our private quarters, I glanced sideways at her. The pale blue robe was already beginning to cling to her chest. I liked that a lot. Whether I just had a fetish for heavy women with slack, small breasts—or the good years with Margaret had made me prefer that—or it was just that the view brought to mind so much remembered pleasure, suddenly I felt better and sex was more urgent.

As soon as we were in our bedroom we turned the air-conditioning on. If air conditioning had merely been a local religious taboo, we might have defied it on principle—it was very much in our interests to "remind religious locals that they follow a *local* religion," as Shan liked to put it.

But it was even more in our interests to be respected by the locals, and that was the issue here. Both cultures on this planet made a great point of the strength and merit demonstrated by their endurance of the uncomfortable local heat, humidity, and gravity. Therefore to keep ourselves worthy of respect we could not use air-conditioning in front of them. It had to be our private vice, practiced only among ourselves.

We slipped out of the robes and slippers, and lay down on the bed, waiting a long moment for the room to drop to a pleasant temperature, then stretched and sighed exuberantly and in unison. It was as if our bodies had decided to chorus their approval of being out of the heat. That set off a fit of laughter in both of us, and we swept each other up in a great hug. My penis was already hard before it bumped against Margaret's thigh.

A few times I have had sex so perfect that I remembered it forever. That morning was one of them. As I mounted her, awkward and silly with affection and enthusiasm, I leaned back just a moment to look at her. The damp shine of the sweat on her pale skin; her soft, baggy breasts, white in contrast to her big red nipples; her pubic hair, darker than the pale hair on her head, billowing in dense curls from the firm bulge of her belly; the white stretch marks and the great swelling curve of her belly—all of that called up years of pleasure, things I hadn't thought about enough lately. I couldn't remember being so aroused.

From the way she was grinning, I guess she felt appreciated. I slid into her and let my body slide forward to rest on my elbows. Her mouth opened onto mine. Her hands slid down over me, from the pulse throbbing in my throat over my sternum, my clenched belly, and down over my buttocks, pulling me forward.

She cried out in orgasm with every stroke, the little scream smothered in my mouth. The whole thing must have lasted less than a minute, yet as my testicles let go in a great surge, and I fell forward, gasping and thrusting deeper into her, my eyes were wet with tears and my body was dripping with sweat despite the air conditioning.

I was sobbing as I rolled off her, but then our eyes met and we were overcome by giggles. For a long time we both kept trying to speak and being overcome by fresh laughter every time. Finally, gasping and with my sides aching, I managed to say, "Well, *companhona*, I do love you."

She rolled over and pressed her face against me, hanging onto me as if I were her life preserver in a choppy sea. I was afraid for a moment that she would begin to cry, but when she raised her head, though her eyes were wet, she was smiling. I ran a hand through her fine, short blonde hair, and kissed her lightly just under each eye, tasting her tears on my lips and feeling her cheeks tighten into a little smile. "I suppose now the Council will insist that we have to put our clothes on and go earn our exorbitant salaries," I added.

"*Que seretz seratz,*" she said. She said it exactly like Mother. "Or as we say in Caledon, *subj-condit subj-futur ident-futur.* But I sure feel a lot better about the range of possibilities than I did a while ago. Write to me and call, will you? Just to say hello and . . . well."

"Of course," I said, realizing at that moment that I hadn't been planning to, till then. When had I lost the habit of writing or calling every day while we were apart? I had always done that years ago, early in the marriage. "Anyway, I hate to be getting up and dressing when we could be snuggling down to a nap together."

"I know. The world does seem like a really nice place right now. But you're right, we have to go earn our keep . . . . Well. You *will* stay in touch?"

"Every day."

Her face serious, she put her arms around me and hugged me again. I held her for a long time.

We had to dress very quickly to get back to our table on the Embassy balcony before Kapilar was due to arrive. I pulled off the soft, comfortable robe and put on a scratchy brand-new Standard Issue Hot Weather Coverall, the only politically neutral thing that we had been able to figure out that was even remotely appropriate. "Just wanted to say thank you, love you—and watch out—one more time," Margaret said, not looking at me, as she put on her day uniform.

Her words were so welcome and so useless. *"Ja, ja-deu-ja,* I understand," I said, "And I love you too and I'm looking forward to getting back together, and I'm pretty scared about what I might be getting into in Yaxkintulum. But I don't know how to 'watch out.' It's pretty hard to get prepared for all the things that you don't expect to happen. Maybe you'd better just wish me luck."

The sour half-smile she gave me reminded me more than ever of the way things had been when we had first gotten together, so I kissed her. She kissed back, warmly, and then, still holding me, she said, "Shan has always said your biggest and most useful talent was being lucky. So keep being lucky, okay?"

"I'll do my best, *companhona.*"

"*Yap,*" she said, and hugged me close again. "This whole planet scares the piss out of me, Giraut. I don't know if it's that, being a Caledon, it seems to me as if both the cultures here are worshipping idols and demons, or the weird light, or the way almost no one talks to us, or what, but it's just *scary.*"

I stroked her hair and whispered, "Now, don't turn into a bigot."

"I'm *trying* not to, Giraut, honestly, but this place scares me. More than anywhere we've been stationed." She raised her head from my chest, looked into my eyes, and said, "And you're impossible and frustrating and a lot of times I don't see how I can stay married to you for five more minutes *but* all the same I don't want you hurt and I don't ever want to have had my last argument with you." Her eyes were damp and her throat sounded tight.

Probably only the truth would do. I just wished I knew what it was. So I blurted out the best I could do. "Well. I know you don't scare easily. And, um. *Deu.* Isn't it always awkward? I'll watch out, I will. But you know as well as I do, for all that we know, the Maya most likely just want to explain to us that they emphatically want to be left alone. Or maybe they've all taken a vote or the king or whatever they call him has decreed, or however it is they decide, and now they are suddenly going to be terribly friendly. Sir Qrala said that something just like that happened with New Malawi, on Roosevelt, didn't he? A xenophobic isolationist culture just suddenly decided to be open, for reasons that no one but them could understand?"

"We always can hope," she said. "I guess. Nevertheless, be careful, be alert, stay lucky."

I was startled by how vigorously she kissed me. Probably we had kissed more this morning than in the past stanyear.

We both hurried down the hall, so that we wouldn't keep Kapilar waiting. Partly to take my mind off all the confusing fears and the whole complex problem of Margaret, I fretted about how I had looked in the mirror—like a simplified one-piece version of bwana in the old flatscreen movies, except that the shirt and short pants were a single piece coverall and I wore it with a white bodysuit against the burning UV. I hoped the Maya didn't have the tradition of guest-naming visitors, as so many Amerind-derived cultures did, because I was sure I would immediately be named "Dresses Funny."

We had a minute or two to spare when we got back to the table, and Kapilar had not yet arrived. Some efficient robot had set out the fresh tablecloth, pot of coffee, rolls, fruit and cups, so we each had some more coffee and another roll with jam. Despite the always-oppressive heat, Margaret and I sat contentedly, sipping the fresh coffee. For me, anyway, it was as if all the quarrels and troubles, and even all the years, had fallen out from under us like a wave depositing us on a shore, leaving us here on the balcony of the New Tanjavur embassy, silent together in the first light of morning.

Like the first lovers in the world, I thought, *pare totamundetz amoris prim*. I looked at her, long and steadily. Her face was framed by the black shapes of spires, domes, pyramids, and cones behind her, and within that by the blaze of her platinum hair, but her face was still in the sharp, hard shadow and unreadable. "You know," I said, "I even love you with your clothes on."

She kicked me lightly under the table. "You better."

We were still holding hands a minute later when Kapilar showed up, just slightly early as always. He was dressed in a white, baggy version of the *suit-biz,* which was not anything that would offend the Maya if Tz'iquin could be trusted on the point.

I looked him over as he approached and found myself thinking that for someone trying to be conservative, Kapilar had hit on quite a dramatic effect, aided by the low-angle actinic light now brightening to full daylight: the suit was a startling pure white, with very wide lapels. The pale blue shirt under it had no collar, but Kapilar wore a violet iridescent scarf around his neck, tied very loosely, tucked under the jacket behind and spilling in a dark splash across his shirt. A broad-brimmed fedora balanced the wide span of the padded shoulders. He looked perhaps slightly like a gangster or a colonial official in an old flat movie, but mostly terrific. I envied him the dark skin that made the suit work so well for him. *"Deu,* but you're handsome today."

"I was about to say the same thing," Margaret added.

Kapilar beamed. "You've lived here long enough to know how it is with us, by now. I will have to deal with a number of people who will have to be impressed, and so as not to fall short of the need, I dressed for—*awe!"*

Margaret laughed, her hand shaking as she poured coffee for him. "Well, *I'm* awestruck, at least. But doesn't the invitation just say that you will be visiting with Maya political and religious leaders?"

Kapilar shrugged. "It's entirely possible that they will keep us under wraps and out of public sight the whole time we are there. But the invitation did specify that we were to come and live, eat, and talk until we had accomplished some worthwhile thing together. So it sounds like we are going to be there for a while. Based on that I packed for everything from a formal ball to a picnic."

"Makes sense," I said, sipping slowly at my final cup of coffee. I stood up and stretched a few times because this was a chance to do it before the rest of the day got going. Even so, I knew that in the high gravity, if there were a lot of formal affairs, I would be stiff at the end of the day. "But what I hear between the lines is that if you know, or guess, so little, probably no Tamil has ever done this before."

" 'Probably' is the right word." Kapilar spread his hands. "I don't know that *no* Tamil has ever met with the Maya leadership privately. Of course a Tamil who received such an invitation would never speak of it if he didn't go, or if he went and didn't succeed. It would be the kind of thing that might make your neighbors and friends feel that, well, there must be something about you that had, you know, attracted the Maya. They would . . . *wonder* what that might be."

It was about as delicate and polite an explanation of bigotry as I had heard in a long time, which—coming from our top local assistant—was pretty offensive and depressing. But I swallowed that one, as I had most such things since we got here.

Kapilar must have felt some coolness from my direction, because suddenly he began to chatter about all the mechanics of our trip to Yaxkintulum. Maybe he was developing enough *saperefacire* to be embarrassed. Anyway, I had more coffee, and knowing the details as well as he did, let my mind wander while he babbled about it. I watched Margaret watch him; she seemed bored, impatient, and—I wasn't sure what else. There was something she wished he'd say, or some point she wished he'd get to.

"—no regular passenger traffic except for the once-a-week public transit between Mayatown and Yaxkintulum, and that's quite unsuitable to a diplomatic mission," he was saying. "And there's no tradition of landing rights over there either. So we didn't even have a system in place for asking permission to fly over and land there. And the springer's out of the question because they won't even have one for emergencies. So it looked extremely awkward until Tz'iquin volunteered his 'family yacht.' But if he's from a lineage that owns something like that, it makes his presence here all the more of a mystery, unless he isn't the pariah that we all thought he was to the other Maya, which—

again, looking at that yacht—would seem to be likely and therefore maybe they've been taking us much more seriously than we thought all along. It's really very puzzling but then almost everything to do with those people is puzzling."

I didn't bother to answer because by then I thought Kapilar might not even be listening to himself. I gulped the last of the strong fierce coffee, hoping that the heat settling into my belly would bring on more sweat and help dissipate the terrible heat now swelling on the face of the city. Although Kapilar was a bigot, he was probably the least bigoted person in this culture and, given that I didn't know any Maya well, possibly on this planet.

I wondered how well *I* would be able to keep an open mind while meeting with the Maya. Maybe the only difference between Kapilar and I was that I had been trained to look for experiences that would expand my sense of the possible? Never mind all that. Why was it the only time I really got along with Margaret was when I was about to embark on a long trip?

My luggage had already been sprung ahead of me to the "airport." (The old-fashioned word made me think of livery stables and trolley barns). All I had to do was make sure that the right papers and personal stuff were in the pockets of the coverall, and I had checked and double-checked that the night before. So after I hugged Margaret, Kapilar and I took the first step of the journey, a very informal step of about seven kilometers, through the embassy's public springer, there on the terrace, into the big nondescript space of the New Tanjavur Airport.

There had been airports on Wilson when I was growing up. But the stanyear I turned fifteen, the springer had arrived, eliminating every other form of transportation except the recreational ones. Wilson had never had many airports anyway, with our whole population on one good-sized island, easily connected by high-speed rail. After the springer, the few airports in Nou

Occitan had been redecorated and beautified into vast land sculptures, to which big graceful gliders slowly descended from their high-mountain launching places, and from which the little rockets of the ballistic skydivers had screamed into the sky. So every airport I could really remember had had no trace of ugly functionality.

New Tanjavur's airport, which served air traffic from the cities of the four other Tamil sky islands plus the occasional charter flight to Yaxkintulum, was still, in every sense, an old-fashioned *airport*. It embraced ugly functionality with a passion. The high ceiling was supported by an exposed steel truss, painted a nondescript charcoal color. The bare floor was that shade of dark mottled gray designed to look swept for as long as possible rather than to please anyone's eye. There was a list of flights on the far wall, given in Terstad and in the whorly Tamil script I was barely learning to read.

Tz'iquin's "family yacht," whatever that might turn out to be, was going to be a private flight and so wasn't posted. That his family owned one was a status indicator, I knew, but it was hard to see how it could be much of one.

Maybe that was my limited imagination. Historically what you owned had been a way to indicate your status in many, many different cultures. But in the Thousand Cultures, where almost unlimited quantities of almost anything were available for the asking, possessions meant nothing. Anybody enjoyed drinking on someone else's tab, or getting a gift, but the pleasure came from the message implied. Anyone in the Thousand Cultures who had wanted to dress in garments of diamond chain mail or live in a house of solid gold—both silly ideas considering the discomfort—could have afforded it during the last four centuries.

A few of the Thousand Cultures had had sumptuary laws, so that only members of certain privileged castes or statuses could own or display certain possessions. But it didn't sound as if a yacht were in that category. One thing that the Tamils often worked their bigotry up about was the presence of wealth and poverty in Maya society. How a society that could make anything for anyone almost immediately, just like any other of the Thousand Cultures, could have genuinely rich and poor people was another mystery to be unraveled later. Meanwhile that big mystery at least explained the small mystery of why everyone acted as if owning the yacht were terribly important.

"This isn't exactly our most impressive place, is it?" Kapilar had emerged from the springer behind me.

"I'd think with all the painters and sculptors you have, and all this room and flat space, surely someone could have decorated this a little," I said.

"No serious artist would lower himself or herself so far as to decorate a purely functional space!"

"In Noupeitau," I observed, wondering why I was deliberately needling him, "we used to get artists to do public spaces by arguing that it was their duty not to allow their culture to be embarrassed by ugliness."

That made him stop and think, but then he shook his head decisively. "That wouldn't work on *our* artists. Any art you put into a space like this would be irrecoverably shamed, and that's that. Shall we go out and get aboard? I imagine Tz'iquin is waiting for us."

There was so little sound in the almost-deserted terminal that I could clearly here the echoes of the soft slaps Kapilar's low-heeled pumps made on the floor, and the thuds of my boot heels. The rightmost gate was marked "PRIVATE AND CHARTERED."

The only thing on the asphalt had to be the yacht. It looked like a beautiful silver version of the old "airplanes" from the first century of flight: stretched-ovoid fuselage, big forward wing, and smaller aft fins. The curves were graceful, soft, very art deco, but as we approached it, I saw that every curve ended in a sharp edge, nipple, or row of nipples—clearly the propulsion system was electrostatic, another ancient technology. Charges on the sharp edges would induce charges in the air around them, causing it to flow over the airfoils and control surfaces, lifting the yacht and pulling it forward. When it was in motion it must be alive with St. Elmo's fire, coronas, and brush discharges.

As we climbed up the steep stairs into its belly—easily three meters off the ground—I said to Kapilar, "This really must be something to see when it's flying at night."

"It is," a voice said from above us. Tz'iquin sat there, by the entryway, grinning at us. We climbed the steps toward him and he said, "The whole surface of it shines, brighter at the forward and rear edges so that it seems to be outlined in white sparks and blue flames."

"Zenzar, companhon," I said.

Tz'iquin grinned at me and gestured for us to follow him back into the central body, somewhere aft of the main wings. He was wearing a black hat with a broad, flat brim, a narrow orange poncho with intricate decoration I couldn't make out in the dim light, a blousey white shirt, and baggy black pants.

"Not knowing your customs," I said, "Would it be rude of me to say just how becoming your clothing is?"

"Not at all. The pattern on the vest is a very elaborate lineage history, I suppose because I belong to a very elaborate lineage. Perhaps the time will come, while you visit us, when you will be able to read it. The Maya system of writing is really extraordinary, you know, a system in which each matrix represents an idea, so that you might—at least defensibly—say that all our writing is just a calculus of differences. At least that's what one scholar said, about a thousand years ago. I happen to think that he was wrong. But time enough for everything later, eh?"

The moment didn't seem to call for an answer and besides I was thinking. Tz'iquin had just mentioned, however jokingly, that he came from an "elaborate lineage." Yet every Tamil I met in New Tanjavur seemed to believe and repeat that Tz'iquin was an outcast from his culture and family. If so, he was a highly respected and honored outcast.

Further, I had never heard a word about his status from

Tz'iquin himself. I wondered how many other things that everyone knew here were going to turn out differently in Yaxkintulum.
No doubt a lot; it was often that way on these missions.

Most of the way to the rear fins, we climbed down into a one-
way-silvered bubble that Tz'iquin called the observatory. It was
like a very small parlor—cushioned seats and chairs arranged in
a circle—except that you could see straight down through the
floor, or out through any wall.

Takeoff was disconcerting. First we saw the ground fall away
from us, as the yacht rose and lifted its supports. Then the tar-
mac two meters below began to slide backwards faster and faster,
and, with no sound or vibration, fell away as we gained speed.
The supports folded into the belly of the yacht like the claws of
an owl.

At one moment we had been just settled into our comfortable
chairs, and now we were off into the sky. By the time we had traveled a kilometer, we were at least six hundred meters high, yet the
yacht had stayed level the whole way and the cloudy pink liquid
in the glass Tz'iquin had handed me had only slightly leaned toward me. It was more like a subtle shift in gravity than a takeoff.

I felt a surge of kinship; an Occitan could understand doing
things more beautifully than necessary, with cool indifference to
difficulty.

We climbed higher, sweeping over the spires, towers, and sharp
pyramids of New Tanjavur, its brilliant white punctuated with intricate points and whorls of pure primary colors. *"Deu, que
bella, que gratz, que gens,"* I whispered, talking to myself.

Tz'iquin chuckled. "I don't speak Occitan but I can guess what
you were saying. I felt the same way the first time I saw it from
the air. Now there are going to be more people than just me who
know that each of Briand's cities is a glory to the eye."

"I haven't seen them all yet."

"I have faith in you," Tz'iquin said. "And in you, Kapilar."

Kapilar squirmed in his chair. Perhaps a compliment from a
Maya was more than he could bear. But he did say, "Well, from

up here, you can't hear them call each other names, or see them throwing rocks."

We all just sat, appreciating the view, for a long time.

Below us, the city fell away, and the surrounding red scrublands descended into a deep blue-green jungle like a dark, blotchy wash over the land, parts of it almost mauve, other stretches darker-than-phthallo green. We were headed out over Cape Kilaiyur, a long strip of high ground, framed by two high ridges, that thrust almost due south for thirty kilometers from Tamil Mandalam, along the west half-pi of longitude. Below, to either side, the land fell away to the abyss.

Both cultures clung to the highest peaks near the south pole, and most of Briand was a murderous cauldron of water-saturated air at seven standard atmospheres, only about 40° K below boiling. The upper slopes were inhabited by engineered life designed to keep the stratosphere cool and oxygenated. As for the deeps themselves, no one had really settled the question of whether what was down there had crossed the fuzzy boundary that divides complex chemistry from simple biology.

Far down below, to east and west, I could see the pale greens, light blues, and cabbage-reds of upper abyssal life going about its business.

"We call it Xibalbá," Tz'iquin said, as if he had been reading my thoughts. "The kingdom of the dead and a place of unending torture in the old Maya stories; many of our heroes are supposed to have journeyed there to bring back the things human beings need."

The peninsula below was slashed and spotted with veins and patches of white, pink or black stone, not yet digested enough by soil-making nanos and therefore not yet covered by the jungle. It was still an hour till noon, but that was late enough in the day so that the Kaveri River, which ran a weaving path between two long ridges, was well past its crest. It left a sandy wash that steamed in the blazing sun, surrounding the thin trickle that would dry by late afternoon.

Motion caught the corner of my eye. That blur in the muddy exposed riverbank must be stranded mudfish migrating into the jungles higher up the ridges; they would wait there in the relative cool under the trees until the night hurricane washed them back into the stream, where they would cling to rocks till the flow grew slow enough for them to swim safely again. Only about two hours of their day were spent behaving like fish; perhaps the *toszet* who had genetically engineered them had put in something to make them think it was worth it.

We all stayed quiet, just sipping our cool drinks and watching the land fall gradually away. The downward slope of the Sahyadri (the great sky island on which Tamil Mandalam sits) is gradual. As the land descends, the jungle gives way to scrub, the scrub to grassland, and the grasses to the upper abyssal microecology. From where we were we could just see some of the deep canyons where the lower abyss stabbed into the polar ranges like fingers squeezing stiff clay, and far out on the southern horizon the rolling, bubbling opacity of the deep abyss itself.

Scant centuries before, no doubt the gently sloping shelf below us had been a wild jumble of rocks, potholes, hillocks, and little bits of volcanic formations sticking up—before terraforming this area had been subjected to a nightly rain of harsh acids, and the Kaveri, before there was vegetation to hold back the runoff, had roared through in an hour or less per day, sweeping far down the shelf and carrying immense amounts of rocky junk with it. The tamer world where clear, pH neutral water ran gently down onto the plateau had done little, in these first few centuries of human settlement, to soften the ancient scars and rips in the land, but the lichen and other vegetation that foamed over the lumps and gashes in a thick blanket of yellow-green scum, shadowed by patches of cyan and teal, gave it a different, softer quality, as if we were flying over a moldy moonscape.

Below the indigo sky, its shadows blotched and blurred by the thick air over them, the yellow-green land looked like a badly developed photograph, sloping down into the dark clouds along the too-close horizon.

We seemed almost motionless in the sky, and not just because we had climbed to an altitude of fifteen kilometers. "This thing isn't really very fast, is it?" I asked.

"Four hundred kilometers per hour," Tz'iquin said. "It will take us nearly eight hours to fly to Yaxkintulum. But we have everything on board to keep you comfortable until then. And you know, we have a saying—when Ix Chel made time, she made a lot of extra, and it's up to us to use it all before the cycle ends."

"The cycle . . . " I said, and I recalled some of the Maya material that had been loaded into me via the emblok. "Oh. The *great* cycle, thirteen baktuns?"

"That's the one," Tz'iquin agreed. "We are currently in the sixth Great Cycle, third baktun, second katun, eleventh year."

"How long till this Great Cycle ends?" I asked.

"Plenty, if you're worried. A Great Cycle is thirteen baktuns, and a baktun is just under 395 years. We're only starting the third baktun at the moment, and after the end of this Great Cycle a few thousand years from now, we still have seven more Great Cycles to go. The universe isn't going to end till Standard Calendar Date 14 November, 43,015. So there's plenty of time for everything to happen, still."

We flew onward. The land fell farther away, first fading into translucent mists streaked with fog, then disappearing completely beneath the colorful clouds. We had another round of the sweet-tasting punch as we watched the billowing, bubbling mass of bright colors under us. "Do you have any way of knowing if there's land or water under that at the moment?" Kapilar asked.

"I can check the map if you're really interested. But there's no big ocean in this part of Briand, anyway. Lots of salt-saturated lakes that aren't quite boiling, or aren't boiling at this moment, due to the pressure. But the real oceans, which do boil, are a long way north."

Kapilar nodded. "Funny, we've lived surrounded by all this, but I couldn't begin to draw a map of the abyss."

Tz'iquin shrugged. "Well, even we Maya don't bother, really. There's not much point in knowing, since we don't get anything of value out of Xibalbá, and there's no reason to go after anyone whose aircraft goes down there—no possible rescue, at least not once you're away from the edge of the plateau. If the yacht were to start to go down, we'd all just go through the emergency springer."

I was startled enough to blurt the obvious question. "You have a *springer* on this thing?"

"Why, yes. There are about ten springers in Yaxkintulum, and maybe another dozen on aircraft. All secret and private."

Kapilar sneered. "So your upper class gets springers—"

"And works on devising a way to get them to everyone else," Tz'iquin said, impassively. "Without shaking our society to its roots, without causing civil war, without tipping us irrevocably into the kind of anarchy that leads to assimilation. Or rather *some* of us work toward peaceful, gradual change. Others oppose it very much. I know that we have tried very hard never to let you see any of our internal politics; have we really succeeded so far that you have no idea that there is conflict?"

Kapilar shrugged, his face set. "Naturally there are rumors. There are always rumors. That there is a liberal somewhere among the Maya, that there is some member of the aristocracy who favors change, all of that. There were rumors like that in my grandfather's time."

Tz'iquin had a half-smile; it reminded me of nothing so much as the way, back in Noupeitau, a dueling opponent smiles when he knows his opponent is worthy. "Well. Can you be so sure that every one of them has been false? Perhaps they were true even in your grandfather's time and the sad truth is only that nothing ever came of them.

"And in any case, this is not a rumor. There are some of us who are actively seeking change. There are others, with, well—

backward and stupid ideas. And right now my side's greatest strength is that since any public appearance of dissension is anathema to the other side, they cannot bring themselves to move to stop us. So we shall make things happen very fast and hope to see what we can do while they are off balance. You are part of that plan.

"Try to be less easily surprised. A springer in a Maya aircraft is only the first of many shocks you will be having. It will help a great deal if you can shrug off more preconceptions."

Kapilar's lips pressed together, but he made a small, correct bow. "And may I ask, before the springer—"

"In a bad year we might have lost a dozen people to aircraft crashes, which is perhaps twice what you were averaging," Tz'iquin said. "There was no room for more of us in Tamil Mandalam, we weren't welcome to stay there and we didn't want to, and at the same time the obligations to lineage shrines made it impossible for everyone to move to Yaxkintulum, and families needed to stay in touch. If you factor in our traveling the longest air route on the planet about three times as often as the average Tamil traveled your much shorter routes, you'll find it was proportional enough. The chances of dying from an aircraft crashing in the abyss were probably less than the chances of drowning in the tub."

"Or *starving,*" Kapilar spat out.

"Or starving. I do believe I said that some of us favor change, and implicitly I asked for your help."

Kapilar sat frozen and tense; I put a hand on his shoulder. Before I had time to draw a breath, he said softly, "I will try to be of some help to you. I doubt I will be any good at it."

"That's not required," Tz'iquin said. "I am honored that you will try."

Kapilar and I sat back and looked out at the cloud-covered abyss far below. To people from worlds with gentler atmospheres, "cloud-covered" would usually mean "featureless" or "monotonous," but this wasn't. Great hot clouds of water, acid mists, complex organics, and *deu sait* what else boiled up constantly as pressures and temperatures shifted. A kilometer-tall geyser of something bright yellow shot up through a brown-and-white mushroom cloud, and as it fell back into the upper part of that cloud, the surface was wracked with explosions. A purple blob leaped from the bland white hills and valleys of a bank of water clouds, breaking through the surface like a trout rising to a fly. It climbed on out of its cloudy birthplace, trailing black tendrils from its purple jellyfish-body; it had to be easily a kilometer across and half a kilometer tall.

Tz'iquin said, "Watch what happens when it hits the tropopause."

It was rising very fast until it broke and scattered. The twenty or so purple cloudlets raced around madly for an instant; the black tendrils moved inward. It looked like twenty octopi doing a contra dance, their tentacles all meeting at the middle. Then the "bodies"—the little purple clouds—fell back toward the abyss. They fell only a short way before they began to explode and burn.

"In effect they pick up a water coating on their way up, so they only trail long filaments of carbon ash. When they hit the tropopause and break up against the warmer air layer above them, the water gets mixed inside, so that when they fall back into the lower atmosphere they're ready to burn," Tz'iquin explained. "Sometimes you'll see the filaments get sucked all the way up and then follow the clouds down."

Kapilar pointed down below my feet and said, "Godfart."

I bent forward before I realized what he had said; when I looked up at them, Tz'iquin said "Watch."

I looked down again. A pale, shimmering bubble was rising through dark opaque masses below.

"Wet one," Kapilar said.

Tz'iquin grunted agreement. "Look at that color. Bet it makes it to the free oxygen layer."

The bubble kept right on climbing as we passed it and turned to watch it behind us. It was less and less visible as it rose into higher, more transparent air. Eventually I couldn't see it, and was just about to wonder why they had wanted me to look at it, when abruptly a sphere of white formed behind us, which then burst in a huge cloud of flame. Seconds later the yacht pitched gently, tipping forward and rearing back two or three times, as the shock wave hit us.

"Flammable gas," I said.

"Right. At that temperature and pressure down there, on such geologically young surfaces, every so often things come together to make hydrogen, or methane, or propane—all kinds of reducing gases. Usually a godfart rises till lightning or something ignites it while it's in an oxidizing layer, like acid clouds way down, or chlorine just at the edge of visibility, or oxygen up higher. But if there's enough water in it to protect it, it can get all the way out of the weather below. In that case usually when the water condenses it releases the latent heat, and that's just enough to take it past the kindling point." Tz'iquin seemed to be enjoying showing me this; but then I don't think I've been to a planet where a local wasn't proud of *something*.

"Sometime before you leave you really should see a godfart storm at night," Kapilar added.

"Oh, sure," Tz'iquin said. "If I'd been thinking we could have done this flight at night, and really enjoyed it."

The ice seemed to have broken between them; at least they weren't sparring and sniping as they had been before. I let them continue pointing out different events in the atmosphere to me, which was something they could both enjoy doing, and as we followed up the punch with a pleasant bitter chocolate drink, they taught me to identify "streamers"—explosive uprushes of burning gas; "rollers"—turbulent tubes of dark gases rolling like a wave over the cloud tops; "slinkies," tornadoes whose tops would bend down toward the lower atmosphere until they formed an inverted U, then lose their original bottom, form a new bottom around their former top, and grow back erect, over and over, so that they seemed to "walk" across clouds below.

Three hours into the flight we had a light meal, a goat-meat tamale with a light spattering of mole sauce and a chile dressing; it was tasty enough but still so foreign to my palate that I didn't quite know whether I liked it or not yet. As we finished that, I asked, "If it's not a painful subject, can you give us more of an idea of what the internal political struggle you were describing before is all about? It helps to know what game we're playing."

"I imagine it does," Tz'iquin said, not looking up from where he was mopping his plate with a piece of flatbread. "And indeed, Grandfather asked me to brief you about all this well before we arrived, so I'm only doing what I'm supposed to do. But it isn't easy. These are things I was taught never to speak of and never to hint at."

"We understand that much," I said. "We'll try not to interrupt or make it any harder for you."

"I appreciate that. All right, here's what I think is the truth, then. Very rightly, you might ask, if there are springers concealed in the homes of our political allies in Yaxkintulum, why are we flying there when we could have gone there in one step? And the answer is that this makes it easier to keep the springers concealed; in any case the yacht would have had to make the trip and we would have to be seen getting out of it when it landed, to preserve a decent respect for the traditional ways.

"Now, what complicates this a lot more is that my Grandfather is the chief priest of the Center Temple, which means it is his duty to oppose change of any kind and particularly change that would lead to greater contact outside our culture. So it would be especially shameful if he were seen to embrace change in his public role, even though that is exactly what he means to do privately. So, *Donz* Leones, we use the family yacht, and to preserve Grandfather's position I must now pretend to quarrel with him about this, and he must pretend to go along very reluctantly. The little prestige he loses by seeming to accept you too quickly, he can gain back because this will be an important event and it will be his family that participates. And if we preserve his prestige, he will have enough power and influence so that he can continue to act for change.

"And *that's* just the *basic* politics of why we are taking the yacht. There are several other reasons I don't have time to explain. Now, if one small flight between two airports gets this complicated, I want you to try to imagine how much *more* complicated it all becomes when we get into detente with the Tamils, rapprochement with the Thousand Cultures, and in general our breaking out of the cultural prison we've built for ourselves. I think Grandfather will want to explain it to you in his own way; he says I don't respect tradition enough when I talk politics." Tz'iquin stretched and yawned. "Meanwhile, I could use a nap, and both of you might want to take one as well. We can set the alarm to wake us when we're approaching Yaxkintulum."

We followed Tz'iquin back up the ladder and down a corridor to a the rear of the craft, where there were six one-bed cabins. Mine was comfortable enough, but after I stretched out I slept only fitfully. It was the wrong time of day and I had too much to think about. I wasn't worried about staying within the correct bounds of behavior for Maya society, even though I was ill-prepared. I had faked my way through so much ceremony and social maneuver in so many different cultures that I didn't think they could surprise me much. And the Council of Humanity was now getting somewhere with this planet; we would at least be talking to both cultures, and that would be a start.

No, silly as it was in the circumstances, most of my thoughts kept returning to the problem of Margaret and me. Or maybe just to the problem of me, and my own moodiness and depression. Why was it that every time I got bored, I began to daydream about life as a *jovent*?

In Nou Occitan, we have an expression for people who can't leave their *jovent* days behind—*tostemz-toszet,* which is sort of like *puer aeturnus* but could also be translate as "always just a guy," that is, fixated forever on the trappings and behavior of first manhood. It's an insult. I was beginning to wonder if it wasn't also an accurate description of me.

I opened the blind, feeling that sleep was futile, and watched a long string of godfarts explode, down low in the atmosphere, far away. Tired and drained, I lay back down and tried to sleep again, but couldn't find a comfortable position.

Maybe it was Margaret rather than me. Maybe there was someone or something she wanted to grow into, and maybe I was in the way, and that was why nothing I did was right? But that was contradicted by the little whisper of reality that told me that I usually knew perfectly well which of the several things I was doing would really irritate her. The problem was in refraining from it.

Perhaps we were just growing apart?

I had always hated people that used that rationale—it seemed to me that what such an excuse really meant was that they had already been ignoring each other for a long time.

Maybe I just missed the sense of having it all in front of me. Even visiting a hundred cultures or so on a dozen different planets couldn't possibly live up to the dreams about life that I had had as a young man. Maybe the only thing that would really satisfy me would be to move to Earth and take the long dive of plugging into the world of shared virtual adventures, slowly rotting away in my little wired-and-plumbed coffin.

That made me laugh, slightly, because I had always despised those people. I thought a nice honest final suicide would surely be preferable. All I really wanted, I thought, was to get over this weird fear of something I was missing, something I wasn't doing. My little "humph" of amusement at that turned into a yawn, and finally I slept. I don't remember what but I think I dreamed ironically.

When the soft alarm chimed, I rose, splashed water on my face from the basin, used the urinal, and combed my hair. It was getting thinner. Trying not to fall back into the train of thought that led from Margaret to me to my lost *jovent* and back to Margaret again, I experimented with a couple different ways of combing it, all of which made the situation worse. Occitan men share an advantage with cats—whenever the world is insolubly unpleasant, we can always devote our full attention to grooming. I sighed. No one could look good anyway in this silly bwana outfit, so I gave up and went aft to the observatory.

Kapilar and Tz'iquin were already there, engrossed in an exchange of inside jokes about the New Tanjavur artistic scene. It all went right by me, which was fine since I wasn't really up for conversation just yet. I sat down, poured myself an iced bitter chocolate from the pitcher, and quietly watched the land roll underneath us. We had crossed the abyss and were nearing Yaxkintulum, flying over its surrounding plateau. Below us there was dense jungle broken by broad clearings, which grew thicker until we crossed a rocky ridge. On the other side the land plunged away, revealing a great canyon below us, and across the canyon, I caught my first sight of Yaxkintulum.

The city had been built where a high promontory broke through the side of a volcanic dome. The canyon before us cut into the dome at the foot of the promontory, so that the straight drop could not be less than six kilometers, and the bottom of the canyon was in the lower abyss. We were approaching from the north and west of the city, flying down the canyon, so we saw it in profile, the knife-sharp ridge breaking out of the great rounded swell of the volcanic dome, ending in a great knob that plunged down into the depths of the canyon to where the air became opaque.

The long ridge that led back into Yaxkintulum proper was lined with buildings. The city itself swelled across the volcanic dome, rising perhaps two hundred and fifty meters across a kilometer, extending over the top of the dome.

The yacht banked, swung out wide, and then flew straight toward the promontory, as if we were going to fly directly down the ridge. The group of buildings that crowned the promontory had the symmetrical perfection you see in computer reconstructions of the Athenian Acropolis (before it was destroyed forever in the Third World War), in the Peace Spires that once circled the Eiffel Tower (before Paris was lost in the Slaughter), the Pyramids (before they were partially melted), or the Taj Mahal (before it was shattered by atomic fire). Or did I only think that later?

There were many beautiful places among the Thousand Cultures, and I had always been prejudiced toward my own culture's soaring imitation cathedrals, but the city of Yaxkintulum, approached (as it was designed to be) over the Temple Height, still glows decades later in my memory.

Toward the peak of the promontory, a sheer white stone wall rose a full two hundred meters on the cliff face. Above the wall the tops of five steep stepped pyramids rose, arranged so that the center was largest, the two closely flanking pyramids were shorter, and the smaller and squatter outliers were spaced more widely. Each pyramid was red-brown dressed stone, and long steep staircases cut through the wide, high steps.

On top of the two outlying pyramids sat identical temples, of two stories: a lower one square-columned and open inside, with thick reinforced corners topped with a heavy slab, on which sat the second story, a gracefully cut-away half-cube with a single wide door on each face.

I was still too far away to see any of carvings and reliefs in detail, but we had drawn near enough so that the intricate play of shadows on the red-brown walls, and on the white stone face, told me that virtually every square centimeter must be carved in relief.

My gaze drifted up to the flanking pyramids, asymmetric in mirror image of each other. Three story temples like extended versions of the outlying ones, with two column-and-slab sets stacked under the upper half-cube, graced the tops of long stone-block platforms, but at their inside ends, so that they seemed to crowd in toward the central pyramid, the far bare end of the platform and the top of the temple forming a line that drew the eye to the base of the central temple.

The yacht was drawing close to the city now, and the great mass of the central temple filled my field of view. It was wider than it was tall, a lower part four stories tall flanked by fiercely steep stairways on all sides, so that it seemed like a truncated pyramid on top of the central pyramid itself. A squat building perched at the center of the lower part, rising three more stories; the flat surfaces were pure white, with columns of the red-brown stone, and the top rose in a graceful corbeled dome.

The whole effect was so elegant that I forgot all about the mission, since that was nothing I could do anything about at the moment, and just let it wash over me. The white top building cut into the black sky with enormous force and utter finesse, blazing in the blue-white light, at once graceful and immensely strong, like the body of a wrestling champion. *"Zenzar!"* I said, falling not only back into Occitan, but into cliché; but this time the cliché was exactly right, it was beautiful in a way that grabbed the eye like a light shining in the darkness. The usual Terstad translation of *zenzar* is "shining," but that means so much less— a metal gutter in sunlight shines, but it's not *zenzar*. Things which are *zenzar* shine in the mind, cutting through ordinary memory like a welding laser through a sheet of paper, so that your first impression of them is that this particular instant of beauty will be with you to your grave, and that having seen this you will never be the same person again; and your second is that it is already over, that the image burnt into your mind is of something long past and always treasured.

That was what the Center Temple did to me, the first time I saw it.

The dizzying view down into the canyon opened beneath us, and then we swept on over the city wall. With a negligible change in momentum, the yacht sat back and hovered above a wide courtyard behind the central pyramid. We sank until the temple rose past us, and continued down, as smoothly as an elevator, until the supports softly swung out of the belly of the yacht, and grabbed the pavement. To one side of us, the mighty steps of the pyramid led up until I lost them at the top of the observatory window; to the other side, Metallah, now much of the way down the sky, burned too bright to look at.

Tz'iquin rose from his seat. We followed him to the front exit and descended the steps to the ground; about a hundred Maya, dressed like Tz'iquin in broad-brimmed black hats, white shirts, dark trousers, and wildly bright red-yellow-orange vests, were there to greet us. "Here comes Grandfather," Tz'iquin said in my ear. "I hope you have room for some more surprises, *Donz* Leones."

An older man came forward and embraced Tz'iquin. "It is good to have you here, grandson."

"It is good to see you again, grandfather. This is Kapilar, a representative from Tamil Mandalam; I claim him as my friend and guest. And this is *Donz* Giraut Leones, representative of the Council of Humanity. I claim—"

"No, grandson, I claim *Donz* Leones as *my* friend and guest. I do not mean to slight you, but it seems to me that the chief priest of the Center Temple is a more fitting host to one who speaks for all the billions of people of Earth and the Thousand Cultures." He had a warm, friendly smile.

Tz'iquin bowed. "As you wish, grandfather. They are here to hear us, and to speak with us."

"Good talk leads to good deeds." It sounded like a formula. He bowed very slightly to us. "My name is Pusiictsom; I am the lord and keeper of the Center Temple, and daykeeper of Yaxkintulum. If you will accept my hospitality, perhaps soon we can discuss what we should do next."

Kapilar and I both had just enough phrases of Mayan in the embloks we were wearing to say that we accepted gladly. There was a pleased murmur in the crowd.

Pusiictsom smiled again. With a winning grin like that, he'd have made a great politician back home in Occitan—but then again, that might well be what he was here. No one outside the Maya culture had any idea how, or if, they drew the line between politics and religion. "Then before we talk more seriously, let me first share my friends and family with you," he said.

What followed then was the most familiar drill in a diplomat's life—the receiving line. We were introduced to about thirty people, cousins, children, friends, friend's children's cousins for all I could tell. Both Kapilar and I exchanged some pleasantry or other with each of them, and then complimented Pusiictsom on his good luck in having such a connection. It took quite a long time.

The sun was very hot and bright—we were almost $\pi/10$ lower in latitude here. The gravity was as high as ever and so my feet and knees, and especially the small of my back, began to ache pretty badly. Still it went on. "Hello, yes, you are an exceptionally attractive young lady, so poised and with such beautiful manners; my lord Pusiictsom, you must be very pleased to find yourself the great-uncle of such a fine young lady . . . " and on to "Goodness, what a splendid young man, so beautifully muscled and with such intelligence in the eyes! My lord Pusiictsom, your friend's son honors me by his presence . . . " and on, and on, until I was exhausted and befuddled. Pain charged up my calves, regrouped in my back, and made a concerted drive on the back of my scalp. Kapilar too was visibly fading before we got to the end of that line.

At last, though, we had admired the last child, complimented the last beautiful youth, and been impressed by the credentials of the last bureaucrat, scholar, or artist. They all bowed to us, collectively, and we returned the bow. Then they filed out of the courtyard and Pusiictsom said, "It is good. You are accepted."

He beckoned us to follow as he walked into a covered entranceway that led down under the base of the huge pyramid. To judge from the now-long shadows, we had spent the better part of an hour on greetings. It was a relief, to the point of delight, to be walking. I could only hope this would eventually lead to urinating and perhaps to sitting down in the shade.

After so much harsh blue-white glare, the dark of the passageway seemed frozen, opaque, solid. As our eyes adjusted enough to see the dim guidestrips in the floor, we walked deeper into the pyramid. I still had no idea whether in the presence of a temple lord I should speak before being spoken to.

The passage bent twice, and serpentined through one long set of curves. The geometric forms and spaces looked like the pictures I had seen of those of the Maya back on Old Earth, before the Slaughter had reduced most of Central America to a desert of glassy ash, but the material was very different—this pyramid was not made of compacted earth and cut stone, but of grown stone—indeed the "blocks" of stone were not really separate blocks—the walls had been programmed to grow with rectangular seams on their surfaces.

Though muffled by the walls, there were footfalls and voices all around. Probably the pyramid, for all of its appearance of solidity, was almost all hollow, made of ordinary diamond rebar with stone grown in a geodesic foam pattern around it—strong, light, and not at all as massive as it looked. There could easily be several large office buildings' equivalent of space down here.

We came around another turn to a bank of elevators. Following Pusiictsom, we got into one, stood in it for a few seconds as it either rose or descended (the motion was far too smooth for me to tell), and finally walked out into a short hallway that led to a small room lined with low cushioned platforms that might equally be beds, benches, or couches. A strip of padding perhaps forty centimeters wide ran along the wall, as a back rest.

Pusiictsom sat on the platform opposite the door, a little stiffly, cross-legged with his back against the padding strip. "Please sit also," he said. "Tz'iquin, please close that door. The guest who is joining us later knows that he is to open it."

The feel of the couch-bed was exquisite. Some part of it sensed that my buttocks needed more support and that my legs needed to sink a little more for perfect comfort, and the cushions adjusted to do that. The pad behind me swelled, shaped itself to my back, and gently warmed. I felt the feathery, soothing touch of neuroducers, pressing a galaxy tiny pinpricks through the fabric of my coverall, contacting my nervous system, blocking the soreness and relaxing the muscles in my lower back.

A moment before I had been sore and tired. Now I was so utterly comfortable that it was almost a shock.

Beside me I felt Kapilar sigh. The furniture must be working on him as well.

"Well," the old temple lord said, "Now, here, at last, we can speak freely. I do apologize for all the folderol, but I'm sure you've both had some acquaintance with such things. And it seemed best for your safety if we made you a special guest-friend of every significant lineage that we could gather. Besides, it forces them all to acknowledge each of you as my guest, and that is a warning and guarantee."

"Not knowing your customs, but needing to," I said, "what if you had not done that?"

He shrugged, a long slow gesture that seemed to contain a thought in every micromovement. "Possibly nothing. Possibly some unpleasant insults and some undermining of the whole process we are trying to begin. And possibly one of you being poisoned or knifed. When a customary kind of communication is used so rarely, you know, it's sometimes hard to know what it is saying. There is much less violence within our politics than there used to be, but there is still some, and who can say whether you are covered by the older or the newer customs? I can't say what I warded off, because now we'll never see that—and if anything *does* happen to either of you, well, we didn't ward that off."

"There is a certain logic to it," I admitted, showing more *enseingnamen* than I felt.

Pusiictsom beamed at me as if I had done just the right thing. "Well, then. Business. I shall begin indirectly, as comes most naturally to me.

"Nearly everything we do is by family and lineage. Our internal politics is so complex that there is almost no concern for the outside world at all. For example, we could feed everyone here easily, and this would erase one of the most odious insults from the Tamil vocabulary at no real cost to our culture. Seven old priests, who happen to occupy key seats in three temples, have made it impossible to do that, and so we have continued to lose lives to starvation in every generation, and to starve people to death, for which every other culture rightly condemns us.

"Well, we belong to a distinguished lineage, Tz'iquin and I; we are Peccaries, a senior lineage—which means we have an unbroken male line in primogeniture, leading back to the arrival of the Maya on this world. Though we began as ordinary farmers in old Kintulum, we have risen steadily, priesthood by priesthood and temple by temple, until in my generation we captured the titles of Lords of the Center Temple. And here in the Center Temple is where we Maya preserve the oldest customs, worship the most ancient gods—and by these things, we anchor the rest of society.

"Now it happens that I believe we must change a great deal if we are to survive as a culture. But it is my duty as the Lord of the Center Temple to preserve—not to change. Thus I must act privately and personally in a way very different from the way in which I can act publicly and ritually. So here is what I have thought of. If it is acceptable to you it will be acceptable to me."

I nodded my acknowledgment.

"Good then. What do you know of our prophetic tradition?"

"Only that you have had some very important teachers at various times," Kapilar said, "who have, in one way or another, drastically revised your religious and social thought. Many times they come from lesser families. I understand that if a prophet's teachings come to be accepted, his lineage rises in status, and his closer relatives receive better appointments and higher-ranking marriage partners in the next generation."

"Not a bad perception for people observing us from a distance," Pusiictsom said, and once again he flashed that winning grin. He seemed to be having a marvelous time, or to be enjoying some spectacular private joke. "Yes. Prophets serve the Maya in a number of ways. A successful prophet in a minor lineage can at least temporarily elevate it to more important status. If a truly successful prophet appears, as they occasionally do, it elevates his lineage permanently. It so happens that we Peccaries were fortunate enough to have two prophets in our background back in old Kintulum, before the eruption of Old Grandfather. So we are extremely respectable.

"Now what may *not* be apparent to an outsider is this: the prophets are not an institutionalized revolution, as one of those eccentric Tamils that studies us once wrote."

Kapilar chuckled, and Pusiictsom raised an eyebrow at him.

"Oh." Kapilar said, apparently embarrassed. "The person you are referring to is almost certainly my uncle. We had a saying in the family that it was good that he understood the Maya, because that was all that he seemed to understand. It is interesting to learn that he didn't understand the Maya, either."

"We have a saying that though every elder deserves respect, some deserve respect only as elders," Pusiictsom said. His face was set. "The truth, anyway, is that the prophets are anything but revolutionary. On the contrary, the prophets are one of our most conservative forces, and reformers like the Peccary lineage have been struggling for a very long time to prevent the irruption of another prophet into Maya affairs. Through our prophets we assure that any change we must make will always be phrased and expressed as calling our culture back to its center and returning to the ways of the ancestors; it makes change possible but it also rules out certain kinds of change—notably the kind that the Peccaries have favored for four generations.

"But setting aside the past, and thinking only of the next prophet, a thousand of our tales would tell you that under the pyramids that hold our temples up to the sky, there are always passageways reserved for the prophets. The radical prophet and the reactionary priest meet each other and settle whatever it is that must happen next. This is a thing everyone knows. This is a thing no one sees. This is a thing no one speaks. Is this something you know?"

"I know now and will remember." I hoped that was the right answer.

"And our Tamil guest?"

Kapilar tensed, but he said, "I understand. I won't speak of it to others but I do understand it myself and will remember." He drew a long breath and I wondered what he might be about to blurt; before I could touch his arm or catch his eye, he spoke. "May I ask a question about this?"

"If you will accept that whatever I say will be the answer."

"I will accept it if I can."

"Ask."

"Among the Tamils there are rumors of what you have just told me, and they are very far from the true version you have just told me; it is rumored that you have a secret police whose job is to control thought, and that the prophets are their primary instrument, used to attract the attention of would-be dissidents so that they can be entrapped and destroyed. Furthermore that story is repeated and believed by people who would harm the Maya if they could. When I hear lies repeated in my presence—and I will—what should I say?"

"What your best heart tells you to say. You are about to observe a prophet at close hand, for some time; compare that reality with the story, and say exactly what you would say if your honor, courage, and truth were perfect. And that is what you should always say, anyway, is it not?"

Kapilar seemed to relax completely. For a moment I thought he might faint, and almost reached to catch him when he slumped forward. Then I realized he was bowing over his crossed legs, pressing his face almost to the floor and extending his arms toward Pusiictsom.

The priest inclined his head gravely, and Kapilar sat back upright. A tension, which had been there but which I had not felt quite aware of, now was absent from the room. At last I realized:

this was the way Kapilar, or any of the Tamils, would have behaved in the presence of a brilliant exposition of the Kural. He had found a way to make sense of his contact with the Maya, at least for the moment.

Pusiictsom nodded again. "This is good. This has hope. Now, what I am about to say next will surprise my grandson more than my guests. I have invited someone to come up the Prophet's Passage, and you will be meeting him in a moment. It seems to me that now that the springer has come, the rapprochement with the Tamils, for which we had so long been quietly working and gradually winning support, is urgent and can no longer be pursued at leisure. We could resist one other culture that was merely twice our numbers, especially since they had little desire to know us and no desire for us to join them. We cannot hope to resist the Thousand Cultures, or the almost-as-large population of the Home System. So we must make contact or have it made for us.

"But this is not the sort of thing that the Lord of the Center Temple is supposed to do. This duty it supposed to fall to the Eastern Temple; if things were working as well as they possibly could, it would be the Center Temple which was to resist as much as possible. Yet despite all my pleas the Eastern Temple has done nothing of the kind and threatens to do things which will—in my judgment—make matters much, much worse. So if what I am about to do is to work, I must do it in defiance of what is expected and customary, and therefore it must be done very, very well. The man who is coming to see us, I think, is capable of the task; I think he can lead us to make peace, embrace the Tamils, and reenter humanity."

Kapilar coughed softly and said, "I am sorry to say that—"

"That some of the Tamils may not care to be embraced? You have seen how strong our resentment and anger can be. You will see how much stronger our love and patience can be."

Again Kapilar bowed, just as he would to a teacher of the Kural. Fortunately that was reasonably close to the proper way to treat him within Maya society.

The door opened silently. The man who came in was middle-aged, his face deeply lined and his skin darkened by exposure to fierce Metallah. He was more fat than thin, with prominent nose, cheekbones, and forehead pressing out against the soft cushion of his face. A thin wisp of mustache looked carefully groomed.

He was in ceremonial clothing, almost naked—a pure white breechclout with an elaborate brightly-colored wide belt of knotted cords, and a helmet-like headdress that bound his waist-length hair into a whorl of curls, spikes, and curving braids, leaving one long thick beaded and feathered braid to fall down his back.

He was barefoot. His ears and nose were pierced with a beautiful array of gold jewelry, softly glowing in the warm dim light. He stood as straight and tall as any twenty-year-old ballerina or martial artist, barely moving but radiating strength and grace. Bowing low to Pusiictsom, he kissed the old priest's extended hand, then sat down across from me, in perfect still grace, all his attention focused on the temple lord. I felt, rather than thought in words, that if only I understood what I was seeing, I would think it very beautiful.

Kapilar and Tz'iquin both had straightened and taken on a formal, still expression; Tz'iquin, moreover, seemed stunned, as if he had seen something else.

There is an Occitan proverb, *Necsetz savare marves mai non possetz savare tota tostemz,* which means, loosely, "You always need to know everything right now but you can never know everything all at once." That was my problem here; clues to what was happening were everywhere but I needed to understand what was happening before I could understand the clues.

After a long still moment Pusiictsom said, "The task is very great. You have prayed and thought as I asked?"

"I have." The prophet's voice was a warm, pleasant baritone; as much as his appearance drew the eye, his voice compelled attention.

"And you think it can be done?"

"I do."

"Then the task is yours. You are to take the name, which I give you now, of Ix. Be known by no other name again."

Tz'iquin audibly gasped. Even the prophet—now Ix—seemed taken aback, as if a venomous snake had slithered into the room and he were trying to hold still.

"Yes, this is how seriously we take the matter." Pusiictsom glanced toward Kapilar and me. " 'Ix' means several things depending on context, but its main meanings are 'blood' and 'jaguar.' It also is the name of this day in our calendar. It is the name of strength, birth, death, and fury. It is the darker root from which our thought of ourselves first sprang.

"I gave this prophet that name because he will need its power. I gave this prophet that name because he must be the prophet of a strong love. It is the love that comes from the dark, fierce and hot and devouring, which is strongest. Also I gave this prophet that name because it is a name for beginnings. Now, my first believers—and it is a great thing that the first believers are one Maya, one Tamil and one from the rest of the human beings— call him Ix, pronounce his name."

"Ix," we all said in unison. It was as if the word had formed under my tongue and just tumbled from my mouth without my will. And it seemed from where I sat that the name itself seared into him at that instant, so deep that he and the name were inseparable forever.

After many years of training and conditioning, it was second nature to notice that these sensations were likely the result of a mild hypnotic trance. I began the inner litany to free myself from them, but I regretted the need of being free, for it was a lovely hallucination.

I thought all this during the long silence before Pusiictsom spoke. Now he didn't sound as if he were worrying about the sound of the words in the history texts, but softly, informally, as if he had merely been a witness. "And I also name this prophet Ix because it is the most logical and expectable name for a prophet of hate, which we could have expected to see launched at any time. Now that you hold it, we have locked one very powerful symbol away, out of the reach of the Eastern Temple."

Ix spoke. "It seems wise to me. I take it that I am to be opposed when I teach in the city?"

"Yes, you will be. You will be forced to flee."

"To flee? But to where could I flee?"

"To Mayatown in New Tanjavur. You are to be the first great prophet of that place."

Ix winced. "I must do something that desperate? Then the situation is worse than I had thought."

"It is. And more urgent. We have far less time before there is serious trouble than anyone imagines. At least that is what my informants here and in Mayatown tell me, if I listen carefully to the little gaps and evasions in their reports, and pay attention to which of my questions are not answered. And there is one more very hard thing, Ix."

The new prophet visibly swallowed hard, and licked his lips. I learned later that "Mayatown prophet" was a contradiction in terms to almost all Maya, and there was a Maya saying that a broken prophet dies young, meaning that a prophet who fails to win disciples and converts has no place in the world and can't be expected to stay there.

Pusiictsom nodded, acknowledging the fear. "You must seek, quietly at first, to be joined by at least a few Tamil believers," Pusiictsom said.

Ix sat still for a long time, looking down at his knees. "And that is the full scope of the task?"

"It is."

Kapilar stirred beside me. "Er—"

"There is information you can share with us?" Pusiictsom asked.

"There is, I think. But I am surprised that you had not thought of it yourself. You do know that if any Tamils at all were to convert to your religion, this would trigger more and worse violence from the Tamils, and many more calls to expel the Maya from New Tanjavur, than you've seen up till now?"

"I had thought so," Pusiictsom said. "And yet if we send a man to teach peace, do we not have to send him to both sides? He will not preach our gods or customs, I am sure." Ix nodded, and Pusiictsom continued, "We of the upper class here only believe in much of it as metaphor, anyway, and in another generation or two we can hope to have virtually our whole population converted to that point of view. But still there must be some Tamils who will go beyond discussing Ix's teachings, to something that will indeed look very much like religious conversion.

"On the one hand, can we tell those Tamils, 'We want you to learn and believe what Ix teaches but his religion is not for you?' Would that not be a more serious insult, and one to our friends rather than our enemies? And on the other hand, could anything bind us together more, later, than the memory of Tamils who sacrifice themselves and endure hatred and scorn for the sake of a Maya prophet's message? Can we turn them away from doing such a good thing?"

Kapilar sighed deeply, and his body sagged from the still, erect posture he had held for so long. "Everything you say is true. And I am glad that you had thought of this. But still, there will be anger and violence, and I cannot welcome them."

Pusiictsom started to speak but the old priest was cut off by the new prophet. Ix said, "No matter what, there will be anger and violence, because there is anger and violence now. And there will be anger and violence if we take the slightest measure of any kind to alleviate it. So I will do what is right, say what is right, be what is right, and let others hate me if they insist on it; if they want it they shall have violence, but only from themselves. What other choice is there, really? All I can do is my own actions, all I can say are my own words, I can only be myself. If I make those right I have reached my limit. The rest I must leave to others."

Kapilar bowed to him, the same deep face-to-the-floor-over-crossed-legs bow that he had given to Pusiictsom earlier. "There is a long, long tradition in my culture of wise men and poets who bring the people to new wisdom. I hope that it will be in that tradition that you will be seen. And I offer myself as your first Tamil student."

"And I accept you," Ix said. "I will begin to teach in thirteen days, because that is an auspicious number and it chances to fall on an auspicious day, and we will do things in accord with established custom as far as we can. You will hear of where and when. Come and listen then." Nodding to Pusiictsom, he said, "I understand that you will have to contend with me, in the way a father wrestles with his son, to make him strong so he can preserve the house in the next generation. I honor and love you for what you will do."

"And I you, for what you will do," Pusiictsom replied.

Ix rose from the couch, the warm red of the room light shining on his deep-brown skin, and passed through the door the way a dream fades. When the door closed again behind him there was no sound.

The old priest looked again at the three of us and said, "There is little for any of us to do until Ix completes his solitude and returns to teach in thirteen days, but if you return to New Tanjavur during those thirteen days I am very much afraid it will start ugly rumors here in Yaxkintulum."

"It would in New Tanjavur," Kapilar said, and Tz'iquin nodded his agreement.

"We will remain, wait, and study," I said. "And thank you for your openness in letting us see how you have established this prophet."

"Peace begins with truth," Pusiictsom said. "Grandson, as no doubt you are aware, you and I must deal with a great deal of family business, but I have pressing appointments at the moment. Perhaps we should save our long discussion until tomorrow, especially since you already know the biggest news and it will take you some time to think of what you would like the family to do about it."

"As you wish, Grandfather," Tz'iquin's voice had an oddly strained quality to it that I could not place; all I could tell was that he was upset in some way.

The old man accepted Tz'iquin's obedience with a mere nod; then he rose to his feet and said to all of us, "An attendant will settle you into a guest apartment and see you all made comfortable." He stood up, and since Tz'iquin bowed, so did Kapilar and I.

Seconds after Pusiictsom had gone, a young man dressed like Tz'iquin, except his vest was much plainer, entered, nodded to us once, and turned again to go out the door. Plainly he expected that we would follow him. We did, as he led us to the elevator, and then, after a brief ride, down another succession of corridors.

"I believe your grandfather said there is big news in your family?" Kapilar asked. "Is it anything you can tell a friend about?"

"You could say that," Tz'iquin said. "The man you have just met as 'Ix' is my father's eldest brother, and the heir to our lineage. The inheritance of office within the lineage will now change, and besides that 'a prophet has no lineage'—we will never be quite the same again. My uncle was one of my first teachers, the one I learned many stories from; later he and I disagreed about many things, some of them important, and so he has always been one of the most important people in my life. So—well, you might say it is something of a shock. But Grandfather's choice is right—he has picked a fine man, *and* signaled how serious the matter is, by choosing his own son and heir, giving up a great deal of the family's strength and hopes to further this message. It's a bold stroke and it will be widely admired, at least in some quarters."

"But I thought prophets generally came from undistinguished lineages," I said, "and helped the lineages to rise."

"Undistinguished relative to the task. Ix is going to rewrite the whole Maya culture; no one is distinguished enough for that! And though we Peccaries are among the top lineages, there's always a step from 'among the top' to 'the top.' I can only hope no other lineage is able to paint this as a power play (which it is, in part) and exploit it against us."

When the elevator doors opened, bright sunlight was pouring down the corridor in front of us. "And furthermore he put us into an apartment right up in the temple itself, rather than below ground. One more way to say that he thinks what we are doing is important."

The attendant led us down the corridor, our long dark shadows reaching out in front of us. "The door faces directly solar west," I said. "And with so little axial tilt, this is going to be true almost all year. You must live your lives in a diagram of the sky."

Tz'iquin smiled. "You could say that. Since you will. Partly in imitation of our ancients, partly because we've learned to find it beautiful ourselves, every feature of every temple is aligned with sunrise, sunset, or noon. In our old home, on Earth, where we lived not far from the equator, that formed straight lines. Here, so far into Briand's antarctic, we lose something of the pure orthogonal symmetry of the Maya cities of Old Earth, and our city is laid out in gentle, graceful curves, mirroring the sun's path through the northern sky."

Without speaking the attendant turned and gestured toward one door in the corridor. Though Kapilar and I thanked him, he just walked away without responding.

"He's probably under a vow," Tz'iquin said apologetically. "He isn't allowed to speak. I remember that was a difficult year of my life."

The little apartment was three rooms off a small central parlor; each room in turn had a small bath with a toilet, basin, and tub. The parlor and all three rooms were furnished only with the customary encircling padded bench, with a backrest attached to the wall. On a small island in the center, the common room had a refrigerator and a foodmaker, a lot like what my mother had had when I was a boy, before the springer-order food slot.

The foodmaker modules in the refrigerator featured a standard intercultural menu: some Occitan and Tamil dishes and a large number of Maya dishes that I knew nothing about. "Very thoughtful," I said.

"And much appreciated," Kapilar added. "I'm going to try the Maya dishes, later, but just now I'm exhausted and something familiar is exactly what I need." He dialed a staple Tamil meal, curried vegetables on rice soaked in buttermilk; I imitated Tz'iquin and selected a dish called *ceehel uah,* which, when it arrived, turned out to be something I had encountered in three cultures before, always under the name "tamale."

Whatever its proper name was, it smelled good, and after a couple of bites to get accustomed to the mix of chocolate, tomato, and a spice or two I couldn't quite name, I liked it. None of us said a word until the food was completely gone.

Finally, when we had all pushed our plates away and sighed with satisfaction, Tz'iquin suggested, "There's a wonderful view that you should see, from the East Terrace, right about now."

With nothing better to do, we followed him down the corridor. When we reached the eastern door, the only trace of the sun was a dim orange glow, reflected all the way down the corridor, touching the high corbeled ceiling of the passageway.

As we emerged, there was a surprising amount of light from the city below and before us—glowing windows, lighted plazas, fountains that danced with light, beacons on top of temples. From the air I had not had a real sense of the scale of either Yaxkintulum or of the Center Temple; the temple was immense and the city must stretch for several kilometers to the east of it.

"Why is it called the Center Temple if it's all the way to the west?" Kapilar asked.

"Because it's at the center of the west side, and the west side is the important one," Tz'iquin said. "A better translation into Terstad than 'Center Temple' might be 'the ritual place and worship center used by the priests of the most ancient and important gods, standing in the place of the heart of importance,' but that would probably require even more explanation."

More of the city opened before us as we crossed the terrace, which was about the width of a soccer field. Engraved figures swarmed across the blocks under my feet—so far as I had seen, almost every public surface was carved everywhere, either into the stone, or in bas relief, with much of it painted or frescoed. The complex patterns looked like those of the hieroglyphics I had seen in training, but subtly different. We were walking too fast for me to try to make out any pattern in the carvings passing beneath my feet; I got an impression of vast numbers of people, in flattened perspective, fighting, talking, making love, running, dancing, praying, under trees of many kinds, magnificent snakes and birds, and oddly distorted figures that might be animal or human. "Are all these carvings writing, or are some of them decorative?"

"They are all writing, but very few of them were written," Tz'iquin explained. "This city, like any other, is built by nanos directed by aintellects. The aintellects used our literary tradition to generate many, many legends, stories, and histories, which the nanos have laid down across the city, so that you can read a story in the carvings, frescoes, and statuary along almost any possible straight line within the city."

Kapilar and I must have looked foolish, gaping at him. I finally stammered out—"But . . . why don't your poets and storytellers write your literature? How can you just machine-generate it?"

Tz'iquin seemed faintly amused. "Both of you come from a culture that favors the writer, the 'maker', the poet, whatever you wish to call the one who creates new work, and so you think that every literary culture must be dominated by them. We Maya don't much make new works, but we develop an ever-better understanding of our old works. In that regard, at least, we are not unlike you, with your endless expositions of Kural, Ettutokai, and Pattuppattu. The difference is that we don't write about the same old work over and over; we discipline ourselves to the adventure of endless reading, seeing how many more things a thing can mean rather than trying to find the one right meaning for it. And to us, it does not really matter where those old works came from, or whether they are perfect or models for anything else, so long as they are truly Maya. A carefully done transform of a Maya myth is as Maya as the original, is it not?"

"I think that's for the Maya to decide," I said.

"Exactly."

We had now come to the edge, and Metallah's last light had flickered out in a sudden flash of green. Above us, the polar stars of Briand danced brilliantly, twinkling more fiercely, in the swirling upper atmosphere on the brink of its evening storm, than any stars I had ever seen before. For just a moment, looking out over the brilliant lights of the city below and then up into the whirling, dipping, splitting stars above, I was a bit more *trobador* and a bit less diplomat. With an inward, unvoiced sigh, I brought my focus back to human matters, lowering my gaze to look out on the city stretching beyond this temple complex, down the ridge, up the hill, and over the horizon.

We stood for a long time, looking over Yaxkintulum. Like the cities it had been modeled on, it had no streets. Plazas joined to plazas at the corners, in patterns of irregular diagonals; the city had grown by fitting new squares into the voids left by the old ones, with each square added where it completed, maintained, and enhanced the pattern. From where we now sat, you could see lines of balance and proportion laid out in the working lights of the city, running through it like bone, nerve, and vein.

At one place just left of where the ridge connected this temple complex to the main part of the city, the lines of a stepped building pointed to the apex of a pyramid across the square, and that pyramid, with its twin in the next square, framed a view into a row of plazas, all just the size of their bases. South and east of there, a row of buildings and plazas formed a rising, crenelated staircase that led the eye to a quad of pyramids, which in turn pulled one's focus in toward a much smaller pyramid on which rested a beautiful little temple.

Farther off, I could see that each structure or space in a square also had a place and function in the array of squares that formed a quad, each square a place in its cluster of quads as well as in its quad. As my eye adjusted and I began to be informed more than dazzled, each building appeared to be meaningful not only in the square structures to which it belonged, but in its row, and its column, and all by itself. It was like the vast acrostic thought of a god written in lights and stones.

I let my gaze wander, strangeness confronting and order comforting me by turns, as the wind rose from a soft sigh to a breeze, and the stars overhead went from twinkling and jumping to dividing, shaking, and bouncing, as their smooth cool light was torn to bits and flung about the sky by the thermal chaos of the polar atmosphere's shift from day to night.

I found myself writing songs, or fragments of songs, in my head, something I had not done much in the last few stanyears. It was a strange feeling because in my *jovent*, as a *trobador*, I had done this constantly. I had almost never had an emotion or an experience without forming it, almost immediately, into song, and thinking even while it was happening of how I would perform it.

Now as I thought of scraps of song, the bits of melody and lyrics that came to me seemed intolerably jejune and sentimental. To break the silence, I said, "Tz'iquin, I have to concede you were right; Briand is a planet of glorious cities."

Kapilar cleared his throat and spoke softly. "This is astonishing. All we ever saw of this place in school was a few pictures of people in bright clothing standing in front of carved stone walls. I had no idea this was here."

"And you didn't have any way to get here, anyway," Tz'iquin said. "We can hope all that will change."

We stood and watched a while longer; at last Kapilar said, "Tz'iquin, would you say you are optimistic about all this?"

Tz'iquin sighed. "As long as I don't think much." He drew another breath. "Well. That's cowardly, now, isn't it? You see . . . well, we Maya divide the world differently from the way everyone else does. I know, I know, every culture makes its own divisions of the world around it, but in our case . . . well. Let me be specific. In most cultures rulers' politics or politicians' sides are their own to choose. Or at least so my reading tells me. The President, Pope, King, Generalissimo, Warlock in Chief, Tuan, or whatever, can be conservative or liberal, strict or loose, allied one way or another, without much regard for anything other than his or her taste and whatever public might be relevant.

"But with us, you see, the ideas and beliefs are supposed to come with the job, not with the person who holds it. It's not just Grandfather's job to perform ceremonies, exercise authority, supervise the calendar calculations, and chant the stories. He also has to stand up for and defend the ideas that the Lord of the Center Temple and Daykeeper of Yaxkintulum is supposed to have. His *duty* is to be the most conservative person in the city. And I do think he would probably do it well enough if it were not . . . . well. You heard him speak about the priests of the Temples of the East. They are traditionally supposed to be the proponents of change, but the position has fallen into the hands of the Quetzals, a lineage which is quite reactionary. So the only changes they propose are ways to bring back more of our past, to become stricter and stricter in our adherence to cultural ways, and beyond that to retreat into isolation and hate.

"So to be conservative, Grandfather is driven to create a demand for change. He says the way he can do this is like a story from *Popul Vuh:* When Hun Hunahpu and Vucub Hunahpu faced the lords of Xibalbá, they were doomed to fail, but their defeat could also be looked on as what the lords of Xibalbá had to do in order to bring about the pregnancy of Lady Blood, the birth of Hunahpu and Xbalanque, and thus their own eventual downfall, which freed the human race from Xibalbá's control. Or was it that Hun Hunahpu and Vucub Hunahpu did those things to gain their place in the sky and their position of permanent power? Or did neither side intend what both made happen? The events of the story are sacred, because we read it. Is that clear?"

"I'm sure it will get clearer," I said. The oncoming evening storm was forming so many vortices and instabilities in the air over the city below us that the city lights were now dancing and splitting as much as the light of the stars overhead. I thought of my *jovent,* when I too had made up stories and we had all claimed to live by them. What a gray shadow that had been, compared to the way the Maya lived their stories!

After a long while Tz'iquin said, "So much of what we have done—including things that I must admit shame me and many others—has been to keep the stories real. If we are all to be farmers and warriors, well, then the solutions are two. You Tamils chose to separate the spiritual from the literal, so that you feel yourselves to be farmers and warriors, without the hard work of farming or the danger of going to war."

"As you must know, some of our critics rail against that very thing every night in some café or other," Kapilar said.

"But what if they were to think of the alternative? We have trained *real* farmers—farmers for whom their activity is not a cultural hobby, but a genuine reality. But what is the basic real experience of farming? Well, of course, it is the experience of depending on the land, and your skill and luck, to feed you. Living a harvest away from disaster. And this means that when the harvests fail . . . " His voice trailed off. The pause dragged on interminably.

"And so," I said, "if they are to be real subsistence farmers, when the crops fail, they have to starve. You can't tell them that with foodmakers, nanos, and electric power you could make all the food they could possibly want. I see."

"We really do starve people for our principles," Tz'iquin said. "I suppose the first generations were programmed very heavily by the people from Earth who wanted us to exist, and since then we have been running their program. It is the same reason we don't tell people about the possibility of the psypyx. The basic religious experience that would make any sense of our stories is living in fear of going down to Xibalbá and never coming back. They can't be spiritually themselves if they live with the knowledge that anyone who dies young can be recovered from their last recording."

"We too ban the psypyx," Kapilar pointed out. "It would trap the soul on its way to its proper reincarnation."

"But that's different," Tz'iquin said, "and, it pains me to say, probably less false and harmful. You tell people they may not interfere with their reincarnation. We make sure they never know about anything that might cause them to question the concept we have given them of the soul and the afterlife and all the rest.

"You see, the belief of the great majority of the Maya in their own stories is sustained almost entirely by the efforts of a dozen important lineages. We are the real rulers of Yaxkintulum, and we have taken it on ourselves to tell people lies that we think will preserve our society. In most cultures the stories serve the people—they are there for people to use to get through what they must. But here, people exist so that the stories can be believed." He sighed. "I did not mean to ramble on so long, but it helps me to get matters clear in my own mind. The problem is that we Peccaries are about to succeed in something that we have been moving toward for four generations—since Grandfather's father first came to understand how much the old stories had become our prison. We are working our way toward telling the great majority of our people who they really are and how they really came to be here. And we Peccaries are also working on becoming the one, true, and omnipotent priestly lineage."

"That's the real reason for Mayatown, isn't it?" Kapilar asked. "The Maya in New Tanjavur know too much."

"It's far from the only reason, but, yes, the Mayatown lineages are our skeptics and doubters. They stayed behind for the lineage shrines, just as I said, but living next to a great city, they could hardly help encountering ideas that told them the old stories could not be true. If nothing else, there were no Tamils in the old stories.

"So now the moment is here. We Peccaries make our move to bring down the prison of myth. Grandfather says temples come and go but people abide, and I agree. It is time for us to break our people out into the wider world. But . . . well. The man we will all call Ix from now on is a man of uncommon force and intelligence, who has risen to very high rank at a very young age. He is one of the most prominent of his generation among us. To have *him* be the next prophet . . . and yet who else should Grandfather choose when he is unleashing a prophet with a broad and sweeping mission to change the whole culture?

"It all makes sense, and the time had to come, and it might as well come now. But still—Grandfather is putting *everything* into play. The Peccaries will win or go extinct; the Maya will succeed on our road or curse our names for as long as they last.

"What Grandfather is doing, you see, is not 'managing' Change or 'guiding' it. It's more like leaping onto Change's back and kicking it with your spurs, and then holding on through the bucking and the wild charge and all the rest of the terrifying ride until finally Change leaves you in some other part of the universe entirely. That is a spirit that is strong in my lineage, and so it is no surprise that we conquered the highest position our culture offers.

"And that is why when I think about us Maya, in the long run, I shudder. The aggressive families who love change and will push for it rise to the top over the generations, and once they are on top, their job is to fight against change. They may not love doing it but they do it, and they are capable and aggressive and take pride in their work, so change is resisted. Meanwhile the less capable, the falling, the mediocre climbers, take the lesser positions where they are supposed to press for change, and they do a poorer and poorer job of it. Eventually we reach this point where Grandfather must do the Quetzal lineage's work as well as his own, and then must somehow lose at the game he is supposed to play and win at the game he should not be playing at all.

"And all this, you see, looks desperate to me, like a last expedient. And I find myself wondering, even if this works, in this generation, for this moment, as things come to be done less and less well and as change continues to become the domain of the mediocre and conservatism that of the talented . . . well. Well. You see my question? How long can this go on? How long before even this expedient will not work? How long will there be Maya, and how long will the Maya be Maya?"

He sat on the edge of the terrace, legs hanging over the edge, a good forty meter drop beneath him. Sitting as comfortably as if he were in a chair, he leaned back on his hands and settled his weight, relaxing until he was down on his elbows. Kapilar and I sat down in more or less the same position beside him. My feet hanging over a long fall into the dark, the glowing city in front of us, and the whirling flashing stars above focused my mind; I felt no need for words.

I glanced sideways at Tz'iquin, silhouetted against the city. His strong, sharp features were very like those of the ancient sculptures and pictures. At last he spoke. "Or on the other hand, perhaps the problem is that it *has* worked. Here we are. More than four-fifths of us speak no Terstad. In all the Thousand Cultures, we are the only one with large numbers of illiterates, and the only ones who have known starvation within living memory. All of this because it was the will of—our gods? our designers? someone somewhere once?—that we lead the ancient style of life. Many of us here do not even know this world is not the world that was made by Ix Chel. The Home System and the Thousand Cultures have not seen anything like us—a lost people with our own ways and own tongue—in a very long time, have they? And now you and your Council of Humanity come to us, determined to have us join you.

"Really, I think most of us only hate the Tamils and blame them for everything out of force of habit. Their springer is not what brought this about, is it? You would have come and gotten us, no matter what, wouldn't you?

"Well, here we are." His voice had gotten softer and softer, and his gaze had slowly risen from the city to the sky, where a ring of dark clouds was beginning to close on the zenith, shutting out the stars that leaped about as if in panic. The night storm would hit in minutes.

"We have done what we were supposed to do," he said, so softly that Kapilar and I had to lean in close, our shoulders almost touching his. "We have been loyal to the instructions that sent us out. The founders, dead five centuries, ordered us to live our lives based the way they read the Maya texts, that we be the Maya of their imagination. And we have done that. So here we are. Now, what are you going to do with us?"

The ragged ring of black clouds lunged across the sky to join overhead. We scrambled back across the terrace for the door, reaching it just as the night storm hit, rain and hail spattering and hissing on the engraved pavement behind us, washing all the messages there clean for another day, as the night storm had done every night for generations.

We stayed in the Center Temple for thirteen days, an auspicious time because there are thirteen day names in the Maya calendar. We had arrived on the morning of Ix; the days cycled away toward the next Ix while Kapilar and I, loosely supervised by Tz'iquin, studied Mayan, got a feel for their art and music, and listened to some of the temple acolytes expound their sacred stories.

It was a pleasant enough time for me. I had had to learn the rudiments of so many cultures that this was extremely familiar. A couple of days of bafflement during which one kept learning things wrong was eventually followed by a gradual awareness of what the right questions to try to answer would be, and finally a few days of breakthrough when the culture became, not understood, but *understandable*—which was as far as a Council of Humanity diplomat usually needed to go.

That is, we had to reach a point where we no longer felt that these people would never make any sense, and where we stopped thinking of them as a great amorphous mass of incomprehensible eccentrics; in the stage after that, though we might never really learn their motives, we could still feel that they could be learned, and thus we could negotiate as if there were hope in the negotiations. At least that was the cynical explanation Shan had once given me.

Margaret's explanation, which I liked better, was that you had to learn a culture until you knew whether the person on the other side of the table was following a cultural norm different from yours, or just an asshole.

So after the stress of life in New Tanjavur and my ongoing problems with Margaret, sitting down to learn the Maya culture was familiar and reassuring. I spent all my time studying and learning, but it felt like a vacation, as I told Margaret when I talked to her via private com every night.

One evening she seemed particularly discouraged, and I asked her what the matter was. "Kannan," she said. "Unfortunately, his hatred of the Maya and his hatred of Kapilar are working in the same direction: if he can build up enough opposition to your mission, perhaps he can keep it from succeeding here, even if it works out in Yaxkintulum." She started to speak, glared with frustration, and then began again. "He's been putting out an issue of *Palai* every day. Theory of why the Tamils shouldn't talk to the Maya, poetry about raping Maya girls, articles about the mechanics of expelling all the Maya from Mayatown with particular emphasis on destroying lineage shrines, an adulatory interview with a judge who gives very light sentences to anyone convicted of assault against a Maya . . . you get the idea. Plus some long sections about Kapilar's inadequacies as a poet, critic, and thinker, and the danger that he will come back polluted by Maya ideas and propagate them elsewhere."

"Well," I said, "Kapilar is . . . well, he's fascinated by the Maya, these days. Sometimes in a positive way and sometimes not, but he's certainly engaged in it. And I do think he just may be ripe for a sincere conversion by Ix, when Ix comes out of seclusion."

"How does he seem otherwise?"

"There isn't much otherwise," I said. "We eat and study, talk over dinner—always about our studies—and then go to sleep. There's not even a gym to work out in. He seems to be happy enough, except when he runs into something or other that just offends him to the teeth. When that happens there's an hour-long outburst of bigotry, then some sulking, and then he's back into the studies. Usually the next day he's worked his way around to a completely different view of it, and he's as cheerful as ever. I think he really likes this work and we might want to think about recruiting him for Council service."

Margaret looked thoughtful. "Well, that's a pleasant thought. But he's, uh—he doesn't appear to be having more trouble than—the usual?"

"Why?" I asked. "Is there a reason he should be?"

"I don't like your tone." She hung up. I was afraid to call her back. I had no idea what I had said.

The next day she apologized for her abrupt disconnection, and blamed a headache. I didn't believe her, but I was hardly going to argue with her. Besides, we had something new to talk about: a new problem in cultural relations had arrived in Margaret's inbox: a compilation of complaints from scholars all over the Thousand Cultures, about letters they had been receiving from the scholars of Tamil Mandalam.

Classical Tamil literature, especially the poems of the Cankam anthologies, was one of humanity's two dozen or so great literatures, somewhere up there with ancient Athens, medieval Provence, Heian Japan, Renaissance Spain, Industrial Age South America, Interbellum Africa, or the post-Slaughter Lunar refugee literature. Thus almost any world with a college, university, or academy had a Tamil scholar or two, and the body of work on the subject was a good thousand years deep, not counting the extensive criticism that the Tamils themselves had done for a millennium before the rest of the world discovered their books.

There were even two other Tamil cultures out there, one group from the Jaffna region that had settled on Dunant in the Alpha

Centauri system very early in the colonization age, and another that had come from the old Indian state of Tamil Nadu and settled on Moneta in the Epsilon Indi system. Both had been ethnic rather than literary cultures, but the Cankam anthologies had played a big part in their cultural development.

All of this helped to explain why it was infuriating to scholars everywhere, and to the other two Tamil cultures in particular, to abruptly receive letters demanding that they immediately change their interpretations, reading, and scholarship into conformity with that of the scholars of Tamil Mandalam, who had peremptorily claimed complete ownership of something as universal as *The Sheep-Well, Mahabahrata, Hamlet, The Dream of the Red Chamber,* or *No One Home A Thousand Kilometers Later,* and were now loudly issuing orders to some of the more respected minds in the human race. "It's not a crisis yet, Giraut," Margaret said, "but I wouldn't call it good news either. And you know how stubborn some of our Tamil friends can be when it comes to the Eight-and-Ten. It's their whole reason for existence. They aren't going to understand that other people have a right in it too."

I shrugged. "One day they seem ready to rejoin humanity right now, the next day I think we should just quarantine the lot of them."

Margaret nodded emphatically. "For more bad news, Giraut, there's the following: nine incidents in the city yesterday, which isn't a high number, but there were three fatalities. Not flukes, either, like infants caught in the crossfire. Two Maya and one Tamil deliberately killed, all in separate incidents. All women, of course."

I nodded. I knew what she meant by the "of course"—it had been axiomatic for a thousand years that where you had endemic ethnic violence, the bulk of it fell on women one way or another. They were physically smaller, they were often out and about more (because of the need to do the marketing, attend to children, and so forth), and most of all there was a great deal of sexual violence that operated under cover of traditional hatreds.

Furthermore, it was often a more effective provocation to the other side; millenia of effort for female equality had not wiped out humanity's fixation on mothers and daughters as the embodiment of a culture's purity, even on Earth—and many, many of the Thousand Cultures, Nou Occitan among them, had been founded purposely to exaggerate gender differences. Margaret was from one of the few cases of a culture that had sought genuine equality. Perhaps that was why we quarreled so often now? Perhaps I had not overcome my upbringing?

I was so lost in thought that I had missed her last sentence. Maybe my problem was that I didn't listen to her enough? "I'm sorry, *midons,* my fault, I didn't pick up your last—"

"It's all right, this world makes me moody too. No, I was just going to mention that Paxa Prytanis dropped by earlier today. Remember her? The one we met at the hotel in Manila."

Margaret's referring to the OSP training camp as "the hotel" meant that she wasn't sure the line was secure. Probably she was worried that Kiel might have it bugged. *"Ja,* I remember her. I ran into her a few days ago myself."

"She mentioned that her husband, a man named Piranesi Alcott, might drop in to see you sometime. He's part of the Council mission to the Maya, I gather."

"I didn't know we had one."

"Apparently the back door contacts via the merchants are more than Kiel knew about. I think she, or your old friend" (she had to mean Shan) "wanted you to know that there's a dependable ally in Yaxkintulum if you need him."

"I appreciate that."

"The other thing she had come into the Embassy for was medical treatment. She was one of the nine incidents yesterday."

It took me a moment to realize. "The nine incidents of ethnic violence? You mean a Council rep was assaulted? By which side?"

"By the Tamils. Sir Qrala says he's been dreading this for quite a while. The Tamils see our attempt at being evenhanded as encouraging the Maya. Same thing that always happens when an overlord culture meets a superior power that doesn't share its bigotries. Luckily she's an old hand commercial rep, she's been in some rough places before—" again, I figured Margaret was reminding me that Paxa was part of the Shan organization and had at least had some training in fighting—"and so she was carrying a neuroducer wand and a neural bomb. They blocked her trakcar, tipped it over, threw stones at her, and tried to rush her. Other than bruises from the emergency stop, and the first couple of rocks she was hit with, all the damage happened to the other side; she was bruised and shaken up, and she's angry as all hell, but she's fine otherwise. Six Tamils, all men, are in the hospital, with various damage."

"It sounds well-deserved," I said. A neuroducer wand convinced the brain that whatever part of the body it touched had been severely burned or battered into hamburger; a neural bomb put out hundreds of neuroducers on microwires in all directions except the one it was thrown from. Probably the Tamils would be in the hospital for months, heavily sedated, as the memories were soothed away from their nervous systems, and the doctors used drugs and hypnosis to persuade them that they had not really been dismembered and flayed alive. And perhaps it would be the salutary sort of lesson that, in many cultures on many worlds, had made it clear to the local population that joining the Council was a one-way business; once in, in for good, and without any special local provisos.

"I have to admit I got some pleasure out of the news, once I knew Paxa wasn't hurt badly," Margaret said. "Unfortunately, at the moment we seem to have created a martyr. There's a special double issue of *Palai* to expose the Council's particular wickedness, with profiles of each of the honored goons who suffered for the sacred cause of the right to beat up tiny women. Some street demonstrations as well. At least for the present, Kiel has barred all Council personnel from going outside the Embassy on any mission that isn't essential, which means that as a tourism rep I'm *truly* useless here. Kiel seems to think he'll be able to lift the order in ten days or so, but till then . . . . well, wish you were here."

"I do too," I said.

"How are things with Kapilar?" she said.

"Same as always," I said, "he eats and sleeps and studies. Which is what I do. Five days left till Ix comes out of seclusion and we can get moving again. Whatever it may be that constitutes moving."

"Well, good luck. Talk to you tomorrow." Her awkwardness made me wonder what the matter was, but she clicked off before I even said goodbye. I stopped myself from muttering "I love you" at the now-blank screen; no Occitan makes a gesture like that without an audience. Feeling sad and discouraged, I went to bed almost immediately afterward, and the dreams I had were all sad, or frightening, or both.

The next morning I talked it all over with Kapilar. He was optimistic enough about the problem of the insulting letters to scholars in the other cultures. "Well, I think it will die out in time," he said. "At least if you can go by my own reaction. The thing is that the anthologies, and the other literature, is probably ninety percent of what we study in school, and we all consider ourselves to be experts. And you know there's nothing that gets its back up further or behaves more rudely than an expert confronted with a view of his subject he's never encountered before. I think this is more in the nature of a spasm than a permanent movement. Right now the people who wrote those indignant notes and riled up every scholar of Tamil literature in human space are sitting at home, having the horrible second thought that just maybe someone off planet knows something they don't, or might be right. And it's not like anyone is going to throw bombs about it."

On the other hand, he shared Margaret's and my sense of foreboding about the attack on Paxa Prytanis: "This is very bad," he said, "and I don't think you're going to find much comfort in her having fought them off successfully. It might almost have been better if she'd been badly hurt rather than her attackers."

"Better for her attackers, I'm sure," I said. "Look, it may be Tamil custom to attack the women of strange people, but it is the custom of the Thousand Cultures to put that sort of thing down hard. And it is very much the custom of women who work for the Council of Humanity to defend themselves, no matter what parochial mores they offend."

"It is *not* our custom. All I meant is that they are now martyrs, where she could have been a martyr—"

I had been losing patience before, and now said emphatically, "A martyr is of remarkably little value to anyone, except the people who live after and are lucky enough not to be martyrs. You know, Pusiictsom takes a more realistic view of the long run prospect here; at least he knows that the struggle is hopeless, and tries to look over the horizon. In a couple of generations New Tanjavur will be dominated by the Thousand Cultures' Interstellar metaculture. You won't like Interstellar. I didn't, when it came to Nou Occitan. It's bland and insipid and dull—and alive. And vigorous and oriented toward the future.

"Now, what do you think will become of your Tamil martyrs in any history written by Interstellars? They'll be an obscure footnote, at best."

Kapilar shuddered. "You know, when we reconnected to the Thousand Cultures, it wasn't presented to us as a complete loss of our independence and our own natures."

He looked disconsolate, but by this point I didn't care much; I'd heard enough about cultural rights, while the partisans of them went right on killing. "Don't fret about it," I said. "None of your descendants will wish they had remained like you. They may form nostalgic attachments to the past, but they won't really want to go back to living the way you did—certainly not out of any feeling that they owe you a debt. Look at our Maya friends here—the only way that they keep everyone on their particular program is to not tell most of them what's going on. How long do you think their old order will last once people find out that they didn't have to lose the baby to starvation five years ago, or that they don't have to spend most of their lives stirring the dirt with a pointed stick?"

That got a rise out of him; he glared at me. "You know," he said, "if I had said that, you'd have called me a bigot. Perhaps you don't approve of the goals their culture was established for, or their way of doing things. I don't, myself. But they have been doing the best they could according to their lights. No other culture ever had to be entirely relocated. No other culture succeeded in maintaining a believing population against the *radio* from the stars, and here you've got one that might well resist the *springer.* No doubt it all looks silly to you people from Earth, and probably someday the Council *will* be telling our great-grandchildren what to remember, but meanwhile, whether you like it or not, we Brianders are going to go on being ourselves!"

He stormed into his room and slammed the door. I sat there for a long moment, and then let myself develop a great big grin, the first since I had landed on this hot, heavy, humid mess of a world.

We Brianders.

He didn't speak to me for the rest of the day. That night I summarized the conversation for Margaret, and added that although I hoped Kapilar was going to forgive me, that his having been driven into feeling solidarity with the Maya seemed to me to be well worth it. The longer I talked about the conversation, the more bored and annoyed she seemed to get, so I told her that I missed her touch, I missed her company, and I wanted to be home with her, then rang off as quickly as I politely could.

One thing that did make learning the Maya culture easier was that it was still relatively whole. On Roosevelt, where Margaret and I had been posted before this, although all 128 cultures on that crowded planet had long since blended into universal Interstellar, almost every person still identified with at least one of them, and each insisted on maintaining a crucial something-or-other about it. You had to remember which. Novy Belarus kept hagiology and icons; Ile de France kept its food; Orleans Trois its music, peculiar vocabulary, and holidays; the three Jewish cultures all kept separate versions of the dietary laws; the Noviromani maintained an elaborate list of ways in which household gods had to be propitiated when entering and leaving a home, and so forth. Yet, for the most part, most of them, in the whole vast polyglot, lived in similar houses, ate similar dishes, spoke Terstad with the same Roosevelt accent, and intermarried fairly freely. It had been a whole planet full of people who were tolerant and accepting in general but each of whom was looking to be offended in some small, specific way, for the opportunity to make someone else apologize and say, "Oh, dear, I didn't know you were an X."

I had hated it. The worst of it was the divergence between what you were told about a culture and how it turned out to be practiced. Here, since the whole culture really remained in practice, there was no such problem.

"On the other hand, you only *had* to learn isolated rules for certain kinds of behavior. You could just learn them as exceptions to what you would normally do," Kapilar pointed out as we took our second break of the evening, a couple of days later, relaxing over cups of the hot bitter chocolate that was the basic drink here. The stormy argument of four days before had vanished without a trace, if for no other reason than that we had almost no one else to talk to. "You and I have to learn the whole Maya culture as one—which means we can't just tell ourselves it's 'normal with variations.' Instead we have to confront all of its strangeness all at once.

"And I confess that at least twice a day I hate them with more passion than Kannan or any of the other bigots I know. It makes me wonder if the idea of bringing us together is a good idea at all. On the other hand, about twice a day, I wish I had been born Maya."

"Normal reaction to studying another culture." I took a sip of the chocolate to conceal my smile. "The first culture I learned after my own was Caledony, where Margaret is from. I used to write long, long letters to my friends at home, telling them what an awful place Caledony was, and then twenty minutes after sending the letter I'd be overcome with the feeling that I had never had a real friend before I came to Caledony, and that only Caledons really cared about anything important.

"It's like the problem medical students get during their training. They think they have every disease they study. Supposedly that's because when you tell somebody that, oh, say, her knee *could* possibly, some day, be full of burning, tingling fluid, she has to imagine, for a while, that it is, just to understand the idea. Humans crave to know their whole range of possibilities, so if you've never had, say, mastitis, once you know the symptoms, you have to try them on mentally. So the same thing happens with a culture. You learn the name of an emotion or a quality that your culture doesn't name or know, and all of a sudden you have to see if you can feel it, and it always turns out you could, which questions your previous existence but also opens another possibility to you . . . you see?"

Kapilar nodded. "I can even see why you and Margaret chose to do the work you do. When you study another culture you're always meeting someone else you could have been, eh? And sometimes you like what you find and sometimes you don't. When you do, you wish you had developed that part before, and you're in love with the culture that introduced you. When you don't, and you discover someone you could have been or something you might have done that disgusts you, the other culture has just given you bad news and you hate it. Hmm. Do you ever get immune to the mood swings?"

"I wouldn't say immune, but you learn that they don't mean much," I said, stretching and yawning. I was getting pretty tired and thinking of early bed. "But in a way that's the sad part. After a while you learn to pick up the mechanics of a culture without ever even feeling those possible places in yourself. Once that happens life just isn't as intense as it used to be. Maybe it's just that the bigger your self gets, the fewer things you can get a cramp in your head about, but I think it's also callousness and ability to fake. Like the first love affair versus the fiftieth seduction: objectively speaking your technique and knowledge might be a lot better, but nothing is going to match the intensity and the discovery of the first time. You won't ever have a more intense experience or one you remember more thoroughly for longer. So enjoy it. Especially enjoy the mood swings. They mean you're still alive to the process."

He was grinning. "You know, I didn't realize it before, but I *am* enjoying it, mood swings and all. I guess I just didn't notice it before."

We chatted about everything and nothing for a while afterwards, speculating about what Tz'iquin was up to that day; we knew he was involved in some complicated politics that had to do with transfers of power and prestige now that his uncle was out of the lineage. We avoided discussing Ix himself, in my case at least because it's not easy to think that somewhere out there there's a man sitting and quietly thinking about how he plans to tear the fabric of history.

When I went to bed I found that at first I couldn't sleep.

I wondered where and when my intensity had gone.

The very first mission, back before I had been a regular Council rep or OSP agent, when I was twenty-two, had been the most intense time of my life. My time in Caledony still burned vividly in my head, and I still retained the faces, names, and voices of even the most minor acquaintances there. I had lost some good friends to death there—Caledony had psypyxes and used them, but the leaders of the coup there had deliberately wiped many of the recordings. I had seen some of the most spectacular country known to human beings, and learned a thing or two about love. Most of all I had met Margaret there.

It didn't seem to me that I could ever feel that intense about Margaret again; the first time with her had coincided with a time when I was growing and changing, emotionally, very fast, and she had been part of the whole excitement of discovering that I could be someone other than an arrogant Occitan *jovent,* that there might be more to life than conquest followed by bragging. In the culture in which I was raised—not "in which I grew up," you can't really say a true Occitan ever grows up—art, violence, and sex were all frauds alike, and so the encounter with a less-pretended world had been quite a jolt.

And, too, because Margaret was coming out of drab, repressive Caledony, just when it was suddenly waking up to art, music, fashion, and the rest of what makes people worth bothering with . . . well, I had been her personal pathway into a much wider world, and so she had loved me in a public, passionate way that couldn't be sustained—sooner or later she had to see how many flaws I had—but a year of being worshipped does things to a *toszet* too.

Was all of the squabbling with Margaret just because both of us could feel ourselves getting older? One reason Romeo died at seventeen was because if he had lived to be twenty-two he might have found out he was Don Juan.

The next day was the thirteenth day, which meant that in the Maya calendar the name of the day was Ix—and on our calendar, it was the day when we were to meet Ix. We had no idea when, or if, Ix himself would be contacting us that day, so there wasn't a strong reason to stay inside, and on that particular day it just felt unbearable to spend a whole day inside reading, watching recorded performances, and listening to music, always waiting for the com to chime and the rest of the adventure to begin. No doubt it could find us when it was time. I suggested to Kapilar that rather than wait around, we might want to see if our

skills had come along far enough to read some of the inscriptions
on the front wall that fell away into the abyss from the west side
of the Center Temple.

"Absolutely," Kapilar said. "I'd like to remind myself that I'm
not a prisoner, for one thing."

The inscriptions and reliefs on the front wall, like the ones
running through the most important plazas in the city, were actually ancient rather than machine-generated. When the Maya literary culture had been defined, some bright fellow in the design
team had come up with the idea that the Classic Maya and their
descendants down to the Spanish Invasion had lived in places
where nearly every wall, stele, step, floor, ceiling, lintel, and rail-
ing was inscribed and illustrated with the traditional stories and
chronicles. Thus part of the experience of being Maya was defined as growing up among inscribed walls, and when, after forty
years of robots and aintellects laboring to get the original Kintulum fit to move into, the colony ship had arrived with its ninety-
six adults in suspended animation and its millions of frozen
embryos, almost every surface of the city center of Kintulum had
borne copies of Maya writing, from the codices and inscriptions
of Old Earth. Every possible text had found a home somewhere.

But the plans for what to do with a growing population had
been deferred to the second generation after settlement—a common enough way to deal with the problem, for the designers of
the Thousand Cultures had envisioned that each culture would
be self-sustaining and dynamic. Therefore in every culture some
issues of culture design were deliberately deferred anywhere from
one to eight generations, so that they could evolve.

The wisdom of putting off some decisions for the culture itself
to make was nowhere better shown than in the case of the Maya.
When Old Grandfather erupted and Kintulum was lost, Yaxkintulum had had to be grown in less than two stanyears, and there
had not been nearly enough geomancers and planners to lay out
what inscription should go where, except that the most ancient
should run along the major axes of the city. It had been impossi-

ble to think of allowing duplicate texts—since each physical location was unique, so must each inscription be. And there were
nothing like enough scribes to compose the enormous volume of
new text, eight times what had existed in the old central temple
district of Kintulum, that would have to be there to cover the
whole city. Nor could Yaxkintulum have been made with only
the central district inscribed—some force, democracy or a religious change or a new decree, had required that from now on *all*
Maya and not just the aristocracy and the priests, must live in inscribed space.

The aintellects had been put to the job of writing the vast
amount of new text that would be needed. Besides *Popol Vuh*
there were only four codices, plus a few hundred thousand pho-
tographs of stone inscriptions taken before Central America had
been vitrified in the Slaughter. With a limited number of motifs
and combinations in the traditional literature, and duplicated
material known to vary in predictable ways, it had been possible
to have the aintellects create the enormous quantities of new
chronicle, poetry, myth, and prayer needed to cover Yaxkintulum, by recombining material according to traditional patterns.

Only an occasional specialist knew or bothered to know exactly which inscriptions were from Old Earth and which were
chronicles of the wholly imaginary Briandian Maya history that
stretched from the supposed beginning of a migration from Central America to Briand (by extremely unspecified means) around
standard year 900, through the claimed Maya abandonment of
Earth around 1450, and on through the supposed founding of
Kintulum at the end of the fifth Great Cycle in 2012, followed by
the chronicles of seven imaginary dynasties across the 702
stanyears following until the destruction of Kintulum by Old
Grandfather.

That absurd culture history stretching from 900 to 2460 (the
date of the founding landing) was typical of many cultures; what
was atypical here was only that belief in it was relatively
uneroded. During the century after the Slaughter, when the

Thousand Cultures were all designed and the Inward Turn was just starting, no one had thought that the different cultures would ever want, need, or have much contact with each other, even on the eight planets that had more than a hundred cultures each. In that era of formalization and intensification, it had been thought that all cultures would want to develop separately, each in its own isosemiotic episteme. Thus each was granted permission not only to invent part of its history, but unleash the aintellects in its libraries to rewrite every historic reference into accord with their particular version of history, so that their descendants would grow up knowing no other version.

The culture designers had responded in a wide diversity of ways. I had grown up believing that various French Symbolists and Romantics had led the American Empire and its allies right up through World War Three; when I had hit advanced study at university, and been compelled to learn universal history, I had been upset to learn that Picasso and Braque had neither killed James and Eliot in a drunken brawl, nor had to flee to Paris in the airplane invented by Yeats.

Margaret's culture had been founded out of a mixture of North American fundamentalism and Austrian economics, and so she had been raised to believe that various forgotten crackpot economists were Christian saints. The warrior culture of Thorburg thought they were descended from an exiled band of mercenaries who had actually existed only as characters in a popular adventure hypertext game. The people of some other cultures were raised to believe that they had been created by some god or other, right where they now were; others that they had been exiled by an imaginary tyranny; still others that the culture they supposedly created, and not the Council of Humanity, had dispatched them to settle their appointed patch of a terraformed planet. In all the cultures of the Thousand Cultures, only the Hedons—who I liked better and better the more I saw of other cultures—had raised their descendants on as much of the straight truth as they wanted.

So it wasn't unusual that the Maya had a fictitious history. It was unusual that most Maya had never had access to any other, that most of it had only been read, never written by anyone, and that the great majority did not even know much of their cultural history. In effect, the Maya had spent hundreds of stanyears reading one vast book of permutations of the fragments that had come down from the long-lost pre-Columbian Maya. If you supposed that most meaning was inherent in the fragments, as the Maya tended to do, rather than in their arrangement, it made little difference.

On the other hand most Western-derived cultures tended to assume the meaning was in the arrangement—which meant, as I was inclined to read it, that the Maya were living at the end of a false history written by random number generators, and would now have to cross over to an impossibly different reality, with farther to go faster than anyone else had, due to their long isolation.

All of this had been running through my head, in one form or another, over and over as Kapilar and I made our way down through the outside stairs of the pyramid, to the landing leading to the stairways that descended the face of the front wall to give access to the ledges that ran across it, one ledge per line of writing.

Tz'iquin had mentioned that in some cases the carvings extended below the altitude where a human being could breathe without a respirator, but we weren't going nearly that far into the canyon. We had chosen a ledge a few levels down, because there was a relief there that was highly admired, and, just right of it, a story that was the focus of numerous exegeses. "If you want to learn a culture, you have to learn how to like what it likes, rather than go looking for something that you like," I explained to Kapilar.

"I understand *that,*" Kapilar said, from a few steps above and behind me, as we gingerly descended the nearly vertical, less-than-a-meter-wide steps. Climbing these in 1.3 g must give all the

Maya great calves and thighs, and on this particular flight of steps, with a multi-kilometer drop to my right and no guardrail, the evolutionary process had probably also worked overtime at eliminating any genetic tendency to vertigo.

Kapilar had been babbling on and I hadn't been paying attention due to combined fear and discomfort. I made a point of listening again. "—understand we need to understand, but I don't understand why understanding requires scaring ourselves silly on this high wall, especially since all this stuff is computer indexed and we could have just accessed it back in our rooms."

"Didn't you want to get outside for a change?"

"The Maya have a point about change not being good, you know."

We finally reached the ledge we wanted and stepped across onto it. We still had to go single file, slowly.

"You haven't answered my question," Kapilar said.

I shrugged. "This is the way the Maya say one sees it best. By definition, they are the best guides to their culture. So what we want to know is why they say this is better than seeing it on a computer screen in a comfortable chair."

"Well, so far it *really* is a mystery," he said.

The figure we had come down to admire was about half scale or so, a bit under a meter tall, and was a representation of one of the maize gods, copied from Copán on Old Earth. He was carved with such a precise and sensitive touch that the curves of his lips, the flare of his nostrils, the set of his eyelids, all made him seem just about to move. "It is beautiful," I said, "at least as realism. And it seems to . . . well, there's a mood here. Look how pensive he is. He's wrestling with something inside."

"The workmanship is very fine," Kapilar said, "and it must have been an amazing job when the Maya first carved it. Here, it's just a copy anyone could make with the right nanos."

His sniping was annoying, but I didn't want to snap at him, so I made a point of moving on to the story, closing the discussion of the relief. Probably he was just being unpleasant because he was hot and sweaty and his feet hurt.

Even with the emblok, reading the text was difficult. Mayan is built around the linking of stems (or word roots), so much so that early grammarians regarded a link between two stems to be equivalent to the sentence. Consistent with that, Mayan prosody is built almost entirely on powers of two—e.g. one stem pair per line, four lines per 'stanza,' so that there were eight stems to a stanza.

A line is written as a group of four characters, with each group arranged

$$A_1 \quad A_2$$
$$B_1 \quad B_2,$$

so that you read the group as $(A_1\&A_2)\&(B_1\&B_2)$. The resulting combination might mean two phrases or one, or the beginning of a phrase that continued in the next group, in a partly phonetic, partly syllabic, partly ideographic relationship. Tz'iquin had told us that producing a good reading of Mayan texts was a difficult and highly admired skill; I was beginning to understand.

I took off my hat for a moment to wipe sweat from my forehead. The first group of four was a familiar pattern:

4   AHAU

NAME   KATUN

With diacritical marks it meant "4-Ahau is the name of the katun when." A katun was a period of 7200 days, or about 100 days short of twenty stanyears, so this was not a precise date, even if the event being reported had actually occurred.

I began to work my way along the wall, trying to make out the story, and after he saw that his sulking was having no effect, Kapilar joined me in puzzling out how each quad added to the story. Pawaha was born—"Is Pawaha the name of twin brothers or of a lineage?" Kapilar asked.

"I would bet it depends on these marks here, but I can't make them out," I said.

"That's not the part that I instructed the acolytes in the temple to guide you to," a soft voice said beside us, so gently I didn't start at all—a good thing on the narrow ledge. On the other side of Kapilar, Ix stood calmly, hands at his sides, just watching us.

He wore a plain white shirt and pants, nondescript slippers, no jewelry, and a simple broad-brimmed hat; his beautiful long hair had been chopped off and what stuck out from under the hat now was a plain bowl cut. He was the first really plainly dressed Maya I ever saw.

"Sorry," he said. "I didn't mean to startle you. But I confess to some impatience. I could have waited till you finished reading, but I wanted to talk with you about something."

Kapilar sighed and stretched, working the kink from his neck. "Well, I'm in favor of anything that gets me off this ledge quickly. Uh, off this ledge and back into the city quickly, I mean. It sounds as though you had something to do with whatever text the acolytes were sending us here to read."

"I did. And what impression have you formed of our literature so far, before coming down to this wall?"

"Well," I said, "no more pattern than I see in any other culture based on a pre-industrial literature, and I've known several of those and come from one myself. As far as I can tell we've mostly been reading straightforward chronicles of wars and kings, plus stories about the gods, who spent most of their time playing ball, going on quests, resurrecting, and copulating."

Ix nodded. "Not a bad summary. What would you say about the Maya pacifist tradition, from what you've read?"

We both gaped at him. Kapilar recovered first and said, "There isn't one."

"Exactly," Ix said. "Will you walk with me to the place where

I'm staying? There are things to talk about and I would like to have you present while they are talked about."

Without waiting for an answer he turned and went back up the steps. Kapilar glanced back at me, I shrugged, and we followed. My calves ached at the effort of hauling my extra weight up so many stairs, and the drop-off, centimeters away, seemed to get closer and longer with every step. I was sweating even more than was usual for the temperature and humidity by the time we crossed the temple courtyard and descended the ridge into the city.

It was a very ordinary Maya house in the middle of the city, off an open plaza faced by blocky rowhouses on two sides and two nondescript temples on low pyramids on the others. If you read the carvings along the walls, you found that the house stood at the intersection of two of the stories that ran wall-to-wall and building-to-building in long straight lines through Yaxkintulum.

The specific passage that ran along the rowhouses, west to east, was from *Popol Vuh,* the story of how after Hun Hunahpu and Vucub Hunahpu were defeated by the Lords of Xibalbá, Hun Hunahpu's head was hung in a tree till Lady Blood came by, when it spoke to her and ultimately impregnated her by spitting onto her hand. The house Ix led us to was mainly covered, on the north side facing the plaza, with a bas-relief of the head of Hun Hunahpu spitting into Lady Blood's hand.

The most distinctive thing about Maya art was that it mixed realistic line drawing with iconographic imagery in a jam-it-in-any-old-way topological composition. The relief of Hun Hunahpu's decapitation on the rowhouse east of this one depicted a very real-looking head hanging on a very stylized tree. Hun Hunahpu's body stood in a pose that showed off fine detail of muscles, but from its neck erupted a cluster of snakes representing blood. And yet along the stylized tubes that indicated the snakes coming from his neck, detail re-emerged, so that the snake-heads too were very nicely detailed (though drawn in a flat perspectiveless style, unlike the rounded body).

I stood for a moment before following Ix and Kapilar in. My eyes traveled down from the indigo sky to the shocking white corners of the house and into the dense complexity of the narrative band and finally to the three-meter-high carving that covered the upper part of the house. There was a whole story in just that picture: Hun Hunahpu, having just spit, looked as if he had had a bare moment of consciousness, now slipping from him. Anger, satisfaction, even something that looked oddly like desire, were all captured in the moment they faded from his face and his muscles relaxed back into death.

Lady Blood held up a squared-off stylized hand. A flower grew from her palm: the icon for Hun Hunahpu's spit? the icon for the instant of the conception of Hunahpu and Xbalanque? Mirroring Hun Hunahpu's face, hers—also depicted in realistic detail—was just beginning to assume joy or awe. Perhaps a touch of sorrow? No one feeling was quite there yet, in her instant blank recognition, but all impended.

And although Hun Hunahpu and Lady Blood were not part of the north-south story that ran through the house the other way, inlaid into the stones of the pavement, yet the picture also seemed to illustrate that story as well. You could as easily see the blossom not as the spit of Hun Hunahpu, but as a gift held up. If so the figure was not Lady Blood but a maiden who had lost her lover when he was executed for losing at the ball game, and was making her final offering to him. The text under my feet said that after this offering she had been ever-fortunate and had gone on to marry the son of the other player and found a great line of warriors.

Thus the bas-relief might be hello or good-bye, love or hate, conception or death. Anyway it was a moment when one part of the story ended and another began.

I felt something on my left side and looked to see that Ix was now standing beside me. "You chose this house for this," I said. "At a moment of great change in two stories."

"You are beginning to understand," Ix said. "Besides, the north-south tale was invented by aintellects but the east-west is one of the best-known parts of *Popol Vuh,* so you could see this as the new intersecting the old, or the invented with the inherited. Furthermore, this place holds two *very* trivial temples plus a residential area, so if by any chance there should ever be a need to commemorate this place, and by commemorating it to say something about who we Maya wish to be, there will be an appropriate place for us to tear down the old and grow a great new pyramid and temple, which in turn can become a force for the new idea."

"How many places like this are there in the city?" I asked him.

"There are many, many public squares. Shall we go in?"

"This is another way the Maya have to deal with change, isn't it? You live right on top of a text so complex that whatever happens is always already recorded somewhere. So you've always got a quick transformation available if you need it, without ever having to admit it wasn't there all the time."

"You could say that," Ix said. "Except that this particular corner meant very little till I chose it, and if I don't succeed it still won't mean anything. As you have been learning, for those who can *really* read, there is an art to reading that is greater than the art of writing. Now, will you come inside with me and see what meaning we will be able to read from our history, into our history?"

I followed him. Everywhere in this supposedly rigid and traditional culture, I saw systems of meaning that had been clearly established to accommodate rapid change. And yet the Maya had tolerated starvation and poverty till quite recently, large parts of their population were being kept ignorant in a way that recalled nothing so much as Tokugawa Japan, every year they killed a number of young boys with the rigors of the ball game . . . and they had done nothing to change that. The cruelty of the culture had been tolerable if one imagined them all as prisoners in the shackles of tradition or the cells of received ignorance. But if they had so many ways to change, then the poverty, ignorance, and suffering here was their choice.

And I was sworn to understand and to learn to like them.

Maya homes were built with thick walls and small deep windows. Passing out of the searing actinic light, I shuddered at the surprising cool, but within a few steps down the corridor I felt comfortable enough.

The room Ix led me to was pleasantly dim, with amber-tinted recessed wall sconces, so that outside of shadows the colors were vivid, and the soft edges of the shadows and the indirect glow pervading the space blurred anything sharp-edged and made it all feel warm and friendly.

The surrounding couches were mostly occupied by Maya in undecorated, plainly-cut shirts and pants similar to what Ix was wearing; each had his or her hat on the left knee, legs crossed, back to the padded strip on the wall, hands folded in the lap. Kapilar had followed their example. Since there was an open seat next to him, I took that and also took up the same position.

As my eyes adjusted I saw that Tz'iquin was sitting directly across from me; I didn't know any of the dozen or so others. Ix crossed to the center position on the couch opposite the door and sat down. He was silent for a few seconds. His weight settled; his breathing grew steady, muscles relaxed, focus reached out to the whole room. When he looked at me, automatically I relaxed and concentrated on Ix.

He was working his way around the room, and Kapilar was his next object of focus. I felt the young Tamil next to me relax, straighten, and concentrate, at Ix's invitation. It's a very elementary kind of hypnosis—you learn it as part of the black belt training in ki hara do—and it has a number of functions, most of them benign like making instructions seem clearer and more powerful, improving retention of things heard, and creating an air of awe or of powerful charisma.

I hadn't seen anyone use it here before, so I didn't know whether everyone else in the room knew what was happening to them. For all I knew they might be admiring Ix's technique as much as I was. Or this style of light hypnotic suggestion might be a carefully-kept temple secret, which the others were experiencing as a mysterious power. It didn't matter to me—I had been trained to resist it by going along, until it was time to quietly diverge from whatever path he tried to take me down. The interesting question was why he wanted us all hypnotized, so for right now I didn't want him to know that I wasn't.

When Ix seemed satisfied that everyone was at least in a light trance, he placed his hands, palms up, fingers spread, on his knees, in the position that designated a teacher in so many different cultures. He drew a long breath. Everyone breathed in unison with him.

As he spoke, time began. No anticipation. No surprise. You were in this pleasant, amber-lighted room, hearing the words that started the universe. Ix's technique was even better than I had thought it was.

He spoke Terstad. At first I thought this was because he wanted Kapilar and I to understand, but then I realized it also implied that everyone in the room was educated enough to know it. He spoke of Jaguar Quitze, Sudden Jaguar, Not Right Now, and Dark Jaguar, the four fathers of the Maya, then of how the Maya had come to live in this world where, in the comfort and pleasant security of their stone homes, wrapped up in a city where every place had meaning and every meaning harmonized, they hung between fierce Metallah's deadly light and heat, and the terrible chemical inferno of Xibalbá.

It was a good invocation and I was pretty sure that everyone except me was falling into the more suggestible state that Ix needed. By the end of it he could have told them almost anything and they'd have accepted it.

He stopped, drew another long steady breath, and said, "Well, then. That is who we are, brothers and sisters, and I want you to see that I include my Tamil brother, and my brother from beyond the sky. I have thought and read and looked far and long, and no matter how I look I am forced to say that our ancient texts are full of blood, death, cruelty, and pride, and there is no getting around this.

"When first our people turned to Tohil, when the gods still spoke and the sun had not yet turned them to stone, he pledged that other people would give up their hearts and blood for us to return to him, that we would be great sacrificers. We are pledged to bloodshed. Our stories recount many times when our people have risen in fury against oppression, then to oppress others, and at each turn of the wheel they have fed bloody human hearts to Tohil and his kin. That is who we are. That is who we have been.

"The Temples of the East call us to be who we are."

I felt sick. It sounded as if Ix had fallen into exactly the ideas that Pusiictsom had been working so hard against. Would there be a bloody uprising, then? Should I break the trance and intervene before this turned into anything more? He spoke again.

"And yet, the Center Temple is also correct: we cannot hope to fight, as one small weak culture against more than sixty-one score, to say nothing of taking on mighty Earth itself. If each of our fighters could kill a thousand of those who fought against us, they would barely notice their losses, and we would be extinct. So even if the Tamils vowed to leave Briand forever, there would still be no escape from living with the rest of the Thousand Cultures.

"And yet, as the people we are, as the people we believe ourselves to be, we *cannot* live with them. They will not consent to be our prey or our inferiors, and we do not have the force to compel them, and we will never have such force.

"What is to be done, then? We must live with them, we cannot live with them, and thus we must cease to exist."

I wondered how much paperwork I would have to do if the Maya all killed themselves.

"What we must do, then, is be something else. Something that is also Maya, but not as we have known it. It is this path I hope we can take."

Again he paused for a deep breath. I saw the shadows shift around the room as everyone else breathed in unison with him.

"I give you, then, three principles by which you will be guided as we make a kind of Maya that has not been seen before. The first of these may be the least. From now on, read our texts only to speak of the struggle within. You will not fight with your flesh against anyone else's flesh any more, nor seek to hurt people even if they hate you, nor look for any power or force over the people who choose to be different from you. But you will still hold the texts sacred, and practice the art of reading them, and think on them always. You will understand, however, that when we think of Tohil's promise, we will use it to mean that we accept (that is, we embrace and strive to comprehend) the hearts (that is, the essential natures) of all people, Maya or not. You will never again read it to mean that we tear the living muscle from their chests.

"I wish the Maya always to be conquerors, but only of things inside themselves. Each wrong thing inside you is a person you might have been, and so you must look into that person's eyes, cut them open on the left side, tear out their beating, dripping hearts, and give it up to Tohil. And that is the first principle and that is what needs to be said about that."

He looked around the room from person to person, breathing with each, clearly waiting till he saw assent. He looked at Kapilar for only a single breath. From the corner of my eye I saw both of them, locked in each other's gaze, smile very slightly as if sharing what would become a grin sometime long after this. Whatever agreement Ix sensed in Kapilar, it was more than he had asked and it delighted him.

Ix's gaze came to me at last, and as I returned it I reminded myself that my knee ached slightly from an old injury, the small of my back was a bit compressed, and both my buttocks were getting tired from sitting so long in one position. For good measure

I threw in a memory of a nice little piece of Hedon jazz, an odd little piece in 7/2 that demands good rhythm. As I watched Ix try to get me into a trance, I breathed in time with that song in my memory; since he was trying to get onto my rhythm, this at least gave him a challenge or two to deal with.

His rhythm wasn't quite up to it. It was a direct, if subtle, challenge. I had to know whether Ix was going to be the sort of religious leader the Office of Special Projects could work with, or the sort we would have to work against. We don't *have* beliefs, we *use* beliefs. Ix would be all right if he were willing to use us right back, but didn't care about our indifference to his vision. He would *not* be all right if he set about trying to capture the Council of Humanity itself for the faith—such religious leaders always turned against us when the attempt proved futile.

Before he even finished expounding his basic doctrine, I needed to let Ix know that he could have cooperation but not commitment from me and the people I represented, and I needed to see how he responded to our setting that limit.

He watched me as I sat, openly friendly, accepting his gaze, but refusing to fall into a suggestible state. At last his shoulders rose and fell, not more than a millimeter, but distinctly. We had a deal.

"Brothers," Ix said, "here is the second principle, more important than the first: exclude nothing, bring all things in. For many centuries we have declared more and more things to be not-Maya. 'Since our ancients did not know of it, and could not have named it,' we said again and again, 'it can be no part of us, it is not Maya, we will not see it or know of it, we will prefer our old text to the new things we see and hear all around us.'

"But I say to you, when you see a new thing, let it shine in your mind, so that it lights up the old text and finally the text itself grows to embrace it and all the world becomes Maya. Or I will say it to you simply: be Maya in the world and trust the world to be Maya."

He paused again. Because everyone else was in a state of deep suggestibility by then, I may have been the only person besides Ix himself to know that he hesitated and wet his lips before finally acquiring the composure to go on. "And this last is the most important of all, and the hardest to do.

"We must, as a people, cease our pretense of belief and commit ourselves to the way we know the world to work. We must no more whisper to each other that the Tamils are descended from the subhuman Wood People of our legends. We must take our stories and our customs, walk through the springers into the Thousand Cultures and back onto the Earth and on into the many cultures to be founded in the future, and say to everyone else: 'Here. Share with us. These are our stories and these are our customs. We think they are very beautiful and we hope you will like them too, but they are merely our stories and customs. We would be honored if you would share yours with us, and then let us go, together, to see what is true, to do what we can, and to see what all our poets can make of us after we are gone.

"We must set a boundary in Maya thought, now and forever, between what is true everywhere and for everyone, and what is true for our time and place. And we must accept that once we set such a boundary, the Maya culture itself will slowly dissolve, for slowly our ancestors, myths, and teachers will retreat across that boundary into our past."

He bowed his head for a long time, and when he looked up his voice was softer than a whisper, barely a sigh, but perfectly clear. "I will teach this with all my force tomorrow, in the square in front of this house, one hour before the sun sets. Many will come and understand, and others will come and be angry, and there will be conflict so that some great temples are thrown down, and other great temples are raised up. And my truth, finally, shall conquer.

"You will bring as many of the Maya as you can to the square tomorrow, and do not ask what their lineage is, or whether they are man or woman, or whether they can read and write, or work with their hands, or are great priests. All are invited. Bring them all.

"This gathering is ended."

He rose, quickly and lightly, and was gone before anyone else moved. The door closed silently behind him.

We sat for a moment, all of us like saints in our niches, or plaster Buddhas on a shelf at a souvenir store, in the glow of the sconces, outlined by deep shadows.

Regular flat-white light came on. We might have been in any ordinary room in Yaxkintulum. Everyone shook and shuddered; their breathing desynchronized, and they looked shyly at each other, as if to ask "What was that like for you?"

I stood up, and Kapilar rose beside me; Tz'iquin crossed the little room to join us. "So," he said.

"Yes," Kapilar said.

Each of them had the most blissful smile of sheer joy, and of pure purpose, I had ever seen. In that moment, even knowing that that smile was there only due to their being incompletely recovered from a hypnotic trance, I could hardly help envying them.

Quite early the next morning, Tz'iquin was already out trying to round up people for the great meeting that night in the square, Kapilar was taking a shower, and I had just settled in to try to read yet another essay about Mayan prosody, when there was a chime at the door. I opened it and Ix was there. I asked him to come in.

He sat on one of the benches. I sat next to him, and he said, "This is something that troubles my heart. You are to be my teachings' contact beyond Briand with all the Thousand Cultures. It does not trouble me that you do not believe; I trust you to report accurately, and if the idea is reported accurately, I think enough people will believe. What concerns me is that you may not listen as well as you should, for you seem to be preoccupied."

"I am," I admitted. Perhaps he was trying to think of a reason that his hypnotic techniques hadn't worked on me, and he didn't know about the basic tactics of resistance. Or perhaps he was able to tell that I really was preoccupied. In either case, telling the truth was probably the wisest thing to do, at least until I figured out what all this was about.

"You are a man who is having trouble with the love of a woman," Ix said firmly. "You can't help thinking about her often, wondering why she is angry, blaming yourself, trying to puzzle out how things have gone so badly."

This was a pretty good act but I'd been to a lot of cultures and I knew what a good fortune-teller or mentalist could do, and besides, I very much doubted that Margaret's and my troubles could be remaining entirely within the Embassy; even if Kapilar had been discreet (which I doubted), who knew what the other Tamils among the Embassy employees might be saying, and to whom? What Ix had given me, anyway, was a general-purpose description of what it felt like to have marital problems.

"You are thinking about how many different ways I could have found out about this," he said, "and I didn't mean to try to impress you by knowing it; I thought it was common knowledge, based on what Tz'iquin had told me."

Well, there's nothing more convincing than honesty—and that too can be a tactic. "What exactly did you have to say to me?" I asked.

"Only to beg a favor of you. Only to ask you to open your heart to what I say, and to understand that although I am part of Pusiictsom's political games, and part of the Peccary bid for greater power, and part of the reform movement within our religion—although I am part of all of these, and each of them is a consideration for me—I am also the keeper of an idea which can genuinely help to bring peace. To us, to the Tamils, to the Thousand Cultures . . . and to one marriage, perhaps. Therefore I beg that—as busy as your mind must be with your politics, and with your marriage, and with other things that I probably don't know about—*please* will you do your best to listen and comprehend me accurately? I know it is no part of your job to become a disciple, I know I cannot expect or ask that of you, but please make sure my words reach others accurately."

"Accurate reporting *is* part of my job."

He seemed lost in thought for a long moment; finally he nodded. "It is good that the Council of Humanity and I can find something in common, and that for the moment you can serve us both." He looked down at his hands and said, "Do you see how my ideas can bring peace, perhaps, to your marriage? I would like to bring you that peace, so that you can concentrate on these other matters."

The last thing I wanted was a volunteer marriage counselor, especially one that thought he had a hot line to a variety of gods in which I did not believe. Yet, for my mission it would be good to appear willing to be instructed. Moreover, for all I knew, Ix's advice might be good. He was certainly a smart man of wide experience, and good with people. "Well," I said, having temporized far beyond the point of being polite, "I will listen."

"I want you to talk, also. Now do you see the first principle, that you must find the persons you could have been, who threaten who you are now, and rip out and eat their hearts?"

"I don't much like the people I could have been," I said, imagining myself a dead drunk like poor old Marcabru, or a stuffy academic, or a *tostemz-toszet,* or—

"I did not say you must like them. Second principle. Do you see the importance of finding a way to make the new a part of you, instead of rejecting it as not-you?"

"I've lived in a lot of cultures. I think I'm already pretty good at that."

"Then you should easily be able to do it in your marriage. What is the reason you don't?"

I was taken aback; my first thought was *"What could he be talking about?"* and almost at the same time *"How did he know?"* A moment's thought, though, reassured me that this was another old trick; people with relationship problems nearly always are having trouble accepting some change or other. "I understand what you mean," I said, "but I think it's a common problem to all relationships."

"Could you love Margaret if she were someone else?"

"I could try. I might. Depends on who else."

"Think about that. Now, as for the third principle, that of facing reality . . . do you love this woman?"

"Of course."

"There's no 'of course' about it. I know she's your wife, I know you've been through a great deal together, I know you don't like to discuss your problems outside the couple. I know all those things because they'd be true of anyone in your situation. What I am asking, however, is whether you honestly do love her."

"*Deu-ja!*—uh, yes."

He nodded. "Have you sincerely tried to love her more since the trouble began?"

I nodded, slowly.

"Has it worked?"

"Not at all," I blurted out. "It seems to make matters worse."

"There's the thing you need to face, then," he said. And with that, he got up and left. It was a good curtain line, and it sounded wise. Against my will and better judgement he had impressed me. This was essential if I were to see him as a saintly wise man.

It was such a cunning act that instead of studying, writing reports, or doing anything productive, I spent the rest of the day trying to figure out what he had meant by that parting shot. That last sentence—*There's the thing you need to face, then*—was merely a shrewd-sounding purposely vague aphorism, the stuff of miracle-mongers, oracles, and phony psychics since civilization began.

That did not keep me from turning it over and over in my mind.

I suppose I should not have been surprised at the immense crowd in the plaza that evening. A dozen men and women, in the twelve hours that each of them probably put into it, can talk to a lot of people, and the people they talk to can talk to a lot more people, and so forth. Besides, although Yaxkintulum was technically backward by the standards of most of the Thousand Cultures, still, like all of them it had all the technology that had existed up through the Slaughter and the beginning of the Inward Turn, six hundred years ago. The Maya had all the knowledge they needed to construct computer nets, self-replicating power satellites, food assemblers, nanos, telephones, neroducers and neurobloks, DNA retrodesign, and psypyxes, though they chose not to use some of those possibilities. Certainly there were means enough to ensure that the great majority of the adult population of the city knew when and where Ix was to speak by the time he did. Probably most of them had heard some fairly accurate description of what the new prophet was going to be preaching.

Still, even after explaining that to myself several times, standing there at the front of the house where Ix had spoken, a little back in the doorway to be inconspicuous, I still had to marvel at the size of the crowd. I wanted Margaret here, more than ever, to share the sight with me.

Ix had chosen to speak from the steps of the east-facing pyramid—in Maya symbology, this would signify that he was hearing/asking for the revelation of a new truth. Or perhaps he just preferred not to have the sun in his eyes, or he wanted it in the crowd's eyes so that he would appear indistinct and bigger than life.

The crowd was a mixture: some who would not have looked out of place in the bas-relief on any surface in the city, and others who could have been any tourist in any warm city in any actinic light environment; small children in their mothers' arms, and people so old it was hard to believe they were alive.

The crowd buzzed the way any crowd does when they're all waiting eagerly for something undefined as yet.

Kapilar was leaning in the entryway beside me, out of sight of most of them, hidden by shadow. His dark skin would have been at least as conspicuous as my light beige, and much more likely to draw attack. Locally speaking I was a freak and he was anathema. When Ix started to speak, and the chances of anyone looking over here decreased, we would move to where we could both see the prophet.

Kapilar was watching what he could see of the crowd. "They *look* like enough people to pull down one mighty temple and raise another, don't they?"

"*Ja, m'es vis.* Or if they don't like what Ix says, they look like enough to make him a martyr, or a laughingstock." I turned my shoulder to find a more comfortable way of bracing it against the stones of the doorway. High gravity makes fidgeters of us all. "Considering how hot it is, even this late in the day, I'm amazed that this many people are willing to be in a public square. I suppose prophecy might be, for them, what art, poetry, or music are for your culture or mine."

"The thing their life turns around," Kapilar said, too solemnly. Clearly he was again in the phase where he was going to admire them immoderately. "Yes, I suppose so. They really are quite an astonishing people. I can't imagine I've been living within a kilometer or so of Mayatown all my life and yet never really perceived them before."

I could have reminded him that he was still being hit by the emotional response to his first cross-culture contact, but I didn't see any reason to patronize him. Probably he remembered what I had already told him and was just enjoying this step in the process.

Whatever the case, I let it go. My mind was drifting back to my own first few missions for the Council of Humanity, when I first understood that to say Occitans valued art and honor, or that Caledons centered themselves on righteous work, or that Spartans treasured physical fitness, or that Thorburgers were all soldiers—was all so much crap. We all pursued our various values and cultures for one reason, human space's one real and only supreme value.

We were trying to stave off boredom.

In a world without poverty, where the answer to any question that *could* be answered was available from a machine, and every school of every art had been brought to formal perfection, where even death was rapidly becoming a temporary nuisance, we were all just players at history. I had gotten a song out of that thought, "Echoes After the Aftermath," and the recording of it had been well-received in many cultures. But I hadn't come up with a solution for that problem, any more than anyone else had; describing it was the kind of trivial thing a competent artist can do at twenty-five, solving it was out of reach for fifty billion humans in six hundred years.

So I kept my mouth shut, because although there was truth in my thoughts, there was a sense in which Kapilar *was* right. The Maya, more than any of the Thousand Cultures, had turned their backs on all the other cultures and tried to slide away into their own myth. And though the myth had no more made them real than any of our myths had made any of the other cultures real, what it *had* done was to isolate them and give them an elaborate structure of denials and barriers to protect them from reality.

This had crippled them from the standpoint of coping successfully with the rest of the human race, and it might well mean the immediate end of their culture instead of the slow dissolution and assimilation that had happened or was happening to most. In a general way I had grounds to hope that no sudden or catastrophic collapse would happen: the higher ranking Maya, who had to interact with the outside, were in most ways just shy extreme eccentrics in the greater world of Interstellar metaculture. If they retained their places in the Maya culture, then no doubt they would be able to steer the rest into a gradual and successful accomodation with this new, Interstellar age. It would be difficult, of course, due to the lies that the Maya ruling class had propagated to their ordinary people, allowing them to forget that they did not have to raise food to eat, that most of what they did with scraped hands and aching backs could have been done for them better by machines, and that the powers of their priests were not gifts of the gods but the execution of priestly specifications by the aintellects that ran the powersats, nanos, neuroducers, and assemblers. But lots of cultures had recovered from the exposure of worse and bigger lies, and at least Ix's ideas included the importance of exposing the lie; not all of them would have to be dragged unwillingly to the truth.

And yet despite all the reasons why these things had to be, and all the reasons to hope that the process would not be impossibly painful, I couldn't help feeling sorry for them; it seemed to me that they were about to lose something unique in the Thousand Cultures, something that I wasn't quite sure how to formulate. I thought *they got to be somebody purely by being allowed to forget that nowadays everyone is nobody.* Just for a moment I wondered if Shan and the Office of Special Projects were right. What harm had the Maya ever done anyone by just living where they were in the way they did?

The "undisturbed" Maya were living out the fantasies of the elites; no one had asked them if they wanted to be isolated, let alone whether they wanted starvation or disease to be part of their lives. And thoroughly as the elites might believe that a naive misery, ignorant of the possibility that things need not be this way, was good for the lower classes, they would never test their hypothesis, because they themselves would never be ignorant in that way.

And always there was the OSP's overwhelming argument for why we were pushing humanity back together again as fast as we could: the aliens. Twenty-six ruins on nineteen different worlds, including the little radio listening post recently discovered on Charon. A dozen long dead probes found orbiting various suns of human space. Four ghost ships in long cometary orbits. All of the sites and objects dated from the early second or late third myriadium before the present, insofar as they could be dated at all. None bore any mark of being intentionally left for us or anyone else. Indeed, the ones on Nansen and Dunant looked more like long-term survival camps than anything else, presumably built by castaways.

Whether those particular aliens would ever return did not matter nearly as much as the possibility that someday, somewhere, as humans expanded out into the space around us, humans would meet aliens, and whenever we did it was vital that they meet a unified humanity. Remember, in human history, what happened to every group of indigenes unlucky enough to be in disarray when they were found by a more sophisticated society.

It would be better still if whoever the aliens first met were some group of people who would represent humanity as it was, rather than some local mythic version of it. Humanity lived in a three-pronged lump of space with huge gaps in its surface— thirty-nine worlds (counting Earth itself and the seven permanently settled worlds in the Sol system) dusted very thinly into the 150,000 cubic light years that a sphere embracing all of human space would have to be. For all we knew there could be ten alien bases closer to Earth than some of the colony worlds, and a thousand starships a year could be entering and exiting "our" space without ever coming to our attention.

The thinness of our settlement, and the vast distances between settled planets, meant that was no real "frontier"—the first aliens who approached us were just as likely to suddenly appear at the post office in Tehran as they were to land here on Briand, or on Addams, the two settled planets farthest from Sol.

Therefore no matter where the aliens showed up, whoever met them needed to be someone representative of the whole. All I had to do to convince myself of the importance of this was to imagine an alien spaceship showing up in orbit around Wilson before the springer had transformed Nou Occitan. Half the Occitans would have leaped up to make demands of the aliens, probably mostly that the aliens settle all artistic questions right now, and the other half would have demanded that the aliens be forced to go away. And as for any impression that the aliens might have gotten about what the human race in general was like—well, it was just very, very fortunate that no such thing had happened.

Humanity under the Council of Humanity might be a lot less varied, and the Office of Special Projects was encouraging it to become dull and disappointingly bland. But at least this way whoever made first contact would represent all of us and would not *deliberately* foster misunderstandings.

So, I reminded myself, the Maya had to be like the rest of us on the vanishingly small chance that they would have to represent us.

I didn't like that train of thought. In my early twenties I had spent a lot of time fighting on the losing side to protect Occitan culture, brawling with the Interstellar-minded Occitans who were trying to join the rest of humanity. If the springer had never happened, I would, today, be teaching lute, tending a small vegetable garden, making a little wine, and probably writing elegant despairing verse as I felt the first pangs of age. Compared with this crazy, dangerous business, that seemed pretty appealing.

By now many people in the crowd had inflated the small air cushions everyone here carried, and sat down cross-legged on the pavement of the square. Because of the high gravity and the way the sun heated any exposed surface, no one went anywhere without the means to sit down. If you had more than a short wait, you popped the cap on your cushion, squeezed the activate, and sat down on the little torus that looked a lot like the gadget my father had had when his hemorrhoids were particularly bad.

"Curious," I said. "See how they're willing to stand on the stones inlaid into the pavement, but not to sit on them?"

Kapilar nodded. "I just saw a young mother move her child from sitting on an illustration. I wonder how the rule works? Among us Tamils the *feet* are profane and we'd worry about keeping that off sacred text. But I suppose another way to look at it is that one way to get to know a sacred text is to walk it. Or maybe standing doesn't prevent other people from reading— they can wait till you move—but sitting does."

"Your guess is as good as mine. I just thought a consistent

pattern of behavior was interesting." The crowd noise sounded like they expected something to start right now, so I leaned out a little distance from the doorway, looking up toward the temple. No one was looking our way, anyway.

Ix wasn't there yet, but they had begun to lean toward the temple as if to pull him out, a focus and intensity spreading through them like ground waves in an earthquake. The buzz became softer, faster, more excited, the way a person does when he's telling a very private story with an exciting ending. Gesturing to Kapilar that he could follow, I moved out of the doorway, inflated my cushion, and sat, avoiding inscriptions and illustrations. Kapilar sat beside me a moment later. Everyone was so intent upon the temple in front of us that we might as well have been invisible.

When Ix came out of the temple and part way down the steps, he looked like a giant. Then my eyes adjusted and I saw that despite his new short haircut, he was wearing a shoulder harness, rigid decorated girdle, and high headdress. To my inexpert eye the style looked not just traditional but archaic.

The crowd fell silent as if cut off with a switch. Ix's face, shadowed by the overhang of his headdress, was invisible. When at last he spoke, I could hear him clearly, eighty meters away, and also the echoes of his words, a second later, bouncing back to me from the row of houses at the back of the square. I heard every syllable distinctly but since he spoke Mayan and my grasp of the spoken language was still chancy, about all that I could tell reliably was that he was mainly speaking in verse.

There were many allusions to familiar myth. From the occasional simple sentences at the conclusions of sections, I gathered that he was setting forth the three principles we had heard the night before. The crowd reacted to them with gasps, moans, and a low buzz of excitement. Ix had said, when we had seen him briefly in the Center Temple in the late afternoon, that he was aiming for a very conservative and traditional expression of novel ideas, so that people could not complain about esthetic lapses nor pretend they hadn't understood him. He wanted to give them little choice but to reject or accept what he said, to make it impossible to ignore him or distort his words into some simple easily-rejected formula.

I could tell they were excited but I couldn't tell whether they wanted to hear more or him to shut up. Whichever, he had their attention.

He went on. In a period of a few moments, the quick-but-not-instant sunset of Briand swept through the square, shadows visibly lunging across the space, darkness flowing like thick cool syrup over the hot pavement. The crowd seemed more intent on Ix's less distinct form, moving in time with his cadences like a single beating heart. The shadow of the temple rolled over the edge of the crowd, then poured up the wall of rowhouses at the back of the square. Still Ix continued to preach, and did not even sound tired.

After a while, the wind was rising, first signal that the night storm was on its way up out of Xibalbá. I still could catch only scattered phrases of what Ix was saying, but it sounded like he was working his way through the permutations of the stem-anagrams of his "three principles." If I understood the little bit of Maya prosody I had learned, this was traditional in a prophet.

The rising wind, steady rather than gusty, was deliciously cool. Above I could see just a few bright stars overhead; the rest of the sky was rimmed in dark—the onrushing ring of clouds that would bring the night storm. Taking my attention away from Ix, I sat back and looked straight up to watch the sky iris shut.

Ix's voice rose in volume and deepened in pitch. Probably he was reaching for power for his conclusion. The clouds closed around the last small cluster of stars.

From all directions at once the square exploded with light. I was looking up and so took the worst of it in my peripheral vision but that was bad enough; with my pupils dilated by the darkness, the light was hot oil in my eyes.

We had barely time to gasp—thousands of people all at once,

like the cry of a great wounded monster. Before I had gotten my hands over my eyes, the fierce throbbing siren spiked my ear drums. People everywhere around me bounded up, but, blinded and deafened, could do nothing more than grope about wildly, with no direction or purpose of motion.

Every time I have ever seen riot police hit a crowd, before or since that night, they have come in slowly, creating an impression of massive force grinding inexorably toward the crowd. It's a way to get a crowd to break and run. The few people who are dumb enough to stand their ground, or unlucky enough to fall under the advancing police line, get hurt, but normally a line of riot police allows most of the crowd to escape, so that the fleeing front ranks spread panic, indecision, and flight back through the crowd into the rear ranks. After all, the point of riot police is to *disperse* a riot. If you want to stop the riot, it's more effective to make them all run away from each other than to hit each of them individually with a nightstick.

But there was no riot here and the cops had no intention of merely dispersing us. They charged in fast from all directions at once, not in the usual walls and phalanxes of riot shields, but in tight little knots of flailing clubs, laying into the crowd as if they were chopping brush.

This happened in no more than the time it takes to draw two breaths. Then the siren switched off. That was worse—I could hear the screams and cries of those being struck and the moist massy thud of nightsticks on ribs and bellies.

Kapilar, standing beside me, took a quarter of a step toward the milling, rushing, terrified crowd, but I caught his arm and shouted into his ear, "Nothing we can do! This is what they always planned to do—no way to stop it or help—" I dragged him back through the doorway into the rowhouse where we had met Ix and his disciples the night before. The door fell shut behind us, closing off my backward glimpse of a Maya cop standing over a fallen man, holding his head up by the long hair and jabbing the end of a baton against his nose and teeth.

For one long second after that blessed door closed and reduced the pandemonium outside to a distant devil's cacophony, I stood gasping, still gripping Kapilar's shirt, the sound of my own breath roaring in and out and the blood bulging my eardrums in subsonic pulses, almost drowning out the screams and cries of the beaten.

I caught my breath and let go of Kapilar. We went down the hall to the inner chamber where we had met the night before. Three others—two men and a woman—from last night's original group were there before us. They sat in the corner, huddled against each other, weeping.

I should have said something to them or tried to lead them to safety, but I was so shocked and disoriented that I just sank to the padded bench next to Kapilar, in a stupor. My only conscious thought was relief that I could no longer hear the screams.

Kapilar leaned forward beside me, his head in his hands. "Oh, Murukan, Murukan, why did they, I mean, did they have to, oh Murukan . . . "

I ached all over from much more than the high gravity. Tears leaked from the corners of my eyes. I wiped them away angrily with the heels of my hands. "We weren't listening," I said. Unbearable clarity rang in my head the way a sucker-kick takes a beginning martial artist in the gut. "They even told us. That he had to preach his message. That he had to be rejected. That he had to flee, and be driven into fleeing by the authorities. You see it, don't you, *companhon, deu, deu,* this is all just Act One of some incredibly elaborate show that they mean—"

The door swung open. The Maya cop who came in held a baton up with one hand and beckoned with the other. We and the three Maya got up and followed him down the hall. At one junction our Maya comrades were handcuffed and led away. I asked several times where they were being taken and what was going on—feeling ridiculous, knowing that whatever happened to them was merely calculated for some effect that Pusiictsom and Tz'iquin wanted to achieve, and whether they were released tomorrow or tortured to death tonight depended only on the exact show that the Center Temple priests and the Peccary lineage intended to put on.

No one bothered to answer me. I wondered if the prisoners knew they were just part of an elaborate drama, or if any of the police did.

After the three Maya prisoners were led off, a Maya cop, out of uniform but still very obviously a cop, came in and asked Kapilar and me who we were, as if any other Tamil and any other pale Caucasian might have been found in this place at this time. We let him look at our papers to confirm it. I tried to invoke diplomatic immunity. He gave me a long stare.

He said we would have to come with him. After a long ride in a police truck I discovered another point of cultural consistency: in Yaxkintulum the prison cells have surrounding benches, just like every other room.

I was sick about what had happened, especially considering that Pusiictsom had as good as told me what they were going to do and I still hadn't seen it coming, but I wasn't worried about my safety. I doubted that they would dare do much to a Council of Humanity diplomat. I had been through a number of rebellions, coups, and disorders, and as a general rule my job had been to hang around in a state of acute boredom until the time came to look presentable and calm and pretend to be on top of the situation.

The moment the cops showed up in this building, I had set off a little transponder concealed in the button of my trousers. Probably right now Margaret was leaning across Ambassador Kiel's desk and telling him what he was going to fix and how soon. Shan was very likely on the line as well—Office of Special Projects communiqués have been known to work miracles.

Not that I was especially valuable. I was a middle-quality bureaucrat with a record of good luck. But as a matter of principle, the Council of Humanity never dithered around or waffled when any of us were in trouble.

A big part of what power and effectiveness the Council had depended on maintaining an image of being bad to get on the bad side of. That image demanded that they show no tolerance at all for even the slightest mistreatment of employees. So anything from bail, lawyers, and bribes, right up to a couple of companies of CSPs—whatever it took—would be arriving soon.

Once we were out of here, whenever it was next to their advantage, the Council would settle scores, and I doubted that Pusiictsom would enjoy that either, so there wasn't even much point in fretting about getting even with the old bastard—that too would happen in good time. Meanwhile the reasonable thing to do was to get caught up on sleep.

I could have slept if Kapilar had not decided to spend the night pacing, fretting, and asking questions. You'd think the high gravity would get someone to stop pacing after a while, but apparently worry was a more powerful force than sore feet. Not knowing whether the cell was bugged or not (but I'd have been surprised if it had not been) I couldn't exactly explain things to him. So I stretched out, ignored Kapilar as best I could, and thought about the one thing that was still puzzling me: how Ix would get over to New Tanjavur's Mayatown. I expected I would know that by the end of the day tomorrow at latest, but at least it was a moderately interesting puzzle for the moment. I didn't make much progress on it, but then I was tired, upset, and harassed by Kapilar's pacing and questions.

Still, I managed to nap now and then, and was able to look human when Pusiictsom, Tz'iquin, and a couple of acolytes showed up, opening the door and gesturing for us to follow them.

There was no trace of any guard in the corridor. Probably they had been pulled.

The two acolytes looked nervous and upset, and considering that they were carrying nightsticks and handcuffs, I tried not to do anything to alarm them. Pusiictsom and Tz'iquin appeared calm and comfortable enough.

We walked a long time, far enough so that my already-tired legs began to get more score. Now and then we'd take a turn to the left or right, always into another corridor just like the one we had been on, windowless and blank except for an occasional un-marked door. Sometimes we got onto an elevator, rode briefly, and then resumed our long walk through the corridors.

No one spoke during the whole long walk, probably more than two kilometers (though I was so disoriented by the alikeness of every passage and the quiet that I would not be surprised to learn it was more than five kilometers or less than one). In all that time the only sounds I heard were people breathing and the soft scrape of sandals on the carpet. Finally we entered another corridor, no different from any other, and stopped at a door that looked just like the hundreds we had passed. Pusiictsom opened it.

Ix was in there, asleep on the couch opposite the door, dressed in plain pants and shirt as he had been when he first preached to the small group of followers. He jumped awake at Tz'iquin's touch. The way he moved told me he'd had a beating, probably not enough for serious injuries but more than sufficient to leave him sore in most of his large muscles. They had spared his face.

He smiled, recognizing us, and said, "I've been expecting you."

"Indeed," Pusiictsom said, not returning the smile or even looking at the prophet. "There's not much time. *Donz* Leones, I am told that you are a martial artist?"

"I have a black belt in ki hara do. I haven't practiced in half a stanyear."

"You're more than sufficient for the purpose. Would you please beat these two acolytes, and then, if you would, would you and Kapilar please tie them up?"

Suddenly I knew why the two young men had seemed nervous and frightened. They had known this was coming; they were being set up as the guards who had been overpowered.

I hesitated a moment while I thought of how to proceed. Even in the rest of the Thousand Cultures where there were flying springer-ambulances and emergency on-the-spot neuroreplacements and organ substitutes, concussions and body blows were dangerous. It was too easy to rupture something or give someone permanent damage. With the more primitive medical facilities here, accidentally killing these poor bastards was a real possibility. I studied the acolytes for a long moment, which I'm sure only made them more afraid.

I had no other plan and there was no escape available except this one. Pusiictsom knew his local situation better than I did; maybe this really was the only way.

I only hesitated a second or two. I'm sure that was too long for those poor acolytes. I moved toward one, faked a blow that made him jump back, and then grabbed the other by the tunic with both my hands. I knotted the fabric together between my fists, spun in under his balance point, dropped to one knee, and threw him hard, saving just enough so the back of his head didn't hit. It brought him down on his back in a hard slam that would leave his ribs bruised and sore.

I turned out of the throw and hurled myself onto him, knocking the wind out of him, then put him into a tight cradle hold. "Tie his hands and feet," I told Kapilar, "and be careful that you don't tie *mine.*" I tightened my grip, feeling him gasp with pain.

Bits of fabric flipped over and around my head and arms as Kapilar tied him. (We found out later that they were torn from some of Kapilar's clothing that they had taken from his luggage, and he was furious that they had done that without asking him).

When the acolyte was thoroughly tied I pulled out and sat up. The poor *toszet* looked a complete mess, and somehow I had given him a bloody nose that was getting all over everything. I turned him on his side so that his nose could drain, muttering. "Sorry." He just panted; perhaps I had overdone the pain.

I turned to the other acolyte, who had been watching all of this, and reached for his shirt.

He fell limp in a faint.

I fought down the qualms about hitting an unconscious man; this was probably better for both of us. Then I kicked him hard, several times, in large muscles where he would be bruised but not seriously hurt, I hoped. Kapilar and the others looked away while I did it. When I saw that, I really hated them.

When I finished, Kapilar knelt and tied up the second acolyte, still unconscious. "He's all right," I said, after checking his pulse. "I guess he's the lucky one."

The other acolyte, his face still bloody, groaned.

Pusiictsom kicked him, hard, and he cried out in pain.

"Quiet," the old priest said. "Remember your vows. Concentrate on how much depends on your keeping your story straight. Do that well and you will advance; make a mess of it and you will be in Xibalbá before you know it." He turned to Kapilar, Tz'iquin, and me. "You are going to steal the family yacht and fly with Ix to New Tanjavur. Ix will inform you of any special needs after he arrives. Grandson, you are to convert to Ix's prophecy on your arrival. I envy you that; I won't be able to convert, myself, for at least two more stanyears, I think, and it is a very beautiful prophecy, one of the best our people have ever had, in this old man's opinion."

Then, looking at Kapilar, he asked, "Does it seem good to you?"

"The prophecy is indeed beautiful," Kapilar said, "even to a Tamil, and I'm sure at least some of my people will be fascinated by it. You can find some support, anyway, among our younger poets, who will gladly do anything that offends their elders."

"Young poets are alike everywhere," Pusiictsom said, smiling for the first time that evening.

"I'm afraid that there is nothing that will convert *all* the Tamils," Kapilar said. "It is not in our nature to be an 'all.' "

"We must learn that from you," Pusiictsom said, "just as you must learn how to be an 'all' from us. There is much to talk about if we can get our peoples to talk at all. May what we do tonight bring it sooner."

He turned to me and said, "I will not disparage your intelligence by pretending that you don't know what's going on. May I ask you to tell me frankly where the Council of Humanity will stand on this matter?"

I pulled my concentration together through the curtain of weariness, trying to ignore my disgust at what I had gotten into. "Well, we favor peace and unity. We are not above using deception to get it. And we believe in working with local people by local methods whenever we can. It will be necessary for the Embassy to formally protest my arrest, and that of my assistant, and they will also emphatically defend our decision to escape with these two political refugees."

Pusiictsom bowed slightly, a smile twitching at the corner of his mouth. The second acolyte was now waking up, groaning in pain, and Tz'iquin kicked him and told him to be quiet. Then he turned toward us and said, "That is what we expect the Council of Humanity to do. It will strengthen our position here, and that will strengthen our mutual cause."

"Let me remind you that *I* am not a convert to the new prophecy," I said. "And if any of our regular Embassy staff show any signs of becoming converts, we will spring that person to a mental hospital back on Earth immediately."

Pusiictsom nodded. "Regrettable but understandable. Now, I very strongly suspect that rumors will circulate in both the Maya and the Tamil communities that your escape was a very daring and exciting thing. You will find a version of the story of your escape for your study in the family yacht, which I suggest you all memorize and then destroy before arrival. It is in accord with what a variety of witnesses will becoming forward to say here. And that, I think, is all the preparation we *can* make. From here on improvisation will actually be better."

He bowed again, solemnly, and then added, just to Ix, "As I said, it is a fine vision and a splendid prophecy, which will live to become part of the Maya. I feel that very surely." Then he nodded once more and left us.

Leaving the "guards" tied, Ix, Kapilar, and I followed Tz'iquin, nearly running, through another seemingly endless tangle of corridors. My feet were aching again long before we burst around a corner and breathed dark, cool outside air, at the base of some pyramid within the city, definitely *not* the Center Temple. During our long time below ground the night storm had passed, leaving the stones slick with water and the air damp, fresh, and bracing.

The yacht stood there in the courtyard, a black shape glinting with silver, like a giant sculpture of an Industrial Age airplane, its curves marked mainly by the way they blotted out the stars and the soft glow of the buildings beyond, highlighted at various points by little streaks of gleaming silver where some stray light caught a surface.

We crossed the pavement to the steps, ascended into the yacht's silver belly, and headed back to the observatory, following Tz'iquin. We had barely seated ourselves when he said, "Now fasten the safety belts beside you. We're about to do something authentic-looking." Before he could get his own belt fastened, he fell sideways as the yacht lurched fifty meters or more into the air. I grabbed his arm and steadied him; he pushed himself back into his seat and yanked the belt on hastily. As he was fastening it, we dropped several meters, then rose again. The yacht began to move forward, rapidly picking up speed.

There was a bright flash below and in front of us. "Was that—" Kapilar asked.

"A shell burst," Tz'iquin said. "Absurd as it is in this century, Yaxkintulum has an air-defense system, which is trying to find us through a virtual fog, induced by a special virus that the temple technicians fed it earlier tonight. Supposedly the one thing it can't do is shoot where we are."

Those temple technicians must have done it right, because though the yacht jumped all over the sky as it rose, the explosions remained an interesting fireworks display rather than a threat. Knowing that they were shooting near-but-not-at us made the whole experience into a dull dramatization of an escape. I just wanted the shooting to be over so that I could get some food and sleep. Within a few minutes we had danced and bounced our way through the sky above the vast expanse of softly shining pyramids and temples, on out over the surrounding plateau, flying low, I assumed, to drop off radar as quickly as possible. No doubt we were doing something to evade overhead satellites as well, and no doubt it was just as staged.

"Just what other weapons have you been concealing over here for all this time?" Kapilar asked. "You have an air defense system; what else do you have? Nuclear bombs?"

"No nuclear bombs to my knowledge," Tz'iquin said. "The air defense system is a compromise, and an absurd one, which also protects us against orbital attack, supposedly. A battery of high-velocity guns, electric-boosted ones, that throw explosive shells like the ones we just saw. It couldn't stop a real attack for ten minutes."

"That's not a compromise," Kapilar pointed out, "that's a violation of the colonization charter you settled under, and it's also a violation of the treaty in which we ceded you the land for Yaxkintulum. And if you've been hiding one set of weapons from us all this time, what's to keep you from hiding a lot more?"

"It's a domestic compromise," Tz'iquin said, impatiently. "You know perfectly well we have a lot of hotheads and romantics who think that we should never have given up warfare. Their excuse is always that the Tamils might attack us any time. And many of the Maya listen to them, especially because so few Maya know any Tamils. So there was always a great demand that we arm ourselves. Those of us with more sense were able to keep it to purely defensive weapons; none of those guns has a range over a hundred kilometers. That's all. And I'm telling you about them now. Yes, we have a lot of secrets, but we'll drag them out into the open, eventually, all of them."

Kapilar shook his head, stubbornly. "The Maya had no right to build weapons. And with the hatred there is between the two peoples, you've given the Tamil every reason to be afraid of you—"

"Which is why there must be no hatred, someday," Ix said. "The weapons will be thrown away when they are seen as what they are, toys for lunatics. And what we must do is hasten the day when that is what is seen." He turned to Tz'iquin, who was nodding in a very satisfied way, and said, "But that day must be *hastened,* and so I assure you, we *will* demand—our whole movement, Maya and Tamil—that you disarm *now,* without any preconditions."

"That's going to make a lot of trouble," Tz'iquin muttered.

"A lot of trouble is just what's needed," Ix said.

Tz'iquin glared at the floor, clenching and working his hands together. "It seems to me that a prophet of peace would want to—"

"Peace is good. So is truth, so is justice. Not least because peace itself requires both. First we settle the outstanding wrongs; then there will be space and time in which to live at peace. Meanwhile, let *your* peace be internal, because in the wider world we are surely going to make an uproar, Tz'iquin. We can't do otherwise. You yourself suggested revealing the air defense system to Kapilar as a gesture of our trust in him."

"I didn't know he was going to react like this!"

"You are obligated to tell people the truth. They are not obligated to like you for it."

After a long silence, Kapilar murmured, "Tz'iquin, I trust you, personally, to be honest with me."

Tz'iquin nodded but did not look up. At last he said, "I am sorry that we violated our agreements. I am working to make my people live up to their bargains."

Kapilar nodded. "I see that."

We were leaving the shell bursts behind us, creating the impression that we were pulling out of range. Then four shells exploded in rapid succession not far behind us, and the whole craft shook and bounced. We all jumped and cried out—for an instant

I thought that Pusiictsom had changed his mind, or that the aintellects that controlled the guns had recovered from their virusing.

Then, looking around at us, and pointing to himself, Tz'iquin laughed. "It's one thing to know the plan and another thing to remember it while it happens," he said. "That was supposed to be the signal for us to stop taking evasive action, so that should be the end of the dramatic part of the escape. Let me order some breakfast, and then we'll all get to work memorizing the harrowing details of our daring escape."

It took two hours to get the story completely straight between all of us. By the time Metallah rose, roiling the cloudscape of Xibalbá, we were more than halfway back to New Tanjavur. We had been studying diligently, memorizing critical details and explanations, eating *ceehel uah* hot and greasy from the little galley oven and drinking bitter chocolate. We all took a break to watch the crimson sunrise run out ahead of us, lighting and shaping the clouds, turning them from red to white in less than a minute. The deep shadows from the low-angled sun showed the peaks, spires, bubbles, and domes of the lower atmosphere in sharp relief, as if we looked down into a soft, gently rounded hell.

After that none of us had energy to go on trying to get perfect versions of our stories memorized. We went to our cabins, with time for nearly five hours' sleep or so before we would have to be up and about for the approach to New Tanjavur. I dropped off so quickly that afterward I didn't remember getting into bed. My dreams were wild and dark, full of blood and vague threats, and I wandered through them looking for Margaret and not finding her.

Part Three

Not Right Now

Kurinci

Not Right Now: Third born of the people. Things to come. Hopes.

Kurinci: strobilanthes, a blue flower that grows only above 1800 meters and is said to blossom every twelve years.

In the akam poems: The mountains. The night (friendly to lovers). The place of the monkey, tiger, bear, elephant, peacock, and parrot. The people stand guard over their fields of millet, gather honey, play and bathe in the streams and waterfalls, and eat millet and mountain rice. Union. The lovers meet and are joined.

In the puram poems: vetci, the cattle raid; prelude to war.

The world dominated by Murukan, Siva's second son, called Skanda in Sanskrit, a smiling lover, god of wisdom, learning, poetry, beauty.

The first thing I did when I got back to the Embassy was to sleep all day. Margaret said she could keep people away from me for a while, and she had filed a memo that would stall Shan until I was fit to make a full report. It felt wonderful to just let myself collapse. I was dimly aware of a quick hug from Margaret and then of the pillow touching my head again.

I woke up near sunset, feeling grotty all over and drenched in stale sweat. When you move around the Thousand Cultures all the time, you're constantly exposed to one version and then another of the common cold and flu bugs. Miss a day's sleep or take on too much stress, and something or other attacks, despite all the immune boosters they keep pumping into us. At least it felt like I had slept through the worst of it.

Gingerly, I pushed the covers off and stretched a leg over the side. My aching muscles, cold sweaty skin, and musty mouth all confirmed that I had a minor infection. Aside from mildly sore ears, it seemed to be on the wane.

You don't spend a decade of getting these without developing a ritual to cope with them. I went to the food slot and punched in for a tall hot glass of Old American—the mild watery coffee some people like with breakfast—and, when it slid out a moment later, used it to take some ava's (the standard aspirin-vitamin-antivirals from my travel kit), plus a couple of caffeine tabs. I drank the rest of the coffee straight off, enjoying the warmth and moisture in my throat and sinuses, and then took a hot shower.

As usual the aspirin, caffeine, and steamy air worked miracles. I would just have to trust the antivirals to do their bit. By the time I turned off the shower, I was hungry, and feeling no worse than a little tired. Margaret was waiting and handed me a big, hot towel, a small gesture that pleased me very much. As I toweled off, she and I at last got to talk.

"Well," she said, "You have a knack for a dramatic exit. On your way out of here, you give me the best time we've had in bed in years. On your way back you shoot your way out of a Maya prison, with the bloodhounds baying after you, and hijack a high official's yacht. What shall I pack for our next transfer, a pistol and a parachute?"

"I liked the first exit better," I said, "and if it's up to me, that's how I'll take all of them." I dragged the rough warm towel over my back and pressed it into the aching small, getting one more little touch of warmth onto the place that had hurt ever since I came to Briand. "And the real story of the escape isn't nearly as exciting as all that, but it's something you and I need to talk about, and pass on to Shan. Also, I seem to be starving. If you want to order a huge dinner, over which I can tell you what's really been going on, I would have no objections."

"Already ordered it," she said. "A hectare's crop of potatoes and a boiled sheep should be turning up any minute, along with a whole huge compost heap of smelly vegetables."

Boiled dinner was a favorite of mine but not of hers. It was a traditional Caledon meal, something she had grown up eating every few days, and her years of travel had given her a taste for many more exotic flavors than plain bland Caledon food. I had first encountered boiled dinner in Caledony, along with hard physical labor and a truly nasty climate, all of which help one appreciate plenty of soft meat and starch.

"And we have the night off," she added. "Shan is expecting no report till late tomorrow and there are no meetings. So I suggest that after you get dry you just stay as you are—we have no particular reason to leave the apartment."

"Agreed, if you'll wear a matching outfit." It had been a while since I had seen my wife naked, and I was looking forward to it.

A few minutes later, as I finished drying, the apartment springer chimed, and I heard Margaret open the door and wheel the serving table in. A rich steamy smell of cooked meat and vegetables filled the room, and I hurried to dry off, my mouth already watering.

When I came out of the bathroom, dry and combed but naked as requested, Margaret was nude as well, smiling shyly. I took her hand and seated her at the table. I couldn't quite remember the last time we had spent an evening like this.

I glanced again at her and liked what I saw; every curve, line, and plane of her was familiar and comforting.

At first we just ate. When we had settled in and relaxed, and the need to get food into myself wasn't quite so urgent, I told her the whole story of the escape, leaving nothing out since she needed to understand that Pusiictsom and Tz'iquin, while currently on our side, were dangerous, smart people with few scruples.

The major news in New Tanjavur was that there had been several trakcars overturned by a Tamil mob, and a number of Maya had been beaten, none fatally, that day. It was believed that the mob had originally gathered to go to a reading of the new issue of *Palai*, but that could not be established and Kannan was denying any connection—while running editorials insisting that all those arrested should be released at once.

After dinner we sat on the sofa together, with one of my better recordings playing softly—it was the "Love Found Again" cycle of songs by Guilhem-Arnaut Montanier, in my arrangement for two lutes, recorder, and voice. As a child I had sometimes been moved to tears by that music and unable to listen to it because it was too intensely sad. As a *jovent*, when I had made this recording, I had found it to be profound. In later years I had felt embarrassed when people in a variety of cultures congratulated me on the recording, for I found it silly and sentimental, a reminder that I had once been very naive in my idealism. Now, listening to it at the age at which Guilhem-Arnaut had written it, there was irony I had not detected when I was younger, which you had to have suffered irrevocable aging to understand, combined with a joyful leap into a love affair that Guilhem-Arnaut knew he was too old for, but refused to resist.

I wondered how, when I was a *jovent* of twenty-one stanyears, I had managed to find that particular feeling, without knowing it was there.

"I'm glad you put this one on," Margaret said. I liked the firm press of her heavy body against my ribs and hip, and the slightly uncomfortable weight of her head on the peak of my shoulder. "It's always been one of my favorites, and there was a long time when you didn't like it much."

"I'm thinking that during the break after this trip I'll get my voice back into shape and record it again. I was really just a boy when I sang it and I don't think I understood enough of what I was singing."

"Aren't you afraid that now you'd understand too much?"

"I suppose that's always a risk, but I'd like to do it. Our Wilson-year anniversary is coming up, anyway, and I might want to do it so that I can dedicate it to you for that."

One advantage of living a life of constant springer trips was that it gave you more anniversaries to celebrate. We had been married just over twelve stanyears, but the stanyear only corresponds to the year on Earth. We had also been married for four and a half Nansen-years (the year of Caledony), and because Wilson circled Arcturus at such a great distance, we were just about to have our first Wilson-anniversary, a big occasion back in Nou Occitan.

She squirmed. Like an idiot, I asked, "What's the matter?"

"Well, it's just . . . you've been good about birthdays, Caledon holidays, and anniversaries, and all that, Giraut, I don't mean that you're ignoring anything, but . . . well. I don't—that is." My heart sank. When Margaret had trouble getting words out, usually she was upset. What had I done? "Um," she said, "it's just that I know the Wilson-anniversary will be very important to you, and I know that's because you love me and all that stuff, but Giraut, sometimes I just wish I didn't always get the feeling that

Nou Occitan was the only real place in all of human space to you. Does that make any sense? Or am I being unfair?"

"Never unfair, *companhona*," I said, denying the thought before it had time to emerge. "I . . . well, I suppose I do think of Nou Occitan, very much, as home. And we don't get back to Caledony often enough, I know, and your parents are getting older."

She turned away angrily. "That isn't what I meant at all. I'm not making sense to you, am I?"

"I'm trying, Margaret. I'm trying. If you feel that my feelings are too bound up in Nou Occitan, well, you know me best, and if it hurts you, well, then I need to—"

"*No!*" It was almost a shout. "Let me—that's not what—oh, shit, shit, shit, Giraut, I told you I couldn't explain it. I feel like our whole life together is one long vacation that you're taking until you die, and then they'll put your psypyx onto your clone and you'll get to go back to being a *jovent* in the Quartier. I feel like this is all some long dream to you, like you don't treat this like it *is* your life. And I don't *want* to go back to Caledony any more than I have to, and I don't *want* to go to Nou Occitan either, I just want you to commit to *me* and the *OSP* and the *Council* and all the other things that you supposedly work for and quit treating your life as a hobby to kill time before you die. I don't want my marriage to be a reason for going to another big party at Elinorien!"

"Then we won't," I said.

"But that's not right either! You see you're not even committed to being really Occitan, Giraut, you can give that up just as easily too."

"Now wait—" I said, still more bewildered than angry.

"No, listen. This is what drives me crazy, Giraut. You do so many things so well. You do things with such . . . oh, hell, sure, you're Occitan, you do them with a lot of *merce* and *gratz*. But I can feel how easily you could let it drop, Giraut, I'm your wife and just about the only friend you've had this long, and I never see anything move you one way or another. I don't think you ever really put yourself into anything."

I was still confused, but this sounded like something I could try to be reasonable about, so I said, "What would make you feel like I *was* putting myself into our marriage?"

She gave me a hard, solid slug in the ribs that made the air woof out of me and half-froze me with shock. *"Don't be so damn reasonable, it's too important, come on, just act like you care about something!"*

"Don't hit me," I said, and got up. "I care about that. When you can talk without hitting me I'll listen." I went back to the bedroom, meaning to slam the door. I didn't; I closed it and sat down on the bed, rubbing my ribs. She had landed a hard one. It seemed silly that I had spent all my time in Yaxkintulum wanting to get back to her.

She opened the door and came in silently; she sat down beside me and used the analgesic spray on the place where she had hit me. "I'm sorry," she said. "Some of it's me, anyway. I fell in love with a heroic young man who didn't seem to care if he lived or died as long as he could make art, triumph at fighting, and have fun while he lived. I loved the way that the world wasn't serious to him. And here I am attached to a middle-aged bureaucrat who doesn't take the world seriously. And half the time I want my young hero back, and the other half of the time I want my bureaucrat to settle down and be a real daddy-type."

Silence stretched on and on while we sat on the bed. I ventured, "Do you mean you want to have children?"

"Not necessarily. Maybe no. Maybe not unless I thought you would at least put some of yourself into being a father. And . . . oh, well."

There was a lot more silence. Slowly she leaned over against me until we were again side by side with her head on my shoulder. I could feel big wet tears plopping onto my arm. This time there was no music. I was annoyed—if it had been up to me we'd have stayed on the couch where it was comfortable, and talked about things we enjoyed.

Her skin, as always, was a bit damp and clammy. More than usual, I was noticing the rolls of fat that partially circled her belly, probably just because she was slumped over.

"It's not going to work, is it?" she asked. I could hear the tears in her voice and when I slid my arm around her, her shoulder muscles were tight as lute strings. My first thought was to ask her *what* wasn't going to work, but that was a dumb question. She might well take that as my pretending not to understand, and either hit me or stop talking to me. I thought of saying that yes, yes, it would work, I would change if she needed me to, or help her change, or we would just change things, or whatever, but surely it would work. But I didn't really believe that myself, so I said nothing and sat there feeling like a fool. Margaret stood up and said, "We should sleep. We have a lot to do tomorrow. You can take the main bed and I'll fold out the couch."

She was halfway to the door before I could blurt out "Talk to me." I was sure I had just said the wrong thing.

She turned around and sat down beside me, but didn't say anything, until I repeated, feeling foolish, "Talk to me."

"Well, I would like to. Truly I would. The problem is that every time I think of something that I really want to say, it sounds stupid to me. Does that make sense so far?"

"So far. It explains why you're not talking but I don't think I can judge your thoughts without hearing them, so I think you'll have to say them out loud."

"You'll think they're stupid. Either that or you'll patronize me and the only reason you won't think they're stupid will be because you're worried about me and my feelings, even though I can take care of myself, and . . . is it any use, Giraut?"

"I'm still here," I said, feeling more helpless than ever.

"And if my thoughts are really stupid, will you say so? You won't lie? You've lied enough already."

"I didn't think—"

"For example I know you don't find me attractive but you do like me, and I have a pretty good idea of the effort you go to to persuade yourself that you're aroused. And I know you're often homesick and you really miss your youth and think those were your best days—hell, Giraut, I agree, that's the time when I fell in love with you and you *were* at your best—and you keep lying about not minding getting older. Oh, hell, Giraut, the hardest thing is to see you lying so hard and not be able to believe you when I know you want me to feel happy."

That was her interpretation, no doubt, of this and that: my interrupting her too easily, my pushing off trivial details for her to take care of, the way I brought all my troubles to her but celebrated triumphs with casual friends.

"You see," she said, "you know it's all true. And you're a very good liar, Giraut, I believed you for years and years, but now I'm seeing that what you're doing is just throwing your life away because you can't bring yourself to tell me what you really feel, and I can't stand to watch you do that."

"That isn't how it is," I said, dully, wishing I could shout it, but feeling like I had lost every bit of strength in my body. "Margaret, I do love you. Really. I do love you. I don't know what to say except that."

"It's a start. I'll try to believe you, I guess." She got up and left the room; I heard her setting up the couch to sleep on. I went out to try to talk her into coming to bed with me, or at least letting me take the couch, but she just finished setting up the couch, turned off the light, and lay down, her back pointedly turned. Tired and sick at heart, I went back to the bed we had shared through twelve stanyears, all over human space, and got in, curling up and wrapping my arms around myself.

My first night back, still sleeping by myself. Dull misery and acute self-pity kept me awake half the night and filled my sleep with eerie, threatening dreams. The next morning when I heard

Margaret moving around in the apartment, and got up to join her, I felt as if I hadn't slept at all.

After the mob attack on Paxa Prytanis, Kiel had ordered personnel to stay in the Embassy for a few days, hoping to calm things down. He had scheduled the expiration of the restriction for four days after the day when I arrived home. But two days before the restriction was to expire, there was a huge demonstration in Mayatown; Ix spoke to a crowd of about 40,000, and the police didn't try to break it up. As far as we could gather from video reports, the message was the same three principles he had preached in Yaxkintulum. The next day's rally was smaller, but when the cameras panned the crowd you could see that there must have been two hundred people in the plain shirt, trousers, and broad-brimmed hat that were becoming the mark of Ix's followers. From then on there were more of those at every demonstration.

On that second day of rallies and demonstrations, there were also a few Tamils in the crowd. On his way home, one of those Tamils was recognized, set on, and beaten by other Tamils, badly enough to have to spend a couple of days in the hospital. That led to Tamil demonstrations outside the hospital, and rocks thrown at the windows; the police broke that up with clubs and gas, and there was some rock-throwing and brawling as the crowd dispersed down the side streets. A couple of them turned over a trakcar but then were unable to force the elderly Maya woman inside to come out before police arrived to rescue her.

Then Ix announced that he would be holding a peace march, going from Mayatown right up to the temple of Murukan at the center of New Tanjavur, in a few days. He was denied a permit; he announced he would do it anyway. He was told that the police would arrest and detain every single person on the march if need be; he announced he would do it anyway. It became clear that no more than a few hundred Maya and perhaps a dozen Tamils would take part; he announced he would do it anyway.

Looking the situation over, Kiel decided to extend the ban on going outside the Embassy indefinitely. I guess in his place I might have done the same; the situation looked very unsettled and dangerous. Just the same, it crippled my work and Margaret's, and from a thing or two that Sir Qrala muttered into his wine at dinner one night, and some hints that Paxa Prytanis (who was now living inside the Embassy) dropped, it wasn't helping matters for intelligence work or for commercial contacts either. Probably just the classic case of a choice that was bad no matter what you tried.

The march was peaceful, to everyone's astonishment. The police had rounded up some of the more active bigots proactively, and it was clear that Ix had everyone on their best behavior, but still it was a miracle. There was some yelling at the Maya, who did not even yell back, but nothing more dangerous than an insult was hurled.

The day after, a group of Tamils killed a young Maya woman walking with her little girl. Two Maya retaliated by sneaking across the line in the middle of the night and smashing an idol of Murukan. Ix spent all night pleading with all of the guilty parties; by dawn they had confessed, the police had taken them into custody, a judge had been found who would declare the cases to be emergencies and pass sentence immediately, the book had been thrown at the murderers and desecrators, and by the time most people got up and turned on the news, it was all over. The city seemed to hold its breath for an instant, and then to relax into its normal routine. Again peace held for a few days.

Kiel watched all this closely, and called us all in to discuss it every few waking hours. But he maintained his ban on travel outside the Embassy, only muttering, when we argued, that this backwater city was nowhere to lose an employee over.

We received only short notes from Tz'iquin, about once per day, which essentially told us only what we already knew: that Ix's appearances were causing a sensation, that he was teaching a lot, and that his message was highly controversial. "I could have guessed that much," Margaret grumbled, reading the third such message.

"Maybe he's trying to hide something," Kapilar suggested. We were having breakfast on the Embassy terrace, which was still allowed; it gave us a chance to talk with Kapilar in a location that *might* not be bugged.

"I suspect he is," I said, pouring coffee. "And what he's hiding, I'm pretty sure, is that he doesn't know a thing. And has no idea what to make of what's happening. Your local media can get many of the Maya to talk to them, all of a sudden. For generations none of them would voice a thought in front of a camera or a microphone, especially not one held by a Tamil, and now any Maya in a plain white shirt will pretty much say whatever he or she is thinking."

"Oh, that's been noticed," Kapilar said, grinning. "Kannan was saying something quite rude about it not long ago. I had to explain things to him."

Margaret got a funny, puckish smile. "Not another explanation. Did this one happen in front of Auvaiyar, as well?"

"No, but I'm sure she heard of it," he said, smiling back.

"I have a feeling there's a story that I haven't been told here," I said. "By 'explaining,' Kapilar, you mean—"

"I mean I hit him. Hard. In front of his followers. And dared him or any of them to do anything about it. It's funny how some people who have a philosophy built around violence have no idea what to do about it when it happens."

I glanced at Margaret; I wasn't sure why she could be smiling like that. It had an unpleasant quality that I couldn't quite identify. "And this was the second time?" I asked.

"It was," he said. "The first time was for a very similar occasion. A couple of nights ago at a party, Kannan was saying something about my presence at the peace march, and it seemed very insulting to me, not to mention bigoted and stupid. I saw that Auvaiyar was smiling at him for it—and as an old and losing rival, I just thought I'd get out some long-suppressed feelings, *and* start to solve the Kannan problem, right then and there. So I hit him. It does wonders for an evening. I hadn't gone home so early or so happy in ages. And then last night, Kannan made a joke, or as near as he could manage one, about how Ix had made the Maya so talkative that the next thing you knew they'd be asking for food, and I decided further instruction in public behavior was necessary. For a man who preaches massacres and pogroms, he doesn't deal with a bloody nose well."

I had been watching Margaret intently, trying to figure out what she was feeling. She looked very amused, but behind the dark glasses I wasn't sure. She was getting some kind of pleasure out of hearing Kapilar tell that story. Of course anyone who had had regular dealings with Kannan liked to hear of him getting punched. Or perhaps there was some private joke between her and Kapilar? (The two of them were friendly again after a brief period right after our return when they had been angry about I-didn't-know-what.)

When I heard Ix's voice behind me, I jumped. "Kapilar," he said, "I strongly recommend that you not hit people who deserve it. It can lead to your discovering that it is fun, and from there you will find out that it is fun even when they don't deserve it quite so much, and after a while you won't care whether they deserve it or not."

"I don't think that will happen to me, sir," Kapilar said, standing up.

Ix nodded and gestured for Kapilar to sit. "Your employers were good enough to tell me where to find you. I am assuming you are Margaret?"

Margaret nodded. "And I hardly need to be told that you are Ix. What brings you here?"

"In a very limited sense, my feet. In a larger sense, a need to talk about politics. And in a much, much larger sense, the needs of the human soul."

I thought he was laying it on pretty thick, especially in front of people who knew every detail of how he had gotten to be a prophet. "Well, sit down," I said, "and that will take care of your feet. Politics is what we're here for. And I would suppose a prophet can tell us whatever he wants to about the human soul."

Ix pulled up a chair and refused the coffee; then he leaned forward and said, "Giraut Leones, you don't believe you have a soul."

Usually when I am startled I tell the truth. "Well, no. I don't have a soul. Nothing goes on after death. If you checked through most of the Thousand Cultures, there are only a small number of people who do believe in the soul—not more than two billion out of the thirty billion of us. And nobody at all in the twenty-five billion in the Sol System."

Ix grimaced. "I said nothing about life after death. I said I don't think you believe you have a soul. I don't think you believe there's a you inside you that matters, that you don't get to choose, that is just what you are."

I nodded. "You're right, I don't believe that either."

Kapilar was now looking a little shocked; he turned to Margaret, who said, "Well, if you insist on asking, I don't either."

Ix sighed. "So I suppose we must seem very backward to you here. And perhaps we are. We preserved illiteracy, hunger, ethnic strife, caste . . . all sorts of things, far, far beyond their proper time. And when you see us hanging on to the notion of the soul . . . well, you can hardly help concluding that it is for the same reason."

"More or less," Margaret said. "I am Caledon. Quite a few of my fellow Caledons still believe there is some essence to a human being, something that makes a person unique."

"And you don't."

"I don't. I see that people who believe in anything beyond plain physical reality are mainly engaged in making themselves or others miserable."

Ix stood up. "I don't think this is our time to talk, just now. I think I need to think about how to talk to you before I am ready to try it. Kapilar, will you walk with me? If we start walking now, we can be all the way back to Mayatown before it's really hot."

Kapilar nodded and got up. "I believe that if I'm to be your eyes and ears—"

"Go," Margaret said, sounding extremely bored.

There was a long awkward pause, and then Ix and Kapilar left. "Well," she said, "I think you gave them something to think about. Isn't that odd, that they're so disturbed by the way we feel about the soul? For my part, I felt like they were suddenly asking me about witchcraft or my astrological sign or my IQ."

"Odd and sort of creepy."

She nodded, and then said, "Pardon my asking you this, but by any chance would you like to, er, go test out the air-conditioning in our quarters for a few minutes? Our next meeting with Kiel is not for an hour, and no Tamil staff will be coming in for at least that long."

I was startled, but then, these things happened so rarely that it seemed worth a try. I would probably have thought it was worth it in almost any circumstances.

To my surprise, the quick sex worked perfectly for both of us, and it was wonderful. We were both a lot more relaxed in all the meetings and conferences for the rest of the day, and that night we went to bed early, falling asleep holding hands. I didn't dream at all.

The next day, as we were dressing to go out on the terrace (uniforms rather than robes today, because we had a breakfast meeting) I said, "It's selfish of me, and I know we have work to do, but I wish I could have you all to myself this morning. When things are going well I just want to—"

"I know," she said, "and Giraut, I love you too, but you know, the way you act—well, it's smothering. Can't you let things get just a *little* better instead of insisting that everything now has to become a big passionate romance?" Her voice had an ugly undertone to it, and when I glanced at her, she was bent over to put her boot on, so that I couldn't see her face.

I fought down all those atavistic Occitan feelings that told me I should shout and storm out. "Is that a general rule, or just for today?"

"What?" She glared at me and I thought we *would* have a fight.

"All I'm asking," I said, "is if I smother you *often,* or it's just *at the moment.*"

"Often," she said, returning her attention to her boot.

"Then I'll try to do it less. See you out there."

I was half way out the door before she said, "Thank you."

"For what?"

"For trying. Especially when it's not easy."

"Well, uh, you're welcome." I went out the door to prevent more conversation.

Today we were supposed to have breakfast on the terrace with Sir Qrala, Ambassador Kiel, and Tz'iquin. I expected Kapilar as well—it was free food and he was the next person we'd be talking to anyway—so I wasn't surprised when he turned out to be the first there. "Any news in the city?" I asked. "I haven't turned on a broadcast."

"No *news* exactly," he said, "but the usual. Some scattered violence, no fatalities or hospitalization. Lots of people saying vicious things about the other side. More splitting and arguing in the Tamil community. Kannan is changing strategy: he's trying very hard to get the authorities to consider an application for the *Palai* group to become the Fourth Cankam. His argument is that if they wait too long, there's a danger that the Tamils will be too culturally contaminated to properly maintain or respond to a new Cankam. I'm omitting the usual crap, of course—"

"For which I'm grateful," I said. The robot came up and we both ordered coffee and fruit juice. Dawn wasn't long away, to judge by the low parabola of cobalt blue just forming on the eastern horizon. "So we're where we were yesterday, and today—"

"Maybe," Kapilar said. "I don't know how Ix is going to take the things he found out about you yesterday. I'm not so sure how I can accept them myself. You really believe you have no immortal soul? How can you believe you don't exist?"

"I certainly don't believe that."

"I can tell. But the soul is the part of us that's most real, the part that isn't just leftover things that influenced us, or old habits, or all the trivia—"

"Who says those things are trivial?"

"They might be important, but compared to the soul—"

"I believe I exist. I recall when many of the pieces of me came to be—all those pasts and memories and things. I'm also aware of a part that just happened to happen, somebody for the things that happened to happen to—"

Kapilar shook his head. "And there you lose me again. It seems as if you're claiming you don't have a leg, or an arm."

"Or a wing," I said.

"Hello, are we talking ontology today?" Sir Qrala said, coming in and sitting next to me. I missed the characteristic whiff of gin. My nose might be mildly plugged, or perhaps he wasn't drinking today, or maybe he was managing to hold off till afternoons. "I see we're one more than scheduled—or rather two more, because I was going to mention that Ms. Skine will be joining us as well."

"No reason to worry as long as they don't send the bill to any of us," I said. "Is there an agenda for this, or is Ambassador Kiel just keeping in touch with everything?"

"Both," Kiel said, emerging from the Embassy door with Skine trailing after him. "My main agenda was just to see whether everyone is ready for us to lift the restriction to the Embassy. We really mustn't let restrictions on movement go on so long that people think of them as customary, but on the other hand I don't want our people hurt, or worse." He sat down at the table, nodded politely to all of us in turn, poured his coffee, and said, "I asked Ms. Skine to join us here because she has a number of se-

curity and intelligence reports of considerable interest. She and I
will be meeting with each working group in the Embassy all day
long; then, always assuming that something doesn't utterly
change everything all over again, we'll make our decision this
evening. I do want you to know that I'm very biased in favor of
lifting the restrictions."

Sir Qrala nodded vigorously. "Can't happen too soon. We're
getting more and more out of touch and our contacts are feeling
bolder and bolder about feeding lies to us."

"I agree," I said. "I'm useless until the ban is lifted, and there's
a lot going on out there."

Margaret had come in and she slipped down into the chair beside me. "Quite a gathering," she said. "The robot with the food
is on its way up. I think there will be plenty for everyone, even
with Kapilar here."

It seemed like a friendly, teasing joke to me, but Kapilar didn't
look at her and appeared to be pointedly ignoring it. I felt irritated with him, and sorry for Margaret, so I explained, "We're
actually talking about whether the restriction on travel outside
the Embassy ought to be lifted."

Margaret didn't look at me. "Then we'd go back on our regular schedules?"

Ambassador Kiel nodded without looking at her. "That's it
exactly."

"Well, then I'm very much in favor of it," Margaret said.

There was a very long, awkward silence at the table, as if she'd
said something embarrassing.

Kapilar cleared his throat. "Feelings are still running high in
the city, but it's possible that more visitors would remind people
that you're human beings, not monsters. Possible. On the other
hand, I think the risk of another incident like the one with Paxa
Prytanis is worse now than when the restriction was put on."

In the awkward silence it seemed as if everyone were speaking
in some secret code that only they knew, that somehow the language I was hearing was only superficially Terstad. Everyone was

looking away as if one of us had just suffered an embarrassing accident of the bowels. Beside me, Sir Qrala quietly laid a hand on my arm, the way a friend might caution a friend against doing something rash. I had no idea why he was doing that, but decided the one thing that would probably not be rash was to say and do nothing.

Fortunately, at that moment the robot cart arrived with the food. It was just standard Embassy kitchen food, good but not the least bit special, and yet everyone was exclaiming over how good it was. I shrugged, figuring I would know the truth sooner or later, filled my plate, and sat down to eat.

After we finished, Skine looked around at us and said, "The reports I have don't tend to agree with Kapilar. There are a sizable number of businesses in the city that were negotiating under our limited import program, a lot of cultural exchange candidates, and all sorts of other pro-Council and pro-assimilation groups that are being frustrated by the absence of our support. Covert polls show that we're no less popular than before and most people seem to blame the attack on Ms. Prytanis on the Tamils who did it, not on any behavior of hers. Quite a few people spontaneously express shame about it."

Kapilar fidgeted. "I hear more starvation jokes and more people using words like 'savage,' these days," he said. "That's anecdotal and not statistical but—"

Skine shook her head. "Oh, the covert polls definitely show that anti-Maya bigots are being more public and vehement. And the true counts of incidents of harassment and violence bear that out (pretty much) as well, though the drop in incidents initiated by Maya, and the number of times that the Maya seem to be avoiding confrontation, are starting to have an unpredictable effect. But none of that really matters for the issue at hand, because none of our Embassy people is Maya."

Kapilar shook his head. "Well, I just have a very bad feeling about the whole thing. But it's always possible I'll be wrong." He got up from the table and added, "I have several reports to write so I guess I'd better get to them." With a little bow to the table, he left.

"He's upset," I said, after he had gone. "That's the first time I haven't seen him get extra helpings at breakfast. Perhaps he does know something or intuit—"

Sir Qrala kicked me under the table. Still having no idea what was going on, I shut up.

Skine waited a for a very long, awkward moment, and said, "Anyway, I may be overrating numbers that are being gathered under very difficult circumstances, but I do think that all the indications are basically favorable."

"Thank you," Ambassador Kiel said. He was running his fingers up and down his long, thin nose, his eyes closed as if in contemplation, or as if he were trying to solve, without scratch paper or a computer, a very difficult problem.

For a breakfast that had been so exclaimed over, everyone finished very quickly, and after seeing the dramatic rise of Metallah, people seemed to flee to their offices. I waited for Margaret to get up. Everyone else left first. Finally she said, softly, "Giraut, I feel really bad."

"Are you sick, *midons,* or is—"

"I'm going to spend the day in our quarters. I might feel better by afternoon. Just go about your work and don't worry about me." She stood up and went through the door, leaving me standing and staring. After a while I went down to our office and busied myself with trying to read every single document I had been ignoring for months; I spent an hour reading the specifications for how much weight I could pile on my desk.

At lunch time I elected to go eat in our apartment, partly because Kapilar was being strangely, irritatingly cheerful and, though he didn't speak, constantly calling my attention to himself by whistling, drumming on his desk, stretching and sighing, and the thousand and one things that a coworker with too much energy can inflict on one. Margaret was in bed; I asked her if she was all right and she grunted. "Talk to me when you're ready," I said, "unless you're sick."

"Only metaphorically," she said. "That sounds stupid. I mean . . . oh, I hate it, Giraut. We'll talk sooner or later I guess. Get your lunch and go back to work, will you? And please don't worry so much. Just let me be."

I shrugged, more for my benefit than hers, went to the food-slot, and dialed up *ceehel uah*, which, now that it was on the Embassy menu, I had been having a couple of times a week. So far it was probably the thing I appreciated most about the Maya culture; just possibly it was the only thing I could understand.

The internal com chimed softly and I picked it up on the room screen. It was Kapilar. "Something the two of you should deal with. Ix just arrived at the back door. By himself. He says he needs to talk to just the two of you." Kapilar made a face I couldn't interpret. "Or to be more accurate about it, he's saying that he thinks the two of you need to talk to him. Shall I send him up?"

"Give us ten minutes."

Kapilar nodded and clicked off.

I told Margaret; luckily she had gotten into bed in her clothes, and needed just a couple of minutes to wash up and get focused. I tried not to watch her too closely, but she looked bad: as if she had been crying most of the morning, or had suffered a shock. But with an important person coming to see us, I didn't want to ask any question that might upset her.

Margaret and I quickly straightened our little parlor, in the familiar drill. We had just put a few books back onto the shelves and sprung the waste paper and dust to the Embassy's central trash bin when—exactly ten minutes after I had rung off from Kapilar, I noted by the parlor clock—the doorbell rang. I set down the cushion I had been about to brush off (it wasn't dirty but we did all of them automatically, because we had been doing this in so many embassies so often for so long) and got the door.

When I opened it, Ix had a warm, friendly smile, as if he were bringing the best news in the world. He came in quiet as a shadow, taking the door handle from me and closing it behind himself. "Time is limited but I think there are important things to talk about here," he said, "and I thought this might be the quickest way and the one that drew the least attention. There are some very important things to discuss, some of them political and some of them personal. Margaret, when we first met I forgot to tell you that it speaks well of you that Giraut missed you so terribly while he was in Yaxkintulum."

She seemed startled. I don't know whether it was because she was surprised that I had missed her, surprised that he knew, or surprised that he paid so personal a compliment in so abrupt a manner.

"Come in and sit down," I managed to say, after an awkward pause, "and tell us whatever you think we should know."

He took a seat on the couch, sitting cross-legged; I suppose that was the nearest thing to the way he was used to sitting at home. We dragged chairs up close to him. Not judging whether it was deliberate or meant anything just yet, I noted that he had set up a situation where we would have to look up at him, unless we wanted to stand. "This room is secure, by the way," I said.

"Secure. You mean that it is—"

"Free of listening devices, particularly listening devices from hostile forces."

"And you know this because—"

"We sweep it electronically daily and we scan everyone coming in," Margaret explained.

"Strange, a building where the rooms are secure and the people aren't. I mean no offense by that. But surely if you talked only about things that it was all right for everyone to know, you would have no such problems."

I said, "That is a strange criticism, coming from one who was prepared to be a prophet by the very people who are now pretending to suppress him. What would happen if we were to broadcast all the details of how you were made a prophet to

everyone on Briand?" That was blunter than I had intended to
be. Perhaps I was still irritated because he had presented Margaret with that surprising comment right at the beginning, and I
feared he might upset her more on what was obviously a bad day.
Or possibly I myself, short on sleep and long on worry, was just
more sensitive than usual, and I hadn't liked his sniping at a perfectly normal security matter.

Whatever the reason for my irritation and blunt response, he
didn't seem to pay any attention to the anger or hostility. He
considered what I had said for a long time, as if it were profoundly hard for him to understand. Finally he said, "I don't
know what made you say that, but that *is* what I came here to
talk to you about. I have been thinking that I might divulge the
whole thing at the next big rally."

Margaret and I gaped at him. "The whole thing?" she said.
"You mean tell them how you were made a prophet and why?
Reveal—"

"Absolutely everything," he said. "It seems to me that it is
perfectly in accord with the third principle I claim to be teaching,
that we should acknowledge all the stories as merely stories and
get on with our connection to the world we live in."

"And that connection is—" I began.

"Oh, stories, of course. But that's the important thing to remember is that we work with a story, within a story, until the
time comes to let the story fall apart and weave a new one. And
it seems to me that I cannot stand in front of them and say I am
anything more than one more story to be read before it is tossed
aside."

"But won't it destroy your credibility?" I asked. "To expose
falsehood and so forth is one thing, but exposing your own
strikes me as—"

He shrugged, an eloquent gesture of disdain. "It will destroy a
credibility that is quite undeserved, one that the Center Temple
created for me. It *may* establish a credibility that *is* deserved, and
if so . . . well, then. Good enough. If not, it will be a vaccine

against future lies. And in any case, because I'm quite sure it will cause Pusiictsom to reject me completely, it will free me from having to have any considerations for the future of the Peccary lineage, or for the Center Temple, and allow me to try to move in the direction in which things most need to go, for the Maya and all the people of Briand. I can't do that as long as I'm still trying to watch out for Pusiictsom's concerns."

"He *is* your father," I said.

" 'A prophet has no lineage.' "

My head was beginning to hurt. I got up and ordered three bitter chocolates from the food slot. Margaret and I could probably use a drink, our guest might like the gesture even if he wasn't thirsty, and a few moments' delay would at least allow us to regroup emotionally.

"So you feel as if—" Margaret began.

"I don't feel it, at least I don't think so. I know, I think. In the ways a prophet is supposed to know."

I blurted out a question without thinking what the implications might be. "Are you a *real* prophet?"

He laughed. I think it was a laugh. A wild furious sound burst through his tight throat. "Now, in what sense do we mean *that? Real.* I am at least as real as the last ten or so prophets about which I know anything; all of them were pawns created for one temple or another. So in that sense I am exactly what a prophet has been historically for two hundred stanyears or more. Then again, I am teaching something new in terms of the old language, which is the function of a prophet, so since I am doing a prophet's function, you might say, based on that, that I must be a prophet, just as one who prepares food is a cook, whether the food is any good or not.

"And you know, there isn't the slightest bit of evidence that there ever was any such role as 'prophet' among the ancient Maya; it's the interpretation of a small minority of scholars long after the ancient Maya were extinct, from a few scraps of text in a few places, that there was a tradition of a preaching holy man.

For that matter we have no idea how much the ancients read their own books, or how seriously. Maybe they wrote it all down and then ignored it.

"We are *not* the ancient Maya, and we are *not* their descendants, and we are *not even* the descendants of the Maya who lived in Central America until most of them died in the Slaughter. We are the evolved version of some culture-designer's idea of the Maya; we are an embodiment of what some mostly-European academics—motivated by their love of their own eccentric readings of the few texts, and Asian quadrillionaires, motivated by a grotesque sense of guilt—made up about the Maya. They copied Maya genes into embryos, and Maya texts into computers' memories. Then they loaded it all onto a colony ship and sent us off to be the thing they wanted us to be.

"So in that sense, since we are not real Maya and the real Maya, so far as we know, had no prophets, I cannot possibly be a real Maya prophet.

"But if your question means what I take it to mean—am I a prophet in the way that a prophet that was envisioned by our culture's designers?—well. Now that *is* a question, isn't it? Do you believe that such a thing is possible, that someone could fulfill such a role? Do you believe that it can just happen that someone takes on that role? Do you believe there is a 'true' reading of the ancient writings—and the many more writings produced by a set of clever aintellects with random number generators—that I might possibly be finding and expressing?

"Because I don't know, myself, how much of that I believe. All I can tell you about is my own, overwhelming feeling that the only way to peace will be through truth and therefore I had better start speaking it, all of it, just as effectively and persuasively as I can, in the hopes that others will do so too. Is that enough to make me a prophet? Or does the message have to be *really* true? And what can 'really true' mean in a world where most of the past is invented anyway?

"You see, at least, I hope, why I needed to talk to someone

who was not Maya, already knew what I know, might be willing to entertain the possibility that I was right, and might even be neutral on this issue.

"Sometimes I think that the little word 'prophet' has taken over everything and I'd have been better off without it. But then I can't think what I'd have done if I weren't a prophet. The days when I wasn't seem to be fading; it feels like soon I'll remember nothing before the first time I preached."

I didn't quite know what to say, but Ix seemed willing to wait all day for me to find a response. What should I do? Usher him out quietly and call Pusiictsom, tell him that the prophet he had sent us was cracking up? Use this opportunity to try to get control of the prophet, myself, for the Council of Humanity, and thus cut the Maya leadership—who were unreliable allies at best—out of the loop? Decide if he really was a prophet within a tradition that I myself understood badly?

While I was thrashing among the alternatives, Margaret jumped in. "What do you think is the best that could happen?"

"That the Maya and the Tamil might get control of their stories, instead of vice versa. That we might just stop, sit back, and choose to live our lives and tell our stories in such a way that something will go on after us, something we might not approve of but that will approve of itself, that will be able to live in the new world of the reconnection, perhaps even go out and make a place for itself among the Thousand Cultures, because our old cultures surely can't."

"And what would be the worst?" Margaret's voice was so soft I could barely hear it.

"That everything might collapse into violence. But here on Briand, for at least a generation or two, we will *always* be at risk of that. We may by great good luck avoid widespread violence but we cannot abolish its possibility for a long, long time. The best hope is only that in a generation or two we can raise enough children who are *not* filled with hate, that they will get a chance to take over, and then if they succeed more than we did, perhaps in a century or so the risk will be gone. So for any course of action here, the worst does not matter, for it's always the same, and always highly probable. Rather we should ask, if I don't divulge what I really am, and it is widely believed that I am a prophet, and my teaching does indeed take hold in both communities, what is the best that can happen?

"Only that the Maya will have learned a way to provoke the Tamils less, and perhaps also a way to have more patience for them. Tolerance is sometimes all that can be achieved, but it cannot end conflict; only love, charity, and pity can do that, and it seems to me that we must try to end the conflict, not merely contain it and pass it down to our children. If I had a poisonous snake under my house, I would crawl in with a sharp stick to kill it, taking a chance that I might be bitten, so that my son would not have to deal with a nest of them. I would not merely feed the snake some sleeping pills from time to time, and hope that it had no offspring, and would die of natural causes.

"If this present conflict really does risk death to both cultures—and that's what's at stake as far as I can see—then we must try, not merely to contain it, but to end it if we can, and ending it means letting go of the things that keep it going. I can offer the opportunity for people to do that. Whether they take the opportunity or not . . . well, I am not responsible for choices others make. Nor are you."

Margaret sighed. "Tolerance is what keeps half a dozen of the inhabited worlds from tearing apart. There are many cultures that hate each other, and it is hardly surprising that the ones that hate each other tend to be neighbors on one planet or another. I have visited those places and walked their streets, bought in their shops, talked with people on all sides, and I can tell you this: there is no love or charity there and precious little pity. Yet people live. Yet children grow up. Yet the years go by and though now and then someone gets hurt, most people have the time and space to just live. Tolerance is often the very essence of the gift of peace, it seems to me, and—"

"It's a very cruel gift," Ix said, leaning forward as if confiding a secret. "Because it isn't peace. They still live in fear. They still hate their neighbors. And they still cannot drop the things that stand between them and their neighbors."

"But you're talking about risking—about risking . . . "

"Everything. In the hope that what comes of it will be better than what we gave up. What else do you suppose love is?" Ix looked down at both of us from his higher seat, and I found my vision of him splitting, so that at one instant I saw the clever politician selling his line of action to his coconspirators, and at the same moment I saw the prophet who could not do anything but what his visions told him. "I don't know how far down this road I can go," he said. "I don't know whether a whole planet of people can reach as high as love itself, and stay that way long enough to change forever. I do know that if we don't find the way to make that dangerous leap, all we do is delay the day the murder begins again."

"Delay is a great thing," I said, feeling like Kiel or Shan explaining things to a new diplomat. "Every year that no one dies—"

"Is another year of Tamil mothers frightening their children with tales of Maya cannibals. Another year of Maya boys being taught obscenities about Tamil girls. Another year for the poison to sink in deeper."

"That is a cost," I admitted, beginning to lose my patience, "but it's not the cost that blood in the streets is. And for every bit of hatred engendered by an unpleasant story there could be a thousand times as much from violence crying out for vengeance. It may not be the best way to live but it doesn't risk the worst—"

"And your way," Ix said, impassively. "Does it guarantee that there will *not* be an orgy of violence, revenge heaped on revenge, eventually? Does it save you from that?"

I had answers, and Margaret said later so did she, but we didn't get to talk just then, because Ix leaned forward and added, "Let's consider an example. Look at the two of you. The way you sit, the way you look at each other, the way you can't think of anything but each other—in the middle of trying to keep my planet from ripping itself to bits—so afraid that if you face what you don't like about each other, that you may fly apart, and that very fear is exactly why you're both starving for love.

"You are both geniuses at tolerating each other, do you know that? But it makes you *fools* at loving. You tell yourselves terrible stories about each other, and then you so-nobly don't do anything about the hatred that the stories lead you into, and that keeps the peace, doesn't it? Each of you all by yourself. Each of you wrapped up in those comforting stories that justify your anger and fear, and the even bigger and more comforting story that you are such a noble person that you can bear with the harms your partner does you. Well, what if you just dropped your stories and loved each other?"

He stood between us, and laid his hands on our shoulders. "What if you just dropped the story of all the little wrongs between you, all the things you dislike, and most of all the story that you bravely bear with each other's failings? Suppose you just loved each other?"

He was using hypnotic technique again, resting his hands on our shoulders in order to gauge and synchronize our breathing. Knowing that didn't matter. He had me. I had to listen to him.

"Drop all those stories. Love each other, in the real world and not in the stories you tell yourselves," he said, "and once you do that, then you'll know something of love and wisdom. Meanwhile I confess I am a great fool. I came to two people who are afraid to love to get their advice for a great work of love. Perhaps I should have consulted a blind man about a painting instead."

He pressed down on my shoulder as he headed for the door, and I looked up. Here is the strangest thing of all the strange things that happened to us on Briand: I swear by whatever gods might be that to this day I can *feel* his hand on that shoulder, inexorably firm yet light and gentle, every pad of his palm and press of each finger. And I know that he looked at me, winked, and nodded toward Margaret, as if to say *Friend, I have done what I can, now it's up to you.* Just as if I heard his voice in my head, though I know he did not speak aloud.

Margaret remembers him doing exactly the same for her—the pressure, the wink, the nod, the same words heard in the head but not spoken aloud. Yet he couldn't have done that in both directions at once.

If we had ever asked him, I suppose he might have told us that some stories are lovely enough to be worth remembering and retelling. Or he might just have called us fools again. With Ix you never knew, not then and not ever, and you just had to make what you could of him.

He went through the door without a word, leaving Margaret and I to turn and face each other. Her eyes were leaking tears down over her cheeks; my cheeks, too, were flooded. We reached for each other, perhaps at first just for familiarity and comfort, but then things took over.

Strong emotion, I know, often manifests itself in sex, and perhaps it was only that Ix had upset us so badly. Or perhaps for some inscrutable reason of his own, he had planted the suggestion, or then again maybe he was just our excuse. Maybe he really did have some power that we never did grasp.

Whatever the cause, without a word, we undressed, and, with solemn joy, grinning like maniacs with tears pouring down our faces, we fucked on the couch.

In less than a minute we both finished in a glorious spasm, and sat up with our arms around each other. "I am sorry for a lot of things," I said.

"So am I," she said, "but let's not talk about what we're sorry for right now. You must have told him everything about our relationship, but I surely don't blame you; thank you for finding us that wise man. I begin to see what the Maya see in their prophets."

"Er," I said, "I never told him anything about us. I think he just knew, without my having to tell him."

Her eyes got wide, and she shook her head. "By everything you and I both know, or have any way of knowing, his crazy plan to go public with his real origin is going to be a disaster. But he might have a way of knowing differently."

"*Companhona y donz de mi cor,*" I said, "Before we talk any more business, would you mind if I said I loved you?"

"Me first. I love you, Giraut."

Late that afternoon Kiel called me into his office. The moment I got there, and saw Ms. Skine, whose face was set in sharp lines of anger and disappointment, I knew that something bad had happened, and that it must involve Ix.

Without preface, Kiel showed me a video recording. Ix spoke before a crowd in Mayatown, and made his announcement, revealing everything. The crowd broke into a thousand factions—some flocked to him, but these were a minority. Some tried to rush him, but his few remaining disciples clustered around him and the angry mob seemed to lose its energy and drift away, after shouting a few insults.

"He told you he was going to do this," Kiel said.

"Yes, sir, he did," I said, seeing no advantage to lying.

"And you didn't see fit to tell either Ms. Skine or me that something like this was impending?"

"Sir, I had no idea he was going to do it today, and no idea that they would react like this."

"Well," Ms. Skine said, "Perhaps you should know that a lot of the Maya went direct from that religious meeting to wandering across the line into New Tanjavur proper, and quite a lot of them seem to have gotten into fights. Ix has been burned in effigy by crowds of Tamils. There's been more violence in the last half-hour than we'd had in ten standays. So first of all, we are going to have to cancel that plan to let Embassy personnel leave the Embassy again; I do hope every single one of them comes around to thank you. And secondly, I think what is happening may fairly be described as ethnic rioting, and anyway, whether I think so or not, that's what it's being called on media all over human space. After several days without a headline, we've just become the most important story in the news media again.

"In short, where things were almost quiet, this protegé of yours has now brought things into a state as bad as any since we got a springer connection to Briand. Now, I really doubt that you planned or intended any of this, but I understand he was right here in the Embassy talking about something with you and your wife just a few hours ago."

"He was," I said, "and he did tell me what he was going to do. I'm very sorry I didn't notify you promptly. I really didn't know he was going to go do it at that very instant, and I really didn't know how much trouble he was going to cause, but I must admit that I should have told you at once, and I'm sorry, and you are entitled to reprimand me."

Kiel sighed. "You answered the important question. I don't think you helped to set up anything for Shan here. I was afraid this was going to be some pretext for bringing in the CSPs and that the whole thing was a fraud for that purpose. That's not what you're acting like; every Shan agent I ever knew gloated when he sprang the trap." He shrugged and said, "We all make mistakes of one kind or another. Be more careful about keeping us posted. Meanwhile, the city police seem to be getting it under control, and I think we're probably already past the peak of fighting. It's hard to keep a riot going on a planet this hot and uncomfortable, where it takes so much effort just to stand up." He gestured toward the door. "You can go now. We'll get the details from you and Margaret, later."

Beginning two days after the rioting stopped, Ix held more rallies and marches. Though the attendance was now smaller, it looked very much like the *rate* of conversion to Ix's prophecy was much higher; any new face that showed up at a gathering of Ix's followers, especially one at which Ix preached, was extremely likely to show up at another one as well, and within two or three such events, to begin showing up in the plain white shirt, broad black hat, simple hair, and dark trousers that set Ix's followers apart from other Maya. Almost all of the Tamil followers of Ix stayed with him through the uproar, and their numbers began to grow again as the violence subsided.

Kapilar told me that Ix was the single obsessive topic in all the young artist cafés in every tank in New Tanjavur. Tz'iquin said that the remainder of Ix's disciples seemed fanatical and passionate in a way he had never seen before. What had been lost in numbers had been gained in intensity. Dutifully I reported all this to Kiel and Skine. Though they were civil enough in thanking me, it was clear that I was always seen as the bearer of bad tidings. Anything to do with Ix was bad news as far as they were concerned.

The ban on going outside the Embassy remained in force. The people inside got a little crazier each day. As for Margaret and I, the love that seemed to spring up from Ix's touch evaporated just as quickly. We were fighting again, about everything, more than ever, within a day. When we shared the bed, we lay side by side, snapping at each other, or crying in loneliness, centimeters from each other's touch, till exhaustion brought on sleep. I wrote song after song in my head, but I never wanted to record or publish any of them. For the most part I didn't even try them on the lute or sing any of them. They just came to me, and though I tried, I never did forget a word or a note of them, not even years later.

If Skine really intended to scapegoat me for the restrictions' continuing, she did a very poor job of it; nobody else seemed to feel that way, and my relations with other people within the Embassy were as good—or as superficial—as they had been before. Meanwhile things out in the city became stranger and stranger; by the time we were allowed out again, we might have to learn everything over.

Shan's messages to Margaret and I were brief and perfunctory.

We couldn't get out among the people, so he didn't have much for us to do. Paxa Prytanis said it was much the same way with her; the only thing she was doing for the OSP was acting as a conduit for her husband's reports from Yaxkintulum.

Well, if it wasn't possible for us to go to the people we were supposed to be contacting, perhaps we could get them to come to us. One morning at breakfast, Margaret suggested that we might throw a young artists' and critics' reception and thus at least get to hear some of the ideas floating around in the city, or at least some of the gossip. Kapilar said, "That's a pretty good idea. If the ambassador will tolerate it, I've got a way to make sure you get the right crowd, too."

"Oh, he'll tolerate ideas," I said. "It's *us* he has trouble tolerating. What did you have in mind?"

"Invite a bunch of Tamils of liberal persuasion—plus Ix and some of his followers."

"Really?"

Kapilar shrugged. "Absolutely everyone who is anyone among the poets and the critics—except Kannan and the hard-core bigots—drops everything every afternoon, just to catch Ix's preaching. There have been brawls about people working Maya loan-words into Tamil poetry. Auvaiyar's hangers-on have even been doing what they call 'Briandism,' which is Tamil lyrics with lots of references to New Tanjavur, the Maya, trakcars, springers, and terraforming—all things no one would have been so rude as to mention before—and often with a lot of Maya loan-words. Tz'iquin assures me those words are quite often misused and the Maya find some of it hilarious, but the intention seems to me to be what matters. I understand in the next issue of *Briandia*— that's a new journal Auvaiyar has started—there will be a few pages of Tamil verse 'in Maya form': four idea pairs, AB-CB-DE-FB, like Jaguar Quitze, Sudden Jaguar, Not Right Now, Dark Jaguar, or Brave Quetzal, Beautiful Quetzal, Life is Short, Dead Quetzal. Except these are *kurinci* poems, the most admired of all among us for centuries. I happen to know one of them—it goes:

'My lover by the stream in the mountains
As darkness falls on the stream in the mountains,
The tiger finds its mate,
And we unite, by the stream in the mountains.'

Admittedly, it's not brilliant, but—"

"By any chance is it yours?" Margaret asked.

"Oh, I wouldn't say by chance. I wrote it on purpose. Auvaiyar was having trouble getting enough of them. How she knew I'd be willing to try one, I don't know. She also extorted a short essay from me, in Tamil, about Maya poetics. Which I'm quite sure Tz'iquin is laughing about secretly, but he *said* it wasn't too bad. Anyway, I was going to say lots of younger artists hold views close to what the Council would like, and, for them, Ix would be a draw. And if they got along with him . . . well, then we might have started something, if you see what I mean, or at least gotten something to move further in a direction we would like. If you'll trust me to work out a guest list, I think we can make the whole thing work."

Margaret and I agreed at once, and to my mild surprise, Ambassador Kiel thought the idea was workable as well. "I won't attend it myself," he said, "this time. If you can make such receptions a regular thing, I might get some political mileage out of them. Many of the important people here seem to have a fetish for poetry, so much that they often neglect their real duties, and so it wouldn't be a bad idea for me to learn a little bit about how to talk about that, and to socialize with some of those poets they're so interested in. It can't *possibly* be as dull as learning golf was when I was posted to New America."

Thus, about ten standays after Ix had revealed his origin, early in the evening, Margaret and I found ourselves performing the familiar ritual of preparing for a reception. We had invited a variety of the more liberal Tamils, including Kapilar and Auvaiyar, plus Ix and whatever Maya he chose to bring along.

Somehow, even the comfort of ritual wasn't working this evening. I was setting out plates of food—a careful mixture of the Maya things that Kapilar thought might please the Tamil palate, Tamil things he thought the Maya might like, and a diversity of Occitan and Caledon food that would help give people things to talk about with Margaret and I, in case the conversation were in danger. So little of my attention was required that my thoughts were free to wander down gloomy well-worn paths.

There is a saying among those of us who have careers with the Council of Humanity that skiers, cooks, painters, and diplomats must work with what is in front of them. I knew that even if we won over every Tamil at the party, we would never gain much by it. The café society of one culture just wouldn't amount to much in all of human space's fifty-four billion people. Yet though the little gathering of self-appointed artists and critics who met in the tanks every day to argue endlessly about long-settled questions, long-accepted manifestos, and long-dead artists seemed irrelevant, it was no more and no less so than anything else human. Everywhere in the Thousand Cultures, most people lived in some version of a permanent summer camp, doing some form of endless, fruitless self-development. The only real differences were whether they played at art, religion, science, or lifestyle. In Margaret's home culture people pretended to seriously follow a stern god and to work at hard physical labor; in mine, they pretended to care passionately for an imaginary honor and to live for the sake of beauty.

I had seen many variations on the theme of killing time. There were cultures full of people pretending to pray (to all sorts of absurd supreme beings in a conspicuously empty universe), people pretending to advance knowledge (that is, getting in the way of the aintellects that did all real scientific work), people pretending to violate codes of behavior that ten generations of their ancestors had pretended to violate, and so forth. All of us but the very young really *had* developed to our full potential, usually in several different areas of study. Human space was full of average poets, mediocre physicists, second-rate athletes, and ordinary mystics, each competent enough but none able to rise above the millions of equally privileged and well-trained people. Most of humanity could reach far enough to appreciate how far the geniuses stood above us, but not enough to stand with them.

Almost everyone in the human race had to invent reasons not to wipe our psypyx recordings and take voluntary euthanasia. Humanity as a whole was bored, and incapable of self-amusement.

At least in their hatred for each other the Tamils and the Maya had found something greater than their personal lives to be engaged in, and that was more than much of the human race had.

While thinking all that, I set out the Occitan canapés and the Caledon fruit wines, checked the musical selection with a team of aintellects to make sure that nothing even faintly offensive to either Maya or Tamil would emerge from the speakers, and occasionally fussed with the absurd necktie and uncomfortable collar of the ancient *suit-biz* I had elected to wear.

I couldn't wear the dress of either culture without immediately giving offense to the other. I couldn't wear the bureaucratic uniform, because that would mean official support. And in either the Maya or the Tamil cultures the implications of my Occitan clothes would be wildly sexual.

Margaret was just as stuck as I was, except that her Caledon costume would merely have made her look like a convict. So she too was in ancient formal clothing, a jacket, shirt, tube skirt, and tiny ribbon tie with a pair of absurdly uncomfortable high-heeled shoes.

Margaret must have caught something in my glance at her clothing, for she said, "I'm sorry, I know I look like a bad sofa, but—"

"I understand. It's not easy, is it? It's hard for anyone to manage an important social function, stuck in clothes you don't feel are attractive—"

She sighed and looked down. "You don't understand at all." She turned back to the tray behind her, to rearrange an arrangement that was already perfect.

I tried going over to put my arms around her, but I felt her stiffen, and it made everything worse. I left my hands resting on her hips so that she could move into my embrace, but she didn't; she clenched her fists and stared at the floor. "I'm not sure what's wrong, Margaret. I don't want to lose you but I don't seem to be doing anything very effective about keeping you. But I don't *want* us to get further apart."

"*Yap,*" she said. "Me either." She heaved a sigh and relaxed her hands, resting them lightly on my forearms. "Our guests will be here any second. Tz'iquin said he was going to try to be early. So . . . later . . . "

"There's an expression I haven't heard in a while. '*Yap,*' " I said, teasing her. "You can get a girl out of Caledony but you can't get Caledony out of a girl."

She looked down and smiled. "*Yap.* I must be reverting. Perhaps I should set out some bowls of plain oatmeal and dry bread, and maybe some lukewarm drinking water, for our guests?"

"Sure, and I'll put on Occitan clothes and look like their idea of a boy-whore, and that will give them something that upsets them more than each other."

Margaret grinned at me. It was a great moment. So the doorbell rang.

I went to get it. It was Tz'iquin. He had a sardonic half-smile, as he often did these days. He allowed himself to be steered to a chair, and said, "I wish I had more real news. But here's what's going on as far as I know. Half a dozen of Ix's friends and disciples bolted at the last minute. They said they didn't want to be an exhibit for a gang of style-crazed Tamil poseurs. Having been just such an exhibit myself many times, I'm afraid I didn't have the conviction to argue.

"Now, among the purported artists and their hangers-on, every Tamil who is really serious about style is in a dither, anxiety cranked up as far as it will go. No one is going to pay any real attention to anything around them, and thus you will have a whole roomful of people staring at themselves in their mental mirrors, and, in place of a party with thirty people, thirty separate simultaneous anxiety attacks all held in the same room."

"Just like in Noupeitau," I said, "if there's a significant guest coming. Social occasions that involve anything new are always that way. But at least Ix himself is coming, isn't he?"

"Oh, I think that's all but certain," Tz'iquin said. "There is going to be a group of potential listeners, so he'll be here, along with at least a few disciples."

"Well, we can hope. With luck the urge to be friendly will win out—"

"And the wine will finish the job," Margaret added.

I snorted, but she shook her head and said, "*Nop, nop,* I'm serious. The best thing that could happen this time would be for the two groups to get so drunk that they don't know what anyone's saying, but they do know they're very, very happy. Then they can all be quite sure that somehow all the differences are trivial and deep down we're all the same, and hang all over each other getting sloppy with sentiment, and the next day—without being able to remember any specifics at all—they can all believe they had a wonderful time, and say to each other 'Why can't it always be like that? Why must we fight? Why can't we just all live in love and peace and harmony?' "

"You're right," I said. "A vast sloppy outpouring of sentimental good fellowship would do a world of good. Is that why you set out those apple wines?"

"Yap. Sweet, so people won't realize how drunk they're getting. If courage can come out of a bottle, maybe peace can too."

Tz'iquin looked unhappy. "You don't really mean you want to get them all drunk? How good can an idea be if you have to sedate everyone first?"

"That's the idea," Margaret said. "There are *no* good *ideas.* Not in this situation. If you want human beings to get along, you'd better make sure their heads are empty. What we want are feelings. Big, sloppy, loving, affectionate, indiscriminate, completely irrational *feelings.* That way—"

The doorbell rang again.

"Hope that's not Ix," Margaret said. "I suggested that he be late to make a better entrance, but a Maya who is being late is often earlier than a Tamil who's on time." She bustled over to the door.

It was Kapilar, and he was grinning. "You have fifteen people standing on a street corner a block from here," he said, "all desperately confirming to each other that they are appropriately dressed. So even if you don't get anyone to like each other, at least it's a giant stride for manners and fashion."

I ushered him in. He was wearing an undecorated white shirt and black baggy trousers, not quite Ix's followers' uniform but not decisively different from it either.

"Good choice," I said, looking him over.

He looked at my *suit-biz,* nodded back to me, and said, "We seem to have all gone in for bland, eh?"

"It's common sense to be inoffensive," Margaret said. "I just hope our Tamil guests don't stand on the corner so long that they meet Ix out on the street. *That* could get unpredictable."

The doorbell rang once more. Somewhere along the way the fifteen Tamils that Kapilar had seen had become about twenty-five.

I let them in, bowing and saying hello to each. They had made quite a variety of choices about how they looked and how they presented themselves. Among the men, there were two *suits-biz* like mine, several very simple shirts and trousers in imitation of Ix's style, and a few who had chosen the traditional Tamil long wrapped skirts. The women were in a diversity of dresses ranging from bland-everywhere to this-minute-New-Tanjavur.

Even though they had all arrived en masse, once we got them through the door and to the drinks and food, they all had to catch up with everything everyone had been doing, just as if they hadn't all been continuously in each other's company for years. I remembered that from my *jovent* days; humans demand a certain amount of news and if there isn't really any (as there hadn't been for some centuries) then they get the habit of making smaller and smaller things into news.

Like any conversation about nothing, it was lively, with a dozen good arguments going within minutes. Since they were ignoring me, I continued to fetch drinks and carry around trays of food. My mind wandered back to Margaret.

It was always pleasant and comfortable to have her as a *companhona,* a close and deep friend with whom I could share anything. I didn't want to lose that, yet I did miss the wild irresponsibility of my *jovent:* fighting and verse-making, preening in front of *donzelhas* who were rarely serious but who didn't always laugh at the trivia of life . . . in short I missed everything I had been glad to be done with when I had married Margaret. Perhaps she sensed that, and that was why she was always angry.

I gulped the rest of my apple wine and went back to get another, realizing I had been standing all by myself for at least a full minute, staring into space—hardly the appropriate behavior for either a host or a diplomat.

After I filled my glass I looked around for somewhere to behave as I was supposed to, and slipped quietly into a group of poets. They were all locked in a vigorous argument, using absolutely stock ideas and phrases, about whether there had been any survivals from the First Cankam in the form of quotations in the Third. It was the kind of question that kept parties going until the next sunrise, not too different from the ones I'd had in my youth about whether Alain of Lille's manuscript reflected custom or exaggerated it, or the ones Margaret remembered about whether, if God required everyone to follow their reason at all times, then if reason led one temporarily into atheism, a Rational Christian must temporarily become an atheist. More timekilling for a species with nothing to do.

At least the apple wine was good; it occured to me that since most people would not have seen me take a couple of scrubbers before the party started, and Caledon apple wine is ferociously strong stuff, they were quite possibly assuming that I was morose and getting drunk.

I nodded politely to the people I was around and drifted over to where Tz'iquin was talking about growing up on his family farm. This played well to a group of Tamils, of course, because of their Velalla tradition. Tz'iquin was just going on about his mother's cooking (I doubted very much that she had ever cooked, except as a hobby), following his father around in the fields, and the feel of damp, warm, dark soil on his bare feet as a little boy. Two of the Tamil women were standing closer and closer to him with their eyes shining. Looked like there might be some rapprochement between Maya and Tamil, but nothing political was about to happen. I swallowed the last of my wine.

What was it about café society? There was some form of it in every one of the Thousand Cultures even where they tried to suppress it. Except for overtly anti-artistic cultures like Thorburg or Saint Michael, almost every one of the Thousand Cultures produced far more well-done art and intellectually respectable criticism than it could possibly consume. So young poseurs who claimed to want to become "serious artists" had to be willfully not knowing that it was ludicrous to hope for an audience. Hence the substitute that was universal around the Thousand Cultures: taking *each other* very seriously and pretending that the objects of their babble were the true centers of the universe.

It made me sad to keep coming back to the question, but just what in all the dark reaches of the universe *were* we alive for?

I had finished off two glasses and made polite noises in two conversations. The Maya were still not here. Kapilar and Margaret stood talking in a corner to the two Tamils in *suits-biz*. The topic was the discomfort of wearing a necktie. Some subjects just go on forever.

By now I had surely convinced everyone (except Margaret, who knew me well enough) that I was drunk and unhappy. The trick, now, was to use that impression for something. One of humanity's most enduring myths is *in vino veritas;* very well, then, I would let people think I was really drunk, and see what information, if any, they tried to pump me for, and what causes, if any, they tried to enlist me to.

On the other hand, if no one wanted to talk to me when I was drunk, it would be about as clear a piece of evidence as there could be that no one here thought the Council of Humanity had anything worth offering. That was what I suspected, and it wouldn't please Kiel if we reported it, but our job was not to tell him what he wanted to hear.

I checked the time; my first dose of scrubbers would be wearing off soon. With a slight nod to Margaret, who blinked at me hard once (our little signal for "I'll play along if you need me to"), I backed out of the room and went down the hallway to our apartment.

In the bathroom, I opened a drawer, grabbed the injector and the caps, loaded the injector, loosened my tie, undid my collar, and gave myself a quick pop in the neck, far down where it wouldn't be seen once I re-fastened my collar. Now I could drink heavily for another couple of hours without feeling it. I dropped the injector back in the drawer and closed it, then splashed a little water on my face.

I wished there were such a thing as a despair scrubber. Maybe it would all go brilliantly *and* they would all like each other *and* they would all go home early *and* Margaret and I would work things out tonight. Maybe I'd get a com call from God and he'd tell me how to do all that.

I splashed more water on, dried my face, and opened the bathroom door. A Tamil woman I had never seen before was in our parlor, admiring one of Bieris's paintings on our wall.

Her dress, close at the waist but full above and below, was a bold mix of colors, a vivid pattern that danced in the cool clarity of our decor. Her hair was very thick, black, and lustrous, her smooth skin dark even for a Tamil's, and when she turned and smiled, her teeth flashed a beautiful white. She looked at me for an instant, then turned back to look at the painting. "This is by *the* Bieris Real?" she asked, pronouncing it as if it were French, diphthongizing and omitting consonants, so that it took me a moment to realize what name she had said.

"Bee-*air*-eess *ray*-all. She's an old friend of ours," I explained. "I've known her since childhood back in Occitan and she was part of the mission on which I met Margaret."

"Her painting is very fine," she said, and turned back to look at it, at an angle that displayed a lot of hip and breast.

She was small and slim. Her eyes were huge, round, and very dark, her nose fine-boned and thin, lips wide and soft-looking. Her breast, seen in profile, was large and very high on her chest. It was an effort for me not to stare at it, or at the slim, perfect, deep brown leg sticking out of the fold of her dress. Her ankle was decorated with three thick gold bangles that must have been terribly heavy in this gravity.

Her body turned more toward the painting, but she looked back over her shoulder at me, with an arched, teasing expression, her chin held a little up.

It was a fast relief for depression, but I wasn't *altogether* crazy. "Er," I said. "Are you aware you walked into our private quarters? I must have left the door unlocked."

Her eyes widened and she smiled. "Oh, I'm sorry. I just was bored at the party, and thought you would be going to a kitchen or something and thought I might at least get to talk with you more privately there. I didn't know you'd be going to a private area, let alone to the bathroom, and then I didn't want to look like I was sneaking in and out of your quarters all by myself."

Not exactly an answer, but it wasn't *not* an answer, either. I was all the more attracted to her, because it was just the sort of *jeu-donzelhi* I had grown up with, but I had a mission to get accomplished, and less than twenty meters away, I had a wife with whom I hoped to make up, and being flung into a pubescent game of "do you want me?" annoyed me more than it aroused me.

"Well," I said, "It *is* our private quarters, and it certainly doesn't look proper for you to be here. Why don't you go out the private springer to, oh, the station a block from here—" I said this as I guided her to the springer door, my hand planted in the middle of her back—"and then walk back?"

"Sorry to inconvenience you," she said, smiling sweetly. She was wearing some remarkable scent, coconut and cinnamon with a touch of rose, and I carefully avoided breathing deeply. I set the code and she stepped into the gray field and out of existence. Then I sighed, stretched, and told myself that all in all that was well-handled. When I checked the lock memory on the door to the private quarters, I found that I *had* locked the door. I went back to the party.

I caught Margaret as she was floating over toward another conversation, at a pace intended to make sure anyone who wanted to could interrupt her. I set a hand heavily on her shoulder so that anyone watching might think it was the drunken husband threatening to quarrel. "Something you ought to know about," I said, very low, in her ear, and quickly told her about the mystery woman.

"Think she was sent by someone who researched your tastes?" Margaret asked, just as quietly.

"She'd be to the taste of any hetero male," I said. "She'll either vanish or be back in a few minutes. Just wanted you to know somebody, possibly an organization, possibly a loose group, possibly one particular woman, is getting nosy and aggressive."

"Are you doing the drunk act?" Margaret asked.

"Yeah. How's it holding?"

"Good as ever. I'll try to look worried and upset and see if I get approached by anybody. That was a pretty amateurish approach to you, though. Either it's a very amateur group, or she's an amateur on her own, is my guess."

"Nothing would make me feel better than discovering it's an amateur. I guess I better—"

The doorbell rang. I went to get it, expecting it to be that woman, returned from the springer station. Instead, it was more of the Tamil crowd, the ones who had panicked and decided not to come, now arriving because all of their friends had commed them word that the party was good. I spent a while bowing and nodding and pouring wine; it gave me an excuse to have some more, and encourage the idea that the host was pretty drunk.

In all the chaos and conversation, I did not pay much attention to the door, and so did not notice when the woman I had sprung out of my parlor returned. Perhaps Margaret let her in, or one of the other guests did.

As I went back to the service table, I saw her standing at the entrance to the hallway back to the private quarters. I gulped one glass, filled another, noted the wince on Kapilar's face that meant that he, at least, was taken in, and then sauntered, too casually, over to the woman by the hallway.

"Well," I said, "looks like you found the place again. Were you looking for a chance to get the rest of the jewelry and silverware? I'm Giraut Leones, by the way, your alleged host." I stuck out my hand.

She shook it, apparently unperturbed. "Auvaiyar. Sort of a poet, more of a critic. Known, for my acumen and wit, to dozens."

So this was the Auvaiyar who was the subject of so much gossip. "The editor of *Briandia*?"

"Yes. Have you read an issue?"

"Kapilar told me about it."

She nodded. "He's going to be one of our leading contributors. Mostly because I can't get many other people to contribute. Right now I'm thinking the next issue may have to be our all-death-threat special, since that's the only thing most people are willing to send me. Of course that may not be because of our editorial stance; more likely it's because I'm a critic."

"The critic is a vital part of any art scene," I pointed out. "Someone has to take responsibility for all the failed artists. How else could so many of them fail without your being there to distort and conceal their work?"

She smiled, a lot more than my feeble sarcasm justified, and arched her back slightly—a pretty effective display of her remarkable body. "Well, really, I don't know why I do it. Or how. Most of the poets I cause to fail, fail before I ever hear their names. It's an uncanny power." She straightened, as if from an uncomfortable position; it moved her a step closer to me. I felt as if her body were radiating heat like a stove.

If I backed up a tenth of a step, it would signal "no" and I'd be out of this.

I leaned back against the other hallway corner myself, letting my hips roll forward slightly. I felt we were speaking in an elaborate code—I just hoped I wasn't the only one reading it.

Slowly, deliberately, Auvaiyar took a balanced, dancerly step backward, gazing into my eyes with a wide smile. "So are Ix and the Maya ever going to get here?" she asked. "They need to start soon if they're going to corrupt and co-opt our cultural leadership, which is what four journals were saying this morning. Journals edited by people you failed to invite, notably Kannan."

I sighed. "Well, we couldn't invite everyone, and a known bigot has to pay some price for ignorance and stupidity. With luck maybe we can make him look like a whiny child. That's how he reads to me."

"Me too," Auvaiyar said. "I spent a year with him, writing waspish little articles for his journal and sleeping with him after every party, and it was *depressing*. All those lectures about cultural autonomy. Even when it was just the two of us talking he went right on as if he were speaking from an outline, but every time I was alone with him he couldn't keep his hands off my breasts. I could never decide whether I was more bored or sore."

She stroked one hand lightly down her ribcage, as if she might be about to run it over her breasts. It was quite a show but she'd overdone it this time and I laughed. To make it seem more like I was just drunk, I added, "Well, host-duty compels," and went off toward another conversation. I figured that the mill of rumor was now grinding along. I didn't want it to rev up any further until I knew what Auvaiyar was after.

It was possible that she liked me, but that wasn't my first bet. A person who clearly had some past involvements with people the Council of Humanity had strong reason to distrust— suddenly sexually fascinated with me—was probably not evidence of my charm.

At least this party wasn't dull.

I caught up with Margaret again; she glared furiously at me and whispered, "How's it going?"

I let myself fall sideways against a wall, made a wobbly, apologetic gesture, and said, very softly, "Perfectly, I guess, *companhona.*" Switching into Occitan, I added, "She's after something, anyway. And I doubt it's me."

"*Quer-expecto subj:anohito spec:poeta, enpi?*" We often switched languages when we were afraid of being overheard. Anyone could record us and translate it, but the odds of anyone other than us instantly understanding both our culture languages was vanishingly small.

"*Yap,*" I said. "*Tropa impudetz, m'es vis.* Even for me. Any reaction out there so far?"

"Just from Kapilar who felt he should warn me, you know, as our friend. Auvaiyar is a noted source of public scandal. Know who her last boyfriend is?"

"Kannan," I said. "She found a way to tell me, which involved telling me how much he liked her breasts. Kapilar's been with her too."

Margaret's eyes opened wide. "You're ahead of me, then. I had it from more than one person that she had a big blazing scandal of an involvement with Tz'iquin. Rumor is that he had to be *ordered* to break it off, directly by the Grand Council back in Yaxkintulum. He barely kept his job here. Supposedly."

It didn't sound at all like Tz'iquin. It did sound like two isolated moves in some incredibly complex game his grandfather had been running.

Margaret had a speculative look. I probably matched it. It was a bad idea for us to look too obviously curious, so we both nodded, and she put on the scolding face. "Pillow talk tonight?" I murmured, slumping down as if ashamed.

"See you at the mattress," she agreed. "Let's go. There's posing and posturing to do."

I grabbed a large jug of Caledon apple wine and began to circulate, refilling empty glasses and drinking generously from my own, as I went.

I had gotten about halfway around the room and was laughing too loudly at the jokes of some poets. Margaret's back bumped mine, and I glanced over my shoulder to see her holding a tray of canapés up for several people to grab. She had just a moment to murmur, "I just did the jealous wife routine on Auvaiyar. Low grade acting snotty. You should probably encourage her a little."

"Ja, donz," I said. I continued on my way, filling glasses as I went and stopping to talk about some technical issues in Tamil poetics I didn't understand, assure people that the Maya would be here soon, praise the architecture of the temples, and agree that the thunderheads that rolled in with the evening storm were among the most beautiful things I had seen on many worlds. (Every world has something beautiful if you squint hard enough.)

Finally, the bottle empty, I turned to find myself face to face again with Auvaiyar. She had the same smile, and said, "Oh, my. And I was hoping for more of the Caledon wine. You can really get drunk on Caledon stuff, can't you, but isn't it awfully sweet for everyday?" She was pointedly staring at Margaret, across the room.

I said, blandly, "Once one acquires the taste, nothing else is ever quite so satisfying."

"Still I would think you'd need frequent breaks from it to keep your palate fresh," Auvaiyar said. "I mean—" and she stared at Margaret's big buttocks "—it's so *thick.*"

I was beginning to feel irritated, and I needed to act seduced.

Auvaiyar's body was wonderful but her approach was unsubtle to the point of insulting.

She was standing closer. I had let my thoughts drift off into a vague focus inside myself; probably I had been standing there without saying anything for a half minute, and probably it looked more than anything else like some mixture of drunk, thunderstruck, and horny. "Well," I said, letting the room seem to spin, though the wine was just so much apple juice to my scrubber-filled bloodstream, "well, um, I can tell that we'll need to have many more conversations before all of this can be settled." I let the sentence hang for a moment, to make sure she noticed the vagueness of "all of this"—I might be too drunk to remember what we had just been talking about, or not. "Some conversations with good Caledon stuff and maybe some without. You know. Let me get you another glass."

As I walked over to the rack of bottles, she followed, and moved in close to "help" me pour. I felt her full soft breast pressing through the stiff fabric of my *suit-biz,* against the back of my upper arm, and deliberately pressed back gently. She didn't withdraw.

We passed some more conversation, about the wine mostly, before she wandered off into to the party again, the sway in her walk making her skirts swing back and forth and her ankle bangles jingle. In case anyone was watching, I sighed softly, leaned back against the wall, and took a big gulp of wine.

"For Margaret's sake I think I should tell you," Kapilar said, appearing at my elbow, "that aside from being the most prominent slut in New Tanjavur, Auvaiyar has an unparalleled record for causing trouble for important men."

I smiled slightly. I couldn't tell Kapilar everything, because we still didn't know, and might never know, who or what his loyalties lay with, but I didn't want to leave him totally in the dark, either, or have him reach the conclusion that *I* was irrational or untrustworthy. "Er," I said, letting myself fall out of the drunk act for a moment and hoping he would understand, "We've got a certain awareness of some of what you're telling me. Part of the job of a transcultural envoy is to seek out the top people in every field."

"Well, you've found *that*," Kapilar said. "And after all, you know, we are a people who have devoted a great deal of attention to the arts of love; I suppose she is an artist of that sort."

"You would know," I pointed out.

"Indeed I do, and I think I might be a little jealous. If you decide to pursue her. It is a unique experience; it's just that the cost afterwards is often rather high. On the other hand, I suppose you aren't brand-new to the game, and for a man who could look after himself, Auvaiyar might make a great adventure."

Why, I wondered, was he suddenly urging me to have that affair? Was he in on some scheme that also involved Auvaiyar? And if so, who else—

He was still talking. "—be careful you don't make it impossible for any reputable Tamil to associate with you. Your Jesus hung around with prostitutes and publicans, but if that was *all* the company he'd kept, no one would ever have heard of him. Though if one of them had been Auvaiyar, he might have enjoyed his anonymity—"

"Point taken," I said, "but I do recall that Murukan was pretty well married to Teyvayanai at the time that he went courting Valli—and that was part of what made him what he was." I needed to divert Kapilar from talking of Auvaiyar for a while, at least; the pressure was getting embarrassing, and I didn't know who might overhear.

"Well," he said, "I can see that as a plausible interpretation, especially for one who is only just learning the Cankam. But consider the exact nature of that parable. We are told that Valli was half-human, half-deer, and that Murukan fell in love with a drawing of her and courted her passionately after that. She only fell in love with him after he put on the guise of the old man and saved her from the elephant, so that she was brought into physical contact. Now, you could read that to mean that there is a pathway to the god that demands physical love, and heaven knows many of our people do, especially when they're adolescent and arguing with their parents. Or you could just as easily interpret it to say that physical love is to be trusted only to spiritual guides (for in his first and second appearances Murukan was a hunter and merchant, very much a part of the world, and it was only when he appeared to Valli as an old ascetic—and her refuge from the charging elephant—that she could run to embrace him). Or you could say, as we do, that it's the story and not the meaning that is primary anyway. On the other hand—"

I almost felt sorry for Kapilar, because just then, as he was getting warmed up and ready to go on for at least half an hour on the technical issues of interpretation, the doorbell rang.

Margaret went to get it, and then all conversation stopped as Ix, and a dozen Maya with him, entered the room. All of them wore the plain dark pants, broad-brimmed hat, light shirt, and hair in the bowl shape that he had made his own. They stood there perfectly still, as Margaret ran through introducing the line of Maya to the crowd of Tamils.

Once all the names had been spoken, there was a long silence while everyone looked at each other. Then Ix said, "We are here to share the pleasure of your company, and to try to make our company a pleasure to you. I *do* seem to remember this is supposed to be a party, is it not? Shall we proceed with enjoying ourselves?"

I hadn't seen Ix since he had come to tell us that he was going to reveal everything, and I was startled at the change in him now. He had greatly gained in stature and authority. Nou Occitan has an elective monarchy, and I've known five or six kings and queens at home—the one everyone called Yseut the Miserable was the *entendedora* (something more than girlfriend and a lot less than wife) of my one-time friend Marcabru. Since then I've probably met a dozen monarchs as I've bounced from culture to culture. But I don't think I'd ever seen anyone *really* move, speak, and act like a king before seeing Ix that night.

Some of it was that he was perfectly centered; the only person I've known who stood like that before was a master of ki hara do. With some individuals it may also have been his hypnotic skills, but it's very hard for even the best hypnotist to work in an environment of constant interruption and unplanned events, and a large party is that way; he might have engaged a few that way, but surely not the whole room.

Yet his rapport and power over people was undeniable. Ix seemed to direct the people around him, as if he always knew what they were about to say and was just a quarter step ahead of them, so that whatever they blurted out always fit perfectly into what he wanted to talk about next. Everything was intensely interesting to him but nothing was personal. Most of all he had a powerful presence that made you want to be around him and hear every word he said—which is nothing more than repeating the mystery of his great gain in presence and authority. It's probably best to say that you could feel it but it was much harder to describe it, and moreover it was even harder to explain than to describe.

Whatever it was, it got to the Tamils. When Ix acknowledged Kapilar by name, he looked down as shyly as a small boy whose mother is recounting his exploits in school. There were two or three other Tamils Ix had already met, and he greeted them by name. When he did, I saw unmistakable jealousy on the faces of several of the other Tamils. Everyone seemed greatly pleased as soon as he learned their names and addressed them by them; his attention seemed to make them all glow. Undoubtedly Kannan and all the other bigots would soon be denouncing them as traitors to their people, but at least in some artistic circles, a connection to Ix's prophecy was being established as chic, hip, *kulturny,* and *tropa gens.*

When dark fell, and the room lights came on, the party settled into a large circle around Ix and a small number of people outside it. Tz'iquin and I stood in the corner drinking together, and one or two things gave me the distinct feeling that Tz'iquin, too, had taken a large dose of scrubbers and was quite immune to the effect of the alcohol. Probably each of us was standing here pretending to be drunk in hopes of taking advantage of the other.

"He seems to be doing well," Tz'iquin said. "They're listening, and listening seriously to him. They used to talk with me, just to shock their parents, but they never heard a word I said. At least not compared to the attention that Ix is getting."

I glanced sideways at him. His face was blank and impassive. "You're not . . . jealous?"

He shrugged. "Well, I've been in New Tanjavur a long time. And I'm not naturally a loner. And for several years the Maya wouldn't speak to me because I associated with Tamils, and the Tamils treated me as if I were a freak show exhibit: they were so fascinated with there being a Maya who would talk to them that they didn't bother to hear what I said. It would have been nice to have someone to listen." He sighed. "If you decide to mess around with Auvaiyar, you'll discover that she *really* doesn't listen. She's better at not listening than anyone I've ever known."

"Is it all that obvious that she's uh, interested?" I asked.

"It's also obvious that you are; don't try to tell me that you were working on driving Auvaiyar away by standing half a centimeter from her for all that time over in the corner."

I nodded, shrugged, and finished off my glass. "She certainly has charm and it isn't unpleasant to imagine getting her into bed."

"There are worse ways to spend time," Tz'iquin agreed. "She's very, um, good at what she does, in a professional way."

"Who does she really work for?" I asked, chancing the question because I seriously doubted it was anyone Maya.

"That's what everyone would like to know. I asked her directly once. She laughed and started undressing, which is Auvaiyar's answer to anything you say to her that she doesn't want to answer. That is, if she's decides you're the man she wants at the moment—which is all the longer she ever holds to that decision." His arms were wrapped around his chest, he was staring at the floor, and his hands gripped his upper arms fiercely.

"I don't think you hate her," I said, "and I also don't think you're indifferent to her. And that's why I should probably tell you that all I'm doing is trying to find out who, or what, is trying to get at the Embassy by using her to attract me. I really don't feel like messing up my marriage to Margaret and *deu sait* I know that young women who look like that rarely pursue men who look like me, not when they have a lot more attractive choices. So you may, if you wish, be jealous about Auvaiyar, but please don't aim any of it at me."

"I understand. Thank you. It's kind of you to tell me that . . . well. My job is also to help bring our peoples together, you know. And so when there was the chance for an affair with a Tamil woman—and a very beautiful one, such a highly respected critic, and a one-time apologist for the worst sort of culturism—well, a fellow can dream, can't he? I imagined that she would turn out to be a lovely person underneath, as beautiful in the soul as in the body, and this long crusade I've been carrying out on Grandfather's orders would be much less lonely . . . oh, what's the use?" He gulped his drink; anyone looking at us was going to think we were the two unhappiest drunks in human space. "You can guess the whole story, I'm sure. It turned out that Auvaiyar will sit there while a man talks about anything, and she'll repeat your prejudices back to you, and whenever you start to think of something serious or ask her if she feels anything for you, she'll initiate sex, right then and just the way you like it, to shut you up.

"And after a while you discover that you don't know anything of what she really thinks. All you know is what she's like in bed, and that aside from that you might as well be talking to a parrot. And if you stay at it as long as I did, as long as Kapilar or Kannan did, you get to find out that you are a fool. There was a time when I was prepared to defy the whole Grand Council, and my grandfather and the whole lineage, just to marry Auvaiyar."

"Why didn't you?"

"She wouldn't say yes. Or no. Or discuss it. Or even say that she wasn't ready yet. Same answer I got about love, and trust, and everything. Do you know, we were together for a full year and I have no idea whether she has any living relatives, or where her house or apartment was, or what foods she likes or doesn't or for that matter anything about what she liked or disliked except in Tamil poetry.

"So I stood in front of Grandfather and said I'd defy him and the whole damned Maya civilization, but by the Four Founders and Hunahpu and all the Lords of Xibalbá I was going to marry this woman. And a few days later Grandfather commed to tell me that he would come to whatever ceremony we had and defend Auvaiyar's presence to the whole Peccary lineage—can you conceive how much love and courage it took for him to offer that?

"And by that time I had to admit that I couldn't get Auvaiyar to take me. I had to explain that to Grandfather, and when I was done explaining he was very kind, very gentle about it, but I swear I could hear him thinking—'What an utter, utter fool my grandson is.'

"At last, after some more endless time like that, one day I didn't call her or see her; then the day following I didn't either, and the day after that . . . and she never even came around to ask why, either. After a while she took up with another culturist poet. So yes, I look at her and I gnaw my heart into sour little chunks. If you have to do anything with her, please try to do it out of my sight, as a favor to a friend, all right?"

"Agreed," I said. "More wine?"

"More wine."

We went over to the table and I poured a big glass for each of us. He tapped his glass on mine, and said, "Damn love to hell."

"I won't drink to that," I told him. "Will you drink to 'better luck next time?' "

He would so we did. Then we topped up our glasses and went to lean against the wall together, and watch Ix try to convert Tamil poseurs to a Maya prophecy.

"Looks like *you* have a rival," Tz'iquin said, teasing me, and nodding toward where Ix sat. Margaret had wedged her way in close to his feet, and Auvaiyar was right next to him, all but sitting in his lap. He was telling some immensely complicated story that everyone found very funny.

Nodding to Tz'iquin, I moved to the edge of the crowd so I could hear better. "But that's the whole point," a young Tamil was saying, "we are what our stories make us. Without them we aren't anything. So if we give them up, who will we be?"

Ix smiled. "That is the heart of the matter, isn't it? None of us really wants to just become one more segment of the vast Interstellar metaculture, do we? Even though it's already here, has been here for centuries in the Inner Sphere, and we couldn't resist it any more than we could undo the Age of European Conquest, the Industrial Revolution, World War III, or the Inward Turn.

"And I won't insult you by asking what's so terrible about it. We are just beginning to comprehend that by the time we are old enough to die there will be no more people like us. The Interstellar metaculture is converting us all into relics, and our grandchildren will be Interstellar, not Tamil or Maya; the only cultural descendants we will have will be readers and critics who study our ways but don't live them. We are facing oblivion and our hearts ache."

He looked around at everyone gathered there; the group was silent and motionless, frozen by his having said that.

"And yet," he said, "there are more and less honorable oblivions. We could conceivably ally with each other, destroy all the springers on the planet, and go it on our own until the next starships get here from Sol or Eta Cassiopeia—a generation at best. We could go down fighting each other and help rid human space of any trace of either of us. We could pass local laws to preserve the old ways, and watch all of history bypass us. Or—we could reach out to other cultures, join them, embrace them, and in exchange for preserving as much of their cultures as we are able to take in, let them preserve as much of ours as they can grasp. The Interstellar metaculture will keep right on expanding, no matter what we do, but if we present our cultures to it properly, we can penetrate it, flavor and differentiate it."

Auvaiyar squirmed; it looked like she was eager to ask a question, but it also very definitely got her body on display to Ix. "But," she said, "but—but aren't most of the Thousand Cultures already Interstellar? The Interstellar trend started in the Inner Sphere *because* they had so many crowded worlds and so many cultures living next to each other. They didn't need it on Earth, where the Inward Turn had already produced a single culture. What if the Interstellars don't want to be 'flavored' or 'differentiated'? I don't think they do, and there are a lot more of them than there are of us."

Auvaiyar had posed a good question: the Inner Sphere, the solar systems that were in close to the Sol System, had much more population than the rest of the Thousand Cultures, and had more than 800 of the cultures. And because Alpha Centauri, 61 Cygni, Epsilon Eridani, Tau Ceti, Epsilon Indi, and Procyon were all so close to each other and Earth, the Interstellar metaculture had begun to develop there before the colonization period was even really over; Terstad itself was the language of the Inner Sphere. Compared to the Inner Sphere, the other four hundred of the Thousand Cultures, scattered across nineteen other solar systems, weren't much more than the debris of humanity. The idea that a world like Briand, with a population less than a tenth that of the New York Transpolis, Ceres, New Honshu, or Klein City, would swing any weight in intercultural affairs, even if its inhabitants all dedicated themselves to doing so, was ridiculous.

I had been aware of all this without thinking it through, just noticing and understanding it while I waited for Ix to say something. Finally, he said, "I believe it was one of the Christian saints back on old Earth who said we are summoned to try but success or failure is in heaven's hands."

Kapilar said, softly, looking down at his hands, "It seems a pity that for thousands of years your people, and mine, have struggled to keep from being absorbed and assimilated, and at the end all we can do is try to be assimilated in a less-unacceptable way."

Ix looked straight at him, and the usual warmth was not there; Kapilar froze first, then everyone around him, then the whole crowd. Finally Ix said, "Remember my third principle. Remember that it commands you not to believe the comforting lies anymore. We are not really the Maya and you are not really the Tamils. If that distinction belongs to anyone it belongs to people on Earth who no longer know anything of their ancestry, or to people in various of the Thousand Cultures who made real, living cultures on new worlds, when their old Earth cultures went out to exile and diaspora in the twenty-fourth century. We are the creation of some misguided scholars and artists who packed up a set of long-dead cultural artifacts and a million frozen test-tube embryos and sent us out here to live by their books. We are not the people of *Popul Vuh* and the codices, and you are not the people of the Cankam anthologies. Rather, we are the inventions of wealthy Asians and Europeans, who felt guilty about the conversion of most of Central America to antimatter-burned glass. You are the results of the dream of a single family of corporate barons who had come to admire the Cankam poetry enough so that they wanted someone somewhere to speak it. It is time to drop their dreams—long past time—and to begin to dream our own, to stop asking what sort of people made the inscriptions and wrote the books, and start asking what sort of people live under blue-white Metallah and the indigo sky. Once we see that *that* is who we are, and not the foolish dreams of the long-dead—then we may well have a story to tell that the rest of humanity will have to listen to, will want to know about. Till we do that, all we are is an echo of things they can get more accurately from their libraries."

He had held them still with his voice and his manner while he delivered that message; he had made them all hear it. But when he was done, nothing could have stopped their reaction. At once the Tamils were on their feet, shouting at him, and an instant later so

were the Maya. I ran forward, forgetting to play drunk in my anxiety to keep anyone from hitting each other or pulling weapons.
Margaret was on her feet, struggling to keep two shouting Tamils
from assaulting one screaming Maya. I had just a glimpse of Auvaiyar's dramatic figure as she cut out through the door; at that
moment I blessed her for being the only sane one here.

The thing that saved us was that they didn't really want to
hurt or fight each other. They wanted to hurt Ix. And since he
stood with such perfect calm, offering no physical threat, right
among them, none of them was quite willing to throw the first
punch or kick. Consequently despite the passion with which the
shouting and arm-waving had started, there were no punches
thrown, just some inept shoving, and it only took Margaret and
I a few minutes to deal with it. It was clear that they were too
upset to stick around and talk it out once they calmed down
(calming down would not happen for hours, I judged) but also so
far no one, other than perhaps Ix, had done anything unforgive-
able. Common sense said the thing to do was shove them out the
door as fast as we decently could, which is what Margaret and I
did. Somewhere along the way she got the clever idea of dispersing them by using one of the Embassy springers to spring
them to a bunch of public springer sites around the city, thus
scattering the crowd and giving them less chance to run into each
other on the street on the way home.

"Great idea," I said, as we sprang yet another couple to a station near their home. "How many are left out there?"

"Just Ix, Kapilar, and Tz'iquin, if you got the tall drunk one to
go out the front door."

"I did. It took some effort because he wasn't being rowdy, he
just wanted to explain to Ix that he was right about the Tamils
but not about the Maya, that the Maya *were* authentic because
the spirits, I guess, had been involved in restoring Maya culture
but not in the Tamil culture."

"Bigotry rearing its—wait a minute. That guy was a Tamil.
And he's saying that the *Maya*—"

"Oh, pretty much the same situation as Kapilar. Temporarily swung from hating them without knowing them to knowing a little bit and loving everything he knows. He'll level off, you know. The problem with getting him out was that he knew perfectly well he wasn't dangerous and wasn't going to hit anybody, and he just wanted to stay and talk to Ix, which really was a reasonable enough request. So I had to make up six or seven things to get him to postpone that. At least he isn't lost to the cause, and I'm sure a lot of these folks are."

"In a couple of cases we can hope that they *are* lost."

"Auvaiyar?" I asked. "Did she get more annoying?"

"Maybe. Or maybe I just got to see more of her. What is it that causes your whole gender to lose all its brains when someone like that comes along?"

"Not my *whole* gender, Margaret, just heteros past puberty. I don't know either. It annoys me, too, whether you believe that or not. Anyway, we should get back to the reception area, and see if Ix and the others are at knifepoint yet."

She nodded. "How do I look?"

"A minor mess. I bet I do too."

She reached up to straighten my tie and smooth my thinning hair back down onto my head. "Better. Now fix me."

She was fine except for her collar. I tugged it into place. The feel of her soft throat next to my hand started a hint of tears in my eyes.

When we got back to the remnants of the party, we found the three men sitting over hot coffee, talking quietly and reasonably. Tz'iquin and Kapilar had already been familiar with Ix's blunt honesty and his analysis of the situation, and knew that this night's abrupt ending had been a calculated strategy by Ix to guarantee that his ideas would be talked about everywhere. "And it's a bit like losing your innocence," Kapilar said. "As soon as they really entertain the thought that their books are made up, they'll be unable to believe in them enough to kill each other."

"I wish I believed that," Tz'iquin said. "Seems more likely to me that the idea is so threatening that rather than admit it attracts them, they're going to be willing to kill people about it."

"Time will tell," Ix said. "But people have to be trusted with the whole truth, I think, before we can expect anything of them. Meanwhile they rejected it in the right way; they were upset by it and went off to think about it and try to prepare rebuttals."

"Do you have a next move in mind?" I asked him, pouring coffee for myself.

"I teach, and I look for converts."

Kapilar nodded. "If I may say so, I was glad to be with you tonight; I will remember it all my life."

"Good," Ix said, "and better if you not only remember it but repeat it."

Tz'iquin had grown curiously quiet while the others had been talking, but now he looked up and smiled. "It's so strange. More progress here than we'd made in many stanyears. And a real prophet—I mean, not just an engineered event—and a really new vision. I feel . . . alive. And a little bit like what I want to do is go make friends with everyone, or go sit on a mountaintop until I see a vision, or something."

Ix stood up. "We should go. Margaret and Giraut will want to get to bed."

They got up and departed within moments, all three of them now chatting comfortably about the evening, declining the use of the springer since the night storm had passed and it was a cool, fine night to be out in the streets. They were going to walk to Kapilar's apartment to finish talking.

The household robots knew what to do with the silver, leftovers, glasses, table cloths, and so forth, so Margaret and I summoned the robots and returned to our private apartment. Once we had gotten into bed, I leaned closer, and she didn't lean away, so I said, "What do you think happened this evening, *companhona?*"

She sighed and rolled toward me, putting her head on my chest, resting a hand on my belly. She was quiet for a long time and I had almost fallen asleep when she said, "You know, even though Ix, Kapilar, and Tz'iquin were very confident, and happier than they had been about anything in quite a while . . . I feel more frightened than ever about this awful world. Don't you?"

"Well, this is without a doubt the most frightening and the least attractive place the Council has ever sent us, for all sorts of perfectly objective reasons, but *midons,* I think something else entirely is bothering you, and I wish you would explain what it is to me. Because I have learned to trust and value your hunches very much, you know, and if you feel something isn't right, chances are it isn't."

"Well, at least part of it is that those three felt so confident after that uproar," she said. "People were almost hitting each other, Giraut, even if it was better suppressed than usual, by local standards. We could damned well have had a bare-hands killing right here in the Embassy, I'm sure of it. And yet all the locals felt that it was a better gathering than they had a right to expect. So . . . *what* do they usually expect?

"They have no practice at tolerance, Giraut. Nothing! There's nothing here to build even a truce on—and Ix is going to walk right out among them and try to talk them into positive love for each other. Do you realize he's *planning* to be martyred?" Her hand on my belly tightened, relaxed, stroked from my sternum to my navel. "God I'm glad to be alone with you right now, Giraut; out of the silly costume and the painful shoes and most of all out of a roomful of people that I had to keep pretending to like and treat seriously, when all I really wanted to do was to shake them and demand to know when they were going to commit their next atrocity."

"This is a very odd way for a diplomat to talk."

"*Yap, yap.* Well, this diplomat feels odd." She sat up for a moment and I was afraid she would leave the bed. "Giraut, tonight I got a few minutes to talk alone with Ix, and—well, he did it again. I feel calmer, and like talking to you. I swear by all God's equilibria I had my guard up against hypnosis."

"I believe you," I said. "Ix is a very remarkable man."

"Well, then. Giraut, it's not you, exactly. What's bothering me is . . . oh, well. I don't know. Maybe I shouldn't tell you till we're out of here, or maybe I should never tell you."

"It's probably not good to keep it to yourself. And you know, no matter what it is, I'm not going to hate you, or stop loving you?"

"I wish I knew that. Or even better, if I just knew for sure that you were really as noble and as *gens* as you try so hard to act. Oh, I don't really doubt you, Giraut. And it probably would be a good thing, in the long run, if I just talked about it." She lay on my chest for so long, silently, that I thought she had gone to sleep; then I felt the warm tears splashing onto my sternum. I held her closer and said, "You've really got to tell somebody, *midons*—"

"I did. That's what I was getting to before. I got into a conversation with Ix, and he asked me—I don't know what he asked me—but as soon as he asked me, everything spilled out in about two minutes, and he answered in about one. And now I think I'm more bothered by his advice than I was by the problem. Giraut, what if he really is a Saiva saint, or a prophet, or whatever you call someone that brings wisdom from the gods? Or . . . even from God?"

"Then it might not be bad to listen to him. I thought you didn't believe in any gods anymore."

"I'm down to just one and I only believe in him when I need it. Like now." She hung onto me as if the bed were floating on a stormy sea. "Giraut . . . oh, let me try to lead up to it, and maybe courage will come and I'll know what to do, and maybe you'll guess and I won't have to say it . . . and maybe we'll just fall asleep like this. It's lovely to hang onto you and feel like you love me.

"So, let me try." She paused for a long time, and then spoke very softly and quickly. "I had a lot of dreams when I was younger too, you know. You looked so . . . well, you were the thing I'd been fantasizing about. Or you looked like it. An artist, handsome, a fighter—well, all the stuff that wasn't supposed to matter to a good stolid practical repressed little Caledon girl like me. I thought you'd never be interested in me, or we'd just be friends or something, and then you picked me over Valerie. That meant more to me than you can possibly imagine. Valerie and I been friends since we could both talk and she'd always been the pretty one.

"And then . . . well, you're cranky and you have weird ideas about rights you should have just because you're a man, and you brood, and sometimes you flirt with other women in a way that scares me, and—it makes me feel stupid, you know, because I knew perfectly well what you were when I married you and I don't think there's any excuse for getting angry because that's just what I got.

"But . . . oh, Giraut, damn, I don't think I can explain this. I was young too, once, you know, I'm younger than you, and I never got to be really young, not the way you did—there was no *jovent* in Utilitopia, nobody Caledon ever fell into *finamor*, I couldn't have been a *donzelha*.

"And I know that if you're talking about adventure, well, we've been to a lot of planets and a lot of cultures on those planets, and we've been shot at and been through more than one revolution and all of it, but . . . well, it just isn't what I dreamed about or thought I really wanted, and I know it's a bunch of little-girl dreams, but when I married you it was because you had walked right out of those dreams, and you never did take me back in there with you. That wasn't your fault, I guess. You were about ready to grow up, and I just wasn't quite yet, and I followed you, and now I'll never have a time like that in my life . . . "

Her voice trailed off into a long sigh, and she held onto me the way she sometimes did after a nightmare. I had nothing to say, but I wanted her to keep talking, so I asked, "And what did Ix tell you?"

"That if the world didn't live up to my standards then I should either tell it or accept it, but that I had no right to just hold a grudge against it silently. At first I thought he was trying to make me feel like a silly child, but he was so gentle and so nice about it that afterwards I said to myself, *nop, nop,* that's me picking on myself, he was just calling things to my attention. And then I felt like he was telling me that my problem with loving you is the same problem I would feel with loving the whole world—and maybe that he wanted me to do both? A saint would want you to love the whole world, wouldn't he, and would know something about how to do it?"

"How could I know? If Ix is a saint he's the first I've ever known, and I probably understand him less than you do. *M'es vis, companhona,* the Saiva saints were always supposed to be a bit inexplicable. Even if he were being extremely clear and coherent, anyway, he's talking about a subject that I suspect I don't understand at all well, because I don't think I'm very good at love, myself. *Finamor,* lust, sentimentality, I can do all those, and I love you, but I'm obviously not *good* at love, because I never know when I'm doing the right thing. The whole subject is pretty confusing."

"Isn't it?" she turned her head and gently kissed me. "Anyway, that's what Ix said. Demand what I was expecting or stop expecting, but hold no grudges either way."

"Speaking just for myself, I don't think I've ever loved anything as much as I love my grudges."

"Me either, love. And you know—" her voice was down to the softest whisper—"that's what makes me so afraid about Briand. The grudges here are so fine and fierce and gorgeous, compared with anything else they have here. There's nothing remarkable about their cooking or their poetry or their sex lives or anything like that, and the few things that are unusual are mostly the little squalid failed things, like the Maya not managing to feed everyone even though food is free, or the Tamils being so fussy and rigid in their criticism. But the ethnic hatred! It's elaborate, detailed, passionate . . . it's what everyone here really loves, and

I don't think they're capable of producing anything else that can compete. Poor Ix. To be a rival to that . . . "

I chanced slipping my arms around her; she didn't pull away. I thought about kissing her, but she seemed to be drifting and I didn't want to spoil this. I thought about talking about more politics, but I had nothing to say at that moment. So I lay there, holding Margaret, and listened to her breathing slow as she fell asleep. I was still holding her when we woke up in the morning; she opened her eyes, saw me, and got up and went into the bathroom. She might have been crying in there, but by the time she came out she was calm, friendly—and distant, as ever, again.

During my shower, I kept thinking about Ix. Maya prophet acting like a Saiva saint? Crazy miserable man looking to be a martyr? Clever fake, brilliant hypnotist, cunning con man, first-rate politician? . . . or just a very smart *toszet* who knew something about love? And where might all those overlap?

The next twenty or so days were a difficult combination of too much information and too little. Too much because reports were coming in every hour, from our monitoring of local media and from people like Kapilar and Tz'iquin, about events involving Ix, and too little because Kiel still wouldn't let us go outside the Embassy, and every news and intelligence report we got was wildly inaccurate.

There were about five of Ix out there. First of all, there was the one people in Mayatown wanted him to be: the one who ceaselessly appeared everywhere, defying police orders time after time, often half a step ahead of arrest for incitement, always insistently beating on the same few themes—full equality, an end to community barriers, an end to separate schooling, the abolition of every public ceremony and custom that in any way was used by the Tamils to remind the Maya that they were resident aliens without formal legal rights.

Then there was the version of Ix that frightened everyone back in Yaxkintulum: the one who denounced much of Maya mythology itself and demanded an end to any Maya custom that separated them from their "Tamil brothers."

The more conventional and conservative Tamils had their own nightmares about Ix, which often strongly resembled the dreams the Maya of Mayatown had about him. Most of the Tamils of New Tanjavur looked at him and saw the overturner of the conventions and norms of order, a lawless radical with a terrifying willingness to put large mobs of angry, noisy Maya into the streets of Mayatown. More frightening still was that a few Tamils were joining him and that many, especially younger students, were attracted to his ideas.

Affection for Ix and his ideas was highly fashionable among the younger Tamils, which led to the strangest of all versions of Ix (at least to me): the living saint and the man of peace who was here to unite the two peoples and to bring Briand together in a newer, freer society, in which the Tamil culture could flourish without the crushing weight exerted by the old Cankam tradition and the emotional deadening of bigotry. Auvaiyar's "Briandism" had caught on like wildfire, perhaps because all thought had tended to extreme, pro-Cankam conservatism for so long that the new kind of argument was refreshing, perhaps as a fad, or even because a large number of Tamils were really persuaded by Ix's message.

This "fashionable Tamil Ix" was the Ix who tended to be invoked whenever the real Ix invited Tamils to the front row of the crowd, ate and drank with them, and might sting them with words one moment but always expressed love and admiration for them the next.

The only Ix that it was hard to get any news about was the real one. To understand what the real Ix was up to, and not what was being added to all the various legends, Margaret and I often had to rely on reading between the lines of reports a day or two later. Even Kapilar and Tz'iquin were less and less help as time went on, because it was clear they were becoming followers of Ix and

Briandists, and hence what they said had to be suspected of promoting that agenda.

I kept dropping notes to Kiel about the potential importance of Briandism and the danger of letting it grow up out of contact with us, and I kept getting short notes back from Ms. Skine saying that the Ambassador read my daily reports and letters with interest and was not unaware of the problem. When I encountered him socially—and with only about forty of us Council diplomats living in the Embassy, that was almost daily—he seemed to be always signaling that this would not be a good time to talk. Knowing him for the cunning old rascal he was, I figured that if he just meant to put me off, he would have found a subtler and more effective way of doing it. So my guess was that there was indeed something that made it necessary for him to delay saying anything, and perhaps he was trusting me to figure that out for myself, and not trouble him until he was ready to talk.

As I explained to Shan, early one morning, on a supposedly-secure com link, "It really does seem like Kiel's serious about this as a matter of safety, without much other agenda. That's why he's so hard to argue with. He feels that the whole works is going to blow apart at any moment, and that it isn't worth sacrificing any of our Council people to a hopeless cause. And—sir, if I may speak bluntly—"

"When have you not?"

"How would you know?"

"I miss you, Giraut." He grinned. "Of course, be as frank as you like. The gods alone know why but I value your judgement."

"Well, then, I wouldn't have said there was any hope, twenty days ago, either. The more you find out about how much they hate each other—and the *way* they hate each other, the underlying symbolism, that memo Margaret sent you about it—"

"I read that. It scared the hell out of me."

"It was intended to," I said. "Well, all in all, looking at the evidence, if I were Kiel, I'd seriously consider that there was nothing to gain here, but that a lot of Council personnel could get hurt or killed. Even if they aren't physically roughed up, the things that are apt to happen in New Tanjavur are so awful that it's just as well if they never form any emotional attachments."

"You keep saying these things as if you're leading up to telling me that you don't believe them anymore."

"I don't *not* believe them. That's what bothers me. It just seems that somehow, Ix is having an effect. Very slowly, the rate of violence is falling off, and since this miserable planet doesn't have seasons, it doesn't seem likely that it's a seasonal change. Sir Qrala tells me that the decrease in violence is statistically significant. Kapilar tells me that at the best parties among the artists and critics, right now, Maya jokes are received with embarrassed snickers, as if they were childish and embarrassing—which they are, but who'd have thought you'd see that reaction among Tamils? And there's maybe a dozen other small signs that something is slowly crushing out the worst of it. I don't think they're just running out of energy, either. I think this is something to do with Ix. He's challenging people to be better, and—not always, but in some numbers—they're rising to his challenge."

Shan nodded. "I might as well tell you that the reports I'm getting from the very few agents in place we have in New Tanjavur are pretty much in agreement with you about that. And furthermore, the effect is spreading to Yaxkintulum; there were big demonstrations outside the Eastern temples yesterday, demanding that they go over to the Ix movement. I suppose we could blame it on the simplicity of his message or his charisma or a coincidence of historical forces, but all those are just ways of saying that something beyond our understanding is at work here. Might as well say it's divine intervention, eh?"

"Sir," I said, "I'd avoid that phrase. It's being used seriously by half the people in the Embassy, including quite a few that I know have been planted here by the Office of Special Projects. One risk you haven't discussed is that we may have some converts right here among Council personnel—if not already, then pretty soon."

Shan nodded unhappily. "There's even a notion among staff here that perhaps we should spread Ix's ideas to the rest of the Thousand Cultures. The argument is that they're more effective than anything we've ever tried for reducing ethnic conflict."

"Well, I think probably they're right about that, as far as it goes. I haven't seen anything like this, sir—of course I haven't seen enough of it, because I've been locked in the stupid embassy, so maybe it's just an artifact of the reporting. But Ix's doctrine seems to be a lot more effective than negotiations, or sending in CSP peacekeepers, or PR campaigns—or anything I've ever seen us try."

He sighed. "You may be right, but I can't get happy about the prospect of the Office of Special Projects becoming involved in spreading a cult. We have enough trouble already with the number of people who think that we're opposed to their particular religion—usually because we don't embrace it enough to suit them, sometimes because they become aware that our goal of human unity is ultimately opposed to anyone who wants to divide the world into believers and unbelievers." He groaned. "And yet . . . and yet . . . there *is* something appealing and common-sensical about fighting hate by teaching people to love. Oh, well, I don't have to decide today, and I'm grateful for that too. Anything else to report?"

"Not from my end."

"Well, then, be careful, keep pushing to get regular access to the city, and when you see Ix again, try to avoid being converted. Good luck."

"Thank you," I said, but he had clicked off without waiting to hear my reply.

Only about an hour after that conversation, Kiel called a big general meeting, for all Embassy staff except the CSP guards on duty. He spent a few minutes hemming and hawing, talking about how well everyone had done their jobs in these very difficult circumstances, but then—just when I thought he'd also be calling in reports from Skine and Qrala and their staffs—he announced that the restrictions on going outside the Embassy were officially lifted as of sunrise tomorrow, and urged all those of us who needed to get out into the city to do our work to "get out there as soon as possible, because even though I've been keeping you in here, I'm aware that our intelligence work is not what it should be due to your being trapped in here. I want you to go find out what I ought to know, and bring it back—soon." With a half-smile, he added, "You may expect further self-contradictions at any moment."

Skine didn't look happy, but Qrala was beaming, which told me that this really was a good thing. Margaret and I went to bed early so that we could get out of the Embassy as early as possible the next day. We didn't speak, and she slept far over toward the edge of the bed.

The next morning, just before sunrise, I sat with Margaret, finishing breakfast on the Embassy terrace, sipping chilled fruit juice and waiting for the first hot wind to blow. I felt contented, as if some great battle had just been won, as if whatever evil the day would bring couldn't compare with the unalloyed good of getting out into the city.

After a long while, Margaret sighed and leaned back, rubbing her hands over her face like a sleepy squirrel. "You know, Nansen is a high gravity world, even if it's not as high as this, and you'd think that having grown up there I wouldn't be bothered by this, but I swear every night I sleep less well, and every morning I wake up tireder. Somehow the difference between 115% of standard at home and 130% of standard here is just *huge,* and it's grinding me down."

"We definitely want our next posting on a light-gravity world," I agreed. "This place gets to me, too." I reached out and took her hand. "You know, officially we're only supposed to be here until the basic cultural problems get back to merely miserable. They just want us to see that whatever happens here turns out to be something the Council can live with. As soon as things don't look like they're heading for immediate social collapse, our job is done. So chances are that we'll be out of here in a couple of stanyears at worst, probably a lot less. That's something to think about."

"Well, yap, yap, it's a nice thought as far as it goes," she said, squeezing my hand but then pulling her hand away and putting it into her lap. "Not very comforting at the moment."

"Oh, I wasn't trying to cheer you up by telling you it would be over soon, *midons*. What I was working my way around to is that in a short time we're going to be off this job and then we will have a lot of accumulated leave coming. Rather than go back to see my family or yours, maybe we should go somewhere very warm, safe, and bland. Some nice place with a slightly salty ocean, wide warm beaches, nothing poisonous or dangerous at all, thoroughly Interstellar so that we don't have to learn any customs or respect anybody's traditions. Then you and I spend a lot of time hanging out, looking at the sea, sunbathing, getting to know each other again, all of that." I took another sip of the juice; it was still cold enough to chill my teeth. I savored it, knowing just how uncomfortable I would be within the hour. I had never thought I would pine for the rocky coast of Caledony, with its twice-daily freezing-rain storms, but right now I'd have given a lot to be on a visit there—hell, I'd have been happy to see Margaret's most stiff-necked relatives just to be where I had to put a coat on again.

At first I didn't think she was going to answer at all, but then, staring off into space somewhere well to my left, she said, "Giraut, I want to tell you something stupid. Usually I can only tell you these things during pillow talk but I'm feeling brave this morning."

"Courage should never be wasted," I said, *"Tostemz enseingnamen, tostemz valor!"*

She smiled and looked right at me. "You know, I think I first fell in love with you because you were always saying things like that, and the funny thing is, that has a lot to do with what the matter is. Giraut, you know as well as I do that Briand is a too-hot, too-heavy, sweaty, hate-filled little pocket of hell. The funny thing is that this is just what I was expecting when I first went into Council service, and when Shan first recruited us for the Office of Special Projects. You keep forgetting that you grew up in a romance, but I grew up longing to be in one. I wanted danger, and excitement, and mystery, and—oh, well. Lots of things, Giraut. I kept thinking how many ways I wanted to live where every day had excitement, secrets, danger, passion . . . ”

I nodded. This particular melancholy was very common in Caledons of her generation, the ones who had reached their late teens or so before the springer. Traditional Caledon culture had not provided much room for an adolescence, not as most cultures knew it anyway, so it was hardly surprising that many Caledon adults wished with all their hearts for a chance to have gone through an adolescence, or that they were attracted to my home culture (where traditionally adolescence lasted ten to fifteen stanyears, sometimes more). I could easily see how the Tamil culture—fighting, poetry, all the rest of it—could exert exactly the same attraction, but here it was a complete nightmare—in Nou Occitan, the worst things had been kept hidden, but here the worst things were in your face all day long. So naturally this place attracted Margaret, and just as naturally it horrified her, and I would have been surprised if it *hadn't* made her nervous and vaguely afraid all the time.

“Well,” she said, “you can guess it, now, can’t you?”

I had no idea what she was talking about. “Guess it? Guess what?”

She paused for a long time and when she spoke again she wasn’t looking at me at all. “I wanted so much to be sent to places that were exotic and dangerous, places where I could live in exhilarating fear and walk into all the dark alleys of intrigue. And instead . . . I have gone from one world to another, hopping from culture capital to culture capital, and found the same thing wherever I went: a spoiled and bored population inventing too many nasty ways to spend its time, because in the posteconomic world the only real problem is boredom. Everywhere we've been up till now, the job was always the same, and fundamentally it was trivial: defusing the nastiness and getting the way the local culture reacted emotionally to societal change, and their expressions of social anxiety, steered back into traditional, safe, bland channels."

"It was valuable work," I said. "I wish to god we had some idea that would work, so that we could do it here."

"I didn't say it wasn't valuable, or that it wasn't what's needed. I said it wasn't the thing I dreamed of when I set out—a world that was crazy, extreme, *dangerous,* not rational or logical—and *not a job.* And you know, that's a disappointment I never expressed to you, Giraut, but I'd been feeling it for years, ever since our first couple of postings taught me what we really were going to be doing.

"Once I realized that our job was basically very safe, I was *so* disappointed and unhappy because I had thought we'd be flying off to place after place that needed heroes, and facing danger, and all that romantic stuff. I'm afraid I really spent too much time watching and reading adventure stories when I was younger . . . anyway, so I had been disappointed when you merely had a heroic attitude but weren't a real hero, *and* disappointed that you couldn't take me to magical, wonderful Nou Occitan because by the time I met you, old Nou Occitan was vanishing, *and* disappointed by finding out I was just a glorified government clerk who traveled a lot—and now all of a sudden, here we are. Just the kind of posting I fantasized about.

"High stakes. Treachery. Violent politics and inexplicable people. Risk of war. Sex and love and hate and death and violence and awful secrets all mixed into the whole pool I wanted to plunge into, back when I was eighteen in good old dull Caledony. *And all I am is scared*—when I'm not angry because I'm convinced the whole thing couldn't possibly be happening if people had any sense. It's making me hate everywhere that isn't home."

She took a long sip of her coffee, making a face. By now it must be tepid, but she raised the cup and gulped the rest down. "Do you see? What I hate most about this place is that it revealed that inside this stolid, sensible, too-reasonable Caledon, who always thought she had a heroic princess inside just waiting for the chance to show her stuff . . . there's a stolid, sensible, too-reasonable Caledon.

"The first time we got together, I pounced on you in your sleep and committed a sex crime that—in Caledony—could have gotten me sent to re-education camp. I was not even sure you even liked me, and I felt so brave and confident for having done that. Then we worked side by side through a revolution, and we jumped into another world, and oh, half a dozen other things . . . and I thought I was going to do so much more. I was so sure of what I would become. And now if I had to stand and face my twenty-year-old self and defend what my life has turned into, what could I say? 'Not a bad job but usually pretty dull?' 'You were wrong and adventures are stupid?' 'Forget it, kid, the truth is you hate danger, intrigue makes you nervous, and what you really want is boredom?' " She looked down at the table and sat still for a couple of long breaths.

I wasn't sure what to say, but I was quite sure she wasn't being fair with herself. "How about that you're a lot smarter now than you were then, and you have some concept that getting hurt is bad, and getting killed is sometimes permanent?" I asked. "None of us could stand being judged by our younger selves. And frankly I wouldn't submit to it. My younger self had a lot of fun, got laid a lot, and wasn't afraid of anything, but he was also an asshole and I wouldn't want him as a friend now."

She dropped the conversation, turning away from me to look out over the city. Her thin, short blonde hair ruffled in the rising breeze of the morning heat blowing in. After a while she drained off the rest of her juice punch and said, "So now we're going to go back out among them, and you know we're going to find that they all are busy thinking about things that don't matter at all to you or I. They want to kill each other and they want to start right away. Even Ix—even if he's a real saint—can only make them pause and think about it, and be aware for a second that there's the possibility of peace, before they set about killing each other. Once they're all done with that they'll put up a statue of him, and blame each other for his failure, and eventually kill each other to avenge him."

"Would you like them to start this morning?" The back of my mind was speaking as if Shan were prompting me.

"*What?*"

"Well, would you? We could probably put out posters and broadcast something or other to get it going. We could have a couple of thousand dead by sunset, I would think."

She stared at me. "Are you making fun of me? Because if you are it's not funny."

"Just raising a possibility, Margaret, and I'm farther from making fun of you than I've ever been. I'm taking you seriously. Look, it would be a bad thing to start it sooner, wouldn't it? This *Gotterdammerung* or day of reckoning or planetary massacre or whatever you want to call it, that you're so rightly afraid of—it would be bad to make it start any sooner than it has to?"

"*Yap. Stip-subj neq-utilimax.*" I wasn't sure if she was answering me in Reason, the almost-mathematical language of Caledony, because it's a language so well adapted to argument and she was getting ready to argue with me, or because it's also the language of Caledon preachers and she was mocking me for preaching a sermon at her.

"All right," I said, "if it's bad for it to happen sooner, can't we say it would be good to delay it? That there's some good in delaying it even a single day, and if we can hold it back for a year—think of all the people that get their first kiss, celebrate another birthday, meet an old friend, make a new one, get a little older and wiser, in that time. All the living that the thirteen million people on Briand can do in a year. Isn't that worth something? Even if it's all going to blow to hell and there are going to be bodies stacked in the streets, isn't it better that people will get to know some brief kindness and comfort before it begins? If lots of lives are going to be lost too early, isn't a year added to them precious?"

"Oh, hell, I understand. We do what good we can. But Giraut, I'm feeling tired and old and I'm starting to wonder if those lives really matter as much as the vacation at the beach that you just promised me . . . since I will never experience their lives but I will experience the trip to the beach. And even though I've felt stir-crazy here, all of a sudden I'm thinking how nice and peaceful the Embassy would be, with everyone out in the city, and no one to pester me or argue with me."

I shrugged, trying not to breach whatever the agreement between us might be. "Are you coming into the city with me today, or not?"

"I'll come, Giraut. I even think you're right. I just wanted a chance to say I hated the whole thing first."

"Good enough, *companhona.*" I noted that I had been speaking more Occitan than usual this morning; maybe from nerves? Or was it because I knew she liked the sound of it and liked to be reminded of her dreams about Nou Occitan, however shattered those might have been in twelve stanyears together?

Out here on the Embassy terrace, looking over the statue-ridden temples, spires, and domes of the city beyond, now glowing faintly as the predawn light started to chase the stars away, it didn't seem absurd that I was having to put more effort into wooing my wife than I had ever had to put into getting her to marry me when we were both young and foolish. It was part of Briand, like the animal-headed gods, the meanings within meanings within meanings, the way that Ix veered between working miracles and running a con game—mad and dangerous, but also part of the job.

We got up and went inside; I reached for Margaret's hand but she pointedly ignored it. Just as we reached the door the hot breeze rolled over the terrace, and I broke into the first sweat of the day.

If there was ever anything that I really learned to love about New Tanjavur's architecture, it was not the many jagged, complex, almost fractal shapes that reached into the indigo sky, nor the broad streets lined with big trees, nor any of the other things which one could find on other worlds. It was the tanks.

Like any system of human geography, the tanks had become encoded with complex meanings, so that the tank where you chose to sit for the day, or to tend children, or to go to meet friends, said a great deal about who you were and what mattered to you. So I was careful this morning to choose a tank that was frequented by the bohemian fringe, but not deep in the heart of it. For one thing, the core bohemians were more often than not political reactionaries; it was the poseurs and the syncretic artists who were on our side.

This place had a great expanse of stone tables with attached benches, on a gentle slope down to the water. "I suppose no mother is going to bring a child here," Margaret commented. "Too easy to run straight down into the tank, and any toy the kid sets down would roll there."

I nodded. "That may be part of the point, you know. The Tamils are realistic about the feelings adults have about children; there are places that welcome them whole-heartedly and places like this that aren't the least bit convenient for them. Different from what I grew up with; in Nou Occitan a child is always looked on as an unfortunate side effect of your sex life, and if you take a kid younger than puberty out in public, you can expect glares and complaints."

Margaret snorted. "I remember how impressed you were with Caledony because you could take kids anywhere, but that's the *problem* there. Any place where adults could gather has to be modified so as not to create the least difficulty for parents. A place like this couldn't exist on Caledony, and not because the tank would freeze. The problem would be that there would have to be pads on all the corners of all the stone tables, and a guard rail around the tank itself, and the floor itself would have to slope the other way, and probably there'd be great big safety advisory signs everywhere. And nobody would be allowed to do anything in a public place that might be a bad influence on children."

I shrugged and moved closer to her on the bench we were sharing. "Weird, isn't it? No matter how messed up and crazy a culture is, there will be some subject on which it's saner than most others. This is one of the few of the Thousand Cultures that acts like it wants children but doesn't act like they're the whole purpose of life. Why do I have the feeling that when Interstellarization is complete, and everywhere is just the same wherever you go, what will happen is that all those sane things will disappear and we'll have a nice even layer of consistent foolishness on all subjects?"

"Because you've been dealing with human beings long enough," Margaret said. She leaned toward me. She had cheered up immensely as soon as we left the Embassy and went out into the city. I wasn't sure whether it was an act, or perhaps the change of scene was improving her mood. Whatever the cause, I was grateful, and resolved not to worry until something went wrong, which I suspected would be soon enough.

This particular morning being our first one out, I wasn't really expecting to do more than say hello to some people and begin establishing a pattern. After a few days of establishing the pattern, anyone who wanted to find us would be able to, for private conversation and maybe to pass along ideas or something that we would never hear through any official channel. And perhaps some such conversation would open up a possibility that none of us had thought of before.

I wondered for a moment which side *I* was really on—the Council? the OSP's? Surely neither of these local cultures? Maybe the Thousand Cultures themselves, maybe just Briand? The more I thought about it the more I had too much empathy with everyone. I saw the need for assimilation into Interstellar metaculture, but liked unassimilated cultures better. But this train of thought would only lead down the usual pathway—wondering why people couldn't be somebody, couldn't be individual, without always standing on each others' toes, filled with anger and hate. Some people, like Margaret and I, had been born with a great deal of xenophilia, but xenophobia was a thousand times more common and a taste that required much less acquiring. So humanity would always be made up of people who couldn't let each other alone, a few looking for love, many more looking for a fight, and almost nobody—

"Well, now here is a pleasant surprise on a pleasant day," Kannan said, sitting down facing us. He was dressed in the traditional loose shirt and long skirt, and wore more than the usual quantity of jewelry. His tight smile seemed predatory, and the tension in his shoulders suggested to me that he had something in mind, something that he was sure I wouldn't like, to surprise me with, and was looking forward to my reaction.

"Good to see you again, Kannan," Margaret said, her voice purring with a warmth that, had it been directed at me, would have immediately frozen my blood. It was the way she sounded when she was establishing a record for being nice, so that whatever happened next could not be seen as a consequence of her hostility.

"Good morning," I said, as neutrally as I could manage. "How is your day?"

"Not bad, not bad. We have another issue of *Palai* about ready to go out, and some very fine new writing that may interest you, if you're still interested in our culture. Things that make use of the Cankam poetry without trying to be it, or be enslaved by it, are so scarce that I'm amazed I've managed to fill an issue. But there's getting to be enough of it. So I suppose I am making a little bit of headway."

"Artistic battles always take a lot of time," I pointed out. "And don't be too eager to win. There's something about suddenly discovering that all your wonderful and original ideas (which used to be profound and exciting) are being seized by pedants and systematically forced into the memories of schoolchildren, something that can take the joy right out. I've written a couple of songs that have become standards and now I can't bear to listen to them."

Kannan flagged a passing vendor and got coffee for all three of us, waving off my offer to pay. "Well," he said, "Just now I would be very happy to have to bear such a fate; I'm seeking influence. To have my ideas become common is just what I'm after. Better still if the teachers insist that they're true." He took a sip and winced; the coffee was still too hot. "Obviously you're no longer confined to the Embassy. Are matters so peaceful that you can afford time off, or are you spying?"

I said, "Well, there are always a number of reasons for anything anyone does, you know." I gestured around at the cool, wide space, lighted by dancing jagged curves of glare from the water that bounced off the high, pale gray curves of the walls. A long clear shaft of actinic light fell onto the water, turning the whole tank a vivid, deep blue. "Surely you will acknowledge that this space is much more pleasant at this hour, than, say, the Embassy terrace, and as it happens there isn't much work that Margaret and I could do there this morning that we can't do just as well here. Then again, part of my job is culture contact, and here I am, contacting a leading editor in your culture, am I not?"

"Depending on how you define leading."

"Doesn't the avant garde always lead?"

"You can only tell afterwards if it led, by whether or not someone followed, true? So it's a mixture of business and pleasure. You mustn't let me keep you from any work you have to do."

"Nor you let us keep you from yours," Margaret said. "Is there any prospect that those of us who don't read Tamil well would get anything out of these issues, or must we wait to hear them talked about and then take our best guess as to their significance?"

"Oh, as you may know, to our shame we have many members of our culture who don't speak or read our culture language well. This happens often, you know, in many cultures."

"Certainly it happened in mine," I admitted. "Even before the springer, most people spoke Terstad most of the time. And why not? It's the language of almost all the news of human space."

"Some people may wish to be human," Kannan said, "whatever human means. Some of us wish to be ourselves, which is to say some of us prefer to be Tamils."

"Or Maya," Margaret said.

Kannan glared at her. "You are trying to insult me," he said, finally. "Perhaps you would care to explain it and thus give offense directly, like a civilized person, rather than like a lout."

"I come from a loutish culture," Margaret said. "If you wish to receive a civilized insult you will have to seek it from Giraut, but I warn you, a genuinely civilized insult is far more offensive than a barbaric one. Finesse and technique, you know. But I didn't mean to insult you. I was just pointing out that you share this planet with one of the very few cultures that mainly speaks its own culture language. Among the Maya only the highly educated upper class and the scientists and engineers speak Terstad. I think it's clear that they too prefer to be themselves, and don't much want to join humanity."

"They are a different case. At the time the Cankam poets were writing—"

I jumped him, trying to play into Margaret's game, whatever it might be. "The Maya were building the first of their mighty cities and filling them with inscriptions of power and astonishing poetry," I said, pointing out the obvious. "It is remarkable, don't you think, that those two great ancient civilizations flourished simultaneously?" Needling local bigots is my favorite part of my job.

He made a bitter face. "Well, I suppose one is forced to say that a culture of stone age savages did manage to pile one stone on top of another and they did have their own crude mythology with some charm. But that's not the point here. The best work humanity does must be local and unusual; we can't *all* be the culture with the finest literary traditions. It's the same principle as that of governing—not everyone can be the wisest person in the group, so you decide who is and then let him govern."

"Or her," Margaret said.

"Or her, in theory, at least, if that should happen. Perhaps it does happen among the Maya, and that explains why matters in Mayatown are such a chronic mess."

"I had thought it was beneath the Tamils to concern themselves with Maya affairs," I pointed out.

"It would be if they would live where they were supposed to," he said, getting up, "and since merely by stating the opinion of a patriotic Tamil, who has known Maya all his life and knows perfectly well what they are like, I have said things which you Earth bureaucrats choose to be offended at, permit me to stop hinting and truly offend you. The Council of Humanity is in charge of enforcing culture charters, is it not? Well, if you will note, the Maya are not occupying the land given to them in their charter, and they are clearly occupying land that was to be Tamil. And we have had to hold our birth rate down and delay building new cities because of this. Now, that happens to produce a wound in the Tamil soul. We have been conquerors and we have been conquered but we have always been great, and our greatness has always been in our purity of purpose, in the way we have fought to keep our culture going and to pass on the precious heritage of the Cankam, which we were settled here to create and defend. We don't harbor any more hate than we need to, and the day the Maya return to where they belong—or go somewhere else—that will solve the problem. As for the Council, bah, it's worse than the Maya. You won't even consider the possibility that what we have here is not merely unusual and good, but unique and perfect, and that it is for you to ask us to share with you, and not for you to decide to abolish what none of the other cultures is capable of appreciating.

"Those issues of *Palai* are in Tamil only, proudly in Tamil only, because they are *for* Tamils only. And what they do is trace the shape of the wound left in us by what has happened—the denial of our rights, the handing over of our land to savages, and most of all the refusal of the gift of Cankam, which we have held out to all the cultures of mankind and which they, through the Council of Humanity, have spurned. You see, it is very appropriate to my journal's title, because allegorically you can see it all as a classic tale of *palai,* a tale of separation of lovers, for we have come to you like a fine young manly lover bearing our one precious thing, and you have spurned us like a foolish girl who thinks that surely we can give her more than that, and will not look inside the casket to see how truly valuable the gift is.

"Rather you express your contempt by creating a prophet out of the savages and sending him to us, with his inane message. And such a clever one, for at first it sounded as if he were merely facing reality, as if he were just helping the Maya to see that their silly, childish myths were no more than that. But what he has been preaching has been reaching Tamil ears too, and it is clear that this Ix does not know, or does not care, that there is a difference between stories like those of the Maya, inventions with charm and some limited meaning but no real force, and stories like those of Cankam—invented by inspired poets and *true* and *perfect*. There can be no peace till you open your eyes and see."

"Open yours," I said. "I give you my word (and Occitans do not do this lightly, and before you respond let me warn you I will fight you, here and now, regardless of consequences, and very likely kill you with my bare hands, should you even hint that you do not believe me). The Council had nothing to do with the selection of Ix or of his doctrine; he is entirely the creation of the Maya, and of his own ideas. You may disagree with him all you wish. I think it is foolish that you do, but that is your right. But do not attribute what he says to the Council. He is not our messenger. My word of honor as an Occitan. Call me a liar and I will break your neck before your heart can beat ten times."

Kannan's mouth flapped. He stared at me. I looked pointedly at his thin intellectual's neck and flexed my hands once, hard. I probably *could* break it. I was rather intrigued by the idea of trying.

He swallowed hard and his posture changed slightly, his center moving back so that he could flee more easily. Whether he knew it or not, he had already given up.

I was trading on the dreadful reputation that Occitans enjoy all over human space; we are thought by many to be violent and cruel because of our love of neuroducer dueling and martial arts, and because of an ugly incident that happened back during the Caledon Revolution and caused the Council of Humanity to decide that Occitans would no longer be permitted to serve in the CSPs for at least a generation.

(Since I had always regarded what happened as perfectly understandable, and the few dead civilians as merely payback for the deaths of a couple of good friends, I found it impossible to understand the Council's action. Before condemning a massacre, ask whether the alleged victims needed massacring).

At last Kannan said, "Then perhaps no one but Ix urged Ix to preach his silly ideas. And perhaps it is only the fault of the Tamils who follow him that they do so, but he does not seem to want to learn about Cankam so that he can steer Tamil and Maya alike in the direction in which they need to go."

"How do you know he doesn't want to?" Margaret asked.

"Because I had a friend make the offer to him directly, and she said he just laughed. But then perhaps a man may laugh when he has just defiled a woman. But then he may also laugh knowing that nothing can defile what's already filthy. In any case, the offer was made, and he laughed. If you wish to know more I suggest you ask him. Or you could ask *her* if there were any truth in her." He stalked off in a fury.

"Well, that's a start on a morning," I observed. "We've helped the Council make a confirmed enemy. Do you have any idea what we're now enemies *about*?"

"Some," Margaret admitted. "But you know, all by himself Kannan is not dangerous. You saw how he reacted when you threatened to hurt him—he just let the accusation drop. By himself he'd never have the stomach for real violence, not against anything that could hit back, anyway, but he likes to stir it up in everyone else. The same kind of ethnic intellectual that we saw so many of on Roosevelt."

I nodded. "When you phrase it that way, *yap,* I recognize the type. Smart literary guy and violent bigot. And you're right, they're rarely frontline types. So why did we pick a fight with him, then, *companhona?* I could tell you wanted to but I didn't have any idea why; it's good to be hated by people like that, but *deu sait* the Council has worked with and even assisted people a lot worse."

"True," she said. "Giraut, I have to confess: the way I treated that rat's-rectum wasn't calculated or political at all. While you were in Yaxkintulum, before Paxa got beaten up, I had a couple of meetings with him. At one of them, he made a pretty blunt point of letting me know that he thought it would be very interesting to fuck a blonde. In pretty much the same tone that a lot of guys in Caledony used on me when I was about seventeen or so, the one that implies that since I'm not very pretty they'd be doing me a favor."

"Midons," I said, "you should have told me." I could feel all my muscles warming and softening and my center sinking; it had been a long time since I had fought, but assuming he was walking he couldn't be more than 200 meters away.

"And have you break his neck about my honor? Not necessary. I already dealt with it. Once I realized he was going to try to 'open a line of communication' or 'establish a relationship' with us, I figured he still thought, somehow or other, that he might get me into bed. I *hate* men who can't understand 'no,' and here was one that didn't understand 'go away and die.' So I got angry and picked a fight before I even remembered that we were out here on duty and you'd back whatever play I set up. So I guess we made an enemy for the Council—"

"A perfectly fine one," I said. "Really a perfect one. One who isn't likely to do anything more dangerous than run his mouth, but is exactly what the Office of Special Projects most wants to fight against. As Shan might say, if you have to have enemies, have the right ones. And this one ought to cement a friendship; I'm sure when word gets back to Kapilar he'll be pleased."

She looked very startled. "Kapilar? Why would *he* be pleased?"

"Well, you know, the dislike and the sexual rivalry between Kapilar and Kannan." She was staring at me as if I had said the most outrageous thing in the world. "You know. Over Auvaiyar. I've told you about it often enough."

She laughed. "Oh, that! It's so crazy the way all of a sudden you can forget something obvious." She sighed. "Anyway, I'm afraid that acting on personal feelings that way was pretty unprofessional and not very diplomat-like. Want to go to some other tank and hang out there? We've had more effect here in one morning than we'd had from the Embassy in fifty standays, and the day is still young."

We took the trakcar; it was hot even with all the vents open, but at least it was unlikely that we would be overheard. "All right, now the critical question," I said. "It sounds like Kannan suggested that Ix learn the Cankam and presumably learn to accept the absolute superiority of the Tamils—now there's a perfect Kannan suggestion, if ever there was one, and I'm surprised Ix isn't *still* laughing. But it also sounds as if he sent it via some particular person, and the impression I get is that person must have been female, Tamil—and in bed with Ix. Was that the way you heard it?"

"Yap," Margaret said, firmly. "That's the way I heard it. I was hoping you were going to venture some other suggestion."

"Ten to one it's Auvaiyar," I said.

Margaret looked puzzled. "Why would anyone use her—"

"I think Auvaiyar is working entirely on her own," I said. "I think she's a climber, like our old friend Garsenda, with the same eccentric talent for finding the man who can make her notorious, at the least, and probably make her look more exciting for the next one—who will be another stepping stone—oh, hell, we've both watched Garsenda play the game, and she's been married and divorced now, what, four times?"

"Four times," Margaret said, "and consort to two different Kings of Nou Occitan, while we're at it. Now that you mention it there is a lot of the same style about Auvaiyar. But Garsenda only does that on Nou Occitan, where the worst thing that can happen is usually a hallucinatory death that they bring you back from in a few days, or a ruined reputation that you live down in a stanyear or so. If that kind of sex-and-power game is what Auvaiyar is playing, she's playing it while surrounded by men who can kill—some of them have killed. She must realize that what she's doing is incredibly dangerous."

"People who haven't suffered many consequences—at least not yet—quite often don't know what's dangerous," I pointed out. "And if you imagine that all she's doing is trying to collect powerful men, then all her behavior makes sense, both her past affairs and her present one. She's naive, not crazy. The person who is crazy, if it's true, is Ix."

We hung around in a couple more cafés, and then had lunch at a third spot, all around different tanks. It was a glorious morning of idleness; nobody else walked up to talk to us, and we spent it chatting about old times, soaking up atmosphere, and gossiping about what we'd heard from people back home.

"Well, I guess our one little visit with Kannan is going to be all the excitement for the day," I said to Margaret, as we rode the trakcar back to the Embassy.

"You're probably right. And then there's all the paperwork

and all the correspondence to handle when we get back," she said, "and then it will be just time for an afternoon nap. But I'm not complaining, Giraut. What a pleasant morning it was!"

"Other than learning that a *ne gens* little bigot had been trying to seduce you—"

"Now, that's not fair. He wasn't trying to seduce me; seduction requires subtlety. He was trying to fuck me. Yes, I know, and other than hearing that our living saint is also a man, and making an enemy of an ethnic leader, it was a dull morning with no events. But what I was thinking of, Giraut, was several hours spent just hanging around talking of nothing. And wandering around in all this complex statuary and bright colors. And just for a few hours having an experience like a tourist."

"Including," I said, "that tourists never experience anything. You know, the horrible truth is, if you are ever able to develop a tourist business here, both cities *are* beautiful, and you'll have thousands or tens of thousands of tourists here in no time. And every one of them will go home thinking about what quaint, simple, pleasant people they had met. They'll think the Tamils are all excitable poets, never to be taken seriously, and the Maya are all gentle stoics with deep spiritual values. I can almost imagine the travel brochures . . . "

"*Yap*. And then they'll go home, and based on their extensive experience here, they'll start drafting peace plans and mailing them to the Council, and eventually some of them will gang up and force a peace plan onto Briand. At which point things will truly turn to shit." Margaret stretched and leaned her head against me. "Anyway, all I meant to say, Giraut, was that it was wonderful to get to *play* tourist."

"Even though tourists don't know crap?"

"*Because* they don't know crap. This city is fascinating and beautiful as long as you don't know what's happening." She snuggled closer and said, "Maybe we can start the afternoon nap early."

"I think I'd like that myself."

"Might just be sleeping next to each other. I'm not sure how I feel today. But I at least got reminded that any time there's nothing to do, I'd rather do it with you. And I do love you, Giraut, I don't think I'll stop loving you even if I decide to leave you. I hope you don't think that's too stupid."

"*Companhona,* the only person who ever calls you stupid is yourself."

"Why do you suppose that is?"

"Comparison," I said. "You've got to stop comparing yourself with you. It's unfair to anyone."

She giggled. "And you're silly. I need silliness, sometimes, too." Her arm tightened around me. "Maybe we will make love. Will you put up with me changing my mind a lot?"

"You put up with me changing mine."

"Different issue."

"Well, then, yes, I will put up with you changing your mind a lot."

"Good. Because while we've been talking I've decided twice that I want to make love and three times that I don't, and we still have some minutes left before we get to the Embassy." She sat close to me for the rest of the ride.

When a delicate situation begins to go well, the universe conspires to throw as many hard slams at it as possible. Infuriating Kannan had invoked the law of unintended consequences—he had made some com calls to put things in motion, so that by the time we got back there was no time for any thought of a nap, let alone of making love or of intimate chat.

If we had happened to turn on the video in the trakcar we'd have gotten some advance warning, but as it was the first thing we knew was when we got back to the office and saw a stack of forty messages waiting for us. When that happens over just a few hours, most of them are duplicates, indicating several different people trying to com you every few minutes. We asked the aintellect to filter for duplicated information and determined that all those messages had come in within the past three hours, beginning just after we had talked to Kannan down in the tank.

One of the many morning gossip programs popular in New Tanjavur had featured Ix as a guest that morning. Ix had apparently been better than ever at getting his message across—everyone agreed it was the best short sermon he had ever given—and had fended off the hostile questions in ways that charmed everyone, including the host. It should have been another success for the new spiritual force.

But afterward, as the host was asking a whole array of questions about Ix's personal life (and mostly getting told that since a prophet is newly born, none of that mattered) the host had decided to spring a surprise question based on several com calls they had just gotten (an OSP agent had traced all of them to Kannan and his friends), and ask about whether Ix was having a love affair with a Tamil woman. Since Ix would not lie, he had told them the exact truth—that he and Auvaiyar were lovers and would be applying for a variance in the marriage laws.

So while we had been enjoying coffee and conversation and drifting about the tanks in the shopping and artistic areas, two of Ix's Tamil supporters had been grabbed in public spaces and beaten by mobs. Someone had tried to set fire to a couple of buildings in Mayatown. One trakcar had been overturned by a group of angry students before they realized that it wasn't carrying Auvaiyar; the woman inside had suffered a concussion but was expected to recover.

Ambassador Kiel demanded that we see him at once. Shan wanted a full report. And a covert message from Ix said that he would be coming to see us later that afternoon.

Ambassador Kiel took precedence, being on site. I knew he would be unpleasant about it. What I hadn't expected was that the "debriefing" would be more like a criminal prosecution than anything else.

"I've served on nine of the thirty-one planets of the Thousand Cultures." His voice shook; I could see he was forcing himself to be calm. "I'm part of the old breed of pre-springer diplomats. I spent years in the tanks in the suspended animation ships, and for what it's worth I'm over a hundred twenty absolute age, even if it's only seventy subjective. I have more experience and more seniority than almost any other active diplomat in Council service. Now, I don't know what the new generation of 'cultural representatives' or whatever they are calling you these days is supposed to do differently, but I do suspect that the reason they sent an old hand like me out here was to be a calming, steady influence.

"When you two have been in service as long as I have, I think you'll come to understand that most of the time the best thing that can happen is for things to stay the way they are. The Council can't and shouldn't be choosing directions for the human race. All the Council can do is act on the side of order and stability, and let humanity have the peace and quiet in which to think through its destiny.

"And all of this is why I am absolutely not surprised that the Office of Special Projects policy—don't trouble to deny that you work for them—imposed from above and running outside the normal chain of command, has brought such a disaster down on our heads. The situation here was bad before all this nonsense began. I think that the Shan clique and their allies have now managed to achieve a much worse situation. If the OSP had any delusions that they were gambling on improving it, well, tell your boss—your *real* boss, Shan—that I could have told the old fool that the gamble was foolish, and whether or not I'm right about that, he lost."

He got up from his desk, straightened his uniform, and came around and sat on the corner, facing us. "Now, look. I don't believe for a moment that you were sent here to *make* trouble. I think someone somewhere made a mistake—either the Shan people overreached themselves, or you did something that wasn't appropriate. Right now, we have to come up with some way for the Embassy to help restore calm, to make it clear that the Council of Humanity stands behind both the culture governments here in their efforts to keep order. And all you need do is make it clear to all these extragovernmental contacts that you've cultivated that there is no Council support for going outside the regular channels and for the sort of street politics—street theatre, I call it, really, it isn't politics at all but competitive display—that is erupting. We need to get things back to something like normality, first of all.

"After that there will be plenty of time to discuss how things came to this pass and to make sure they don't again. And I want you to understand that I will not be out to give either of you a bad record or to fix blame on you. I think you were sent out on a bad mission, that what they asked you to do was a mistake in the first place, and I think that's obvious from what's happened—twenty-eight reported instances of violence in the last two hours. When night falls it will get worse for certain. I'm sure you're capable of perceiving abject failure in a policy, and that's what we have to deal with here. I'm also well aware that failure doesn't always have a single cause, and I want you to know that I am not out to hang this one on you."

"Sir," Margaret said, "I don't know where to begin, but I'll start with the most prominent thing that I thought we reported but you don't seem to be including into your calculations. Ix's mission here in New Tanjavur, and everything he has been doing up until this point, has been an overture by the religious leaders of the Maya directly to the Tamils. We were only invited to act as observers. It didn't happen at our instigation; this is what they chose to do. This *is* local people running their own affairs."

Kiel nodded, looking at her with a slight squint that seemed to make the piercing blue of his eyes that much keener. I wondered how much of his reputation for intelligence was founded on that expression, rather than on any achievements. Quite a lot, possibly. "That's one reason why I don't think that there is any way in which this will become a blot on your record. What I am pointing out is that your staying in contact with the people involved, rather than urging them to proceed through the proper authorities—a government-controlled cultural exchange program, say, or an arrangement for this man Ix to speak in a few Tamil schools, or something like that—well, that's water under the bridge. When you elected to remain in contact with the Maya religious leadership even though they were acting in this quite irresponsible and dangerous fashion, you put our stamp of approval on the whole thing, and now we are tied into whatever madness Ix has come up with—most especially including his bizarre and offensive sexual adventuring. We must now disentangle ourselves—"

"Forgive me for interrupting, sir," I said, "but a couple of points are getting lost here. First of all, nobody on Briand really cares what the Council of Humanity thinks or says; the local bureaucrats and administrators might be willing to nod and smile and act as if they want your advice, because they want the Council subsidies to continue, but the reason they want Council funds is exactly that they don't have much real power of their own. In Yaxkintulum the government officials don't sneeze without permission of the temple leaderships, and all the real politics is the struggle between the temples. That's why it mattered so terribly much that a major conservative religious leader like Pusiictsom was willing to try reaching out for peace. And although Ix is—"

Kiel shook his head sadly. "You can't see why we never get mixed up in local religious affairs, can you? It's exactly because of things like this. If the Maya have a situation where the temple dominates the administration and state, then that's a problem to be corrected, and the way to correct it is to strengthen the Maya state, not to assist the religious leaders in usurping its functions."

He went on and on for the next half hour; meanwhile I suppose there were two or three murders and half a dozen buildings burned out in the city, and *deu sait* how many lesser incidents as well. At first I thought of what Shan had said, that here was a man who never made a provable mistake, but then my mind slid over to what Aimeric de Sanha Marsao, my old *companhon de jovent* and the one who had gotten me into the game of intercultural diplomacy in the first place, had said about the older generation of diplomats: that they had all come from the Inner Sphere where diplomatic contact had been constant and elaborate for centuries, and that most of them were interested only in having everywhere else behave just like the bland, overcrowded Interstellarized worlds, or Earth itself. I had been thinking such thoughts myself just this morning. I listened, but I couldn't help noticing that the Ambassador was ignoring things that seemed plain as day, so that he could pretend that the people he was comfortable talking to would fix the problem for him, like having a pipe break and phoning a lawyer because you feel more comfortable with him than you do with the plumber.

Or, I thought, trying to be honest, even if he's blind on one side, doesn't he have a point? Suppose matters had just continued as they were. There would be no Bazaar and no full economic Connect. The Council had already decided not to trigger any major social dislocations here until there was some stability. Suppose that stability per se had never arrived, but things had continued as they were, with the Ambassador just sitting in his office, answering calls from and dispensing Council aid funds to the bureaucrats of both cultures, for a couple of generations while everyone got used to the idea of the springer. If the lid had stayed on that long, and the bland administrators had been able—

No. You might have kept them from hating each other and fighting, but only if you had given them an occupying foreign army to hate and fight instead. And you might have kept the lid on for a while, in that the governments would mostly not have been the ones conducting the violence, but violence was popular on both sides and if the governments of the two cultures had failed to deliver it, that would only have led to more dissatisfaction with the culture governments, and a faster erosion of their authority.

All this was running through my head as I listened to Kiel with one ear. Finally he let us go.

When we got back to the office there were about sixty messages, which the aintellects boiled down to "Everyone you know or have met is calling you to ask what you're going to do about the fighting sweeping the city." The New Tanjavur city government had declared the situation to be a riot, which under their law allowed them to declare curfew and disarm civilians on the street.

Best estimates now had about seventy dead, ten times that number hospitalized, and perhaps half a square kilometer of destroyed buildings in all, scattered throughout the city. Police were insufficient to secure all the streets and tanks, so exactly where the mobs were, or what they were doing, was impossible to know at any given moment—but all police posts believed the mobs still to be growing in size.

We were pretty sure that Kiel would be monitoring our conversation with Shan, so we confined our report to the facts. Shan didn't look surprised, but he looked worried. He asked quite a number of questions about exactly who was connected to whom, and how, and he didn't seem to like those answers either. "For what it's worth," he said, "the independent intelligence agents have been unable to connect Auvaiyar to anything other than a long string of past lovers, almost all of them socially distinguished. Giraut's idea that she's merely a social climber, just trying to hang around with the powerful, and is attractive enough to manage it, is probably the best explanation anyone has. With his uncle out of the way, Tz'iquin is the heir apparent to the Peccaries, just as you've been led to believe, and it's been whispered for a long time that Pusiictsom is a concealed liberal, so everything connected with that story holds up as well. Ix, it turns out, was a leader of a couple of anti-Tamil, anti-compromise groups in his youth, but hadn't been active for a long time. Kannan is just what he appears to be, so far as we can tell—a young ethnic fanatic who is also unfortunately talented as a critic.

"And Kapilar—well, that's the interesting one. He belonged to a group of ultra-conservative Cankam study groups but also to a couple of the small bi-ethnic pacifist groups, all during the last couple of years. Published a number of articles in literary criticism, very technical stuff about very small points as far as an outsider can tell. Wrote a couple of pieces about ethics in Tamil philosophy that have been rejected everywhere, but nobody could seem to get a copy or find anyone who remembered those. Turned down for teaching posts at several schools, both very orthodox and very liberal—curiously, he never applied to any centrist school. And so forth.

"The theory that most of us would immediately adopt is that he belongs to one group and spies on the other, and that's what almost everyone seems to believe. If so, nobody seems to have turned up any evidence about which one he's loyal to and which one he's spying on. Another possibility is that he's an opportunist, and working both sides. Or that he's apolitical and really only works for his uncle. And then again there's the grim possibility that he may be an idealist with ideas all his own, out to make the world over into his idea of a better place, in which case he's neither predictable nor rational, despite all appearances."

I felt a cold chill and said, "I would bet you that's it. I've talked with him enough to form a strong sense of him; probably he has some idea not too dissimilar from what Ix does, that there's a way to fuse the two cultures so that they attract instead of repel, probably based on an ironic approach to both sets of stories. Which is to say if he ever says what he's really thinking, he'll be dead by nightfall."

"So far Ix isn't," Shan pointed out mildly.

"So far," I said. "Well. So Kapilar will be perfectly reliable till something we need to do is in conflict with his ideas, and then *deu sait* what he will do, eh?"

Margaret groaned. "I think that's exactly what the case is. I've worked with Kapilar more than anyone else. He's very quiet about what it is he believes, but what I heard makes me think he's got some plan he's devoted to, probably all his own, and god only knows what. I used to think he was reasonable, and now I know he is only patient."

"That's consistent with what we've had from several intelligence sources. Giraut and Margaret, you have no real friends there and nobody you can depend on, and from what you say the situation is rapidly becoming dangerous, and could get a lot worse very fast. *So*—do what you can, and then when it blows to pieces, run like hell."

Margaret leaned forward. "What do you mean, *when* it blows to pieces? You don't mean we should give up—"

"I mean *mene, mene, tekel upharsin,* Briand is not going to work out. You may trust me on the point, or not, but Briand is not going to work out. And when it goes it may go suddenly and very badly. I would rather not lose old friends and valued agents. Humanity has very little to gain on Briand anymore, and not that much more to lose. So don't make yourselves part of the final collapse."

"Then why are you trying anything at all?" Margaret asked, angrily. "If that's what you think, then why don't you just evacuate us all right now, along with any Tamils or Maya who have been working with us and want to come along?"

"Because it's always possible that the situation will collapse in a decent-enough way. Things may yet slide gently down the tubes, so that a generation later we can start to recover. But if it starts to take the last plunge down the drain, get out of there. Act on your best impulses. Shore up whatever poor, weak forces of tolerance and peace you can find, do what harm you can to bigots and murderers, bind any wound that falls in your reach, keep articulating reason to them. And *don't expect it to work.* The minute you think it's all over, *pull out your crash card and jump into that springer,* or do anything else to stay alive that you have to."

Office of Special Projects agents carried a passcard that let us re-address any springer big enough to get into, as long as it had enough available power. Usually we used the cards to travel untraceably, but there was another use—to spring offworld to somewhere safe when we had to. Shan had never reminded us of that possible use before. It had to mean that things really were bad; he obviously waited for that implication to hit both of us before continuing. "Now, be careful about it, and do your best, and come back in one piece each. Is that clear?"

"Clear, sir," I said.

"We understand," Margaret added.

He disconnected.

"You know," I said, "Shan seems to know so little that I really think the Office doesn't have more than one or two agents on the ground in either culture. That would make sense. Briand must be a hard place to recruit people to spy for offworlders. What Shan said sounded like what you could get from a couple of people on the street and maybe one or two Embassy people that had close relationships with a Tamil or a Maya. Probably he was just feeding us back a lot of our own reports."

"You don't think that someone in the Embassy is really deeply involved with Tamil radicals?" She seemed really upset by the possibility.

"Oh, honestly, *midons,* if that isn't happening here it would have to be the first world we've been on where it didn't. A lot of Council staff are young flunkies of one kind or another, they don't have enough to do, they dress well, and all sorts of fanatics always hang around an Embassy because they have fantasies that their ideas are so right that they'll convince the Council of Humanity to back them in their local squabbles. Sooner or later one of the fanatics, or one of the flunkies, sees a chance for some fun in bed." A thought hit me and I laughed. "You know what? I bet it's Kapilar. A young, good-looking man like him would manage easily. And I bet whoever he's hooked up with is one of Shan's information pipelines. That's why Shan isn't sure what to make of Kapilar; his main information source is too emotionally involved for objective data."

"Oh, stop, Giraut, you're being Occitan on me." She didn't sound so much annoyed as exhausted. "Intrigues and gossip! You still live for those, don't you? Half of what Shan had, he could have gotten from your conversations with Pusiictsom and

Kannan, mine with Kapilar, both ours with Ix, and our reports on the party. He could get the rest from sending Paxa around to check government records here, and her husband around to ask a few questions in Yaxkintulum."

I had to nod. "Of course you're probably right, *midons.* And yet . . . something about Kapilar tells me that he'd have a hard time behaving himself around the whole Embassy staff. I'd still bet that's one of Shan's sources." She was beginning to look angry, and I realized that I'd better drop it. "Still, as you say, it's not much information. Shan's really flying blind. I wonder if he really knows any more than we do."

Margaret nodded and said, "Well, let's see what's available then." She clicked a few keys to set up the office's main room screen, and wideangled a search protocol to see what she could find.

It looked worse. By getting all the public information channels pulled together, she was able to map out what areas were within a twenty-second run of known occurrences of violence, and to chart out the occurrences from most recent to least recent on the map. Projected on the map of New Tanjavur, with its double-hourglass grid-and-circle plan, it looked like blobs of paint thrown by an angry child; there was a broad smear of pale pink representing places at risk of violence, covering half the city; a maroon blob within it like half a malevolent spider, showing areas where violence had occurred recently; and a scattering of crimson islands, like the jaws and eyes of that spider, that indicated areas that police were now unable to enter without being physically attacked. As we watched, the spider grew, its several legs became hairier, and the "eyes" and "jaws" began to swell and merge into a hideous tumor. A little stub of a leg began to reach toward the southeast corner and the Embassy itself.

"As I read that," Margaret said, "Violence is spreading out from the central area of rioting along the trakcar lines, down the boulevards, and probably through the passageways that run between the tanks as well. Those little dots in the middle are probably the actual mobs; everything else is happening opportunistically. It's growing that way because people are fanning out into the other areas, from places where there's already been looting or fighting."

"But the city they're attacking is their own," I said.

"In part, yes. And the reason that shape is the way it is—well, look at it. That sharp line along the western side is—"

"Just about the border of Mayatown," I said, finally seeing what she was driving at. "Actually a little inside it. So the Maya are holding their lines, or the cops are keeping the two sides separated."

"Bet it's both. If the Maya were doing the fighting you'd see them advancing somewhere along that line and it wouldn't be so regular. But I don't think New Tanjavur has enough police to hold that line against both sides. So my guess is that the police are keeping the Maya from attacking outward—probably there's still some semblance of public order there—and the threat of the Maya counterattack is deterring the Tamils from punching through police lines. That isn't going to last, you know—"

The door chime sounded, and I flipped the screen over to see who was waiting in the vestibule for our private entrance. We already expected Ix, and Auvaiyar and Tz'iquin were not terribly surprising, but I was quite startled to see Pusiictsom himself there. I was so startled that I stared at them for a long second before I finally pressed the "admit" button that let them come up.

"I used the springer from the family home to a public one here," Pusiictsom explained hastily as the group of four came in, "and I think I kept anyone from seeing me, but if I didn't, and anyone who saw me is a Maya conservative or tells one that he saw me using the springer, then there are going to be worse riots back home tomorrow than there are here today. I'm assuming I can get your permission to use the springer in your private quarters, so that I don't have to go out on the street again?"

"Of course. You could have sprung here directly—let me make sure you have the code before you go."

"I didn't want to arrive before the others; I'm afraid matters are complicated," the old priest said, apologetically.

"As you wish—though we're getting pretty used to complicated matters. Now come with me." I guided them to the couch and chairs, gave everyone something to drink, and left Margaret with the job of hostess for the moment. I had to do one more thing before I could join them.

I slipped into the bedroom and commed Ambassador Kiel. "Sir, as a courtesy I wanted you to know that we have several important members of the Maya religious leadership here to confer with us. I wanted to invite you down to talk with them."

Impatiently, Kiel shook his head. "Just tell them to obey the orders of their own civil government. If we can just get the top people from both cultures together we can work something out here, I'm sure—a minor case of miscegenation is not something to have a planet-wide riot about!—but it won't stay worked out unless we can keep the religious and social groups from making a mess of it. Just emphasize how important their cooperation and compliance is, flatter them that you consulted with them, you know, the usual. I have to get back to talking to the justice minister—com me later with a report." And he rang off.

We might have a mutual genocide on Briand, but at least it would be fully and officially deplored by top people. As I returned to the parlor, my heart sank lower than before; before I even opened the door I could hear them all gabbling at once, and Margaret trying to get a word in.

It took more than twenty minutes to establish enough calm so that we could proceed. Eventually Margaret and I did get them to agree to talk about it, one at a time, with the others listening but forbidden to interject. That way, they only interjected occasionally.

Tz'iquin went first, and briefly. "All I want to do is to make some peace here. I have truly no concern for your love life, uncle."

"A prophet has no lineage," Ix said.

"Quiet. You agreed to be quiet while others speak," Margaret

said. Apparently even if she did think of him as a living saint, a
deal was a deal—a very Caledon approach to things, I thought.

Ix nodded gravely. Margaret waited a moment to make sure
she had again secured the floor for Tz'iquin. "All right, now. So
you are here to make peace."

"As much as one can," Tz'iquin said. "I understand that a
prophet cannot be subject to the rules that other people are. But
I also note that a prophet is supposed to be holy. And neither the
Tamil nor the Maya community is going to see a man who keeps
a woman like Auvaiyar in his house as holy; I am sorry, Ix, but
they are not. And if he is not seen as holy he won't be listened to.
With people dying in the streets right now, we need to have you
listened to. That's all. Please, be discreet. Or wait a while. Or
even go through purification—I know that Grandfather here
could invent something—and marry Auvaiyar outright, and have
her go off to do penance for her past life. But please, please,
please, Uncle, you can't go and destroy the credibility of your
words merely because you've found someone that you enjoy
going to bed with!"

"Do you listen to my words?"

"Of course I do, Uncle."

"And believe and understand them?"

"Of course, of course—"

"And yet for the past five days all I've heard from you—which
makes me think, all you've thought about—has been Auvaiyar.
It's not who I sleep with but how open your heart is. Don't worry
about it, people will come around—"

Tz'iquin groaned in frustration and seemed about to shout
something, but Margaret cut him off. "All right, all right. Ix, the
purpose of all this is to find out what everyone thinks. You can
argue about it later, perhaps, if there's any point in such arguing.
But for the moment I just want to know what everyone is thinking and feeling. Now we've heard from Tz'iquin. Let's hear from
Pusiictsom. Do you have things to say or additions to make to
what your grandson has said?"

Pusiictsom sighed. "I know that a prophet has no lineage, but you are my son. You know that our family has encountered this woman before and you know that she very nearly ruined Grandson's life, or at least permitted him to ruin his own. I cannot imagine what reason you could have for the choices you have made, in the middle of carrying the most important prophecy ever into the world. I am bewildered by your choices and thinking, Ix, and wondering if perhaps we were wrong to choose you as prophet. And I dearly wish that you would offer us some defense. That is all I have to say, or to ask."

Ix sat quietly a moment, and then asked, "And if it is my turn to speak, is it everyone else's turn to listen? I would like very much to be listened to, you know, for it has happened very rarely." He sighed and drew a long breath. When at last he spoke again it was directly to Pusiictsom. "All right, then, I think in this little room we can admit that this is all family, and that is good, for I would rather call you 'father' and Tz'iquin 'nephew' than try to pretend that I haven't known and loved both of you. So let me tell you the story, and if it seems to you that it makes me no prophet, then find another prophet, or even condemn me at the temple, and I will understand. But if you can come to understand that I am still Ix, still the prophet—and still a Peccary and as loyal to you as I can be with all my other duties—that would be best.

"You have asked for no defense of my telling the truth about the way in which this prophet was made; I take it from that that you have learned to approve, or you are waiting to see, or you feel that is within my prerogative as prophet to decide. And yet did I not, with that, put my whole prophecy in jeopardy?

"Let me begin my defense by pointing out, father, that I was once being groomed for the chair in which you sit. Indeed because the Center Temple is now ours, you did your best to raise me to be more traditional and conservative than you yourself were, because we Peccaries would have to fulfill that role. I have spent a lifetime reading the ancient texts and studying the ways of reading them, until I cannot think a thought which is not a Maya thought—or so I thought. Then you summoned me to be a prophet and told me to meditate and find a way for the Maya to live on, since it was abundantly clear that if they continued the old way there was no hope.

"And what I arrived at was, as you yourself have said, beautiful. It overwhelmed me, myself, when I first thought of it. It seemed to pull down every barrier in the way, to make the Maya path not one that shrank us and restricted us but a road along which we could grow, for the first time in many generations. And what were the keys to it? Those three principles: read the texts to speak only of the struggle within, exclude nothing, know that our stories are only stories. And from this little beginning—everything. A new road into a much wider world.

"Well, you could hardly expect that I would urge it on others if I weren't prepared to try it myself. And if I am free to use my tradition for my purposes but to discard it where it doesn't suit them—"

Pusiictsom winced. "That is what I was afraid you would say. Is *that* what your prophecy means? Not to have people obey and honor the old texts in a wise and creative way, but—"

"To obey their wisdom, honor their creativity, and use the texts any old way they want. Yes, that would be a fair translation. And as life began to blossom . . . Father, I am forty-two stanyears old, and I have lived most of my life doing what I could to get ready to replace you. I have thought what I should think, done what I should do, said the right words, been the right things, until they all come naturally. And then I created a new way, because you asked me to do it, and at your request I made it a way to freedom.

"Why then are you so shocked that I have chosen to use the freedom? The wife you chose for me disliked me, the children I had by her—when I was much too young to know anything, really—didn't know me because I spent all my time on Peccary lineage business and my studies, and now they're grown and barely recognize me. There is no family or bond to which I can see any reasonable obligation on that side. And what harm to the rest of you, eh? How does my joy and pleasure make you less? So it is not a matter for the family.

"Then perhaps you will tell me it interferes with my prophecy. But my prophecy is one intended to make it easier for people to do things that they have never done before (well, let me assure you, I have never loved a Tamil woman before) and to bring us closer together (which I think speaks for itself) and in all to free us to explore a wider world and seek joy where we can find it (and I must say that is just what I am doing). The love I share with Auvaiyar is not a contradiction to my prophecy, but a fulfillment of it in my personal and private life, and I will not be made ashamed of it or unhappy about it, nor will I deny it if I am asked, or go to any effort to keep it secret."

Margaret said, "This is all very interesting in the abstract, you know, but outside we have people killing and dying, and if it goes on I'm afraid we will shortly have full-blown war and eventually genocide. Stopping that sort of thing seems much more important to me than any individual philosophy or its interpretation, just at the moment. The question is, what can you do to get them to stop killing each other out there?—and how soon can you do it?—and damn the truth if the truth gets in the way."

Ix gazed back at her calmly. "And you, of all people, have no sense of how love can come at a bad time, but still be something you cannot just pass up? Or how somehow it's the very love that shouldn't be that becomes your door to who you need to be in the next time of your life? You of all people can have no vision or empathy for that?"

She stared at him and said nothing. I was sure they had talked about this in their private conversations. Probably it was profoundly wise, but just now I hadn't any notion of what he was talking about or why he was saying it; all I knew was that he had prevented Margaret from saying something that really needed

saying, so I jumped in. "The question, again, is not one of principles. The question is whether we are going to stop the bloodshed," I said.

"I quite agree, *Donz* Leones, and that is why I have no idea
what you are so concerned about. If my family here had not insisted on meddling in my private life, I would already be on my
way, with a time already set."

"Already?" I asked.

"Already on my way to the central square, in front of the temple of Murukan, where I am going to teach them how to have
peace."

"But that's not possible, they're fighting all around there—"

"Well, where do they need peace more than where there's
fighting?"

Margaret had recovered herself. "This is a crowd of Tamils
and they're angry at you, they don't respect prophets the way the
Maya do—"

"Even better. Often we Maya have respected our prophets so
much that we haven't listened to them. And besides, Mayatown
has as many converts as it needs, and the teachers there can carry
my message to all the Maya now. I believe it was your Jesus, was
it not, who said that the well do not need a physician? Well, the
whole town at the moment is sick with intense violence. That
needs to be fixed, doesn't it? And that is a job for a prophet." He
stood. "Still, I must ask a favor of you. If Auvaiyar could stay
here, where she will be safe, that would be a great help to me. I
don't want to worry about her, and she does not have the power
of prophecy to protect her, and in any case there is no need for
her to appear in public." He stood up. "Now, you may choose.
You can stay here or come along with me. I think I can promise
that if you come with me you will see something remarkable, one
way or another, and if you stay here you will hear about something remarkable. Let it be as you prefer."

"But—" Tz'iquin said.

"There is really no choice, is there?" Pusiictsom asked.

354 John Barnes

Ix bowed his head in deference. "No, not for you or me. May I have your blessing, father?"

"You have that always," Pusiictsom said.

"Then I must be going. Who will come with me?"

"I must spring back to Yaxkintulum," Pusiictsom said, "before I am missed. I cannot yet let them know that I have a springer."

"I'll go," I said.

Margaret glanced at me. "Take a stun stick and don't hesitate to use it," she said. "One of us should go and you were *trained* for violence. But do try to come back."

"That's part of the plan, *companhona*. Tz'iquin?" I wanted to specifically invite him because I was having sudden visions of what it would be like to be trapped with the former *entendedora* your uncle had run off with, in a place you might not be able to leave for days if things went badly.

"I'm with you," Tz'iquin said. "I was at the first teaching. I don't feel like I could miss this, even if I wanted to."

I thought about comming Kiel and telling him what we were going to do, but he would have ordered me not to.

Half an hour later, after Ix had made some com calls, we opened the side door to the Embassy, and seeing no one in the street, crossed it, went past the temple of Parvati (every one of us touched it for luck) and hurried through the narrow streets, keeping away from the main thoroughfares, working our way toward the central spandrel as Metallah sank through the deep indigo sky, down to the abyss, or Xibalbá, or wherever it was going this evening. Three times on the way we heard shouts and crashes that meant someone was getting hurt for one stupid reason or another.

Much later, Shan insisted that Margaret had to extensively report on her conversation with Auvaiyar. Now, Margaret is utterly fair-minded, but she already disliked Auvaiyar—women in general didn't like Auvaiyar. So I suppose this might be biased, or not. Possibly it's less biased than anything I perceived with my own eyes and ears and wrote down myself; I don't think I have Margaret's sense of fairness.

After Pusiictsom sprang back home, neither of them had anything to do. Margaret asked an aintellect to alert them whenever any of the local video or audio channels began to carry news about Ix. She set out cold glasses of fruit punch. They sat together on the couch in our private quarters; there was nothing to say.

After while, Auvaiyar said, "You know, I urged him to keep it quiet. I would have been willing to sneak around. For the rest of both our lives, if need be, you know. He was . . . I don't understand him. I've had plenty of men who wanted to show me off, and it seemed a little like that, but also like . . . it isn't me he wants to display, more like he wants to display the *way* he loves me, as if I'm just an example he uses to teach the world how to love. And yet not like that at all, because it does seem to matter very much that it's me, he's not just showing how to love just anyone. But . . . oh, I'm sorry. You're probably worried about your husband."

"No more than usual," Margaret said. "Giraut can take care of himself. He'll get back, and if he possibly can he'll bring Ix and Tz'iquin with him."

There was another long pause, while Margaret thought about nothing in particular, waiting for Auvaiyar to speak again. Finally she did. "You know—did you know that Tz'iquin and I were once, uh, together?"

"More than that, I thought," Margaret said.

"I guess the whole thing meant a lot more to Tz'iquin. He, well, he had this idea he was going to marry me. I played along with it and I guess that was wrong of me, but I didn't want him to go just yet and it seemed so important to him . . . Murukan, now that's an awful reason, isn't it? Well, all the same, that's what I felt. I know he went and defied his family—did you see how his old grandfather looked hatred at me? It felt like ice poured down my back, and I wanted to ask how he could hate me without knowing me. But he only knew that I had been with his grandson and made him unhappy, and now here I was with his son, and it just stopped up anything I had to say."

She got up from the couch and took a deep gulp of the juice drink. "You see the problem has always been that I know perfectly well that Tamil Mandalam is a man's culture. If you want power or wealth or a name or anything worth having, you get it from a man. If you're a woman that means you get him to give it to you, or you have to be so much better than he is that you can take it away from him and make him accept that. I'm clever but no genius, there are plenty of smarter and more talented men out there—smarter and more talented women, too, for that matter, I suppose. On my own I could achieve, maybe, a minor niche somewhere, edit a little review or teach poetics or composition, be nobody. I have bigger ambitions than that.

"And I don't *have* to use my talents or cleverness except to keep whatever I get. Because by sheer good luck I started to look like this—" she pressed her dress against herself with her hands and turned sideways, to show off her breasts and buttocks, and let her leg stick out of her dress (Margaret later said it was positively obscene) "—when I was only thirteen. A lot of girls bloom early, I suppose, but there was something else about the way I looked that, oh, well, from then on men were after me. Not just boys my own age—the boys were afraid of me but the men . . . well, there's a special kind of poem in the tradition of our *akam* poetry, you know, the *akam* is the interior poetry or love poetry? Well, we recognize seven kinds of *akam,* five of which are *akam* proper, that is the five kinds that are proper to noble, grown men and women, corresponding to the five basic landscapes of the Tamil homeland on Old Earth. Almost all of the *akam* poetry is written about those five types, both back in the Cankam era and today.

"But there are two other kinds; there's *kaikkilai,* which is unrequited love, the love that makes a fool of the lover, and then, of course, there's *peruntinai.*"

"Why do you say 'of course?' " Margaret asked.

"Well, now, you would expect me to finish with the one that mattered for the story, wouldn't you?"

Margaret laughed. Perhaps that encouraged Auvaiyar.

"*Peruntinai* is verses about mismatched love. Typically about a grown man who is attracted to a girl who is too young to return his feelings, or even to understand what they are about. It's a special humiliation for the man, but nobody seems to worry much about how the girl would feel about it.

"By the time I was sixteen and beginning to understand what feelings I was supposed to have, there had been about a thousand poems of *peruntinai* written about me. My father was a poet, you see, and a teacher at the university, and so many of his students met me, and . . . well. It was terrifying. That's about all I can say about it. When I was a teenager, if there was a word I wanted to never hear again till the end of time, it was 'love.'

"I guess you could make a case history or a novel out of that, couldn't you? The little girl that grew up too fast, who had too many ideas about how much she deserved from the world, and not enough talent, but she had a body men loved . . . you know, all that could be true. I don't know.

"You know I had a long affair with Kannan, and he was a bore in bed, and cruel, and dull at parties, and so forth, and he was always writing things that just dripped with hate, but nothing bothered me until one day I finally perceived that being an influential critic and editor was all the farther that he was going, that if he started a political movement it would eventually be taken over and led by real leaders, not him, and if he started an artistic movement it would quickly fall into the hands of real artists, not him. I don't mind pleasing a man who doesn't please me, socially or sexually or whatever, but I won't waste a minute on a man who isn't going anywhere.

"It was just the same with Tz'iquin. I just put aside all the skills I had in writing all that extremely traditionalist criticism, all my ability to ridicule new writers and innovative forms, all my skills at promoting Tamil nationalism and disdain for the Maya—and, well, here was a man who was going somewhere, so suddenly I was very liberal on all intercultural matters, and writing a very different kind of essay.

"Not that I exactly picked Tz'iquin out as what I wanted. I met him by accident, after a café performance that he attended, where (as usual) no one sat near him or spoke to him; we happened to go to the same coffeehouse afterward, and he spoke to me.

"I think he was just lonely or something—that often happens to a bright talented man. One big advantage I have, looking this way, is that I'm exactly what a lot of very talented and brilliant men wanted so desperately when they were boys, and couldn't get, then. It's the ambitious and the powerful who have the confidence to pursue me. So I sat and listened to him, because like most men who are better than those around them, and know it, he also felt that he hadn't gotten what he deserved.

"I sympathized when he felt sorry for himself. After some time I figured out that he wasn't a shunned exile of Yaxkintulum, as we had all come to believe, at all—that he was likely someday to be an important man in a great lineage, and anyway he was almost certain to have an important role in politics. And he was easily the most important man that had come my way in a long time.

"So . . . well, you know that part. But I couldn't marry him, I really couldn't. He was a fine man, and very dutiful and attentive to a lover besides, and I think he probably could have fought his way to a high position in his society—but he would have had to do all his fighting to get me accepted. I would have *been* his career. His life would have been spent fighting to break open the Maya and bring them to us.

"Well, I don't think it was the bigotry I learned from Kannan or my father or anyone else that stood in my way; if the Maya and the Tamils were able to get together in my lifetime, that would be a great achievement, and the man who can do it is . . . well, I suppose you can already see that such a man attracts me?"

"That's clear enough," Margaret agreed. She told me later that by that point her major worry was that she would say something catty; what Auvaiyar was saying repulsed her, and yet at the same time it was the key to everything going on, and she had to keep Auvaiyar talking.

"The problem with Tz'iquin was that he might be an important man in his society and he might even be the one who brought the Maya closer to the Tamil, but if he were the one who did that—by fighting for my acceptance—that would be all he could possibly do in his lifetime. I wanted a man with achievements; I didn't want to *be* his achievement, you see? I wanted a man who conquered, not one who just won if he hung on long enough. I'm not interested in heroes, but in winners."

"Well, then," Margaret said, still trying to understand without interrupting the flow, "you must expect some kind of victory from Ix. And though I do admire him, I don't see how he can win."

Auvaiyar turned back to her, and Margaret saw wet trails leading down her face to big teardrops. "That's just it. I don't understand it at all myself, but these past few days . . . sometimes I wonder when the real me is going to wake up and pull me out of all of this. He speaks kindly to me for no reason at all. He's happy when I'm happy. He enjoys just knowing I'm around. And I'd have said . . . well, the old me would have said he's no more than average in bed, but there's something about having sex with someone who—hmm. Someone who likes that this is *my* body, rather than someone who just likes my body."

"I know what you mean," Margaret said, "but . . . well, it's different, you know."

Auvaiyar sat down next to her. "You know I tried to seduce your husband and I'm sure he told you. And as much as Giraut seemed to like looking at my body, he didn't really care. I don't know why, but he didn't. There was something else eating at him and my body in front of him didn't matter."

Margaret sighed. "I don't know why I should believe you; I think he probably dreamed about you for a week."

"Ask him."

"I don't expect him to tell the truth about it."

Auvaiyar made a face, and then said, impatiently, "The only hetero men I don't get anywhere with are the ones who are in obsessive, passionate love—so much that they don't even see me. That's probably part of why I've always kind of—well, no, *really*—hated love. It gets in the way of serious things, if you see what I mean. Now I don't know whether you want him to love you, I don't know whether he loves you the way you want to be loved, but Giraut is in love, and you're the only person around who he could be in love with, as far as I can see." She looked down at her lap. "Well, look at me. That was quite the sermon. And to another woman, and in a situation where it can't do me any good. I suppose I'm lucky that you don't know me well enough to know how strange that is.

"Anyway, about Ix. I have tried imagining powerful men making a pass at me, and I found that I enjoyed the thought of turning them down—because if Ix found out about it, he would be pleased with me. But then . . . well. Ix is something entirely else, you must have felt that yourself, haven't you?"

"Oh, yes," Margaret said.

"I am told that our Tamil proverb about being careful what you wish for because you may get it is known all over the Thousand Cultures, that it goes so far back that no one knows who started it or where it started; perhaps its origins aren't Tamil at all. Well, I have wanted all my life to have a man of great power and prestige love me. So finally at the end of a long, long decade of one powerful man after another, here's Ix. He can do things other men can't, and see, clearly, things that they can't imagine. His name will be known for centuries, no matter how this comes out. He is better at loving me than anyone has ever been before. I'm not so sure I'd call him a powerful man as much as I'd call him an immense force; he's bigger and grander in his soul than anyone else I've ever loved, and he lets it shine out more. When I'm with him I feel like nothing could ever be any better.

"But . . . he wants me to love him back. And I'm not sure I

know how. At least not the way he loves me, or even the way he loves everybody." She looked down at her hands; they were clenched into fists in her lap. "And for the first time in my life I find myself wondering if the man couldn't do better; maybe somewhere out there there's a heart that already knows how to love him. All of a sudden I feel inadequate. I just want to ask him, 'Why me?' "

"Have you asked him?"

"Every day. He laughs and says that it's because everything about me gives him pleasure, or that I just happened to be the first case of exactly what he wanted that ever came along, or sometimes he just laughs. It doesn't help much when they say they love you, if you yourself can't understand why."

"*Nop, nop, nop,*" Margaret said, reverting for a moment into Caledon because her culture language provided a more emphatic 'no.' Auvaiyar didn't seem to notice. "It doesn't help a bit. Sometimes I wonder if anyone who really knew themselves would ever feel love."

Auvaiyar laughed, a sad bitter little cough, and put her arms around Margaret. "You do understand. Is it that way for all married people or something?"

"Not as far as I know, and a good thing too or there wouldn't be much of a human race. Auvaiyar, I don't know what to tell you. It's hard enough to keep love going with a more or less ordinary man, and I haven't tried with a saint. What would it feel like to tell him you loved him, and be sure you meant it?"

"Terrifying," she said. "Absolutely terrifying."

"A crowd is forming at the central square, and it looks as if Ix may speak any moment; five video channels are carrying live feed of the situation," a voice said from the speakers above them. The aintellect had spotted news about to happen.

"Put up whatever the clearest video is on the main screen in this room," Margaret said. "Amplify as soon as Ix begins to speak. Bring his voice up and the crowd down."

The screen in front of them flashed to life; there was a confused moment as the aintellect sampled all the feed, and then it settled on a close-in view of the crates that had been piled there as an impromptu rostrum. "Show crowd," Margaret requested.

Cameras switched abruptly. Both women gasped. The square was so jammed with people that it was hard to see how anybody could move. "Audio up," Margaret added.

The sound came on. Even with the audio turned up considerably, the sound from the screen was soft. "Look," Auvaiyar said. "Hardly anyone's mouth is moving and they're almost all standing still. Now and then they whisper to a neighbor but that seems to be all. The crowd really *is* that quiet." Her voice had fallen to a whisper. They sat and stared at the screen, next to each other, alone with their thoughts and the image of that huge, still, silent crowd.

When we first arrived the central square was almost deserted, but looking down any of the long streets you could see the slow-gathering crowds drifting in toward the temple of Murukan. "You two stand here, by the temple, and no one will notice you," Ix said, firmly. He left us in a niche with a life-sized statue of Murukan, who, as always, was smiling. Maybe Murukan just took the long view of the universe, and individual local trouble wasn't enough to perturb him.

"It was hard to see her again," Tz'iquin said.

"It must have been."

"At least now I feel like the problem wasn't that I was Maya and that ultimately she was too poisoned by the prejudice of her people. Clearly it isn't Maya that she has anything against. Or members of high ranking Maya families. I suppose she might have something against men her own age."

"You're letting yourself get bitter," I said. "That won't help you. Even if you were small-spirited and petty enough about love to take revenge, it wouldn't hurt either of them for you to feel that way."

Tz'iquin leaned against one wall of the niche, in that braced-leg way that everyone does in the high gravity. My back hurt—I had been on my feet a great deal that day but too busy feel the discomfort until now—so I leaned against the wall in the same way on the other side of the niche. The sun was most of the way down, so we were in the shade, but blessedly the stone against my back was still quite hot. The nagging pain in the small of my back began to diminish almost at once.

"Just two stanyears ago," he said, "when I was ready to give up everything in my life just to have her, the man we now call Ix was the one who threatened to throw me out of the family. Once he struck me and it was only Grandfather's pleading that kept me from swearing vengeance on him . . . oh, may the Gods of Xibalbá gnaw his bones."

"I think that's more likely than not," I said, looking over the huge crowd now pouring into the square. "Those *toszeti* out there aren't waving weapons or heaving rocks, yet, but they don't look at all friendly, either. There's a few of them helping him put together a platform and podium out of junk, but the rest look like they're going to stand around and wait for someone to shoot him, then cheer."

"By Tohil's stone heart, *Donz* Leones, I don't understand my feelings myself. Losing Auvaiyar was one thing, and that was very bad, but on top of that . . . well, please don't think me a fool, but I'm really very jealous about something else, too. You know my uncle was always the old conservative in the lineage, the one who wanted no change and especially no change that involved his getting to know any Tamils. And I was Grandfather's tool for seeking peace, coming over here to live alone and be hated and suspected by everyone, to try to build the bridges that someday Peace might travel over. That was quite a set of bridges, let me tell you—hard work to build and forever falling down and the truth is I didn't get very far because it was so difficult, and if I ever heard the song of Peace, it was far away and over the hills, where Peace was singing for somebody else and not for me. And no matter how many bridges I built for her, she wasn't about to come down out of the hills, cross one of my bridges, and live with me.

"Now suddenly here's my uncle, a lifelong bigot and obstructionist, and Peace just leaped lightly into his arms and he carried her over a shallow stream. Sometimes I think I'm more jealous about Peace than I am about Auvaiyar, but either way, Ix opposed and opposed and opposed, then Grandfather makes him a prophet and it all falls into his hands. I know it's not right of me to be jealous, but I defy anyone in my position not to be." He sighed—it was almost a soft groan of pain. "And yet, and yet, and yet. His prophecy is so beautiful. His way of saying things is so splendid. If I follow him and love him and do my best to do what he asks, you know, everything I have dreamed about all my life—except Auvaiyar—will fall into my hands, and I can live the rest of my life in that world that I thought I would have to struggle forever just to get started on. Peace while I'm still a young man, something I never looked for. Well, I don't know if I can *accept* getting it that easily. Because . . . oh, I do love him, you know, I did when I was a child, and I do understand that the gift doesn't necessarily come to the one who works hardest or the one who waits longest, and it's not his fault that it's come to him, but . . . " He fell silent. When I looked, he had begun to cry. Pushing myself away from the wall—my back, which had just begun to feel better, protested bitterly—I took him in my arms.

I remembered that the best friend of my *jovent,* Marcabru, had wept this way when the doctors decided that our friend Raimbaut, killed in a duel, would never develop into a transferable personality, and had taken his psypyx off me and filed it— nominally preserving him but actually deciding that he was dead forever, for psypyx technology, as recently as a decade ago, had had only a small chance of success. I had held Marcabru then, like this—when he was no older than Tz'iquin was now—and he too had sobbed without hope . . . and only a couple of stanyears later we had fought a bitter, final duel, I had humiliated him, and whether because of that, or some embarrassing things he had done, or just because he was always bent that way, he had gone on to become a self-pitying drunkard and eventually a suicide.

I wondered for a moment if my touch carried doom; maybe that was why Margaret felt so uncomfortable with me, for we had each seen some friends die, each seen some hopeless situations, and much like the Council of Humanity itself we had done our best but things hadn't worked out. Maybe everything I touched was doomed, or maybe I only wanted to touch things that were doomed, *qui sait?*

I knew this was a stupid way to feel, but I had been standing there listening to Tz'iquin fall into self-pity, and that's the most contagious disease humanity knows. Tz'iquin was strong, smart, young, and privileged, and assuming he got away from here alive after whatever happened in the next hour or so, he would rise rapidly in his society. He had most of a very good life in front of him and that was nothing to cry about. If anyone was going to pity Tz'iquin, it would have to be himself—and *deu sait* he was doing quite a job of it.

But truly I had no faith that our saint was going to do anything other than perhaps make matters worse while getting himself killed. Ix was merely being consistent in his craziness, and I expected to see him die tonight. In an abstract way I admired his courage; if I'd been younger or dumber I might have admired his faith. Miracles are to be accepted with gratitude, but they aren't to be depended upon.

I'm still not sure what sound it was that I thought ran through the crowd. There's nothing like it on any recording. Perhaps a wave in the silence?

Whatever it was, it got my attention, just as it got everyone else's. I looked up, and Tz'iquin stopped snuffling and looked as well. Ix was bounding up the makeshift rostrum, as cheerfully as a child climbing a tree. I half-expected him to be shot as soon as he got up there, but he stood still, his white shirt glowing against the dark sky, a perfect target, and no one moved.

At last he began to speak. None of us had brought any

amplification equipment, I'm sure of that, and there was none pre-prepared, but everyone heard him. Afterwards I realized that what I had thought of as a miracle was probably just a matter of there being so many hookups near him, so that in the farther reaches of the crowd people were playing his voice on radio. At least that makes more sense than imagining that such a large crowd could all hear him when he was speaking well below a shout.

He began by reminding them of his three principles, and he stressed all of them firmly, over and over, and emphasized that it was a message for Maya and Tamil alike and for the rest of the universe, as well.

Then he described the missionary work of the last thirty days or so, emphasizing how much had been accomplished (and ex-aggerating quite a lot; he had had some converts and many listeners among the Tamils, but I hardly thought he had had the success he was claiming here. For a man who said he wouldn't lie, he was getting perilously close to depending on a self-fulfilling prophecy).

Finally he turned to the matter of Auvaiyar. The crowd, if it were possible, became even quieter.

(Even in that silence, I heard no radios playing among the crowd; perhaps, then, that was not how they all heard him. But if not that, then how?)

He said love was good wherever it bloomed, and that he had come not to impose new burdens but to urge them to set theirs down, especially the burdens of hatred and compulsion. They softened as he spoke, as if the whole crowd shifted from hostile to neutral.

I was just beginning to think that whatever he was, fraud, saint, prophet, lunatic, Ix seemed to know what he was doing . . . when he began to scold them. At first it was in a tone of mild re-proof, but it rapidly became a scouring, soul-tearing thing as he laid into them for their violence, for the destruction they had made in "this beautiful city," for the cruelty and randomness of the riots. He demanded—not asked, not suggested, but *demanded*—that they apologize to their neighbors, make amends, rebuild, and above all else *stop*. Finally he said only that he would speak here again, tomorrow night, and teach them more of the way of peace.

I expected to see them tear him apart with their bare hands.

After he finished and descended the rostrum, before he had reached the bottom of that clamped-together pile of crates, the crowd was pouring out of the square in a great roar of babble. He no longer seemed to be interested in them, nor they in him. A moment later he was standing before us, and said, "Well, then, nothing more for tonight. Let's go back to the Embassy, shall we?"

Back at the Embassy, Tz'iquin commed the police and discovered that his house had been partly burned out. The automatic fire-fighting systems had kicked in quickly enough, so most of his property was all right for the moment, and since the city was now largely quiet, he would probably be able to go back and retrieve it all in the morning. Meanwhile, he sprang back to Pusiictsom's house, to spend a quiet night in a guest bed.

That left us with the problem of Ix and Auvaiyar. Ix had been staying with friends in various homes around the city, and since he now carried nothing with him, it was no problem to put him up on our couch. (I privately rejoiced: neither Margaret nor I could sleep there tonight).

Auvaiyar's house, whose location she had kept secret from dozens of lovers, had been discovered and attacked repeatedly; someone had figured out that shutting off the power, backup power, water, and cryonics, and smashing the household brain with a club, was enough to shut down automatic fire-fighting and let it burn. Destruction was complete, according to the police report.

"Well," Auvaiyar said, "then at least I don't have to worry

about fetching anything from there. If your couch folds out and if you don't have objections, Ix and I could just share it."

I was really exhausted: my back was worse than ever, and moreover my calves and shins were telling me just how long I had been making them carry an unaccustomed load. I wanted someone to tell me what the right thing to do was.

"My guess is Shan's Rule Six would apply here," Margaret said, "so I think you ought to stay."

Once, over wine after a fine dinner—I could no longer remember which culture or planet—Shan had confided to Margaret and me that he had just five rules for getting along; the first one was "don't do anything stupid" and the other four were all "get the paperwork done on time." I was quite sure there was no Rule Six in his system. Nonetheless, if Margaret thought it would be all right, that was more than good enough for me.

We had dinner together, the four of us, ordered in from the Embassy's robot systems. We all ordered *ceehel uah* and had a sort of impromptu Maya feast, though I had a beer rather than try their version of mead again; there was an obscure Tamil joke to the effect that Maya mead was intended to be used as an enema—and, once expelled, was served to guests.

The meal surprised me; it was festive. I thought we were all just keeping each other's spirits up, and then that we were enjoying the relief. Later I understood that Ix wanted joy that night, and was going to have it, and once he had decided that, the three of us couldn't possibly have prevented the room's being filled with joy.

At Margaret's urging, I even got out the lute and played a few songs, silly romantic stuff from my *jovent* days, stirring tales of banditry and border war.

Auvaiyar smiled when I took a break to drink more wine, and said, "You see, *akam* and *puram* are more than just Tamil categories of literature. Interior songs about love and exterior songs about courage and fighting—now what else can hold interest like those two? People who love songs and poetry and books, you know, never do anything, and if you're not going to do it, there's hardly a subject more interesting than sex or violence."

I laughed, and then said, "I suspect that would constitute heresy."

"There is no such thing as heresy here," Auvaiyar said, seriously. "Impurity and wrongheadedness and general obnoxiousness, sure. But the Cankam anthologies aren't holy books with one holy reading, so a new reading is not the automatic problem it is among the peoples of the book. That open-mindedness at least is something we share with the Maya."

"And with almost any other polytheists," Margaret said. "Having been raised strictly monotheist, I always feel very attracted to such cultures; the number of reasons to hurt each other would seem to be smaller."

"Yet here we are," Ix said.

No one said anything for a long time after that; we drank a last glass in each other's company. I put the lute away, and Margaret and I went into the bedroom.

In the middle of the night I awoke to the rhythmic squeak of the couch, Ix's fast breathing, and Auvaiyar moaning. She got louder, and the couch noise became positively unignorable, till our bedroom rang with the sounds of lovemaking coming through the door.

I wondered if they had awakened Margaret and if they would stop soon enough for me to go back to sleep. Not wanting to bump Margaret awake, I lay still and listened as the sound went on and on, visualizing each moment of what must be happening a scant four meters away. My penis became painfully stiff. After they were asleep I would have to masturbate; just the light pressure from the sheet was driving me crazy, and it was hard not to breathe fast.

A soft, wet half-snuffle-half-sob came from Margaret. She sounded so miserable that before I could think about whether this was wise, I had rolled over and hugged her close. She grabbed me in a bear hug and whispered, her voice choked with tears, "I was afraid you'd *never* wake up and you wouldn't want me if you did but god those sounds are making me so horny I could die from it."

I hadn't exactly planned to have sex but it only took a moment to thrust into her, and we were both so ready that it was exquisite. There wasn't much friction so I had to go on for a long time, but all during it the sounds from the other room only increased and became more intense, until Auvaiyar sounded to me as if she were howling like an animal and Ix's breathing had become short, grunting cries; by that time Margaret and I were pretty loud ourselves.

It was Ix's cry at his orgasm that finally released Margaret and I—a strange feeling for me since I would have thought that Auvaiyar's half-dozen wild outbursts would have done it much sooner. I fell forward, letting my penis slip out of Margaret, and we lay holding each other, trembling and breathing as if we had run for miles; my buttocks and thighs throbbed with the dull pain of overwork, as if I had been shoveling mud all day. "What is Shan's Rule Six?" I whispered. "I don't know it."

"Me either, but I figured you'd go along with it if you thought I was quoting him."

"I'd have gone along with it even if you had told me it was entirely your idea, *midons*."

"I know, but I didn't want you to get all noble about loving and respecting me. I thought something like this would happen, and I didn't want it spoiled by the thought that you might be doing stern duty."

Even sore and tired, laughing yourself to sleep beats crying yourself to sleep.

Part Four

Dark
Jaguar

Palai

Dark Jaguar: Last born of the people. The past, which follows, which is always there. At times in stories of the First People, he seems to disappear, leaving only Jaguar Quitze, Sudden Jaguar, and Not Right Now. But he always returns eventually.

Palai: the silvery-leafed ape-flower, a desert evergreen with small white flowers.

In the *akam* poems: The wasteland. Noon, when lovers are exposed to prying eyes; when everything withers in the heat. The place of the wild dog, lizard, eagle, kite, and tiger. The few people are travelers or robbers, who fight or dance in triumph, but do not stay, and find nothing to eat. Separation. Doubt, despair, the breaking of hopes.

In the *puram* poems: *vakai*, victory, achievement, completion of what was always to be.

A world dominated by Korravai, known in Sanskrit as Kali, goddess of war, death, and victory.

The miracle (if that's what you want to call it) of the previous day was not at all perfect. In general people had gone home and behaved themselves, but one small Maya girl was in the hospital with a concussion—a group of Tamil men had thrown rocks at her while she was on the way to school that morning. Three of the Tamils were in jail, bruised and sore from police stunsticks, and not long after the incident some Tamils had stoned police cars patrolling the Mayatown border.

There was a peaceful rally of a hundred Tamils or so, outside the Embassy, demanding that the Thousand Cultures recognize Tamil superiority.

Mayatown was quiet and, reading between the lines of the police reports, it looked like the Tamil cops appreciated that a great deal, and were behaving themselves well in that part of town.

What "fighting" there was happened in the tanks and mostly involved groups of young men pushing, shoving, and occasionally throwing a punch. You can depend on private enterprise for a love of order; the café owners were calling the cops promptly, and the lid was staying on those little brawls, as much as it was anywhere.

We urged Auvaiyar and Ix to just stay with us until sunset, when it would be time for Ix to speak in the square again. But Auvaiyar claimed she had a lot of business to do, including arranging somewhere new to live, and insisted on springing to a quiet corner of the city so that she could look over a couple of possible new sites to grow a house on and meet with someone from her insurance company. And whether we liked it or not, Ix insisted on going out into the city to talk and to teach.

We spent the morning reporting to Shan and nodding politely at the bureaucrats that Kiel paraded through the Embassy. There was a curious, jarring quality about every meeting with them, neither our fault nor theirs. Nearly all the local government officials wanted desperately to talk to us about what Ix might do next, since he had both started and stopped the riot, and we knew him better than any of them did. Margaret or I would have been happy to talk about it, but as soon as the subject came up, Kiel had a way of whisking the officials out the door; he was determined that they, being the "top people" and the "local leadership," were supposed to tell us what was going on, not ask us. They weren't supposed to behave as if a mere religious revival like Ix's movement had anything to do with a basic governmental function like the city police. So we could talk with them about anything that none of us thought was important. It made for very stilted conversation.

We argued with Shan. He wanted to send a full company of Council Special Police—the Council of Humanity's euphemism for "marines"—to bolster security at the Embassy. Just about the only thing Kiel and we agreed on was that doing such a thing was unnecessary if things were going well and extremely provocative if they weren't. Eventually Shan agreed to let us do things our way.

Late that afternoon, at Kiel's urging, the city government imposed a curfew on loitering, a sensible measure because urban riots tend to start among groups of idle people, late in the afternoon or early in the evening.

The trick was to keep the streets swept clear of potential rioters without provoking a riot with the sweeping process. Based on the reports that came in to the Embassy I can't fault the cops on the way they did that job. Where groups gathered on street corners, the police politely asked them to settle in somewhere. There was a sizable budget line for food, because one effective thing to do, if you had ten or so people looking for trouble, was to offer to listen to them "anywhere out of this miserable heat," take them down into a tank, to a café, and get them all something to eat, thus simultaneously tranquilizing them with their own blood sugar and getting them out of public interaction for a while.

Overall the peace still was holding, with scattered reports of rock throwing and brawling, but nothing that looked likely to blow up across the whole city. "I begin to see a little hope," Margaret said. "If they can hold off for an hour and a half, then it will be time for Ix to talk, and if it has the calming effect we're hoping for . . . " She shrugged. "I know that's quite a chain of things that have to work right."

"Yes, it is," I said. I was scanning the current police reports and so far seeing nothing really alarming. "On the other hand yesterday I wouldn't have bet we could be having this conversation. What *in nomne deu* is it about Ix, anyway? Half the time he seems like the typical religious guy in any of the Thousand Cultures, pleasantly vague and full of suggestions that we all just treat each other more kindly. Then again he'll act like a really cunning politician. And just when you think you've got that put together, he does something inexplicable—"

"Like l'affaire Auvaiyar? *Yap.* He's some mixture of the frightening and the wonderful. But that's what a Maya prophet is supposed to be, and from what I've been reading in the Tamil literature that's what a Saiva saint is supposed to be. Visitors from a god are apparently never just here to say 'hi' in a friendly way."

Kapilar came into the office, looking well-dressed but tired, as if he'd had a shower and change of clothes about an hour ago but they had not helped much. "Sorry I've been tied up with other things," he said, "but I'm back now."

"Not a problem. We assumed you were doing some work for Dr. Urruttiran," I said, "or maybe working for Ix. Have you seen him? What he doing?"

"He's sitting in a café half a kilometer from here, down in a tank, with a lot of tired, frustrated police officers," Kapilar said. "As far as I can tell he's preaching to them, mostly by praising them for the job they've been doing. They *have* been doing a good job. They like him, and he could hardly be safer than he is right now, surrounded by twenty cops."

"Well, that's a relief," Margaret said, "because the biggest mystery going on in the city was where a patrol of twenty cops had disappeared to. If you think it would be all right I'll notify the central dispatcher. Probably down in the tank the radio reception isn't very good, and that's why they've been unable to call them."

"That and I get the impression that the patrol commander switched off the com so that they wouldn't be interrupted," Kapilar said. "It's really extraordinary the effect that Ix has been having. If we just had seventy or a hundred copies of him the whole city would be completely quiet by nightfall. And when I ran into Tz'iquin—he's back in the city now, by the way—he said that Ix had spent most of the morning in Mayatown, and that's been completely quiet."

"Human beings always say they prefer peace, but it takes a saint to talk us into not assaulting our neighbors," Margaret said. "Just let me notify the central dispatcher—where did you say Ix and those cops were right now?"

He told her and her fingers rattled over the keys.

"One hour to go," I said, "and then Ix will speak again. I will be very glad when this is all over."

As afternoon shaded into evening we watched the police reports come in; there was an upsurge in small incidents, but not the sharp growth that indicates a riot forming. Half an hour ticked by with none of us saying anything more than a brief comment on whichever police report was scrolling across the screen.

The private doorbell chimed. I flipped on the screen. It was Kannan. "May I come in?" he asked. "It's urgent and private."

"Come in," I said, and keyed the authorization. A moment later he stood at the door.

He was so agitated that at first I thought he was ill. Beads of sweat stood out on his dark skin, his mustache was wet, and his chest was moving in hard, deliberate heaves as he fought to control his breathing. "I have something that I have to show you, or tell you at least, but I think it would be better to show you because time is very short."

Kapilar stared at him. "Kannan, what is wrong?"

"Everything. Or nothing. I can't say. The world is about to change very much." He mopped his forehead with his forearm and worked his shoulders, trying to get calm enough to talk to us, I suppose. "I am sorry. For once I don't intend to be cryptic or poetic, but I must get you to see this, *Donz* Leones, and all the rest of you as well. I don't know what to think or how to react to it; I found it by accident and I don't know . . . I am afraid and excited and confused all at once—"

"I can see that much," I said, getting up and putting on my hat. "How far away is whatever-it-is?"

"Ten minutes' walk. There's no springer closer to it than here and we would have to take the trakcar all the way to the central station and back to get there. And anyway it is best we go on foot and on the surface; in this hot part of the day we shall be as good as invisible."

He had gotten his breath back. Figuring ten minutes' walk was the better part of a kilometer in this gravity, he must have run here, and seen whatever he had seen only ten minutes ago or so. If it was as urgent as he said—I looked at him again. He was standing very still now, his arms hanging limply from relaxed shoulders. A great patch of sunlight from the window splashed the wall of the hallway behind him. He did not move at all.

In a bare few seconds I had said, "I'll go," and Margaret had asked, "Is it safe?"; Kannan had said he didn't know but he thought so; Margaret had hugged me and told me to be careful. Kapilar had agreed to meet us at the gathering in front of the temple of Murukan—"if it is held," Kannan had said grimly. "After what I have to show you—"

"Trust Ix," Kapilar said. "He will speak at the temple of Murukan tonight. He said so. I will meet you there. Go quickly, *Donz* Leones, see whatever you must, and you can tell me about it after we both have heard Ix speak. Whatever it is will be more bearable then."

Kapilar sprang from our private springer to the public station behind the temple of Murukan. I hugged Margaret. Then Kannan and I went out one of the many side doors of the Embassy into the roasting streets of New Tanjavur. Kannan took off so fast he left me hurrying after him, sweating and puffing before I had gone twenty steps. I caught up with him and we walked side by side, through deserted streets in the blinding light and stifling heat.

After a few blocks, Kannan took off his hat, brushed a hand through his drenched hair, and said, "Down this way." We entered a long breezeway, and turned right into a stairway that descended, through a steep vaulted shaft, to a balcony that ringed a sunken garden built around a fountain.

Here Kannan stopped for a moment, and we both caught our breath. A young mother was descending the steps on the other side, headed for the big fountain itself. She held a small boy's hand; he was tugging her forward, down the steps, clearly wanting to join the several other children already playing in the fountain.

"I have heard," Kannan said, "and you could verify it better than I, that children everywhere are much alike."

"Well, it's not entirely true. In Caledony all those children—especially that little boy—would be punished for lack of self-control. In *my* home culture the mother would be telling the boy to be more poised and to move more beautifully. Here, she just lets him be a child. I think that's better."

"Oh?" Kannan said. "And can you hear, from here, what she is saying to him? Do you know us so well that you know the secret words mothers whisper to children, the ones that the child is happy about or ashamed of? Can you read the tiny hints she gives about how to be a Tamil, or know what she will sing to him when she tucks him in tonight?

"It is common to observe that children playing tend to look

very much like children playing, especially when they are doing something as common and ordinary as splashing around in a fountain.

"But it is still a foolish observation because usually people make it as a way of condemning prejudice. And that's ridiculous. The observation that we all begin pretty much alike does not condemn hatred, it invites it. To see that we all start out the same means that the detested Other is much too close to ourselves; it reminds us that they could have chosen to be like us—after all, we did—and that they express contempt for our choice by choosing another road. Is that not completely unforgivable? An intolerable criticism, the number of people who are at every moment choosing not to be us? You can forgive a bird for not being a mammal, a mouse for not being a primate, and even a monkey for not being a man, because none of them had any choice, but how can you forgive a man for choosing to worship false gods, ignoring basic duty, and keeping filthy customs?"

His hands clenched on the balustrade and his arm muscles swelled against his thin, decorated shirt. He sighed, exhaling so much air that his short-trimmed mustache riffled and his head bent forward with the effort, as if he were squeezing out a deadly gas from his lungs, trying to remove every trace.

"Are you all right, Kannan?" I tried to sound as indifferent as if he had only stubbed his toe and sworn unexpectedly loudly.

Kannan's smile was tight, but when he turned to speak to me his gaze bored straight in; he might be mad but he would tell the truth as he knew it. "Very, very good. The Council of Humanity's man in New Tanjavur is very calm even in the possible presence of an enraged madman, in a city already torn by riots. He is able to ignore the ravings of a native lunatic and to concentrate on—"

"I'll thank you not to attribute things to me that I didn't say and never would say."

"Better and better. All in such a carefully neutral voice. I feel honored to be taken so seriously even when I am so clearly raving. I suppose no man can know what his feelings will be in a few years' time. Isn't that what makes so many marriages so absurd? I do hope that long after this, when you think about what I am about to show you, you will understand that I see its logic and its necessity, even though I had no hand in doing the deed."

He turned away from me so quickly I was startled and had to rush to catch up with him. He was about three steps ahead of me as we descended a winding crumbled-stone staircase from the end of the gallery. I had thought that the staircase must spiral down into the fountain courtyard we had been looking down into, but about two meters above the courtyard it forked, one branch sloping out into Metallah's fierce light and the splashing, laughing children, the other away into the wall at a crooked angle, steeply down into space-black dark. Kannan took the dark path to the right, saying over his shoulder, "Yes, we are almost there.

"I'm sure the only reason this was not discovered sooner is the many people staying home today; this little tank feeds the fountain above and it's so small and private that mainly it's a lovers' rendezvous. Which I suppose it is about to be, again. Don't worry, there's a mirror light at the bottom when we get into the tank enclosure."

After rushing through the blazing heat outside, the dark cool of the spiral stairway—despite my rising fear of what Kannan was about to show me—was refreshing and pleasant, and the need to go slowly in the darkness gave me time to catch my breath. I had thought that Kannan might be deliberately toying with me, playing on my nerves and dropping so many heavy-handed exasperating hints, testing the limits of the Council's patience yet again. But as we descended, and a dim wet light began to filter up the staircase toward us, I kept bumping into his back, and something—maybe the obvious tension in his shoulders, maybe the way he leaned back, maybe the slight smell of acrid fresh sweat—told me that no matter how many rationalizations he had constructed up above in daylight, he did not really want to see whatever was down here again.

At last we reached the bottom. Like many tanks, this one had its pool inside an inner, curtain wall that ringed the space, so that there was a hallway circling the space with a few doors opening into the tank proper. At the first doorway he went in. I followed him.

Light came down in almost straight lines from the high shafts above, bounced down via the mirror towers that decorated the buildings far above. The central circular pool itself was black except where the bright shafts stabbed into it and were swallowed, as if the water itself were absorbing all the light. A few fast-racing ripples made dim silver curves on the black surface. A narrow walkway with stone benches ringed the pool. Each bench had, at its ends, stone demon heads leering, their expressions exaggerated by the starkness of the sharp-angled top light, so that all the demons faced other demons on the benches nearest them, about to kiss in an infernal orgy.

High up in the shadows, perhaps ten meters above the pool, something just touched one shaft of light. I walked forward to get a better look—it looked like a bit of curtain hung in an unusual place, perhaps fallen from some valance far above.

I saw it was in the shape of a human body just before Kannan clicked on the emergency lighting, and so I had just an instant to brace before I saw it was Auvaiyar. There was no mistaking who it was; her face was undistorted by strangulation. My first thought, that she had been hanged, must be wrong.

Then I saw the way her dress hung open wide and the shape of her chest. Her feet and legs were covered with blood, and now I looked and saw that the pool below her was not merely dark, but stained deep red. There are eleven liters of blood in a human body, and eleven liters of paint would cover a good-sized room, I thought, one of those distracted explanations that run through your head when you need to keep from screaming. There must be a pretty good filter on the fountain above since this didn't leak there. The filter would be removing blood from the water. Therefore she hasn't been here long or the water would not be so deep a red. Therefore this must have happened very shortly before Kannan found the body, or else he did it.

I looked at her again. Her ribcage had been split at the sternum and then yanked wide open. Scraps of flesh depended from the open doors of ribs, but the chest cavity itself was empty.

"I got an anonymous message telling me to come here," Kannan said. "This is what I found. Part of the reason the ribcage hangs so horribly is that her heart and lungs are missing. Maybe in all the mess they didn't know which was heart, and which was lungs, so they just took everything.

"It was a clumsy and stupid thing to do in normal circumstances, since everyone knows that the Maya of Briand never have practiced human sacrifice. But I am sure that there will be enough people willing to believe, now, just for the excuse to resume the violence. And the Maya of Mayatown will take this as a very direct insult, a mocking of their ancient religious customs. So although I'm quite sure that Tohil had nothing to do with the taking of the heart, I'm equally sure that—given what a bloody and savage god he is—he will be very pleased with its consequences."

I felt sick. Perhaps if she had been hideously mutilated all over I would have been able to look at her like sausage or sliced steak, as just a heap of politically significant meat, or if she had really been hanged, as just Auvaiyar dead. But with her face still beautiful and her lower body still a wonder of graceful curves, but her midsection a nightmare of butchery, I was forced to juxtapose the living, laughing Auvaiyar whose cries of passion had aroused me and Margaret not twenty hours earlier, with this lump of ripped meat. I couldn't begin to—

I heard the footsteps behind me and knew who it must be. I turned and saw Ix, looking wordlessly up at the corpse. He stared for a long time, and finally said, "Would you two men please help me cut her down? This is a terrible thing, but I must hurry because I need to speak at the square."

We found the access ladder and got up to the catwalks above the tank. Cutting the rope was easy enough, but the splash, and the way her ribs opened like the wings of some malign ray as she floated face down, were so overpowering that both of us vomited on the catwalk. It took us a few minutes to get our breath and climb back down.

Ix had pulled her out. He was wiping her dead face, smoothing down her hair, trying to close the gaping mess of her ribcage. He looked up. "There are things I must do," he said, "and a short time to do them. Perhaps one of you will call for a private trakcar, and the other will help me carry her body up to the street?"

I ran to the first public com I could find, up in the fountain courtyard. While I was keying in the code to get us the trakcar, I saw Ix and Kannan go by, on the steps, through the doorway, with Auvaiyar supported between them. In the high gravity, carrying a body was no doubt miserably hard work, but they were doing it together with great care.

We had half-opaqued the windows so that we could see out but no one outside could see in. The trakcar crawled slowly along, stopping often to let people get out of its way, or gliding along behind some pedestrian who found the trakcar track was the fastest place to walk.

A four-passenger trakcar makes a poor hearse; we pulled the seats into the facing-each-other configuration and put Auvaiyar on the floor. We didn't have even a blanket to cover her with.

All three of us had been splashed with blood, or bloody water from the tank, and so our first stop was an automated clothing dispenser on a quiet corner that we thought would be out of the way of most foot traffic. We got duplicates of the clothing we had on, threw the old soiled ones into the regenner, and changed in the booths at the dispenser; as always, the duplication was imperfect and the new clothes were a little scratchy and uncomfortable. We also got two blankets, one to carry Auvaiyar on and one to cover her with.

For the whole ten minutes or so that it took the trakcar to get to the stop in front of the temple of Murukan, there was nothing at all to talk about. When we got there, Ix would do what Ix thought proper, and neither Kannan nor I harbored any illusions that we could influence that. Whatever was going to happen at the square would happen.

The day before, the people in the crowd had looked stunned and dull, like people on their way to a funeral where they knew everyone would bicker. Today they looked . . . not happy, not yet, but alive, excited, as if they wanted to see what would happen next.

Ix said, "The two cultures have been at risk of war, and have lived with violence, for so long that everyone has imagined every detail of it. When it looked like the day had arrived, they had spent their whole lives envisioning and preparing for the monstrosities they were imagining; they had no ability to step outside their concept of what was going to happen. Well, I gave them the possibility that this time, too, we might escape."

"How did you know what I was thinking?" I asked.

"I was going to ask the same thing," Kannan said.

Ix shrugged. "None of us wants to look at poor Auvaiyar. None of us wants to talk. And therefore you looked out the windows, and both of you looked puzzled, and the only thing that was different from any other time was the crowd, because they had such an odd mixture of expressions of hope, even happiness. So I thought perhaps I could explain them for you. It was possible that I was quite wrong; it is easier for me to guess your feelings than theirs." He leaned forward and turned on the video news channel, pushing the screen back to where all three of us could see it. "Let's see if my disciples have been able to do what I asked."

He turned up the audio track; the announcer was gabbling excitedly and the camera was swinging back and forth over the square, revealing—

"The *Maya* are at the square!" Kannan exclaimed.

"That's right," Ix said. "They've walked there from Maya-town, through the police barriers, to hear their prophet speak. Everyone on both sides is nervous, of course, but they are all getting along, so far."

"What's going to happen when you show them this body?" I asked. "Shouldn't you—"

Ix shrugged. "I will do what I am going there to do. If it works you will be pleasantly surprised and if it doesn't you won't have been dreading it for the whole time until it fails. As for what will happen or what people will do, well, common sense should tell you that I cannot know any more than you can."

He didn't seem to want to talk after that, so I just watched the screen. It looked to me like there were just a few hundred Maya in the crowd at the square, but many of them had come as whole families—there were lots of kids and old people. "That's a case of risking everything," I said, as the camera zoomed in on a family that was one young couple, several old people, and several small children.

Ix shrugged. "They are already risking everything, just by being alive in New Tanjavur. If this works there will be peace for them to grow into. If not, well, then most of them will die by violence sooner or later, and the longer they live through it the more hardened and bitter they will become. Perhaps they are only thinking that if one must die in such times of troubles, one would do well to die before becoming a murderer oneself."

The news company was clearly having a grand time with this; the next image they showed us was of two small children who had run away from their frantic mothers. Both wore similar sunsuits, but plainly one was Maya and the other was Tamil. I doubt either child was three years old yet. The cameraman had caught the moment of their meeting face to face, as they stood staring at each other.

"Do you still think that's a provocation to bigotry?" I asked Kannan. As we watched, the two mothers had retrieved their children, shyly, glancing at each other constantly. Now they stood holding the children, exchanging pleasantries (or at least they were smiling and nodding).

"I don't understand it," Kannan admitted. "The same mothers who will stand for an hour chatting about childhood ailments and problems in school, and admiring the accomplishments and beauty of everyone's children, are the ones who teach us whom to hate. I don't fault them for teaching us our identities; someone has to, and identity includes who we hate. Everyone has known since the dawn of time that mothers are the carriers of culture. But what is it that makes them all such instinctive traitors? Why do they drop all they have taught us and stand there smiling at each other's children?"

"Perhaps they are wiser than it is possible to become by just reading poetry," Ix said.

Kannan turned to stare out the window.

The trakcar took the turn into the square and approached the stop. Ix leaned forward and hit a few keys. "We'll park the trakcar and pay to hold it," he said. "I want you men to sit with Auvaiyar's body; bring it out when I ask you to. Handle her gently, please."

The car slid into a parking siding and settled to the ground; Ix pushed the door open and stood. For just one instant he looked directly at us and said, "I suppose whatever happens now, you're going to remember this. Try to remember it fairly, for your own sakes, whatever it may be necessary for you to say to others."

He walked away before we could respond. When the crowd saw him, there was a great, happy roar and they all pressed in closer. The front ranks of the crowd lunged forward trying to touch him, and as he passed he lightly shook or squeezed each of those hands, so gracefully that years afterward it is one of my clearest memories of him. Most of us, confronted with several hundred hands to shake, would look as if we were picking fruit or milking a giant cow, but Ix's touch with each of them was friendly, gentle, firm, individual, as if shaking hands had been the whole occupation of his life. It took him a few minutes more to reach the rostrum, but it appeared that he felt he had all the time he needed.

When he at last stood above them on the little improvised platform, the crowd drew back slightly, as if to give him space, and stopped talking; the only sound I could hear was my own breathing and the occasional wail of a baby or prattle of a small child somewhere in the crowd. When Ix began, I could hear him perfectly, even though he was a good thirty meters away.

He began, as he often did, with the story of the Tamils and the Maya, starting with the dreams of the anthropologists and literature professors, and the gathering of genetic samples from the Earth populations. He was challenging everyone who wanted to pretend to continuity with the ancient civilizations, but no one disputed him. Perhaps those who did were intimidated or ashamed, or more likely they had stayed home.

He led up to the moment when the eruption of Old Grandfather had destroyed Kintulum and made the Maya territories untenable. He was doing some distorting of history himself, I thought, as he described both cultures on the planet pulling together to deal with the crisis. Then his voice became steadily sadder until you wanted to run up to him and apologize, as he described the growth of hatred between the two cultures.

When he turned away from history to the present, he began by scolding them. The night before he had explained to Margaret and me why that step was necessary: he was their best friend, their mother and father, the one person they wanted to tell everything to and be forgiven by, and therefore they needed and wanted him first to reject the evil in their hearts. You don't open your heart and repent to anyone whose message is "Everything is just fine." You don't turn to saints and prophets to help you be, more or less, the same old moral mess you've always been.

Ix kept that part short, and moved quickly to talking about forgiveness, and seeking trust, and about, if there was to be hatred, not letting it come from you. He spoke of the redefinition of the old stories, of making them a public highway to share rather than a fortress wall to divide. It was beautiful and when I hear recordings of it played (it enjoyed quite a vogue in many of the Thousand Cultures, especially in the Inner Sphere), even now so long after, I get tears in my eyes, though I didn't then.

At last he reached the point I had been fearing, and for the first time, he talked about himself. "Now, many of you know who I used to be. I spent many, many years trying to preserve the old Maya way, because I belonged to the Peccary lineage, because I was a priest of the Center Temple, and most of all because it seemed right to me. I thought that we owed it to our fathers to deny that they were wrongheaded and small-spirited, and that if we were to drop the quarrels and the pretensions, and face our Tamil brothers, extend our hands, and live together, that would betray twenty generations of ancestors.

"And yet, here I am.

"These riots and crimes began because an older man, freed at last from an old life and his children long since grown, turned out to be human enough to enjoy an affair with a younger woman— and she happened to be Tamil, and he Maya.

"One might ask whether love is so common that you can afford to discourage it, or whether I became less wise because I was happy, or whether it ought to matter to anyone other than my family and the woman's. You might ask yourselves why you think that stoning a small girl or setting a house on fire would make anyone stop doing the thing that offends you. You might ask yourselves a great number of things, and stare into the void left by your lack of answer, and perhaps somewhere in that void you would begin to see just how empty you are, just how barren, and just how much you need to fill yourselves with love and trust and regard for each other. You are reasonably good at filling your bellies and your bank accounts, but when it comes to filling yourself with the gifts of love and trust, you sit and starve in a vast dining hall with the food of life all around you.

"I might have pointed all this out to you, and then stood in front of you and held Auvaiyar's hand, and pledged that our love would be honorable, and suggested to you that you leave everyone free to love according to whatever was best in them. You might have learned, from watching us, how to love each other. But all those things are no longer possible, for someone earlier today killed Auvaiyar, and my heart is with her in the afterlife now, and I am only briefly visiting you from Xibalbá, the realm of the death-gods, where however long I live among you my heart will always be tending.

"And yet . . . oh, and yet, my friends . . . it is too late for me, but it is not too late for you. Bring her forward!"

Kannan and I jumped up from our seats in the trakcar, and lifted the blanket on which her body rested. In the one-third-above-standard gravity, she was even more of a load than an ordinary corpse, and slung as if in a hammock between us, she was so heavy and awkward that we staggered as we carried her body up toward Ix.

The crowd murmured. I suppose it did seem particularly meaningful, one way or another, that her pallbearers were a preacher of hate and a Council diplomat, but then our martyr for peace had been regarded, by almost everyone who knew her, as little better than a whore just hours ago. But whatever the incongruities, Ix had commanded, and his power—whence-ever it might derive—still had its old force, even then. They stood and stared, waiting for him to make sense of it for them, and meanwhile they were quiet.

"Uncover her," Ix said, "and let us all consider what has been done here." I glanced up at Kannan; he was ash-colored from paleness beneath his dark skin, and I was nauseated myself. We pulled back the upper blanket and revealed the pathetic, shattered body with the obscenely gaping chest; the front rank of the crowd recoiled as though from a snake, and the murmur rose to a passionate buzz.

"Now," Ix said, "I give you my word—a word you have trusted your souls to at times—that I loved this woman with all my heart, and that this crime fills me with bitter fury. But I tell you, nothing I can do can bring her back, and I tell you that if her killer steps before me now, and confesses, that striking him down would bring me no peace, and I would not do it even if he freely offered himself to me to be killed."

He looked out over the crowd, the Tamil and Maya standing intermingled, faces all but unreadable in the deep shadows that Metallah now cast, the square itself still glaring white in sunlight and almost black in shadow. Briand had managed to become old and overripe with hatred and despair, without ever having been young; all its beauties were only the echoes of ancient prejudices still, and no one had ever really looked around to see the real Briand, or to sing of what people might be here; there had never been a morning here in which new things might begin clean and fresh as dew, but rather Metallah had always risen only to reveal the fresh crimes of the night and day before lying on top of the old crimes, like fresh garbage on an old heap.

Something moved in the great sweep of silhouettes in front of me, something that I couldn't quite make out because it was backlit by that fierce white sun. When he stepped out of the crowd I recognized Tz'iquin.

"Uncle," he shouted loudly.

"I am here, nephew. Say what you have to say, ask what you want."

Tz'iquin seemed about to speak, hesitated a moment, and then shouted, "I ate your whore's heart."

"Truly I am sorry for what you have made of yourself."

"I am proud," Tz'iquin said.

I had only an instant to realize that what he was pulling from the folds of his garment was a weapon—enough time to take a single useless step toward him, but he was ten meters away and there was no time to reach him or block his shot. With a clap of thunder, a welding-arc-bright streak formed between Tz'iquin's weapon and Ix's face. Ix's head burst open at the back, bits of burning flesh sprayed into the air, and flames rose from the stump of his neck as Ix fell forward.

Tz'iquin had killed Ix with a military hand maser, set to put all of its energy—normally enough for 2000 man-killing shots—into a millisecond burst. I didn't see it at the time but I am told that the beam also blew the smiling stone head off a statue of Murukan on the temple wall, and shattered walls all the way through the temple; even as Ix was falling, the distant thunder of that beam's passage through the atmosphere was rumbling over us.

Kannan and I tackled Tz'iquin before he could pull out the second maser; I think he intended to fire that one into the crowd. I knocked Tz'iquin unconscious with one shot from my stun stick and looked up to see what was happening.

In the crowd, neighbor turned on neighbor, Tamil on Maya. Beside me, Kannan, a frightening gleam in his eye, rose and stared at the crowd.

Kapilar appeared beside me, his eyes wet with tears, and said, "We have to run. We have to run before anyone thinks of—"

Kannan kicked him full in the face. Bewildered, I turned to see if Kapilar was all right, and when I did, a motion caught the corner of my eye. I looked back just in time to see Kannan grab the maser from Tz'iquin's unconscious body and fire it into his head. Then he shot at a fleeing family of Maya; he walked rapidly toward them, shooting over and over. They fell like rag dolls until finally there was only a tiny, wailing child left. As I watched, frozen with horror, Kannan broke into a run, caught up with it—it was too far away and the child was too small for me to say whether it was a boy or a girl—seized the child by the face, and slammed the butt of the maser onto the back of the tiny child's skull.

"Why—" I said, "what—"

"This is what he always wanted," Kapilar said softly in my ear. "Now, *Donz* Leones, we have to run, really we do." He grabbed my elbow and dragged me to my feet.

I looked around. People were approaching, their faces at once blank and enraged, far too many to deal with, armed as I was only with the stun stick that I still held in my hand.

We turned and ran; in that high gravity and at that miserable temperature, it was mere steps before my shirt was drenched and breath came only in great, wet, painful gasps. Beside me, Kapilar was no better off.

"Where are we going?" I had to fight for the air with which to ask.

"Springer station down this alley," he said. "Get you back to the Embassy."

No one followed us, but there were little clumps of people pouring out of the square and down every alley and street. We hurried, no longer running but walking as fast as we could. "How could he—" I panted.

"Save it," Kapilar said. "The whole world lost for jealousy. The whole world. Because one man couldn't accept . . . oh, it makes me want to vomit."

As we hurried up the street, Metallah set. The shadows scissored together and lunged out to the east, so that by the time we reached the public springer the whole street was dark. The noise of the crowd fighting in the square had become so loud that though we had the street to ourselves, we could barely hear each other.

We crowded into the little booth and I cycled my OSP card and spoke the address of our private springer at the Embassy. The field of the springer formed, a gray featureless fog like white noise to the eye. We stepped through into the corner of the parlor, and the field behind us shut off, leaving a bare wall where the gray fog had been. Four CSPs, masers drawn, stared at us. Kapilar and I both raised our hands.

Margaret had to shout "They're both okay!" twice before the CSPs lowered the weapons. They still looked nervous.

We put our hands down and I said, "I assume you were watching what happened."

"*Yap*," she said. "And after that, too, whenever I could spare the time."

"What was happening here?" I asked.

"Right after Ix was shot someone threw a firebomb against the Embassy wall. Crude amateur job—it did no damage but it sure scared the hell out of everyone. Kiel thinks we're going to be attacked any second. He's got all the springers and entrances guarded and they're fortifying the terrace right now, and he's hollering into the com for all the CSPs the Council will ship. But except for that one firebomb, so far there's been no attack."

A loud alarm clanged and all four CSPs jumped.

"That'll be Shan," Margaret said, popping the video channel of the com on the main room screen and the audio on all speakers.

It was Shan. I had never seen him look so old, so angry, or so frightened before. "There is no time to argue about this," he said, "so don't. I am placing you directly under my orders through the Office of Special Projects. I want you to get into the springer within five minutes. I am loading your destination into your springer's address file at this moment. Do not take more than five minutes. Bring any Council personnel you can with you, but come fast and don't take more than five minutes. That's an order. Explanations later. Bye."

He clicked off.

I looked at Kapilar and the four CSPs and said, "Well, you heard him—come with us."

Margaret ran into the bedroom and came out a moment later carrying my two instrument cases and her keepsake box (I have only a few little mementos and they stay in the lute or guitar case for just such moments.) While she was doing that, I sent an "urgentest" signal to Ambassador Kiel. He answered, saw me, and hung up before I had said more than "sir, I have received—"

"Doesn't trust us," I said, and commed the CSP command for the Embassy.

The officer looked exhausted even though it was less than twenty minutes since the crisis had begun. "I am activating my reserve rank with the Office of Special Projects," I said, typing him my code, and told him to verify that as of about one minute before, I outranked the Ambassador. "A springer address is being transmitted from my springer to all springers within the secure part of the building. This is an evacuation, extreme danger, emergency basis. Get all personnel you can through the Embassy springers to that address, right now. You have no more than five minutes to accomplish this." I had finished my keying; the address that Shan had given me was now loaded into every springer in the Embassy, and they all were powering up. "If you have to use force to get the Ambassador to come along, do so. Have you verified?"

"Uh, no, I—just a second." He drew a breath. "Verify seniormost rank of—uh, your name sir—"

"Giraut Leones."

"Grotly Owens," he said.

I started to shout a correction, but apparently that was close enough for the aintellect to figure it out. "Verified," it said.

The officer nodded and said, "Very well, Mr. Owens." He clicked off. An instant later he had overridden the com pickups everywhere in the embassy and was ordering everyone into the nearest springers. I unlocked the apartment door and propped it open. "We'll leave our springer running and tuned to that address," I said, "for any strays that need to come through. All right, you gentlemen go through first," I added to the CSPs, who appeared to be standing there in shock. I grabbed one and shoved him toward the gray fog at the back of the springer booth. "Come on, hurry up, walk through."

After I got the first one moving, they staggered forward into the gray fog, like badly operated robots.

"Kapilar, come with us," Margaret said.

"No." His voice was firm and level. "I thank you, and I would love to see more of the Thousand Cultures, but my place is here."

"Kapilar," I said, "when we get an order like that, it means something really bad is about to happen. There's not going to *be* a *here,* very likely, any second. Now don't argue. Walk into it and let's go."

"No. I said no. I am a Tamil. This is war. This is the war we have dreamed of all our lives, and I cannot be anywhere but here."

"What would Ix tell you—" I began.

"Ix is dead. That tells me everything. His way was very beautiful and if I live I shall weave it into my own poetry or teachings. He saw a way that Briand could be beautiful and new. But he didn't live. And without him Briand is what it always was, only now with an open war. I might have liked Ix's Briand better, but Tz'iquin has blown his head apart. Now I must be true to who I am. I am a Tamil, and we are sensitive lovers but we are also brave, reckless, cruel warriors." He turned but Margaret grabbed his shirt. He slapped her hand, hard, and as she released him he said, "I made sure Giraut got back. We're even." Then he ran down the hall out of sight.

Margaret cried out and ran a few steps after him, still clutching her keepsake box. I made myself say, "Margaret, we've got to let him go, *midons,* we have to—"

She made a choking noise, looked at me, looked at the hallway, and suddenly, still gripping the keepsake box, she ran through the springer entrance. I saw tears streaming over her face as she went.

We had still heard no sound of fighting or anything else from the outside. I picked up the lute case and guitar case, sighing at the loss of our clothes and furniture, and walked through the gray field of the springer. A momentary disorienting sensation told me that I had crossed over to somewhere with much lower gravity, and then I found myself on a big receiving dock in a space station somewhere. It felt like about one tenth of a standard gravity, which meant we had just dropped practically all our weight, a very big change in gravity for most people—

I had just time to think that before, stepping forward, I skidded in a pile of someone's vomit. I'm immune to springer sickness myself, but lots of people throw up whenever they cross between differing gravitational potentials, and this was a difference of about a factor of thirteen. I skidded forward and then drifted gently to the floor, landing in another pile of vomit. The dock was covered with men and women from the Embassy, mostly on their hands and knees puking. It looked like a convention of sick dogs.

Margaret was a meter to my left, on her hands and knees, face still drenched with tears, trying to move away from the puddle in front of her or just not look at it. "We made it," she whispered. "Where are we?"

The medic robot rolled up to us. It was going around giving people a blood pressure test and administering a mild tranquilizer. I got up, looking at the hideous mess on my clothes, and waved off the tranquilizer.

More people were crashing through the springers behind us, most of them falling forward and vomiting, the few lucky immunes like me falling over them or slipping in the puddles. It was a dreadful sight, and even worse to smell.

A loudspeaker announced, "Showers, clothes cleaners, and medical treatment, available down the corridor in front of you. If you cannot walk, raise your hand and a med cart will transport you there." I got to my feet, picked up my instrument cases, and then stooped to let Margaret grab my elbow to get to her feet. She made sure her keepsake box was secure under her arm, and gasped out, "Rough one. Don't think I've ever sprung across such a big gravity difference."

"Can you walk?"

"I'm fine now. Lower gravity feels good. Let's go slow."

As we walked up the corridor it quickly became apparent that we were indeed on a space station somewhere; the constant upward rise of the floor, the faint Coriolis, and the distinct sense that gravity was higher at our feet than our heads, were the giveaways. Perhaps they had sprung us into the Inner Sphere, to Procyon or Alpha Centauri, or even all the way to the Earth system? There were a few stations around Earth that had bigger populations than some of the less-settled frontier worlds.

At last we found the promised area, and I headed into the male section. There I found a cleanup booth—one among many. They must get quite a few emergency springs from planetary surfaces here. I locked my instrument cases into the locker, stripped out of my clothes, trying not to touch any more of other people's stomach contents than I had to, and tossed the soggy mess into the laundry processor. Since I had had to have clothes regenned back on New Tanjavur, I was now washing a bad, scratchy copy of my own clothes. Just as soon as this was all over I would have to shop for a complete new wardrobe.

When I got into the shower, I set the soap cycle for a disinfectant and a mild skin-penetration sedative, and the rinse cycle for a mint scent close to the one I usually wore. I let myself have five full minutes to play in the soap spray—it was lovely. Then the hot rinse hit, smelling strongly of mint, and the warmth and sedatives relaxed my muscles. I began to feel human. Finally the water shut off and the hot air circulated in the booth; I toweled off my hair and the occasional damp spot, and got out to see how my clothes were coming.

They were fresh, clean, and dry. The washing seemed to have reduced the scratchiness. I put them on and combed my hair, and took my instrument cases with me to a large waiting room, wondering when Margaret or Shan or someone would turn up. I was among the first there, and in the next few minutes I was gratified to see almost all the Embassy staff that I knew, including Sir Qrala. So far I had not seen any of the Tamil employees emerge. Later I found out that only six out of eighty had decided to jump with us; I guess Kapilar was typical of those who didn't.

The room was about half full when Margaret emerged, fresh-scrubbed and looking physically healthy, but sad and old in her expression. I was standing to hug her when a voice on the loud-speaker told us we were wanted immediately and to step back into the corridor.

I expected to see Shan but instead a small motorized cart rolled up to us and said, "Giraut and Margaret Leones?"

"Yes," we said in unison.

It unfolded a springer screen and generated the field. "Step through please." We did, into a small conference room. Shan sat at the head of the table, and most of the seats were taken up with people in consular or CSP uniforms, mostly high-ranking. "Welcome," Shan said. "We are still hoping Ambassador Kiel will spring and join us, but it doesn't look good. Take a seat, please. Coffee?"

We thanked him and parked our luggage in a corner. By the time we sat down at the table with cups of coffee, Sir Qrala had arrived as well.

The screens behind Shan showed an array of scenes; it was night now in New Tanjavur, and most of the pictures were coming from flitters, little flying robots with cameras. The only camera still functioning inside the Embassy showed Kiel's office, the furniture mostly smashed and the paper files scattered and smoldering on the floor.

Buildings were burning at a dozen places around New Tanjavur, and by their light I could see men, women, and children struggling; it looked as if there were three way battle between the general population, loyal police, and the Maya of Mayatown, and though the general population was probably winning overall, nothing was yet settled.

One flitter popped us an image of the square in front of the temple of Murukan, slowly scanning it in the infrared. Ix's body lay where he had fallen, and the center of the square was littered with the dead—and perhaps the wounded, for a firefight was going on between one side in the temple, and another in the government office across the square. There was a lot of shattered stone around the temple. "Probably the Maya," I said. "It would have been the nearest place for them to take shelter and a few of them probably came armed, 'just in case.' " As we watched, one maser shot lashed out from the office building into the square; a body bounced into the air from a steam explosion underneath it. Maser shots flashed from a dozen places on the temple. A wounded woman, pulling a small child by the hand, leaped to her feet and tried to run to the temple. The flitter focused in on her, and we had just time to see that she was Tamil as she approached Murukan's temple, her face lighted by the fires burning around it.

Then her body was torn to pieces, and the child beside her turned to run and was cut down as well. Fusillades of maser and projectile fire ripped across both buildings, and sprays of stone, metal, and glass showered down on the square below.

The flitter image cut out. Meanwhile, I had gotten a look at the infrared image from a low-orbiting satellite. Little flickers of maser fire and detonations of projectile impacts danced across the whole face of New Tanjavur like evil sprites. There was a nasty, bright, hook-shaped curve of them surrounding the dark shape of Mayatown, which told me that the fighting was heavy there.

"Now watch this," a dark-skinned man in a consular uniform said. "Here's an overhead close-up out of Yaxkintulum."

The picture flashed bright; in Yaxkintulum it was still two hours to sunset. We were looking at the grounds of Pusiictsom's private home, where Kapilar and I had once eaten a long, friendly meal.

There were hundreds of Maya cops in full gear, carrying shoulder arms of some kind, standing in a long line; it took me a moment to figure out what I was looking at from this almost-overhead view. They were advancing slowly into the house—

"*Deu,*" I said, under my breath.

The military man next to me—he wore badges indicating several CSP interventions—sighed. "Yes. They're heading into the springer. We don't think they had much choice—there are only two springers in Mayatown and it looks like one of them had already been overrun, so our guess is that the Maya figured they had to either use the chance or lose it."

I glanced sideways at him. "Were they always planning this?"

"For at least a stanyear, or so we think," he said. "The Center Temple probably came up with this plan right after they built their first covert springer."

"We haven't met," I said. "I'm—"

"I know you're Giraut Leones, and that this is Margaret, your wife," he said, nodding politely. "I'm Piranesi Alcott, and since I'm a controller for intelligence ops, I hope to stay at least as unknown as you are known." He gestured vaguely toward the woman behind him. "And you've met Paxa Prytanis, the best intelligence analyst in the Office of Special Projects who happens to be my wife."

Paxa gave us a tiny wave and a weak smile.

"Yes," I said, realizing, "I must have read or heard a dozen reports from you or your agents. So the planning for this attack through the springers was going on in Yaxkintulum, behind the scenes, even while they were talking peace?"

"This and many more things," Alcott agreed. "It was hard to keep track of all of them, because, you know, there's no single head of state there, and no single office that takes care of everything. Every little temple was making its own preparations. But the Center Temple was key, and it looks to me like—oh, my, here we go."

The line moved. On the next screen, a flitter got a lock on the public springer booth in Mayatown. Heavily armed Maya cops were pouring out of it; the effect was almost comical since we were watching one file of cops vanishing into Pusiictsom's sunlit house in Yaxkintulum, and another emerging into the dark streets of Mayatown. They formed up rapidly at their destination, into several columns pointed down the thoroughfares toward the main part of New Tanjavur.

"Uh-oh," Paxa said. "There goes about the last hope."

"What hope?" Margaret asked.

"That they might have been going over to protect an evacuation," she explained. "They're deploying to attack. This is going to be ugly."

Alcott shook his head. "I *never* thought they were making plans for evacuations. The Peccaries were always ruthless anyway. The only questions remaining are, how fast can the Tamils respond to an armed invasion?, with what?, and what will happen when they do? And no matter what the answer is to any of those, it's bound to be bad."

By now the Maya forces had completed the trip through the springer, and at a command, the four columns trotted down the streets of Mayatown, toward the advancing Tamils. Within minutes battle was joined, and soon the screens in front of us showed nothing but wild fighting along the front between the Maya and the Tamil rioters. At first the Maya forces gained rapidly, due to surprise, interior lines, and much better organization (since what they were facing was a mixture of paramilitary gangs, impromptu militias, and plain mobs).

But the New Tanjavur police were quick to respond, and soon battle lines formed as companies of Tamil police counterattacked against the Maya. An officer in a Thorburg uniform, his blond braids swaying as he shook his head, said, "This must be the biggest pitched battle since the Roosevelt Civil War. Certainly the biggest since the springer was invented."

Shan had picked up a private com and had the eyepiece and earpiece up to his face. He was talking very softly, but something about the way he kept saying "I see" told everyone in the room that there was much worse news coming, hard though that was to imagine. By the time he clicked off, everyone was dead silent and watching him.

He set the private handset down and looked up at us. "News

is bad all over," he said. "First of all it appears that after he sent the last CSPs through, Ambassador Kiel was captured alive before he got to a springer. One faction of the Tamil police is holding him somewhere in New Tanjavur. We've just authenticated their message to that effect.

"It's not clear whether his status is protective custody or hostage, probably because the Tamils haven't decided yet which way he'd be more valuable.

"Second and worse, it looks like a Tamil counterattack is about to crash through the covert springer they've had in an industrial plant in Yaxkintulum for a long time. Third—"

At that moment the screen showing Pusiictsom's garden in Yaxkintulum went blank. A moment later so did the screens showing New Tanjavur; two that remained on showed a crazy whirling image—the flitter was being flung about too fast for it to focus.

After long minutes of no signal at all, the technicians managed to find a camera on a polar satellite in a low orbit; it was just crossing the equator and heading south. There were a few more minutes until it passed over the Briandian antarctic, but I think that even before it got there, we knew what we would see: two great glowing patches in the infrared, indicating that antimatter clouds had been projected onto both cities. It was a sight no one had seen since the Honshu Transpolis was destroyed in 2248, in the last reprisal of the Slaughter, six hundred years ago. New Tanjavur and Yaxkintulum had both been vitrified; as we watched, great flares marked the abrupt deaths of the other cities of Briand.

"We didn't want to lose CSPs on Briand," Shan said, his voice as dull, soft, and lifeless as a criminal confessing after hours of denials. "And we knew both sides had antimatter cloud projectors ready to go. So once the fighting started, if we didn't want to lose hundreds or thousands of our own people, we couldn't do anything except evacuate and hope. A good evacuation but a poor hope."

Alcott asked, "How soon can we get forces back on the ground to reconnoiter?"

Shan raised his hands as if surrendering. "With a continuous-feed springship, if they've got one building at Eta Cassiopeia, I suppose we might be able to get someone there in a decade or so. Right now the only springer left in service in the Metallah system is the one through which the robot station is laser-relaying the pictures to us. That has an aperture about the size of my little finger and couldn't move a single gram of cargo. No, either we have to send a ship, or whatever survivors there are—if any—will have to build a springer on their own. As of now, except for our limited ability to take some remote pictures, Briand is cut off from human space. Once that satellite's orbit decays, probably in less than a stanyear, we won't even have pictures. For the first time, we've lost contact with an inhabited world."

It wasn't until late the next day—after another more thorough cleanup, a great deal of sleep, the delivery of some new clothes, and a certain amount of quiet talk with a counselor—that I realized this might be a blemish on anyone's career. Shan pointed it out to the whole working group when we met in general session. "It's too soon to say what will happen, but no matter how blameless we all are, and no matter how inevitable it was that there would someday be a mutual massacre of the populations of Yaxkintulum and New Tanjavur, just the same someone is going to get blamed for this. In a way the worst thing was that Ambassador Kiel either died or was stranded in New Tanjavur, because now all that remains of him is a lengthy set of reports complaining that the Office of Special Projects was meddling and making his job harder; if he were here to be interrogated I think we could have depended on him to reveal some things about his trustworthiness and competence, but now . . . well, *de mortuis nil nisi bonum*. At least that's what I imagine the investigatory committees, and the prosecutors if it comes to that, will say.

"As you know, we all worked our hearts out, and I don't be-lieve there is one of you who gave less than his or her all. It was a failure, but there was never a more honorable one. When they come to question you—and they will—you will tell them ex-actly what you think and whatever you feel to be the truth, just as you would tell me. I will tell them that all of you did as well as anyone could, and I will lay no blame on any of my subordi-nates in this project. If you think I failed, or some of your com-rades did, in a culpable way, say that. But I will not blame any of you, at all, ever.

"Nor will I accept blame myself. I have searched my heart and I see nothing I might have done better, nothing that would not have led to the same horrible result. If they demand that I be held responsible, I will take whatever punishment they mete out, but I will not repudiate any decision or policy in which I had a hand.

"We have lost a whole world, but we have kept our honor. I burn with grief, but I do not feel a drop of shame, and neither should any of you. That is what I will tell them."

He drew a deep breath. I saw how ashen his skin looked, how deep the lines were on his face, how dark the circles around his eyes. Knowing Shan, he had probably been up for thirty hours straight or so. He would still do that for us, his people. It was also alarming to see the toll it now took on him; he had been fairly old when I had first met him, back on Nansen, more than a decade ago. Someday we would be in deep shit and there would be no Shan to get us out—that might be very soon, if they man-aged to pin the blame for the Briand disaster on him. He had plenty of powerful enemies who would if they could.

Finally he spoke again. "Now, I'm truly sorry to have to say this next part, but I need to say it out in the open with a clear ex-planation on record. I do not know how long I will retain the powers I have in the Office of Special Projects. There are many of you who joined the Briand project at a time when you already had many important things to do, or who delayed a long-overdue leave or who abandoned personal business at my urgent request.

And because you all trusted me to make sure, as I try to, that things came out square for you at the end, I feel I must tell you now that I don't know how much longer I will have the power to keep any of my promises to you. I might be relieved of duty at any time; there will be a discussion on that subject in the Council within the next few standays, and my friends there cannot hope to delay it much.

"Therefore I have written a report to the Council in which I declare that all of you have done far beyond what anyone could have expected, that I am very proud of all of you, and that in light of the recent terrible events, I have authorized special leaves for everyone. I need to know exactly what special leaves I'm authorizing, but at the moment I have the power to give you up to a year off with full pay, anywhere. I'll give you all three hours. Get on the com to your families and friends if you need to, or look up every resort in the Thousand Cultures, but get going. I'm quite serious that I want to send that letter out three hours from now. I just hope I haven't given you too *much* time."

Sir Qrala stood up. "Sir," he said. "What about the Office of Special Projects itself?"

"I don't know about the OSP," Shan said. "A lot of powerful interests have been looking to tumble it from its pedestal, you know. And perhaps we've grown too powerful in the last thirty stanyears, and maybe it's time for some sun to shine into our dark corners. But the *work* will have to go on. For those of you who haven't heard the most recent count, we've found another two alien installations—one under a dead sea on Ducommon, within twenty kilometers of downtown New Singapore, and the other at the forward Trojan point in orbit ahead of Gobat. Which means they were everywhere in the Inner Sphere, twenty thousand stanyears before we ventured into space. And still we've never found a grave or a book. And in just about nine more years, the springship on its way to their home system will reach it, and we can send exploring teams there. Like it or not, humanity—which is just starting to realize that the Inward Turn is over—is about to be catapulted into some new age, when for the first time we have to confront the genuinely alien. Those of you who have spent any time at all on Earth or in the Inner Sphere know how much preparation we have to do, still, and that we will probably be far from ready when the day comes. And all of you know that we can't start internecine culture struggles at this time in our history, even though we are absolutely ripe for them. There would have been six or seven Briands before now, without the OSP; and there could still be three or four more. Someone's got to try to stop them, and there's going to be work available stopping them, whether it's via the Office of Special Projects or not. Is that enough of an answer?"

"Enough for me," Qrala said.

Shan dismissed us. Everyone hurried back to our temporary rooms. I had already decided that I would urge Margaret to just pick an attractive, low-gravity, warm beach spot where we could dress well and do nothing but loaf and get to know one another again for a year. I knew she wouldn't mind skipping Utilitopia, and much as I liked Elinorien, we had been there only about a hundred standays before. We needed to take a vacation that was just for us.

When we went through the door into our quarters Margaret crossed the room to the wall and put her face against it, so that her back was fully to me.

I looked at her in that inexplicable pose for a long time, and finally realized I was supposed to ask. "Margaret, what's wrong?"

"I don't know what I feel and I'm too upset to think and Shan's going to make me decide right now."

"He's going to make *us* decide," I said, "and I think all we have to do is pick a place to go heal, somewhere with sun and maybe a beach and—"

"No, I didn't say we." She sighed, and it ended in a sob, and then she was choking out her story, a bit at a time, in little gasps that ended in strangled, emphatically grunted words, as if she were pleading while it was being ripped from her chest. "Giraut, I'm not . . . I'm *not* crying about *Briand.* I'm crying about *Kapilar.* He and I . . . we *broke up* not very long before . . . we broke up *five* days ago. We had been *together* almost from the *first day we met.* He wanted to *do* me *again,* just a *day and half* ago, like *always,* and I told him I *wouldn't* because I *didn't want to* anymore, and I was *lying* about it when *I said it,* and now he's *dead* and I wish I *had!"*

With that, she drew in a long ragged breath, and let it out as a keening, sobbing wail, like an animal in pain. I stood and stared, sorting out the words in my mind, making sure I understood, and then because I saw that she was angrily wiping her face with her sleeves, I got out my handkerchief and gave it to her. It was a relief to have something appropriate to do.

It was the better part of an hour before she was coherent enough to hold a conversation; during that time I held her, since she seemed to want me to, and she drenched my handkerchiefs, and then most of a roll of toilet tissue. When she had cried it all out, she looked an absolute mess, and I felt as if I had stepped into a misaddressed springer and arrived in some other universe.

Finally, when she had been breathing steadily for a while and didn't seem quite so upset, I ventured, rather timidly, to ask if she wanted to talk.

"We have to. You heard Shan."

"You were going to tell me?"

"Yap. Oh, *yap, yap,* I thought maybe when we took that long vacation, but don't you see, I couldn't just go off with you, and have you get up on the first day of the vacation all ready to relax and enjoy everything, you're so damned sincere, Giraut, and I know you really mean to be good to me, and then in the middle of all that I would have to come right out and tell you . . . well, it wasn't fair. If you want to get rid of me or run away or whatever, you should be able to have the year's vacation to do that, it wouldn't be fair to make you spend it with me if you don't want to . . . am I making sense?"

"Some," I admitted. "I think you're trying much too hard to be fair. Very Caledon of you. Me, I'm still trying to sort this out. I want to ask a lot of things but I'm afraid time would run out while we were sorting them out. Was it because—"

"It wasn't *because of anything*, Giraut, probably *you* didn't even have much to *do* with it. It was just . . . oh, god, Giraut, look, Kapilar didn't love me and I sure didn't love him, if that makes it better or worse. He'd never seen a blonde woman before. I looked like a freak to him. Some men *like* freaks, you know? There are men who screw animals. I'm not sure that wasn't what I was to him.

"And he was good looking and . . . well, he had a lot of that Cankam kind of chivalry, you know, very, uh, very horny, actually, very attracted to me, and I needed that badly just then because . . . because . . . "

"Because you weren't getting it from me."

"Oh, well, yes, but—but Giraut, you were trying, and everything you were doing had worked for a long time, it wasn't a bad try, you weren't doing anything badly. It was just that I didn't believe you any more. I saw the look in your eyes when you played your old jovent songs, and I knew what the *donzelhas* before me looked like, and . . . oh, god, you know, your whole life seemed like a wonderful romantic novel to me, Giraut, I wanted you to take me into it, and you couldn't. Nobody can. And I was just . . . Giraut, he was the second man, ever, for me. And I loved that he was only interested in my body—maybe especially that, even if it was only my pale hair and translucent skin. I shouldn't tell you that kind of thing." She started to cry again.

I held her. My insides were crumbling. In a short time I would be so depressed that I wouldn't be able to think at all. Therefore I had to figure out what to do for the next phase of my life, right now, before the depression completely disabled me, so that I could just automatically do what needed doing for a while, until it was time to really live again. That was a trick that had worked for me before.

I didn't have any idea what the right thing would be.

I got more toilet tissue and handed it to her; she and I had been sitting together on the bed, but now when I sat down she turned away.

"Do you want me to go, *midons*? Either just now or for good?" I asked. It seemed like something I would want to know.

"I want you to do what you want to do. What you really sincerely want to do. Not to base it all on how you think I want you to feel."

"It's easier to try to please you," I pointed out. "I'm Occitan. Give me an audience and I'll find a way to play to it. I'm sorry that I was so caught up in nostalgia. I hate looking at my developing gut and my crows'-feet in the mirror. I hate noticing how many mad adventures seem like too much bother anymore. But I don't want a new young *donzelha*. I never really knew those girls at all, you know, just their bodies—"

"And that's why I wanted this thing with Kapilar so much," Margaret said. "The thought of just getting pleasure, you know, without having to know so much about the other person. Not that I don't like what I know about you, Giraut . . . but then on the other hand I'm not so sure that I do . . . oh, I don't know at all, really." She rubbed her hand vigorously over her face, smearing snot and tears around and bringing a red flush to her cheeks and nose. "Oh, damn, Giraut, look, I can tell you the rest of the story. I had to keep the thing with Kapilar going, anyway. Shan asked me to. He said a couple of things that I thought were pretty nasty, but then I suppose he's your friend and maybe he was angry on your behalf; anyway, he basically told me that if I was going to go whoring the least I could do is bring something back for it. And what he had me bring back . . . was a lot of things about Kapilar and the young Tamil intellectuals. You know, there's nothing that gets a man talking like a woman appearing to find him fascinating, and, and, and well—I started to find that I really *was* fascinated. He was so complex, so torn up inside, and he told me everything, you know, about himself and what he thought . . .

"And I felt like I understood him. I felt like I knew what he was, and I thought that maybe he would join the OSP and I would see more of him, or the whole thing would settle back into friendship, or something or other. And then—all of a sudden, right at the end, everything about him that I had thought of as local charm, as part of the fun of knowing someone from another culture intimately—it turned out that those were all that really mattered.

"He turned his back on working for the Council, on being part of the big project of reuniting humanity . . . so that he could go kill little children in front of their mothers and throw bombs into hospital rooms and god knows what all they were doing down there before the antimatter clouds erased it. I had been . . . I had been reduced to nothing again. When he went down that corridor and out into the street—even before we saw New Tanjavur turned to molten glass—I missed him, right then, knowing he was gone forever. I missed his cock, and the rough way he would just use me instead of treating me like fine glass, and I missed the contempt in his eyes, and I admit that all that means there is something sick about me . . . but I also missed the friendship and the way he would listen and how easy it was to talk to him, and knowing that he never told anyone else the things he told me. Men are that way, you know, they'll confide in a whore."

"You're not a whore."

"Are you saying that to be nice, or because you're afraid that your dear old friend Shan is a pimp?"

I sighed. "Margaret," I said, "if you want to make a try at working all this out, it's going to take a year to do it. And I'd rather do it somewhere a long way from either family, preferably some place suitable for contemplation and comfort. The beach is what really comes to mind, and I was thinking very strongly that

Hedonia is supposed to have gorgeous weather, perfect beaches, and exciting cities, and besides I have really liked every Hedon I've ever met. So if you want to work it out, come to one of the beach resorts in Hedonia with me. If you don't want to work it out, that's up to you and I won't chase you down the street begging. And I'll probably go to Hedonia anyway."

I had seen plenty of pictures of Eta Cephi sinking into the sea on the west coast of Hedonia, its fiery light bouncing off the big, graceful, slow-moving waves. My back and feet were still recovering from Briand's gravity, and Hedonia was on Söderblom, which had the lowest gravity of any inhabited open-air world. Seventy percent of standard gravity would suit me just fine for a year, I thought; my spine might unpack.

So I had made my decision. No matter what, I was going to spend a year in Hedonia. There was a lot to look forward to about that, even if Margaret should decide this instant to get rid of me. Now I need not fear doing something stupid while depressed. When the depression hit, I could just let it.

All the same I really hoped Margaret would come with me.

It seemed like a long time before she said, "I don't want to have to make up my mind just now. But I guess I better."

"Make it up to go with me," I said. "There are what, thirty-some cultures on Söderblom? If you hate me, or you hate Hedonia, you can put a whole planet between us. And I won't try to follow you if that's how it works out. Please, Margaret, it's probably the best thing for right now, and you can undo it later if you've made a mistake."

"You're making sense," she said. "I don't know if I want to be sensible, but I suppose if I am, then later on when I find out that I don't like it, I'll have an excuse. Where if I screw up while being irrational, I won't have any excuse at all, will I? All right, Giraut, all right."

"You'll go with me?"

"I said all right."

"We need to tell Shan, then. Shall I com him?"

"Go talk to him. Face to face. I need some time alone. But it's firm, Giraut, my poor idiot-boy *trobador,* I *will* go with you. I don't say I won't run off with some beautiful Hedon gigolo, half my age, in the first week. But I will go there with you."

"*Yap,* yes, *ja,*" I said. "*Gratz'deu* you Caledons keep your word. Okay, I'll go tell Shan. Will you wait for me to get out of jail if I punch him?"

"Depends how long you're in for. Don't hit him hard. Remember he couldn't have done it without me."

"Got you," I said, and tried hugging her, but she stiffened and leaned back away; I let her go and was out the door and down the corridor before either of us could say anything more. No matter how it came out, this was going to take a long time.

Shan was in his little office, holding court. He had just dismissed two men who looked pretty happy; from the way they were holding hands I figured those *toszeti* were off to celebrate getting whatever grand vacation they were going on, and I don't think I've ever envied two people more intensely.

He probably could tell I'd been upset, because he shut the door and ushered me in. "Well," he said, "I think your being here alone tells me something—"

"I'd like to beat your face in," I said, my voice very level and even.

He ostentatiously rested his finger on a button on the desk; I assumed if I moved toward him he would call in CSPs. The way he reached for a physical backup before even trying to talk to me helped to crystallize my feelings.

"Well," he said, "from that little outburst, I guess I know that she's told you everything. I presume she did tell you that I merely exploited a situation that had developed, and it wasn't my idea."

"Good of you," I said.

"So where are you going to recover? And will Margaret let me know where she is going?"

"We're both going to Hedonia," I said. "Where I would not like to be visited by you. One full stanyear and I will hold you to that. For the rest, I think you should fuck your ugly mother up whatever filthy hole spewed you, with a live rat. Sir."

"I can understand your feelings."

"I doubt that very much. I look back at how you always took care of me and Margaret, always so pleasant to both of us, and now I see a pig breeder scratching snouts and dispensing sweets, so that all the pigs just love him, until it's time to convert them all to bacon. I've been a damned fool for you, sir. I thought you were my friend. And Margaret's. And I want you to know she's back in the room bleeding her soul into her pillow, and I don't think she'd be doing that if she'd just had a small, ordinary love affair, just for herself. I think she ripped her guts out doing that for you, and she got more attached to Kapilar than she ever would have otherwise, and in short you play around with human beings in a way I really don't like. Did I mention that you fellate dead goats and love it, sir?"

Shan shrugged. His hand had drifted away from the button. Now that he knew I wasn't really going to hit him, he no longer cared much what I said, except as it pertained to his schemes. He gave me a smile that might have been friendly but was probably just condescending, and said, "The Occitan gift for insult always puts me in awe. Are you just venting your feelings or is there some point to this?"

"Oh, yes there is. When our year is up, *you come back and get me*. I'm still going to be in this for good, whatever my personal feelings might be. The mission is still the most important thing going in human space, and I hope you succeed in keeping the Office of Special Projects open. I'll do the job, as well as I can, till I'm dead or you fire me. I have nothing else to do with my life that's as important. I need this year off, and I'm going to take it and get my emotional balance back, which will take a while. But don't you leave me out of things. You come back and get me and put me back into the game."

"I may not be in a position to make such decisions a year from now."

"Like hell. I don't know how powerful your enemies are or how clever, but if it is humanly possible to survive, Shan, sir, you will. Whether your name is on the office door anymore or not, you're going to run this circus, till you're dead. So I don't care if it's *officially* you. It will be, *actually.* Come and get me. In one stanyear. No sooner, no later. Do you understand that, you senile pandering bag of shit?"

"I don't think you really consider me to be senile. All right. Both of you are going to Hedonia. One full stanyear. I will see you or send someone for you on the last day of that leave. Exactly. Departure tomorrow sometime late in the afternoon; I'll send the precise time to your room terminal." He glanced up at me and said, "If it will help you to know that this whole interview has been very painful for me, and that I do like both of you and wish this hadn't been necessary—"

"I don't know whether it would help me to believe any of that," I said, "but I do know it would help you to have me believe it. One stanyear, Shan. Not a minute earlier or later. See you then."

"I look forward to it."

"Good-bye, sir."

"*Atz deu, te salut,* Giraut."

I closed the door carefully behind me, not wanting to slam it, and headed back to our quarters, no happier but with at least something crossed off the list.

As I walked back I was thinking about things I wanted to ask Ix. I wanted his guidance about the choice ahead of me. I could spend the rest of my life suspecting everything, turning away every friendship and every kind offer, and never be fooled . . . and also absolutely never have any human contact, and end my life as a miserable old paranoid. That might make me useful to Shan, in counterintelligence or something.

Or I could trust people and be betrayed, over and over. Accept the scars along with the friends.

I thought Ix would have said that I could choose what ending to put on the story of my life thus far, accepting that it was just a story that I would have to revise again and again—or I could live forever trapped inside the story.

I missed Ix. Worse, I had missed out on his presence all along. All of a sudden my head was full of questions I should have asked him, things he would have told me if I had only thought to ask, and with a sinking heart I realized that whenever anything puzzled or worried me in the future, I would again wonder what Ix might have told me, and try to figure it out, and very likely make a mess of it.

When I got back to our quarters Margaret was curled up under the covers. "Did you arrange it?" she asked.

"We're both going to Hedonia for one undisturbed stanyear," I said.

"Good," she said. "Coming to bed soon?"

"I need a shower," I said. "After that."

"Wake me up and hold me when you do come to bed, then."

"All right."

I meant it to be a quick shower, but something broke open in me when the warm, soapy water hit. I sobbed, beating my hands against the walls of the shower stall like a lunatic, thumping and keening. My eyes stayed shut because of the soap, and so I flailed around blindly, battering my hands on the wall of the shower stall till they ached, getting soap in my mouth with my crying. Margaret must have heard, but she didn't come to me.

Not having really washed, still feeling sticky and a little dirty, I let the rinse take the soap off me, and opened my eyes. The little stall that had seemed like a cell had a door, and I was in an ordinary shower, on an ordinary space station, cleaning up before going to bed early. Tomorrow I would go on a long vacation, just like any long vacation anyone else ever took, and work through matters with my wife, just like any other married couple with big problems. I let myself stand in the hot rinse water and cry for a while, thinking how, if Ix had been there, he could have told me the same thing, but I would have *believed* it if it had come from him.

I don't remember whether I woke Margaret up to hold her, as she had asked me to do. I guess Ix would have said that I didn't remember because it wasn't important to how the story came out. Probably he'd have told me to make up whichever ending I wanted. He was often arbitrary, especially about small things.